THE ESSENCE CRYSTAL

Essence Wielder Book 2

DAN MICHAELSON

D.K. HOLMBERG

ASH
PUBLISHING

Chapter One

THE SERPENT STAIRS LOOMED IN FRONT OF DAX.

He had taken the stairs twice now in his life, which was two times more than most people had an opportunity to do. Doing so had allowed him to progress to second-tier acolyte, though he still wasn't sure what that meant for him just yet. It would've been easier if he could quantify the essence control that he had, but that wasn't how the progression through the various tiers of power worked for him.

Surprisingly—or perhaps, not so surprisingly—he felt a strange connection to the stairs, and to everything that he felt around him. He had been gifted this essence by the Great Serpent, the entity that he had visited once he had reached the top of the serpent stairs and had undergone his testing, so perhaps he should not be terribly surprised by the fact that he felt some connection to the essence that came from it.

"You keep looking up the stairs," Rochelle said.

Dax turned to look over at her, and he forced a smile.

Her blonde hair hung loose around her face, draping down through the hood of her cloak. She had an easy smile, and there was a friendliness to her that not everyone had. "I keep thinking about what we saw, what we experienced, and... Well, I keep thinking that maybe I could have had another vision of the Great Serpent."

"It wasn't a vision this time, though."

It wasn't. Then again, Dax had never truly had a vision of the Great Serpent. When he had come before, he had drawn upon essence and had filled himself with its surprising power, but it hadn't given him a vision the way that so many other people had experienced.

"I still don't quite know what I'm supposed to do," he admitted, and he looked around at the others who were there. Gia and Cedrick were talking quietly together, and Dax appreciated them having the opportunity. Desmond had departed for a little while, making arrangements, or so he had said, but it had left the four of them—only students, nothing more than that—alone at the base of the serpent stairs while they tried to decide how much trouble they might end up in. "We now have the Order to deal with, but I'm still unsure if we have to deal with the Cult as well."

Desmond hadn't been clear about that.

"Why do you think that you actually need to be a part of the Cult of the Dragon in order for you to serve the Great Serpent?" Rochelle looked up at him. "He said that wasn't necessary."

Before he had a chance to answer, Cedrick turned, snapping his fingers. A bit of pink bubbling essence began to erupt from his fingertips, and he flashed a broad smile. "Are we going to just stand here? I know that my bubbly life essence is quite impressive to all of you, but I don't know that I want to stay here for too long. Where's the old man, anyway? We should be getting back to the Academy."

Gia looked over at him. She was tall and slender, which made her valor skill all the more intimidating. "Are you sure that we need to be going back to the Academy until we know whether or not the headmaster has placed anything there to harm us?" She kept her hand near the hilt of her essence sword. She was skilled with the blade, a talented valor fighter, which made it so much easier for the two of them to get along. Then again, she was familiar with the unclaimed lands, much like he was. "I know your friend is starting to make some preparations, but I think *we* need to make some preparations on our own."

Rochelle and Dax moved away from the base of the stairs. They were enormous, stretching high into the clouds overhead and surrounding a tower that could not be seen from the ground. As Dax stepped back, he cast a slow, careful look over the stairs, his gaze working his way toward the top. He could feel… Dax wasn't entirely sure what he could feel, but there *did* seem to be an energy that emanated from the area. Maybe it was essence within the stairs, or maybe it was simply that he felt the effect of the Great Serpent, hidden inside of the tower that he couldn't even see from his vantage.

"She's right," Rochelle said. "Before we head back, we should probably come to terms with what the four of us are going to do."

"I've got to finish my testing," Cedrick said. "I know that all of you probably have finished yours, and none of you struggled, but I still have my essence manipulation exam, and if you know anything about Professor Jamesh, you know that he'll make it as difficult as possible."

"I'm concerned about that as well," Dax said.

Cedrick shook his head. "Maybe before, but I saw what you were doing in there. I don't know what kind of essence you have," he went on, and he arched a brow, as if waiting to see what Dax might answer, "but whatever it is seems to be powerful."

Cedrick was tall, slender, and had a pronounced nose that seemed to take up much of his face. His shaggy brown hair was more unkempt than usual, and he shifted his cloak, as if to try to conceal the fact that he wasn't carrying an essence blade the way that Dax and Gia were.

"I think we'll all do much better with essence manipulation now than before." Rochelle flashed a smile. She was shorter than Dax, nearly a hand shorter in total, and preferred to wear her dark blue robes rather than any sort of a traveling cloak. She wasn't wearing any weapon, though he would've expected that from her. The more Dax tamped down his own essence, the more he could see the faint greenish-blue energy that emanated from her. He had always seen that essence that radiated inside of Rochelle—that of a healer—but it was something that he had become more attuned to the longer that he had known her.

"I think the most important thing is to get back to the Academy before the headmaster."

"Do you really think he might do anything to us?" Cedrick asked.

"Probably not now," a voice said from a nearby building, coming toward them.

Dax looked over at Desmond. He did not resemble the same man that he remembered meeting in the artisan district. There was something powerful about him, though perhaps it was just the fact that he had seen him handling the dangers inside the testing tower, and he had come out on the right side of it. Or perhaps it was that Desmond had revealed more of himself, more of his potential and his abilities, than he had before. Whatever it was, as he strode toward them, Dax allowed himself to feel like maybe they wouldn't be in any real danger.

Though he knew better.

Headmaster Ames had been trying to take the Great Serpent's essence. He had not been alone, working with others of the Order, but now they had been discovered. Now the Emperor would know.

The real question was what he would do about it.

It had all been a plot of sorts, all of them trying to gain access to that power, a power that Dax still didn't even fully fathom. He had grown up knowing about the Great Serpent, knowing that he would eventually come for his testing and likely be gifted a connection to fiery essence, which would change things for him and permit him to be the fighter along the unclaimed lands that his family heritage should grant him. Only when he had come to the testing, nothing had been as it should have. He had never been gifted fiery essence.

Instead, he was given something that he could only call transference essence, though even that probably wasn't entirely correct. Dax didn't know what kind of essence he actually had, but he had learned that he could use it in ways that were far more beneficial than he had ever imagined the essence could be, at least from when he had first discovered what it granted him.

"I'm not going to sugarcoat it and make you think that everything is going to be rainbows and candy when you get back," Desmond said, sweeping his gaze around the arranged students, "but I have arranged for you to be protected."

"You can't protect us at all times," Rochelle said.

Dax appreciated that she was the one to speak up, especially as he agreed with her. There was only so much that somebody like Desmond would be able to do. He wasn't a part of the Academy, so how was he going to try to offer them a measure of protection when it came to dealing with a dangerous threat from the headmaster?

"The Order has been reported," he said.

"Reported?" Rochelle asked, arching a brow. "And who did you report it to? The cultists?"

He shrugged. "Yes. Should I have reported it to someone else?"

"I think that the Guardians should have been——"

"The Guardians were aware of it from the moment the attack took place," he said, cutting her off. "And your sister," he went on, looking over at Dax, "as a Whisper, will report to the Emperor what took place. We had better hope that the Emperor actually listens. Now, if you don't mind, I think we should make some arrangements inside of town, gather supplies, and then return. You don't have to worry about anybody questioning why you were here, as I have made it clear that I am an instructor from the Academy taking a group of second-year students out to the serpent stairs to examine them."

Dax wasn't about to argue with him, and he didn't know if there was any reason for anybody to question it anyway. Second-year students often would come out to the serpent stairs, occasionally even for additional testing.

Desmond nodded off to a clump of trees and the small essence-guided wagon that was parked there. "We will meet there in an hour. Take whatever time you need, as I have a few more preparations to make before our return."

He started off into the supply town and left them alone.

Everybody was quiet for a few moments, until Cedrick broke the silence.

"So we just wait? This feels a little strange, doesn't it?" He looked around at the others before his gaze settled on Rochelle. "What sort of arrangements does he need to make?"

"Oh, he's probably talking to more of the cultists," Dax said, waving his hand.

Gia watched him. "You speak about that so casually. Does it really not bother you?"

"I don't think it should bother any of us," Rochelle said. "The cultists aren't at all what we thought they were. I've researched them, and everything I've found suggests they *do* want to help the Great Serpent. So maybe we should just give them a chance."

Gia snorted. "Give them a chance? You were in the Academy when they attacked."

"That wasn't them," Dax said.

Gia let out a tight breath. "I know that it wasn't, but it's still hard to believe. And even if we believe that, others may not. How are we going to deal with that at the Academy, especially if the Order decides to come at us?"

"I believe we need to be careful," Dax said, looking in the direction that Desmond had disappeared before flicking his gaze back toward the serpent stairs. "We're dealing with the Order, and with cultists, and with the Great Serpent, and I have no idea how much of all this is dangerous for us."

And he had no idea what would happen once they got back to the Academy.

"Do we need to do this here?" Rochelle motioned toward the supply town. "We have time before we need to go back, and we should take advantage of it."

Dax was tempted to tell her no, but he hadn't actually spent that much time here when he had been here before. He had stayed in his family's wagon, and then gone into a small room that they rented for the night before taking his testing. When he had awoken—several days later, which should have been the first clue that something had not gone right for him—he had immediately been sent with Academy instructors away from town. Now...

Now he had an opportunity.

They stopped at a general store, where Rochelle headed inside. Cedrick followed.

Gia grabbed Dax, keeping him from joining the others as quickly as he wanted to.

"Are you at all concerned about what your family might do if they find out that you've been involved in this?"

Dax regarded her for a moment. "I have a hard time thinking that my parents, in particular, are interested in anything that I do. When I didn't get fire essence, my father lost interest in me. My mother goes along with anything that he does." Dax shook his head slightly. "I'm going to end up like Megan."

"Well, your sister is a Whisper, so that's not the worst thing to be. I'm concerned about my parents. If they get word that I was involved in all of this and am somehow tied to the Order and what's happening with the Cult, they might force me back home."

"They would?"

"They only let me come because they thought that I wasn't needed back home. But if they think that I'm getting involved in something dangerous, they might bring me back. I don't know that I want to do that."

"Isn't everything that happens along the border dangerous?"

"I'm sure my experience there is similar to yours. It's not dangerous. We have some incursions, but they are infrequent. And most of the time, my family and others are excited to deal with them."

Dax had much the same experience, unfortunately.

Gia was quiet for a few moments, and then she let out a heavy sigh. "You know, sometimes it's easier for me to think about what it would be like if I were just to go back to the unclaimed lands. Maybe that would be easier than worrying about whether the Order or the Cult might be still involved in something."

"My mother liked to say that easy isn't always right," Dax said. "We've done something that almost no other first-year students do." Then he flashed a smile, turned, and looked over at the darkened form of the serpent stairs. "We climbed the stairs for the second time. And we have progressed to second-tier acolyte before anyone else in our class."

"We don't know that. Others might have been able to progress during the lead-up to exams. Nobody usually talks about what tier they are at. You just have to wait and see. Besides," she said, "I didn't have another vision."

"Well, I never had a vision the first time," Dax said. "And I'm still trying to figure out what it means that your essence—well, all our essences—are different than what is typical. The Guardians manipulate what essence people get. And if we are all supposed to serve the Emperor, what reason would there be for someone like Cedrick to get his bubbles?"

"And what about my earth variant?" Gia asked.

Dax noticed a flare of darkness within her, the deep brown essence of earth that radiated as she sent some of it swirling outward, but he also felt the rumbling that came through her as she commanded her connection to earth, and the way that it flowed out and into the ground.

"I guess if it's tied to something that the Emperor wants from me, that should make me feel good. It's just that I always thought that it was what the Great Serpent wanted." She frowned for a moment and then headed into the store.

But he hesitated.

His essence wasn't given to him by the Empire or the Emperor. His essence wasn't given to him by any of the Guardians. Which meant that his essence, strange as it might be, was meant for a different purpose. Maybe a higher purpose, if he were to believe such things. And though he didn't think the Great Serpent had gifted him with his essence, Dax did feel as if he'd had some connection with the Great Serpent when he had taken it, one he still felt now. He wished that he would've had an opportunity to experience some sort of a vision the way that others did, some way for him to be able to see what the Great Serpent wanted from him, and some way for him to know whether he had another purpose.

Right now it was difficult for him to think he did.

Whatever purpose he had, whatever reason that he had his strange transference essence, Dax knew that he had to come to terms with it.

And Desmond had said that he had to decide what he wanted to do with it.

Was he going to serve the Great Serpent? Would he serve the Empire?

Or would he try to find a way to serve both?

At this point, Dax didn't have those answers.

Chapter Two

THE FOUR OF THEM STOOD AT THE BASE OF THE TREE AFTER having spent quite a bit of time inside the supply town, wandering from shop to shop. Cedrick had bought a few sweet treats, mostly hard candy, some chocolate, and even a hunk of bread that he had shared with the others. They were all ravenous, which surprised Dax, though perhaps it shouldn't, as they had been away, dealing with the dangers inside of the tower, for quite some time. Cedrick was crunching on one of the hard candies that he bought and snapping his fingers periodically, making bubbles appear. Dax thought that they had given Desmond the power that he wanted, but he still hadn't returned.

"How long do you think he's going to make us wait?" Gia asked.

Dax shrugged. "I don't know. Maybe he had to make more arrangements than he was letting on."

"What kind of arrangements do you think he's going to need to make?" Gia asked.

"I don't know," Dax said. "He went off for a little while

after the attack. Given that this is Desmond, I don't know what he's doing. But…"

"Are you really concerned about Desmond?" Rochelle asked. "You saw what he has done for us."

"I saw what he has done, but not necessarily for us. And besides, he still serves the Cult. We need to try to understand why and what that means for us."

"I think we should be more concerned about passing our tests. Most of us still have a few exams to complete when we get back," Cedrick said.

"And I still have essence manipulation," Dax groaned.

"I've never really liked transference," Gia said.

"I didn't like it either, at first," Rochelle said, turning to the other woman. Gia was tall with dark hair, and there was something much more intimidating about her than Rochelle, who seemed almost as if she wanted to please everybody at the same time. "Until Dax started to show me how transference could be used, and the fact that it didn't hurt any of the animals."

"What about people?" Cedrick asked.

"I didn't use any essence that hurt anybody," Dax countered.

"Are you sure? I feel like my bubbles aren't nearly as strong as they used to be," he said, waving a hand in front of his forehead as if he were going to swoon. "It's such a shame. My power is one of the most important ones in the entire Empire. And now look." He snapped his fingers again, and this time, a smaller bubble formed. Given Cedrick's control over his essence, Dax knew that he could direct the size of the bubbles.

What purpose would there be in somebody who had some sort of bubble magic? It might be a form of life essence, but it was a strange form, and one that Dax still wasn't entirely sure how it could be best used. There were probably others who could help Cedrick with that back at the Academy, or maybe within the artisan district, depending upon whether they were willing to go and ask people there about it.

If they believed that it was tied to something that the Guardians had given them, that type of essence didn't make a lot of sense. But there was another possibility, and it was one that Dax had begun to question seeing that the Great Serpent had been awake. What if the Great Serpent had been involved in distributing essence more directly this time?

If so, then maybe there was a different reason for Cedrick's essence. Maybe different for Rochelle, and even Gia.

"Can we see a valor demonstration?" Cedrick asked. "I mean, a real one, not the kind that they tried to control when we were at the Academy. I want to know what kind of things you both learned at the border."

Dax snorted. "I don't know. I wouldn't want to embarrass a Stonewall."

"Oh, I wouldn't want to embarrass a Nelson—though I think he's already embarrassed himself enough. At least I have the family essence," she said. As soon as the words were out of her mouth, she brought a hand up to her face, clasping it over her mouth. "Oh, Dax, I'm so sorry. You know I didn't—"

"It's fine," he said. "I'm not that sensitive about it. If I would have gotten that essence, I would've ended up at the unclaimed lands, and I wouldn't have been at the Academy to meet all of you." He swept his gaze around his newfound friends, before glancing over to the serpent stairs in the distance. "And I probably wouldn't have noticed that there was something going on in the tower and the testing grounds. Who knows what might've happened?"

Dax realized that he was seeing essence much more clearly than he had before. When he had first been gifted his essence, that was the only thing that he had been able to see. Essence had seemed to flow all over, and it had become almost incapacitating for him to observe it, to the point where he had needed to learn how to tamp down his own essence and bind it deeply inside himself so that he didn't weaken himself. Over time, as he had gained a measure of control over it, he had not had quite the same problem. He didn't know what that meant, though he suspected that it had to be tied to some level of progression. Going up the serpent stairs a second time should have allowed him to progress, even if it wasn't in an obvious way. Still, Dax didn't know how to quantify how far he had progressed, or if such a thing was even possible.

What if he had progressed more than he had realized? Maybe he was more than just a second-tier acolyte. How would he ever know?

The instructors had to have some way of detecting that. And if any of them would know, it would be Rochelle. That was a conversation that he needed to have with her.

"Look at who's gone silent," Gia said, waving her hand at him.

"I'm sorry," Dax said, turning to her. "I was just thinking about your insult and what I needed to do to get my recompense. I suppose I could embarrass you here."

"I don't think that the two of you should do anything," Rochelle said.

"It's fine," Cedrick said, waving his hand. "We have two valor masters, don't we?"

"They aren't masters," Rochelle said, and she looked

over at Dax, irritation flashing in her eyes. "They are still first-year students, and though they might've trained with valor with their families, that doesn't make them experts in it. In fact, I would even argue that it probably makes each of them less of an expert. They think they know more than they do. They need to be careful."

"Well," Gia said, unsheathing her essence blade, and holding it in front of her in two hands, with a bit of earth essence flowing from her and into the blade, "one of the very first things that we are taught is how to spar carefully. At least, that's one of the things that my Stonewall family has been teaching."

"My family is a little bit more cavalier about safety," Dax said, and he withdrew his own essence blade. It was one that he had taken off of one of the cultists, and had a series of unfamiliar runes on the surface. It stored his essence, and it offered him a measure of defense and a way to propel essence that he had not ever experienced before. His father had used an essence blade similarly, only with fire. It was merely a matter of pouring essence into the blade, igniting it, and using the flames to combat an enemy. "But I wouldn't be terribly surprised if I still knew more about safety than any Stonewall."

She grinned at him again. "So are we going to do this? You didn't even want to *really* do this when we were training at the Academy."

"Oh, I was just holding back," Dax said, waving his essence blade. There was a bit of power that poured out of the end of it, and he tried to focus on the energy inside of it, wanting to gain some control over it. As he pushed essence into the blade, he realized that he could pull it back just as well, which made it surprisingly easy to control some of the flow.

Maybe when he returned to the Academy, he would have mastered another aspect of essence that could be useful for his classes.

He already had enough experience with valor, and he didn't worry about passing the first-year class. But the second-year, more advanced valor class involved using essence blades. If he could practice on his own—and having his own essence blade made that much easier for him—he might be able to get ahead of some of the other students. And if he was going to have to worry about the headmaster, and the Order, Dax felt like he was going to have to stay ahead of any other student. He was going to have to try to make sure that he continued to progress, gaining understanding of his essence, and the way that he could use it and manipulate it, so that he could prepare for the possibility of another attack.

Gia took a step back from him, and she braced herself, standing in a traditional fighting pose.

Dax took up his own pose.

It had been a long time since he had truly sparred with somebody. When he had been back in his home, training with his father and his brother, he had never done very well. Part of that came from the fact that he didn't have his own essence that he could use, or hadn't thought that he did, but partly it came from the fact that none of his family members were willing to take it easy on him. He supposed that he should've been thankful for that. If they had taken it easy on him, Dax wasn't sure what he would've been able to learn nor whether he would have pushed himself quite as far as he had.

He waited.

"Is this how they go?" Cedrick asked. "I thought that

we would have more fighting, but this looks like a lot of standing around."

Faster than Dax would've expected, Gia darted toward him.

He noticed it when she began, using a bit of earth, exploding toward him. He recognized the flow of the essence, even if he couldn't tell how she was using it to propel herself. He dropped, rolling on the ground, but a bit of earth slammed into him as he went rolling, and he forced himself up, popping to his feet.

He brought his blade out, and very nearly lost control over the attack when he tried to swing it toward her, wanting to try to find some way to counter the attack.

She grinned at him. She darted back, and earth trembled again.

She was strong. Earth made her strong.

He was going to have to find a different technique to counter her.

There were quite a few different fighting styles that he had learned from his father, and others that he had worked with over the years. Those different fighting styles were important to know, as different creatures that they encountered along the unclaimed lands required a different approach, and some of them were harder to deal with than others. For the most part, his father just went flying into any danger with his sword blazing and took care of the threats that way. Dax wouldn't be able to do that.

But he could push essence through his blade.

He'd already seen that, and had already seen how that would be effective, so he thought that he could try a different approach.

This time, when he felt the rumbling that came from

her, and noticed that she was going to lunge at him, he swept his blade down.

He didn't even move.

Instead, he pushed essence through the end of the blade, and it arced toward her, catching the connection that she formed to earth and snapping through it.

She stumbled.

Dax moved then, swinging his blade toward her.

She brought her arm up.

She was quick, and she was powered by a connection to earth, which allowed her to block his thrust.

He was forced back.

As she sprang to her feet again, he swung his blade again, using another burst of his essence out from the end of the blade, where he tried to cut through the connection that she had to earth. Once again, she stumbled, but this time she seemed to recognize what he was doing, and she caught herself with a burst of earth connection, then went staggering toward him.

He rolled off to the side. He jumped before she slammed into him with another slap of earth, and then brought his blade again, whipping out a force of essence that tried to sever her connection to earth.

She wasn't where he thought that she would be. His essence crashed into earth, and there was a cascade of shattering stone that erupted around where she had been.

She was behind him.

He could feel her.

That was a new awareness.

He spun, and rather than using his blade, he held out his free hand and forced a bit of essence out from her. He found himself drawing from the essence in the ground, or perhaps he was also drawing from the essence around the serpent stairs, as if he were calling upon that power in order to create the translucent beam of essence that blasted out. It struck her in the chest, and she staggered back a step.

"What was that?"

"Transference," he said.

"I thought transference involved drawing off of something," she said. She still hadn't moved, and yet he could feel what she was doing with earth, the way that she was drawing on it at this point.

He was ready when she jumped.

Once again, he carved through her essence, keeping her from getting too close to him.

She landed, and he drew up essence, only this time he was drawing from what she was doing. He countered, using earth.

It reminded him of the mirror essence technique that he had seen from Desmond. He wasn't doing anything other than reflecting her own essence back upon her.

She brought her hand back, and she punched.

The stone around them shattered.

Dax staggered backward.

He popped to his feet, bringing his blade around, and then was forced back by a burst of power.

Desmond was there.

"Was this really necessary?" Desmond asked.

"Come on," Cedrick said. "We were just getting to the good stuff. We don't even know who was going to win."

Dax looked over to where Gia stood, holding onto her essence sword. A bit of a smile curled her lips, and he realized that she didn't know which of them would've won, either. Neither did he.

He wasn't nearly as helpless as he had thought that he

would've been when it came to using essence like that, though. He had fought, and he had withstood somebody with a powerful earth essence.

What would happen if he were to face someone like his father?

Would I be able to withstand him?

"Did you make all of your preparations?" Rochelle asked Desmond, glancing over at the town, "or do you need to make more?"

"I think that it is time for us all to get back. There is much to do and prepare for." He motioned to the wagon and then headed toward it.

Rochelle frowned. When Dax looked over, she shook her head.

"What is it?"

"It's this," she finally said. "It's him. What do we have to prepare for?"

Chapter Three

THE WAGON MOVED QUICKLY.

There was a power inside of the essence wagon that Dax could easily see, especially as the wagon rumbled rapidly across the ground. Desmond was pushing them harder than Dax had expected. It left him wondering what he'd learned in town that he didn't want to share with the rest of them. Could it be something tied to the Order—or to Ames?

He sat in the back of the wagon, resting next to Cedrick.

Cedrick looked over. "I thought you didn't have that much control over your essence," he said.

"I'm still learning," he said. "Somehow, the essence blade makes it easier."

"I've seen essence soldiers fighting before. You used something different."

Dax knew that he had been drawing upon his essence; he was pushing out of the end of the blade, but even as he had done that, he had sensed something else as well. He had been aware of essence around him. Some of it had come from the fact that he could see essence, but increasingly, the more that he focused, the more that he recognized that he could feel essence as well.

Maybe that just came from being close to the Great Serpent, the serpent stairs, and the testing ground. If that was all it was, then the essence in the air—what others referred to as ambient essence—might've been enough for him to do certain things that he wouldn't have been able to do otherwise. Of course, having progressed to a higher tier also changed things for him. Dax still didn't know what that would mean for his essence control, though he remained curious to explore it.

"Well, it sure looked better than my bubbles," Cedrick said.

"You do realize that your bubbles are a form of life essence, and life essence is one of the primary essences. It is an incredibly useful type of essence."

He snapped his fingers, and thankfully, there was enough breeze around them that it caught the destructive life essence bubbles and carried them behind them. "I wish that there were something more to it. What can you do with pink bubbles?"

"You can look cute," Rochelle said, looking over her shoulder from the front seat. She and Gia had been locked in a quiet conversation, so it did surprise him a little bit that she had heard Cedrick grumbling about his type of essence, though perhaps it shouldn't. Rochelle always seemed to notice people talking around her, almost as if she were wanting to be a part of every single conversation that was taking place. "And Dax is right. You have a useful essence. Be thankful for it."

"Did you really say that I was cute?" Cedrick asked.

"Is that what you are taking away from it?" Rochelle asked.

Cedrick shrugged. "I'm cute," he said, snapping his fingers and causing more of the pink bubbles to swirl. "I'm glad about that."

All Dax could think of was how he could gain some control over his own essence.

He tried to think about what he had done during the fight with Gia. It did remind him a little bit of the mirroring technique that he had seen Desmond using when they had been fighting in the tower, but it wasn't completely the same. He wasn't exactly sure what kind of essence connection he had used, only that what he had drawn on it had seemed to connect him to a considerable amount of her essence. She had much more control over it, though, and much greater strength with her own essence. Dax would never have been able to fully counter her.

What he needed to find was a valor style that would allow him to use transference of essence around him, or perhaps a combination of different types of essence, that would allow him to counter anybody, and anything, that came his way.

That was going to be the key to dealing with the threat of the Order, he suspected.

Valor was necessary. He had always known how to fight, but now he started to think that he was going to have to *really* learn how to fight. Maybe there were additional classes he could take at the Academy. Of course, had he gotten a fire essence, his father would have worked with him. And his father was one of the most skilled valor fighters.

Somehow Dax would have to learn what he needed without his father.

But that was a good thing, he felt. His type of essence was unique. It gave him the ability to do things that others could not do with their own essences. And he couldn't help but feel as if what he could do with his essence would be useful if he were to have to confront one of the Order again. More useful than just fire would've been.

As he thought all this while their wagon zoomed across the ground, Dax noticed a strange glow in the sky.

It looked almost like a beam of light.

"What is that?" he asked, pointing toward it.

Everybody looked, but nobody said anything.

It wasn't until Desmond started to slow the wagon, and he looked back at Dax, that anybody seemed to realize what it was. The light had shifted, though Dax still stared at it, trying to make sense of just what he saw. It really was a beam of light, only it looked far too vibrant to be from any natural source. Maybe essence? But if it were essence, he thought that it shouldn't be quite so bright.

"Where?" Desmond asked.

Dax was a little surprised that others couldn't see it, but then again, he was the only one who had that ability. It suggested that it was all essence. When Dax motioned toward what he saw, Desmond directed them to it.

"Climb up here so that you can show it to me. We can't lose it," Desmond said.

"What is it?" Rochelle asked.

"A flare," he said.

Dax tapped on Gia's shoulder, and he started to climb over the seat. The essence wagon was really two rows of seats, with a third elevated perch where Desmond sat, guiding it. The two women sat in the front, while he and Cedrick sat in the back. The seats were hard, and with each bump that they hit, he was jostled more than he cared for.

But if he were to crawl forward, he thought that it would be best if the person who crawled behind him would be somebody who had a different type of essence that might be able to handle the sudden change.

Gia gave him a look that suggested that she wasn't exactly comfortable with this before she scrambled over the back seat, as he scrambled forward. He plopped down next to Rochelle, who looked in his direction for a moment before turning her focus straight ahead of her.

"Where?" Desmond asked again.

Dax pointed at the glowing beam in front of him, studying it and feeling as if there were different mixtures of essence coming through, not a singular type. If it was essence, could he draw on it?

He held his hand out, but Desmond glanced back and slapped his hand down.

"Don't," he snapped.

"I was just trying to see—"

"I know what you are trying to see, and I'm telling you that it's not the way. If there is an essence flare out there, we need to reach it before anybody else does."

"Anybody else?" Rochelle asked. "As in—"

"As in the Order," he said.

"I thought we were just getting back to the Academy," Rochelle said.

"We were, but we follow the flare. We *always* follow the flare."

Their wagon crashed through the underbrush. Dax had expected that the essence wagon wouldn't tolerate it quite as well, but somehow it did seem to handle it much better that he would've expected. It rumbled forward, and he noticed the strange whirring sound that began to build. It came from something at the front of the essence wagon.

Is it cutting down the grasses?

He looked over his shoulder and saw that behind them was a trampled path.

"Wouldn't somebody be able to follow this?" Dax asked.

"Yes," he said. "And that is why we are going as quickly as possible. Once we get there, we can decide what else we need to do."

"What else?" Rochelle asked.

"Well, we may have to deal with a threat," Desmond said.

They reached a denser section of forest. Still Desmond didn't slow.

Dax braced himself. He kept waiting for the essence wagon to get caught by some fallen log, or perhaps some thorny undergrowth, things that he knew were much more common in his part of the Empire, along the border of the unclaimed lands. He had quite a bit of experience with tracking through places like this and was surprised when the wagon didn't slow at all. His father would've loved a device like this.

"Do you still see the beam?" Desmond asked. "I know it's harder in the trees. We need to get there before the others. This is imperative, Dax."

"I…" He looked around, and then he saw it.

It was straight ahead. Now that they were getting closer, the light seemed to be brighter, thicker. More than that, he noticed that there seemed to be a tracing of different colors within it. From a distance, it had looked as if it was a pure white light, but up close, he could see striations of color working through the beam as it shot upward.

A flare, as Desmond had called it.

But a flare for what? And who had triggered it?

"What is it, exactly?"

"It occurs when the Great Serpent awakens," Desmond said, seemingly choosing his words carefully. "There is usually a singular flare. Occasionally there are secondary ones, though not with much potency."

"And this one is the primary flare?" Rochelle asked.

Desmond didn't answer.

"Was there a primary flare?"

"Yes," he finally said. "And it's been addressed and dealt with."

"What do you mean?"

"What I mean is that the flares are not for us. Generally speaking. We can climb the tower. We can visit with the Great Serpent. We can take essence that way. Now. Can you still see it?"

Dax nodded. "I can see it. What happens if we don't get to it?"

"Let's just not think about that as a possibility."

Dax shared a look with Rochelle, and a question occurred to him. The flare was not for them.

So who was it for?

Chapter Four

THE LANDSCAPE STARTED TO SHIFT AGAIN.

They had been heading through the forest, moving as quickly as possible, but suddenly, that had shifted into something different and far more difficult to navigate. The ground became boggy, and the wagon slowed suddenly.

Desmond stopped, pausing near a tree, and he hopped out of the wagon before tapping on it for a moment. As he did, Dax felt a surge of essence come from him, and it flowed into the wagon. Something changed for a moment, and then the wagon began to gradually elevate out of the muck.

Desmond let out a frustrated sigh, turning to the others. "We will have to go across ground now."

"Through a swamp?" Rochelle asked.

"Is this a swamp?" Cedrick asked. He flicked his fingers, and this time, it seemed as if his bubbles were a bit smaller than they had been before. Every time that he flicked them, he looked as if he was trying to make bigger bubbles, but they trembled before popping quickly.

Dax focused on his own transference essence, wondering if he had some similar limitation as it seemed Cedrick did. As he looked over to Rochelle, he noticed that her greenish-blue flow of essence was still there, but it did seem to be constricted down inside of her much more so than he would've expected. Even Gia's earth connection was a bit faded, more so than it had been before.

"We go across the ground, and we move as quickly as we can. If anybody gets slowed down, you can return to the wagon. I will not be able to take my time in this. And I need Dax to move as quickly as possible with me."

"Can you tell us why the urgency?" Dax asked as he started off, already moving quickly over a fallen mossy log.

The others stayed behind them, though they were moving quickly as well.

"A flare is a beacon coming from the Great Serpent," Desmond explained. "Every so often, the Great Serpent will send out flares like this. These are true, raw power. It is essence." He swept his gaze around each of them. "And it is the kind of power that anybody can take. It is different than going into the tower and undergoing a testing. It is an easier way to progress rapidly. At least for those who understand how to control it."

"Easier than just drinking from the pool of essence?" Dax asked Desmond.

"Such a thing is incredibly risky," he said, and he paused for a moment, glancing at one of the massive trees that jutted out of the ground. Roots looked as if they wanted to trip them up. The ground was soft and soggy, and Dax didn't like the idea of standing there for too long, but he had shifted forward so that he wasn't standing on soft ground so much as he was standing on one of the roots from one of the trees. "Most people who try to consume that type of essence find that they are forever changed. Very few find it is for the better."

"But I..."

Desmond locked eyes with him for a moment. "I think you were lucky because you hadn't taken any other essence yet. Otherwise..." He shrugged. "I can't say. All I can say is that it does seem as if you were chosen by the Great Serpent to do something significant. You should thank the Great Serpent."

Desmond lunged forward, using some different form of essence. Dax had only seen him using a mirror form before, but he must've had another essence, much like Dax's mother had a second form.

The essence around them was significant—and strange. Dax drew on it, and he found it increasingly easy to do compared with what he had experienced previously. That had to be tied to his progression.

Rochelle struggled, grunting at one point to jerk her foot free from the boggy ground.

He held out a hand for her, but she shook her head. "I'm fine."

"I can help," he offered.

"Stay with him. We will keep up."

For her part, Gia was having very little difficulty. It took him only a moment to realize why. She was using her essence, and she was somehow solidifying the ground as she walked.

Cedrick had just as much difficulty as Rochelle, though.

"Stay close to Gia," he said, motioning to the other two. "She can keep you moving quickly."

Rochelle moved closer to Gia, and so did Cedrick.

At least he knew that they would be able to keep going.

Desmond had already moved farther ahead of them.

Dax scrambled forward, jumping from one tree root to a fallen log, then to another tree root. At one point, he even grabbed onto a low-level branch, swung forward, coming to land next to Desmond. The flare continued to glow with an incredible sense of power.

"It wants me to draw on it," Dax said.

"It is only essence," Desmond said.

"I don't know if it is," he said. "I can feel something. It feels like—"

Desmond touched his hand on Dax's arm, and it forced Dax to shake those thoughts away, looking over at the other man.

"I understand that it can feel compelling. It is *designed* to be compelling. You would need to withstand it. You are not equipped to take on another essence yet."

"Another essence?"

"That is the possibility that you would find here, Dax. Do not draw on it. Ignore it."

The beam continued to glow, almost pulsating. There was something practically seductive about it.

And every time that he focused on that essence, and could feel the strain of power out there, he noticed that some part of it seemed to swirl within the essence beam, and it was looking to him as if it wanted him to draw upon it, as if he had no choice but to do so. Dax tried to ignore it, but he struggled.

Somebody shouted.

Dax turned. He had moved farther away from others than he had intended.

He saw Desmond facing a long, lizard-like creature that was crawling on four legs toward him. The creature radiated heat, but it also glowed with a pale orange essence.

Dax hurriedly unsheathed his essence blade as he scrambled toward Desmond.

But he couldn't move quickly enough.

He wasn't going to get to Desmond before the creature did, so he did the only thing he could. He pushed his power through the blade.

Essence flowed from it, sizzling as it shot toward the creature. When it struck, the creature froze in place, but only for a moment. Then it turned its full attention to Dax.

Faster than Dax would've thought possible, the creature went scrambling toward him.

Essence surged all around, and Dax realized that the others were attempting to fight alongside him. Other than Gia, he didn't know if anyone would have any ability to actually fight.

He noticed a faint, almost sickly yellow essence flowing through the creature.

Did it give the creature immunity to his essence blasts?

Whether it did or not, it made Dax realize there might be something else that he could try.

He hadn't attempted to use transference on a moving creature, and certainly not on an unfamiliar creature, but why not now?

He twisted, spinning out of the way and barely avoided the creature jumping toward him as it snapped a long, toothy snout toward his foot.

Dax slammed his hand down.

The creature tried to twist, but Dax immediately began to form a transference pattern.

It was a matter of reaching for the essence inside of the creature and drawing it up. If it worked like it did with any of the other creatures he had kept, it should incapacitate the creature—if only temporarily. He pulled. Rather than restraining himself from drawing too much, he tried to withdraw as much as he could so that he could ensure that he could get past this creature, and he could drain some of the power out of it.

More and more began to flood out of the creature and into him. There was a strangeness to it. The essence that he was drawing felt as if it were buzzing, almost as if it tingled everything inside of him. The creature thrashed, but Dax continued to pull, drawing more out of him until the thrashing began to ease.

Desmond rested a hand on Dax's arm.

"I would not hold that if I were you."

Dax didn't have any idea how long he could hold onto essence. With transference, it didn't seem as if there was much of a limitation, but then he had never attempted to test that. He had pulled essence off of others, but it was a recent thing.

"Can't I just hold it?"

"You would think that it would work that way, but there are those who can use what you are calling transference with runes, and they have tested the same sort of thing. It damages a person and destabilizes the essence they are able to hold otherwise. I fear that without knowing the true nature of your essence, there's a real possibility that you would end up destabilizing your own essence before you had a chance to test it and control it."

Dax immediately released the power that he was holding upward. It blasted into the trees.

Dax finally looked down at the long, slender lizard. It wasn't moving, though it didn't seem to be dead.

"What is that?" he asked.

"It is an aligars. Dangerous creatures. They are found in this part of the world, and they have a natural immunity to many types of essence." He looked up at Dax. "And from what I gather, from the way that you tried to attack, it obviously has a natural immunity to your type of essence."

"Apparently," Dax said.

He wasn't sure what would happen given that he had added some of that essence to himself. Maybe nothing. But there was a part of him that started to wonder if perhaps he might be able to use that power.

"We need to get to the flare," Desmond said. "And if we find any more of the aligars, I would appreciate it if you would do what you did here." He eyed Dax for a moment. "That is, if it is not too much of a discomfort."

"I think I should be able to do it," Dax said.

They picked their way through the swamp. There was no other sign of any other creatures.

They reached a small clearing. Dax wondered if it was always a clearing, or if this beam of energy had formed the clearing here. Inside of it, the light continued to glow, shooting upward, arcing toward a central point higher in the sky.

"I feel it," Cedrick said as he started forward until Desmond grabbed him.

"It's everywhere," Rochelle whispered. "But faint."

Desmond looked over at Dax. "And I imagine you see it like a bright sun."

Dax nodded. "How do you see it?"

"Hazy," he said. "Flares are always hazy. And it is unusual that some would be able to see them quite as brightly as you can. I suppose that is good that we have you with us. Now, if you don't mind, we need to find a way through. Give me a few moments as I examine this."

Desmond began to make his way around the flare, leaving the others alone.

Dax stared at it. Up close, the draw on him was nearly overwhelming.

Rochelle joined him, holding his arm, almost as if she realized that he was feeling compelled to go toward it. It was too potent.

Without meaning to, he took a step forward. Then another.

His friends stopped him.

Rochelle held onto him, and then Gia joined her, both women linking arms with him, holding him.

One was healing. Water. Dax could feel her touch, and he could feel the way that she was sending essence through him, even though he couldn't see her flow of essence. Then there was a bit of the touch coming off of Gia, the solid nature of earth that emanated from her. It filled him. He could feel her trying to hold him in place, as if she were aware that something was pulling on him.

Still, Dax tried to fight.

As he did, essence pulled on him. And the power was just too much to withstand.

Chapter Five

STRANDS OF POWER FLOWED WITHIN THAT BEAM OF LIGHT, as if representing different types of essence. He could see pale yellow, green, red, brown, gray, and every variation therein. It left him wondering what type of essence each of those represented. They ringed the entirety of the clearing, the essence beam shooting upward into the sky, practically pulling on him in a way that he couldn't even fathom.

Cedrick joined him, pressing his fingers together and letting some of the pink bubbles flow outward. There was a nervous grin on his face. "You're going to have to teach me how you have such a way with the ladies," he said to Dax.

"He's being drawn by it," Rochelle said, looking over at him. "I can feel it a little bit, and I suspect that Gia can as well," she said while looking over to the other woman, who nodded. "But Dax has transference. Which means that he's going to be drawn more than all of us."

Dax nodded. "And it wants me to go forward."

"The essence wants you to?" Cedrick shook his head.

"Or the Great Serpent does? That's what you're talking about, isn't it? This is essence from the Great Serpent."

He still didn't know the answer. Desmond had said this was a flare, a secondary one at that—but what did that mean?

"Let's find Desmond—"

Dax didn't have a chance to finish.

There was a thundering of essence behind them. Rochelle and Gia were jerked away. Dax spun to see flashes of essence in the trees.

They were faint, especially given the brightness of the beam of essence that was nearby, but he realized what they had to be seeing. Different types of essence flared, much brighter than he would've expected.

The Order.

"This isn't good," Dax said.

He reached for his essence blade.

"No," Gia said, and she tried to get to him, but she wasn't fast enough.

Dax touched his essence blade.

And then, as soon as he did, he realized the mistake.

The essence blade magnified everything. He had known that. He had trained with essence blades, and he had always known that there was a magnification of power that came from them, so that as he felt it now, and as that magnification of power exploded through him, he felt the sudden drawing of essence all around him.

It filled him.

It was dangerous to be so close to it.

But it called to him.

Somewhere distantly, he could hear another shout. Was that Desmond?

If the Order was there for the flare, they needed Desmond.

Dax took another step.

Then he felt the edge of the essence begin to touch him.

He could feel a tingling along his skin. A rainbow of colors scattered all around him, as if he were stepping through a waterfall, seeing a prism of light bending through the stream. It was beautiful. It was powerful. It was nearly overwhelming.

He took another step.

Dax had to keep moving. He had to follow that sense of essence.

He felt a growing pressure.

Maybe it was this flare, the essence of the Great Serpent dragging him.

He staggered forward, moving closer to the center of the clearing. A distant part of his mind knew this was a danger, but he knew he had to keep moving.

When he took another step, he felt more trembling around him.

Was that earth?

Maybe Gia was trying to get to him. Or maybe Rochelle was trying to help him.

Another step.

Then he saw a crystalline structure on the ground.

He bent down, and his head began to swim, almost as if the swirls of color around him, and the essence that he felt pressing all around him, was too much to handle. Ignoring the pain, he grabbed the crystal and held it up. It didn't look like anything he had ever seen before. It was nearly perfectly symmetrical, six-sided, with tipped ends that looked as if they were incredibly sharp.

This was the essence flare?

The only thing he could think of was what Desmond had said. This was not for them.

He held onto it carefully, noticing different striations of color swirling within it, and he held it closer so that he could try to make out the different hues within it. The colors began to coalesce, and there was movement within the crystal.

Could that be the Great Serpent?

It was his flare, after all.

And there was a pulling, a drawing of essence, as if the crystal were trying to force some part of him to pay attention to the power within the crystal. It was a power that Dax could scarcely ignore, though he wasn't even sure that he wanted to ignore it. He tentatively connected to that essence with transference.

And immediately realized the mistake.

It felt as if he were pulled *inside* the crystal.

An image began to form, one that was brighter and more vibrant than anything he had ever seen before. It was a massive scaled creature that swirled around him. It felt like Dax was trapped inside a pool of liquid, or condensed air, as he could still breathe. The serpent moving around him was massive, with unfurled wings that strained on either side of the creature and a long barbed tail that swept through the air. Scales glittered, catching the colors of all the different types of essences, and a long, magnificent face turned toward him, with a ring of ridges along the back of its head looking something like a lion's mane.

The Great Serpent.

There was no doubt in Dax's mind that this was the Great Serpent.

"You are young," a voice said inside of his mind.

"I felt the pull," Dax answered.

"Many do. What will it do for you?"

Suddenly, an image in front of him changed.

There was still a heavy cloud, or at least what seemed like a thickened energy, but now Dax was standing on what looked like a mountainside, with pale white clouds dotting the landscape all around him. The sun shone overhead, and within the sky were small dark specks that swirled.

At first, Dax stared at them, but then he realized that those dark specks seemed to be filled with essence. Every time that the shape shifted, moving and swirling and changing, he noticed more within it. Essence?

There had to be a dozen of them.

Then the clouds began to shift again.

He was still on the same mountainside, or at least he thought he was, but now the ground around him had changed. It was a bit rockier, and there were more trees, grasses, and other plants that were there. Everything around him radiated essence. Dax could feel it, though he wasn't sure why he could feel it the way that he did now. He saw colors. Green of life, blue of water, yellows, oranges, and every other color, all around him.

Everything seemed to be imbued with essence.

He looked up as there was another swirl of energy that seemed to call to Dax—a warning.

A long, sinewy-looking creature was moving through the sky, with long, impossibly thin wings that sliced through the air. It looked like the Great Serpent, but it looked like a smaller version of it. As this creature circled, more essence began to flow from it.

Then the image changed again. This time Dax was standing near a series of different essences, though now they were far more distinct than they had been before—pockets of essence, where before it had been diffuse clouds of essence. And he noticed that animals had gathered all around him.

Creatures would pause, some of them looking like wolves or bears or other mixtures of different animals, and they would pull at grasses, leaves, or even nuzzle their heads down to the ground until they were either eating dirt or rock. Some were lapping at water that was flowing nearby. All of it seemed to be filled with the power of the essence that was here.

This had to be the Great Serpent.

And he knew that he had made a mistake. This was not for him. That was what Desmond had said.

Power bloomed all around him. It felt as if everything was the Great Serpent.

Up ahead, he noticed golden eyes locking onto him. There was his reflection in those eyes, holding onto the crystal, but then even that began to change.

The Great Serpent swirled around him, movement shifting and swimming and making everything within Dax begin to feel as if he were all too aware of the power that was coming from the creature.

And then he felt a flare inside of him.

It was warmth. It was cold. It seemed to be all things.

And it seemed to come all at the same time.

Dax had never felt anything quite like that before. It reminded him a little bit of what he had felt when he had been inside the testing tower, taking the essence for the first time, but in this case, it seemed to wash through him rather than starting inside of him and washing outward. It pressed downward, constricting him.

Everything within him went numb, tingling. He couldn't tell what had happened, only that there was a significant surge of energy that seemed as if it had come from all around him, leaving Dax tumbling with that power, leaving him feeling at a loss for understanding.

The Great Serpent stopped spinning.

The creature turned its face, its attention, upon Dax.

Then he heard the voice inside of his head once again.

"Drink."

Dax shook his head. "Drink what?"

He didn't have anything to drink.

"Drink."

He tried to resist, tried to tell the Great Serpent that he didn't have anything, but at the same time, Dax knew that he was holding something. He could feel it in his hands. He had no idea what it was, but it seemed to be burning, didn't it?

He held it up.

It was a crystalline cup. He saw that it was filled with a pale liquid, and with a dawning of understanding, Dax realized exactly what it was.

Essence.

Pure essence, given to him by the Great Serpent.

Even when he had come to his testing, Dax had not seen a vision of the Great Serpent quite like this. This was what he had believed that he was supposed to have seen when he had gone to the tower in the first place. This was what the stories always spoke of. The opportunity to take on essence and have the guidance of the Great Serpent. His mother had told him that he should be deferential, whereas his father had wanted him to ask for fire.

What did Dax want to ask for?

At this point, he wasn't even sure that he wanted to ask for anything.

He couldn't even fathom what he could do, nor could he fathom the kind of power that was there, within him.

And yet, he needed to know, and he needed to see if there was something that the Great Serpent might tell him. He needed to ask the Great Serpent for something, but he also didn't know whether it would change anything if he did.

Dax felt that essence, he felt that power, and he felt…

He felt the draw, as if he needed to try something more. Dax wasn't sure whether the Great Serpent would give him much choice in the matter, only that he had to find some part of himself, some strength that would allow him to understand what it was that he could do with this power.

So he brought the cup to his lips.

He paused for a moment. He looked over at the Great Serpent.

"Ask," the Great Serpent said, though the words came through his mind.

"I want…"

What did he want?

He had been given a strange gift before, but that gift had not been given to him by the Great Serpent. That had been accidental, hadn't it? Despite what Desmond might claim, and what others might believe about him, the gift that he had, the type of transference essence that he could use, was not anything that the Great Serpent had bestowed upon him. Now the Great Serpent was telling him that it was okay for him to ask.

Did he want fire?

There were so many different ways to use fire that Dax could easily imagine that he could draw upon that power, and he could become more like his family, like the person that his father had wanted him to be. Maybe he could ask for something like water. Healing would be beneficial, wouldn't it? He could work with Rochelle, stay close to her, and he could learn how to help others. There were plenty of uses for that as well.

What about life? Life was the core of so many things, and given that he had a means of using transference, Dax couldn't help but feel as if maybe he could use that connection, and what he possessed with it, to be able to understand transference, and to control it much better than he had before. Or perhaps earth. It was similar to what Gia had, and he could easily imagine how he might be able to use that, especially as he had started to draw upon some aspect of it when he had mirrored her. Or even wind, so that he could become a Whisper like his sister. Would he want to be more like Megan? Learn how to control that power so that he could become something even greater and much more beneficial to the Empire?

If Dax were honest with himself, he kind of wanted all of them.

But what he wanted more than anything, was one thing.

"I want understanding."

"A dangerous request. And one that will be transformative."

It seemed as if the Great Serpent loomed forward, and for a moment, Dax knew a moment of fear, as if he were worried that the Great Serpent might swallow him.

But it never happened.

Instead, it got close, and then everything went black.

Chapter Six

DAX AWOKE.

He felt essence as he came around, and he realized that he was still holding onto the crystal his hands, squeezing it tightly. Somebody was shouting his name.

Dax wasn't sure who it was, but there seemed to be a real panic to it.

He sat up.

The swamp had started to swirl around him, as if he were sinking down into it. Distantly, he was aware of the energy that was all around him. The colors had sputtered, the flare starting to fade already, until it would dissipate into nothingness. Dax suspected that it would fade completely over time, and when it did, there would be no protection for him.

Which meant that the Order would come at him and come for the crystal.

That had to be what they were after, after all. Dax thought that if he could get free, and he could figure out just what it was that they wanted with the crystal, he might be able to protect it, but at this point, he wasn't even sure if he knew enough to do so.

He stood, and as he did, he squeezed his essence blade, trying to draw upon the power inside of the blade, even though he knew that there wasn't going to be any power he could draw through it. Not yet.

But he could help.

The Order might have come, but Dax was strong enough to fight, wasn't he?

He just had to clear the image of the Great Serpent from his mind—and recover from drinking essence. And he still couldn't believe what had just happened.

"Dax!"

It was Rochelle.

He followed the sound of her voice.

Dax reached the edge of the bubbling essence, and he hesitated for a moment, feeling it pull him. It was still calling to him. All he had to do was to draw on it.

And he thought that he might be able to do that, but at this point, he wasn't even sure that he wanted to, as he didn't know if it was safe for him to draw upon that yet. He had to be careful. He had to be smart. He had to be—

"Dax?"

There was a different sense of urgency.

Fear?

His friends were worried about him, and he understood why that would be, as he had been inside of this space for quite a while now—long enough that he might have even lost himself a little bit in the process. He stepped forward and felt the strange tingling of essence washing across his skin, only this time as he did, he began to feel the dancing of different types of essence, enough so that he could almost name them, though he wasn't sure that he had them right. It seemed as if there were earth and wind and fire variants that tapped along his skin, flickering along his flesh, as if trying to warn him.

Then he saw Rochelle.

She had backed toward the swamp. Gia was there, her essence blade outstretched, and there was a dark-cloaked man approaching them. He had a pair of swords in either hand, but neither of them seem to be an essence blade. Surprisingly, though, he had a pair of creatures on either side of him. Neither of them looked like the aligars that they had dealt with before—both of these looked like strange, furless dogs.

Dax focused on the essence around him and pushed it through his sword. Power exploded—much more so than he should have been capable of wielding—and struck the man, who staggered back a step.

He turned toward Dax and whistled. The dogs came bounding toward him.

Earth essence flowed within the dogs. Were they some sort of earth bonded creature? He had seen something along that line on the border before, but he had never had to fight it. Could he do so now?

He thought that transference might work against them, but he didn't know if it would be fully effective for him to pull on that essence. He didn't want to destroy them, just slow them. And he could draw through the sword.

He did so, finding it easier than he should have.

He almost lost control of it. This was different than it had been even after he had visited with the Great Serpent the last time. Had he progressed again?

He really needed to talk to somebody about that, and about what it meant for him, to try to make sense of what level he might be. But for now, he held onto essence, and drew it from one creature, and then the next, until both were down.

Dax looked at the man, but Gia darted forward, driving her blade into the man's stomach.

He fell, collapsing to the swampy ground.

"We need to go!" Rochelle shouted.

"I'm sorry," Dax said.

"Did you get it?" Rochelle asked, looking back over toward the sputtering of essence behind him. "Desmond was looking for a way in, but then when I told him that you had gone inside of it, he figured that you were going to reach the essence. Did you forget it?"

"I got a crystal," Dax said.

"A crystal?" Cedrick asked. "Weren't we supposed to find some part of the Great Serpent?"

Dax wanted to tell him that he had, and that by entering inside of that strange band of essence that he had seen the Great Serpent and must've been given some sort of gift. But he wasn't even sure what he had been gifted, nor did he know the power that would come from it. And increasingly, he was starting to wonder if maybe he had made a mistake in his request.

"We have to hurry," Gia said. "I think there are three more that way," she said, pointing off to her right, "and another three that way," she said, pointing to her left, "and if I'm not mistaken, maybe a half dozen behind us."

So many.

That meant that there were a dozen different attackers, so many that Dax didn't think that they would have any chance of handling them. The only chance they had was running.

But how could they run? Where could they run?

"Do you know where Desmond went?" Dax asked.

"No," Rochelle said.

"It doesn't matter," Gia said.

She danced forward, taking the lead. As she did, the ground in front of her seemed to solidify. Dax was impressed by the level of control that she had.

Branches nearby began to stir, and Dax looked over. Before he could do anything, Cedrick flicked his hand, and a stream of pale pink began to sputter from him.

"It's just not working," he muttered.

But where his bubbles struck, the branches began to draw down, forming a thick blanket around him.

Dax smiled to himself. "Keep trying," he said. "Obviously your life essence has a different sort of reaction here. So keep trying and seeing what you might be able to do with it."

"This is all life essence?" Cedrick asked.

"To be honest, I have no idea," Dax said.

Cedrick started to snap his fingers, waving his hands all around him, and more bubbles began to stream from his fingertips, heading toward the trees nearby as if to attack them. But rather than attacking or burning, as Dax had seen Cedrick's essence do before, the bubbles actually caused the trees to ripple and grow. The power that Cedrick was able to use was so much different than anything Dax had experienced before.

They followed Gia, who was solidifying the ground, and let Cedrick take the lead just behind her to protect them from others.

"Do you remember where the cart was?" Gia asked, looking back at him.

"It should be just up ahead," Dax said.

"I hope you're right," she muttered.

They raced through the forest, and Dax began to see a

path forming. It wasn't just because the ground was trampled here; it seemed as if there was some sort of essence trail that lingered. At one point, he felt something nearby and motioned to Cedrick, who snapped his fingers and sent another flurry of pink bubbles behind them.

"I think this is actually going to work," Dax said.

Then there was a thunderous crack.

Two of the strange stone dogs lunged forward.

Dax reacted the same way that he had before and began to pull upon the first dog's essence, but he wasn't fast enough for the second one. As Dax brought one of them down, Gia struggled with the other.

"They have earth essence," he said to her.

"I realize that." She tried to stab at the creature, but with earth essence, her blade merely bounced off it.

There was too much resistance. Which meant somebody was helping.

Three figures stepped forward from the trees.

"Where is it?"

The deep voice boomed, thundering through the forest.

It wasn't the headmaster, though Dax thought it might've been better if it had been, as at least they understood what they were getting into with him.

"There was nothing," Dax said.

Cedrick snapped his fingers, sending a stream of bubbles toward the three figures. They had started to spread out, each of them carrying a pair of long, blackened blades. When they swept their blades away from them, they carved through the bubbles, and the forest seemed to wither away from them.

"The flare extinguished," the lead figure said.

He was a powerful-looking man. Dax couldn't tell what kind of essence he had, only that it was a dark, hazy sort of power that seemed to work from some place deep inside of him. The man stepped toward them, and where his blade carved through the branches, they withered away.

Gia pointed her essence blade downward, and the ground started to ripple.

It wasn't enough. The man swept his blade through that as well.

"You have some nice tricks," he said, "but students do not pose any danger."

As much as he wanted to argue and say that they were students who had dealt with the Order, they didn't have Megan or Desmond with them to help now. He and Gia knew valor, but that wouldn't be enough—and certainly not enough without any additional ambient essence.

"Hand it over," the man said, "and we will let you walk back to your school. We won't even harm you."

One of the other figures was nearby, blade pointed at them.

Dax reacted instinctively. He jerked his essence blade up, pushed through it, and a bubble of power exploded through the blade.

When it slammed into the man, he collapsed.

They had an opening, but it was not one to fight.

"Run," Dax urged.

Gia solidified the ground in front of them.

Cedrick sent bubbles streaking all around them.

The forest and the swamp seemed to come alive.

Even Rochelle did something, though Dax wasn't sure what it was that she was doing, only that she was waving her hands, expressing some essence around her.

What would her healing essence do?

Not healing. *Water.*

Her water mixed with what Cedrick was doing, and the

combination of water and life cause the forest to bloom in a way that it had not before. It became incredibly dense, filling with vines and small trees and thorny branches, all of which worked to at least slow the incomers.

They ran.

"I hope you know how to start the wagon," Cedrick shouted, sending another stream of bubbles behind him.

Desmond had been responsible for powering the wagon, and Dax didn't know if any of them knew enough about the essence in it to make it work.

"Move," a voice boomed behind them.

For a moment, Dax thought that it came from the attacker, and he glanced behind him, ready to expend another band of essence. But it wasn't.

It was Desmond.

He took impossibly long strides that looked as if he were floating, making Dax think that he was somehow using a bit of wind as he hurried through the forest. He passed them, then sent a sweep of power past Dax. There was a stirring of wind mixed with heat.

They reached the wagon, and all of them piled inside quickly.

Desmond backed toward it, snapped his foot against it, and essence suddenly flared inside of the wagon. "Steer," Desmond snapped.

Dax wasn't sure who he was talking to, but he climbed up to the driver's seat anyway. Desmond sat near the rear of the essence wagon, sending more power out from him as the essence wagon slowly but gradually rumbled up to speed. Soon, it streaked through the forest, accelerating until he feared that they were going to crash into a tree. When Desmond climbed past him, taking over the wheel, Dax let out a long, steady sigh.

"Did you get it?" Desmond asked.

Dax pulled the crystal out of his pocket and handed it to Desmond.

Desmond looked down at it. He glanced at Dax for a moment, then down at the crystal. "It cracked."

"What?" Cedrick asked, leaning over to look.

"The crystal. It cracked. It shouldn't look cloudy like this."

"All that for nothing?" Cedrick asked.

"Apparently," Desmond said.

But Rochelle was watching Dax. She said nothing, but she didn't need to. She knew it wasn't for nothing.

Only Dax wasn't sure what he had gained.

Chapter Seven

EVERYBODY WAS SILENT ON THE RETURN TO THE ACADEMY. The wagon moved quickly. There was no further sign of an attack, though everybody looked behind them, watching for the possibility of another. They had survived an attack, but what did that mean for them? No one seemed to know.

Worse, at least for Dax, was the fact that Desmond didn't seem to be interested in talking to any of them. Dax understood to a certain extent, especially considering he suspected that Desmond was more concerned about what the Order was after, and about getting them back to the Academy safely, but he did want answers.

"I'm ready to get back," Cedrick said, finally breaking the silence as they topped a rise where the city was visible in the distance.

The city grew steadily closer as they approached from the west, with the forest along the border of the city a vibrant green contrast to the dark browns and grays and white spires that stretched into the sky. Dax had spent most of his life on the outskirts of the Empire and had grown accustomed to the quiet found there. He wasn't sure that he was ready to return.

Dax had continued to look behind him, watching for any signs that they might've been pursued, but so far, they had managed to stay ahead of anything. It was probably better that they did, as he wasn't sure he would be able to withstand anything more than what they already had.

"Although, I'm not looking forward to my testing," Cedrick went on.

"You don't need to worry about passing," Rochelle said, though she seemed distracted.

"That's easy for you to say," he said, sitting forward and snapping his fingers once again. Every time he did, the pink bubbles that drifted faded, disappearing behind him. "You've been able to control your essence ever since you first came to the Academy."

"So have you," Dax said.

"I suppose that's true. And now I know my essence can actually be useful," Cedrick said.

"You knew that your essence was able to do something before," Dax said.

Cedrick shrugged. "There's a difference between knowing that I can make pretty bubbles and knowing that there is something *useful* to those bubbles. It's nice."

And that was something that Dax understood, considering that when he had first come to the Academy, he hadn't known anything about his essence nor if there was going to be anything useful about it.

He had started to gain a greater appreciation for what his transference essence could do, though now that he had progressed to another tier of essence control, he was going to have to gain even greater understanding about what that meant. And that said nothing about whatever additional gift the Great Serpent had given him.

"Should we make sure that the headmaster isn't a danger?" Gia asked, leaning forward.

"I think we all need to be careful when we get back to the Academy," Dax said. "Until we can be certain that the Order, and the headmaster in particular, aren't a threat any longer, we should make sure that we're watching out for each other."

The headmaster couldn't have been working alone. There had to have been others within the Academy who had known about him and had been working with him. It meant they had to be cautious—and would need to determine who to trust.

"The only one who knows about our involvement is the headmaster," Rochelle said, shooting a gaze up to where Desmond was seated.

They were rumbling along quickly, but they had slowed as they neared the city. Dax wasn't sure if there was a limit to the essence wagon, or if it was simply that Desmond wanted to give them an opportunity to gather their thoughts and regroup before reaching the city itself. It was certainly a much faster journey to the city than it had been when he had first come down the serpent stairs and had ventured toward the Academy. This was almost unpleasant though.

"But the headmaster would have had influence," Dax said, expressing his concern. "We should be careful."

"I don't know how careful we really need to be," Rochelle said. "We are just first-year students."

"I will ensure you don't have anything to fear when we return to the city," Desmond said.

"How do you intend to do that?" Gia asked.

"I intend to go about it the way that I would go about anything," he said, turning back to her. "Carefully. Much like I would encourage all of you to do everything carefully, as well. Until you know what you are dealing with, and until you know the extent of the threat that you might face, you all should be careful. We don't know how deep the Order penetrated the Academy."

He watched them all for a moment, then he turned his attention back to driving the cart. By the time they reached the outskirts of the city, everybody had fallen silent.

They traveled quietly, and only when they got into the city, and the sounds and chaos of the city itself began to rumble around them, did Dax allow himself to feel a measure of relaxation. He didn't hold his essence balled up quite as tightly inside of him as he had been doing.

He looked around, noting traces of essence all around him. The colors were there—swirls of pale yellow, green, orange, pink, blue, and other hues and shades. Some of those colors reminded him of what he had seen from the crystal, all the different strands and striations that blended into one type of essence that had emanated from the Great Serpent.

If only he understood the difference and the distinct nature of each of those essences. That was perhaps what he should've asked the Great Serpent for. He had asked for understanding, but maybe he should've been more specific.

They passed through several different markets before Desmond parked the wagon and motioned for them all to follow. They got out, and then they began to walk. The city was quiet, at least compared with when they had been here last and had been concerned about the Order. It seemed as if a calm had fallen over the city.

By the time they reached the artisan district, everybody

was talking a little bit more. Dax was probably the only one who could see the concentrated flows of essence through the artisan district, and the vibrancy to it. Still, everyone seemed to relax.

He saw no sign of damage from the attack. Those within the artisan district had recovered quickly, repairing and restoring everything that was found here. As they neared the Academy, he even saw some remnants of the Valor Day celebration from a month ago, as the grounds were still being disassembled.

Dax stared straight ahead, marching with everyone else, lost in his own thoughts.

Rochelle tapped him, and he shook his head, frowning. "It's nothing."

"It looks like you see something," she said.

"I'm just looking at the essence around us," Dax said.

When Desmond glanced in his direction, Dax shrugged.

There wasn't anything more to say about what happened. It was more about what he understood of essence. Right now, it wasn't much. He wanted to better understand his essence, and what it might provide him, but for now, he had to master the type of essence that he possessed and try to understand what it meant.

When they reached Desmond's home, he opened the door, and then paused for a moment. Dax felt the essence that he was using and noticed that he drew it through something in his pocket. It wasn't essence Desmond commanded naturally or natively. It seemed to come from a device he carried. It spilled out—a bit of stone, a bit of wind, and surprisingly, a bit of life essence—and went into a series of markers on the building itself. Dax recognized them as measures of protection, identifying them much more easily than he had previously.

Could that have been what had changed for him?

They headed inside, and Dax and Rochelle knew to pass straight through the long, cluttered hallway of Desmond's home, with boxes stacked on either side. Some of them were holding what looked to be artwork, others relics and artifacts, and still others were seemingly packed with books. Beyond was a main room. It was only a little different than the last time that they had been here, though there was some part of it that left Dax feeling as if he had misremembered things. He always had that sensation when he came to Desmond's home, as if the place or something inside it disrupted Dax's ability to remember things.

Desmond made his way toward the stove, where he put a kettle on and quickly lit the burner, whistling to himself.

Cedrick threw himself down into one of the plush chairs near the hearth. He flicked his fingers, but realized where he was, and swiped at the bubbles, keeping them from catching the top of Desmond's home. Dax didn't know what they would do, but there was a possibility that those bubbles might destroy something, given the kind of power that they possessed. Then again, they were life essence, so maybe they wouldn't.

"Why are we here?" Gia asked. "Don't we need to get back to the Academy? Some of us have tests."

"You will," Desmond said, glancing in her direction before turning his attention back to the cattle. "After."

"After?" She straightened, resting one hand on the hilt of her essence blade. "After what?"

"After we have an opportunity to test the dangers. I sent word ahead."

"And how did you send word ahead?" She looked over

at the rest of us before turning her attention back to Desmond. "You're a member of the Cult of the Dragon. How did you send word ahead?"

"Because there are others in the city," Desmond said, waving his hand and turning his attention back to the kettle. It had already started steaming, and he picked it up, setting it on another counter before grabbing five mugs from a cabinet and setting them down beside it. He scooped a bit of tea leaves into each one, then began to pour the steaming liquid over the tea leaves before looking up at her. "Of course there are others active in the city though. You would have known that."

Dax turned away, focusing on essence. Everything was glowing a little differently than he remembered it, though given what he now assumed was his own progression, he wondered if that should have been expected. Maybe he would be able to make out much more of the essence than he ever had before. If so, what would it mean for him? When he had an opportunity to ask Desmond alone, Dax intended to talk to him about progression and whether there was any way to gauge what level he was at.

He constricted his essence down, trying to amplify his ability, but he didn't even need to do that nearly as much as he once had. Now he could see essence more clearly without the need for that technique. One more sign that he had progressed.

The hallway was aglow with essence.

It seemed to flow through the hall, through the walls, through the ceiling. There were threads of silvery essence, something that Dax had never even seen before, that extended from the door, all the way to the end of the hall, stopping abruptly by the time they reached the living quarters.

He stepped forward, and as soon as he did, he felt something about that essence. Now that he was focusing on it, he recognized the essence itself, and he could feel that flow, even if he wasn't exactly sure what caused it. Dax traced his hand along the wall, feeling something. It seemed to leave tendrils of silver tracing within the walls that he hadn't seen before.

He turned, looking back to Desmond, and saw the old man standing at the counter, still pouring mugs of tea. Everybody was quiet.

Dax couldn't hear anything from them either.

That was odd.

He made his way along the hallway. When he reached the door, he froze.

The strange silvery bands of essence had stopped, no longer working their way through the door. But then, Dax wasn't sure if they ever had worked through the door.

"You can return now," Desmond said.

Dax turned back to him. He was standing just across the threshold.

"What kind of essence is this?"

"It is nothing that you need to be concerned about," Desmond said, waving his hand.

"But I can see something. I can feel something. I wonder if I—"

"I would caution you against using your transference on this, and especially here. You can test it all you want later."

He turned, stepping free. Test his transference later? Test it on what?

It had to be some other form of essence, then. And given what he knew about Desmond's essence and how it was some sort of mirror form of essence, it had to be linked to that. Maybe he could learn how to mimic that type of essence in some way.

He stepped back into the room, and as soon as he did, the voices of everybody else bloomed back into existence. The sudden shift, that sharpness of it, surprised him, and he turned his attention to Desmond, who was passing out the mugs of tea.

Dax realized what that was.

Some sort of a conduit.

But a conduit from where to where?

And how was that even possible?

Chapter Eight

HE SAT IN A CHAIR, STARING AT THE HEARTH. FLAMES crackled in it. Before he had left them, Desmond had lit the fire, though as far as Dax had been able to tell, he hadn't used any sort of flint or fiery essence. Desmond had stores of concentrated essence, so he probably used that to give off a cozy and comforting warmth that radiated through the room.

"Do you want to talk about what he was doing?" Gia asked, looking around the room. She was seated on the hearth itself, knees bent at a bit of an angle, hands cupping the mug in her hands. Despite her protestations about Desmond and his associations with the Cult, she was still willing to drink his tea. Then again, if Desmond wanted to harm them or poison them, it would've been easy to do in any other way. He didn't need to use the tea to do that.

"I don't think that he's doing anything," Rochelle said, shaking her head and taking a long drink of the tea. "Desmond has been helping us from the very beginning."

"Are you sure about that? He is a part of the Cult of the

Dragon. How do you know that he's not trying to get you to serve the Great Serpent?"

"And so what if he is?" Rochelle turned her attention to Gia. Rochelle had found a book somewhere and was thumbing through it. "We should also want to serve the Great Serpent, shouldn't we? That's what the Emperor wants of us."

Gia took a slow drink of tea while leaning her head back. She looked distracted to Dax.

"What was it about the crystal?" Cedrick asked.

Leave it to Cedrick to be the one who asked the question Dax didn't want to answer.

But maybe he needed to.

He pulled the crystal out of his pocket, and he held it in his lap. It didn't have the same colorful appearance that it had when he had been surrounded by essence, but then again, maybe it had been different *because* it had been surrounding him with essence. Now that he was here, seated with the others, he wondered if perhaps the crystal only reflected the colors of the essence around it. Now, the crystal had a bit of a haze that seemed to float inside of it.

"This is the crystal that I was supposed to grab," Dax said, his voice soft. "And I have a feeling that something happened because of me."

Rochelle looked up, closing the book and frowning at him. "What did you do?"

Dax shook his head. "I didn't actually *do* anything." He stared at the crystal. He turned it, and though it still had the same six-sided shape, with pointed ends, when he held it out now, the cloudy haze inside of it didn't show him anything. He remembered what he had seen in the clearing.

These were his friends, weren't they? They had all come with him, and they had been willing to do whatever he had needed, and had been willing to help, all because he had asked that of them.

He needed to trust them now.

Dax looked back toward the door into this place. The conduit.

He remembered what he had noticed, what he had felt, and what he had heard.

There wasn't any way for Desmond to hear anything unless he was here.

Dax took a deep breath, and then let it out heavily. Why not tell them now? He had wanted to do so safely, and he had thought that he was going to need to tell Rochelle, but if they were all here, this was where he needed to talk to them. He needed to see if any of them might know more about what he had seen. They would've had their own sort of Great Serpent visions, and with that, Dax had to think that they might have some answer as to what had happened to him.

"When I went into the clearing, and when I grabbed the crystal, I saw something." He looked up, sweeping his gaze over all of them. He turned his chair, giving him an opportunity to look toward the entrance to the room just in case Desmond might return. "I saw the Great Serpent. But it was more than that. I felt like I was pulled into the crystal. It was strange. I had a series of visions."

He described what he had seen, the way that it seemed as if there were small serpents flying, then gradually larger, until he finally saw the Great Serpent staring at him, and then speaking to him.

"That's when I was told to drink. I felt like I had to follow the command. I think it was the Great Serpent," he went on, "but I never had a vision like that when I went to the tower the first time." The others knew that now. "This was the first time I had an actual vision. And it was nothing like I've been told about before."

Every was silent for a few moments. It was Rochelle who broke the silence.

"When I went to my testing, I entered a small room. It was nothing like what we saw in the rest of the tower when we were there just recently. It was small, but there was a swirling of smoke all around me. The smoke cleared, and then I began to see the Great Serpent. It looked like it was out beyond a window, as if I were watching the Great Serpent flying." She smiled to herself. "Then the Great Serpent turned to me. I felt some pressure, and then I had an opportunity to speak. I didn't know what to ask for, but my parents had always told me that I was supposed to ask for what I wanted, and that the Great Serpent gave me an opportunity to try to ask for what mattered most to me."

"And you asked for healing?" Cedrick asked.

Rochelle shrugged. "I asked for a way to help others. I knew that was the right phrasing, as my parents had warned me that I need to be careful how I spoke, and that if I asked for too much, and in the wrong way, I would not be given the right type of essence. And then when I awoke, I was the bottom of the serpent stairs, and..." She shrugged again. "I had this essence."

"You were in only one room?" Dax asked.

She nodded. "Everybody's experience in the tower is different, Dax."

"Not everybody," Gia said. When Dax looked over at her, she shrugged. She still held the mug in her hands, cupping it carefully. "Most people go into a single room. They stand there, and the Great Serpent comes to them. Sometimes it's surrounded in smoke, sometimes they approach a window, and other times they feel like they are falling into darkness," she explained, and paused for a moment, with a bit of a tremble that left Dax thinking that perhaps the last was what she had experienced. "But most people only enter a single room. It's unusual for anybody to have any type of experience where they get to actually walk through the testing ground." She looked over at Dax, watching him for a long moment, and there was an accusation in her eyes. "I fell," she went on. "And when I stopped, there was a jarring sensation. I was surrounded by darkness. Black. And then I felt something thrust in front of me. I could feel the energy of the Great Serpent. As I drank the essence, I asked for my reward."

"You were in the darkness?" Cedrick asked.

"What was it like for you?" Dax asked, looking over at him.

There was so much that he should have known about before now, but he'd been so fixated on what he had experienced. He wasn't the only one who had expectations about what essence would be like, and the gifts that the Great Serpent would provide.

"Bright light," Cedrick said, shrugging slightly. "When I went into the door, I was surrounded by light. I kept walking, looking for walls, looking for a way out, but then I felt as if I couldn't move anymore. The light flickered, and then I saw an outline of the Great Serpent. I was told to drink, and so I did. Sort of like the rest of you."

"And all of you were inside of a single room," Dax said.

"That's how the testing goes," Gia said.

"Usually," Rochelle said, "but maybe it doesn't have to be that way. We all had different experiences, but they were similar. We all observed the Great Serpent and were told to take essence. But what if the Empire really is directing the essence that we take?"

Dax sensed her unease. And he understood it.

Part of the tradition around the testing was the belief that the Great Serpent was the one who decided what type of essence everybody would take on, using some higher understanding. Dax knew they were given an opportunity to take on essence by requesting a specific type, but they were always told that there was a part of them, and a part of what they experienced, that was determined by the Great Serpent, so that if they didn't receive the essence that they wanted, they would be given what the Great Serpent thought that they needed.

That had certainly been his belief.

But given everything that he had seen so far, and his understanding of the Great Serpent, and what he'd learned about the Guardians who were inside of the tower, maybe there was nothing true about it.

"I don't see how any of this matters," Gia said, sitting back. "We have essence. I have earth, which is what my family has. You have water, which is what your family has." She looked over at Cedrick. "I presume your family has some sort of life essence." When he nodded slightly, she smiled to herself. "And then there is Dax."

"My family doesn't have whatever this is," Dax said, focusing on his own essence and trying to constrict it down even more, hoping it might provide him with some answer. But it didn't seem to make much of a difference. "I don't know what type of essence I have, but my father has fire. My mother has a mixture of two different types. And—"

"Perhaps your family has more types of essence than you realize," she said. "The Great Serpent decides. And if the Great Serpent doesn't decide, then we still serve the Emperor."

Did it not?

That was the question that Dax had, and it was a question he didn't really have a good answer to. He felt like it should matter, shouldn't it? Knowing the Great Serpent, and its influence over their testing, was core to everything they knew about essence, and everything that Dax believed about his own purpose.

"None of it matters," Rochelle said.

"It matters if Dax here had a more traditional type of testing," Cedrick said. "I'd like to see essence like that."

"Maybe we could find another flare," Dax said.

"I doubt we can find another."

"Why not?" Cedrick asked. "Desmond seemed to know about them."

"And he said they were rare," Rochelle said.

Dax studied the crystal. They weren't wrong. But he could see essence, couldn't he? Which meant that he would have an advantage in seeing another flare. The only problem that he had, and it was a significant one, was that he wasn't sure how they would reach the essence flare before any others of the Order—if that was even possible.

"What did you tell the Great Serpent?" Rochelle asked.

"I asked for—"

"Fire," Cedrick said, grinning at Dax.

Dax shook his head. "I didn't ask for fire. I didn't ask for water, wind, earth, or life. I thought about it. I thought that any of the primary essences might've been helpful, especially given this transference, and how I might be able to use the combination of the transference essence and the primary essence to see if there was going to be something more that I could do with them, but that wasn't what I asked for. I asked for understanding."

Every was quiet for a few moments. Dax sat, listening to the crackling of the hearth, holding onto the crystal, turning it from side to side as he stared at it, wondering if there was going to be a way for the Great Serpent to return to him, and perhaps provide him with another image, vision, or some true understanding. But he suspected that the crystal itself was all he was going to get. And any sort of understanding that he was going to get from the crystal, from that essence, wasn't limited. The problem for him was in trying to understand it, and to make sense of what more he might be able to gain from it.

Cedrick broke the silence, as he often did. "What's the point of understanding?"

It was Gia who laughed first, but they all laughed, nonetheless.

"None," Dax said. "As least as far as I can tell. I wish that there was going to be something to it, but so far, I haven't been able to find anything useful."

"Well," Cedrick said. "You wasted that chance, didn't you?"

Chapter Nine

DESMOND RETURNED A WHILE LATER, AFTER THEY HAD ALL been sitting quietly, talking about how they were going to deal with the possibility that more of their instructors might betray them to the Order. They all had different ideas about what it might look like as they tested with their instructors while attempting to make sure that they weren't surprised again. No one wanted to suffer another attack.

Rochelle had spent some time talking to Dax quietly, speculating about what he might have gained with his new essence, but neither of them had any clear idea, other than to say that they both agreed that there was likely a strong possibility that the Great Serpent had given him something. The challenge that he had was in trying to find it—and to understand it.

The irony wasn't lost on him.

When Desmond did return, he smiled at them. "No sign of the headmaster."

"Are you sure?" Cedrick asked.

"Oh, quite certain," he said, waving his hand as he

looked around the inside of the room. He frowned, tipping his head to the side, as if listening to something that only he could hear.

Dax had believed that Desmond didn't have the ability to listen in on their conversation, but what if he did? Maybe there was some way of him recording what they said and keeping that to himself, not that dissimilar to his sister's Whispers.

"Anyway," he said, turning his attention back to them. "I don't think that you have to worry about the headmaster, but from what I can tell, several of you have an exam coming up soon. How many of you have this exam?"

Everybody but Gia said that they did.

"Mine would be after theirs," she said.

"And I still think that you probably should be in advanced essence manipulation," Dax said.

"Oh, don't try to drag me into your more difficult classes," she said with a bit of a smile. "I am perfectly content with where I am, and don't need to be forced to take something more complicated than what I already have."

They all got moving to the hall, where Dax took another moment to study the essence, trying to pay closer attention to the silvery lines within it. Rochelle watched him, seemingly recognizing that he noticed something unusual.

"I will tell you later," he said.

The others spilled out of the door, and Dax hurried forward, stepping past the end of the silvery conduit and reaching the street outside of Desmond's home.

Desmond stood in the doorway for a moment. "I will be here if you need me," he said.

"How do we know if we're going to need you?" Rochelle asked.

"Unfortunately, I fear you will all need me at some point, and I suspect I will need you as well."

He closed the door, disappearing.

Dax breathed out heavily. He wanted to tell the others about what he suspected about the conduit, but now really wasn't the time. It was time for them to get back to the Academy, and back to the routine of classes.

And it meant that it was time to get back to dealing with other students.

Dax had enjoyed the brief respite from some of the others that they had dealt with in their classes.

As they neared the Academy, Gia looked over, and she grinned at them. "Good luck."

"That's it?" Cedrick asked. "Just 'good luck'?"

"What else am I supposed to say? I'm going to go back to my room, gather some supplies, and get ready for my testing. So good luck."

She started away, and Dax snorted to himself.

"What is that about?" Cedrick asked.

"I think that's just about Gia wishing us good luck. Nothing more than that."

Cedrick frowned, but he said nothing more as they headed toward the essence manipulation room, where they arrived with plenty of time for the exam. It still seemed a little surprising that they had been able to get here in time, but then, they really had not been gone all that long. The biggest delay had been finding the essence flare. Had they not dealt with that, they would have been back long before now.

They took a seat, and Professor Jamesh headed to the front of the classroom, looking no different than he ever did. He was an older, gray-haired man who had his own way of doing things, and looked as if he were constantly irritated by needing to teach students like Dax and his friends. Dax was a little worried that perhaps Professor Jamesh had been a part of what happened to them, and that maybe he was in on whatever the headmaster was doing, but the professor was quiet, waiting for everybody to get settled.

Rochelle had taken a seat next to him, with Cedrick on the other side. Cedrick was twisting his fingers together, and a bit of bubbles were bursting along the fingertips, but he didn't release them very much. Dax could see others in the room that were holding onto their essence as well, circling it through them, as if they were getting ready to use it for the test on a moment's notice. The only one that didn't seem to be quite as nervous, despite her comments to the contrary, was Rochelle. Her essence was there, a pale blue that sat deep in the heart of her, but she didn't send it circling through her the way that he had expected that she would.

"Now," Professor Jamesh said, clapping his hands together to get the class's attention. "Today is the first step in your exam and in proving your skill at essence manipulation. We are asking for all of you to be much more advanced than we typically do, but I'm quite certain that all of you will be able to handle this with much grace and dignity. You will need to prove that you have external control of your essence, and once you prove that, you will be invited to continue with advanced essence manipulation."

"And if we don't?"

The question was asked by Karelly, a tall dark-haired girl who had led some of Dax's taunting during his earliest days in the Academy. When Dax looked over to her, she was watching him, a hint of amusement lingering in her gaze. It was almost a taunt.

She knew.

But of course she would know that he wouldn't be able to manipulate his essence nearly as well as what he should have been.

She wasn't asking on behalf of herself. She was asking to figure out what would happen to him.

"I doubt that many of you will fail, but essence manipulation is a core requirement for you to remain at the Academy. If you fail, there will be an opportunity for remediation, but in most cases, we would simply ask that you depart the Academy."

Karelly watched Dax with a grim sort of satisfaction.

And he couldn't shake a sudden feeling of dread. What if he didn't pass this?

He knew that he could wield his essence, but it wasn't going to be straightforward for him, he didn't think. And whatever he did with essence manipulation may be riskier than what he was supposed to do. It might not be anything that the professor would be able to observe, even.

"I will test you one at a time. Unfortunately, that involves a lot of sitting and watching. Each of you will observe the other students. You can learn something if you pay attention."

There were quite a few students, which meant that this was going to involve quite a bit of sitting and waiting. Considering how long they'd been gone, he didn't know how he felt about that. He'd rather have just gone back to his dorm and waited for an assigned testing time.

"This is a waste of time," Karelly muttered.

"Perhaps," Professor Jamesh said, surprising Dax by answering that and offering a bit of a response. Given the nature of the comment, and how frustrated Karelly had sounded, Dax was actually a bit surprised that Jamesh had deemed it worthwhile to respond. "But I am certain that some of you will gain something by watching."

He swept his gaze around the inside of the room, until he paused on Dax.

That couldn't be coincidental, could it?

He didn't think that Jamesh knew all the truth about his essence, nor about how he could observe different strands of essence, but maybe he did.

The headmaster could've told him something.

And of all people at the Academy, the headmaster knew the most about Dax's power. That was unfortunate, as now the headmaster was the person that Dax thought he needed to be most careful around.

They started alphabetically. Aidan went first. He was skilled, using a variant of fire as he stood in front of the professor and clutched his hands together confidently. It looked as if he were concentrating for a moment, then a plume of pale orange exploded from his fingertips. Dax couldn't help but feel as if his father would have been pleased.

Professor Jamesh made a note on his pad and then waved for him to take a seat.

Jamesh wasn't wrong. Watching Aidan using essence in that fashion had been helpful for Dax. He had been able to see the flow of essence through him and had seen the way that he had called that power through him before sending it out of his fingertips.

The next person to come was Katherine Bell, who used a bit of wind. Wind was a bit more difficult to use, partly because it was so transparent—a wispy sort of essence. His sister had once said that she'd had a hard time managing a measure of control over the wind. But once she'd captured it and managed to hold onto it, the wind was a powerful ally. Dax had studied wind essence enough to feel comfortable recognizing some of the contours within it. He had seen it from his sister, and he had a pretty good idea of how Katherine was commanding it now.

Again, Professor Jamesh had made a note in his pad and waved for Katherine to take a seat. One by one, the other students went up, many of them using variants of fire, earth, and wind, and one using a life essence that sent vines crackling along the ground briefly before they faded into dust. When it was his turn, Dax went up to the front of the class and paused for a moment. How was he going to demonstrate transference essence?

Professor Jamesh looked up at him. "Mr. Nelson," he said. "Have you mastered what is required of you?"

Dax thought about what was going to have to happen here.

He hadn't been giving it much thought, as he had been focusing instead on watching the other students and their control over essence, but now that he was here, he realized that he had overlooked the fact that he was going to have to demonstrate something visible to Professor Jamesh.

What could he use?

His essence, transference in the form that he had, didn't have any sort of visible outcome.

He constricted his essence down. That was the first step in using it.

From there, he had to send it out through his arms, legs, or up into his mind. It created threads of essence that worked through him and allowed him to manipulate his control over it.

"I can express my essence out," Dax said. "But I don't have the same control as the others do, partly because I'm still not entirely sure what kind of essence I possess."

He might as well acknowledge the truth.

"Unfortunately, that is not going to satisfy the testing."

"I can show you," Dax said. "But you will probably be the only one who will know the effect."

An idea came to him as he was speaking.

He looked over to see Rochelle shaking her head. She knew what he was going to do. But what choice did he have? For him to prove to Professor Jamesh that he had any sort of control over his essence, he was going to have to demonstrate it, wasn't he?

"I suppose that *will* satisfy the testing," Professor Jamesh said.

Dax regarded him for a moment, and then he took a step back.

He smiled to himself. "Could you use a bit of your essence for me, Professor?"

Professor Jamesh frowned at Dax. "This is your testing, Mr. Nelson, and not mine."

"I know," Dax said, "but I need to borrow something from you in order to demonstrate what I can do. It won't be painful," he added quickly, before realizing how that sounded. Some of the students around him started to laugh. "And like I said, you may be the only one who is aware of what happens here."

Professor Jamesh leaned forward. "I will offer you that much."

Dax nodded again. "Thank you, Professor."

He waited. Professor Jamesh had access to earth. Dax had seen him using it before, and he was not surprised when he began to create a thin strand of essence that spread out from him. It was slow, little more than a bloom of power, but as that bloom spread, Dax began to feel something more from it.

And then he pulled on it. It was a simple matter of transference. He pulled that essence to himself, and then held it inside. He didn't know how much he should draw upon, nor did he know how long to hold it.

But maybe he didn't need to hold it.

Instead, he expressed it outward at the professor's feet. A bit of light stirred, then blinked out with a flash.

Professor Jamesh looked up at Dax. "What was that? What sort of trick were you using?"

Dax shook his head. "No trick. Transference."

"This is essence manipulation," Professor Jamesh said.

"I know," Dax said. "And I used transference to manipulate your essence."

Professor Jamesh frowned, and another stream of essence began to build from him before spilling outward. Dax pulled upon it, using the same technique that he had done before, and let it pool around Professor Jamesh.

There was a danger in drawing too much. Not only did he not want to anger the professor, but he also didn't know if he had the necessary control to draw more safely.

Dax was vaguely aware of others watching him, primarily Karelly and Aidan, but had the reassurance that his friends were also watching him. That gave him some strength.

He continued working with the essence, slowly trying to control it. Then he let it go.

Professor Jamesh sat for a moment, pressing his fingertips together. "You may take a seat, Mr. Nelson."

Dax took a seat next to Rochelle, and he shrugged.

"I don't know if it was a good idea," she said.

"And I don't know that I had much of a choice," he said.

One by one, other students went up, until both Cedrick

and Rochelle took their turns. They both did quite well. Dax wasn't surprised by it. Cedrick created a series of pink bubbles that drifted from his fingertips, while Rochelle sent a swirl of pale blue out from her and formed water droplets that dripped outward from her hand. Dax knew she was much more capable than that, but there was no reason for her to demonstrate anything more than what she already had.

When they were done, Professor Jamesh rose again, looked at the rest of the class, and smiled. "You have done as well as I could've expected. I will review your testing and make notes of your performance, and then I will provide the registrar with your final scores. We will meet again in three days, assuming that you are given a passing grade."

He headed out of the class.

Dax got to his feet, and he looked around at the others. "How are we supposed to know if we get a passing grade?"

"They send notices," Rochelle said. "But I don't know that you have to worry too much. I saw what you did."

"You saw it?" Cedrick asked.

She shrugged. "Not quite like Dax can, but I saw something."

They all filed out and found Gia heading inside, staring straight ahead with a look of resolve on her face.

"She's going to do fine," Rochelle said.

"She is," Dax said.

"I was saying that partly for myself," Rochelle said.

He snorted.

"I'd like to get back to my room, then head to the baths," Rochelle said. "Meet for food later?"

Dax made his way to his room, feeling a wave of relaxation fill him at the return to some semblance of normalcy. That faded the moment that he got to his room. Something wasn't quite right. He didn't know what it was, only that some aspect of his room had been altered. He could see it in the flows of essence around it.

He approached carefully and pushed open the door.

And stood motionless for a long moment.

There was an unfamiliar essence here.

Chapter Ten

DAX PAUSED IN THE DOORWAY.

He hadn't been gone that long, but somebody had been here. It wasn't destroyed so much as it was tampered with. He could feel the essence here. More than that, he had the distinct sense that he was supposed to feel it.

Strangely, he couldn't identify what particular essence had been through here. He looked around for signs of the different strands of essence that he knew, thinking that maybe there was some remnant of Megan and her wind essence, or perhaps even the headmaster, but there was nothing.

He looked over at his desk, checking the pile of books. They looked as if they had been untouched. Only one of his books had been moved, left spread open on his desk. It was like a message.

It was his valor text.

Dax thumbed through the pages, but he didn't see anything unusual. He constricted his essence, but still couldn't see anything that would show him what might have happened here.

He didn't see any strands of essence, nothing like the Whisper that his sister had left, and nothing that would alarm him in any way. He looked under his bed but didn't see anything, then stood and turned in place. Until he knew what had happened here, and who was responsible for it, he wasn't sure that he could stay. There was no telling whether somebody—and in his mind, he feared that it was somebody tied to the Order—had placed something in his room to harm him.

Dax grabbed a pack and loaded books into it, along with a change of clothes and some supplies, and then stepped out of his room before locking it.

The lock probably wouldn't even do anything.

He needed to know if somebody came back, though.

Dax set his books down, opened the door, and then positioned the chair so that he could tell if someone had come in here. He opened the wardrobe slightly, leaving it cracked. Then he stepped back out and locked the door. He needed to find Rochelle and the others.

When he went to her room, there was no answer. But of course there wouldn't be. She had told him she was going to the baths. He didn't feel like eating, nor did he feel like staying here.

It didn't leave a whole lot of options for him. Dax headed out of the dorm and over to the library, where he nodded to the librarians and swept down to the Sublevel III, where he set his pack down.

He didn't have anything in mind to study, as he had just finished his essence manipulation test, and he didn't need to practice anything for valor, as there was going to be no test for that. He anticipated that he had done well with his rune exam, and though he still had transference testing left, he wasn't as worried about that, either. He could use transference very easily now.

He sat for a moment.

As he did, an idea came to him. He left his pack of books and headed to the stack of shelves that detailed different types of essences. He found a few books on obscure essences and took a seat.

He got lost in thought, turning pages, and reading about different types of essences. As he did, he found himself drawn into the reading. Many of these types of essences were incredibly obscure, but all of them were old as well.

There had been no obscure essences recently.

Why would that be?

Dax sat back for a moment, cupping his hands over the book and studying the page.

Unless there couldn't be any obscure essences these days.

The only reason that would have made any sort of sense would be if the way that people were given essence, using what the Guardians provided, didn't allow for obscure essences.

What did that mean for Dax's essence?

He had an obviously obscure essence, something that nobody else had and that nobody else that he had heard of possessed. But if that were true, it did leave him with a series of questions about what that meant for him, and why that should be the case.

He began to read with a different sort of intensity.

One of the books spoke about a type of essence that created a plane of light that allowed the wielder to walk along light itself. He couldn't even imagine what that would be like, and yet maybe that was similar to what Desmond used. Could it be that he was drawing upon some sort of light beam, and that was the way that he could generate a conduit? It certainly had seemed a silvery light to him.

Another one spoke about people who could walk along the clouds themselves. Apparently, they were able to solidify the moisture in the cloud, and they could use it as some sort of a springboard, bouncing from one to the next. That seemed almost more fantastical than real, as he couldn't even imagine how somebody could get into the clouds in the first place.

Others spoke of a way of constricting essence, tightening pure essence directly and using that upon a person. There were dozens of different types of essences that he read about, all with different components, all varied in how the Great Serpent gifted them. That was the key. Apparently, all essences were somehow derivative of the primary essences. Most believed the primary essences to be light, earth, wind, life, and water, but there were some, at least in some of these older books, who speculated that there were other primary essences that very few people knew about, which was what made the Great Serpent unique. Dax suspected that could be the case, especially given what he felt about his own essence.

Then he saw a passage that struck him. It reminded him of something his mother had once said about the essence that was within a person from birth, and how the essences given to them by the Great Serpent were only meant to modify that which they already had.

What if that were true?

And if it were, how would there be any way for the Emperor, and the Guardians, to influence that?

Maybe there wasn't.

For the first time since coming to the Academy, Dax wondered if his mother had known something—and if she could help him. He headed out of the library and made his way to the Post.

There was a Post not far from the edge of the Academy, as he wouldn't be the only student who wanted to send word to family. It was early enough that he hoped it was open. As he made his way to the Post, he framed what he wanted to tell his mother in his mind, thinking about how he could word it carefully so that his father didn't know the details. He trusted his mother more than he trusted his father, and there was always the possibility that his father might try to intercept anything he sent to her.

That wasn't the only issue, though.

Messages were sent using wind essence. They were similar to Whispers, similar to the way that Megan's would have worked, but they used their own unique form of essence to send a manipulated connection outward. They passed it from one to the next, with each postmaster sending the document along until it reached the destination. There was always a danger that the message could be misconstrued, but there was also a danger that somebody might pay too close attention to the Post. It was part of the reason that very few people trusted the postmasters for privileged information, as anybody could listen in who had the capability.

But it was all that Dax had available to him.

The building was small, arranged with a series of desks, with weary-looking wind essence users sitting behind them. Only one didn't have a line, and he approached the young woman, who looked up at him through her glasses, shoving them back on her nose. Her wavy hair was a bit tangled, and she had an ink stain on one cheek.

"Write your message here," she said, pushing a piece of paper forward and handing him ink and a quill.

Dax wasn't sure what he had been expecting to find and supposed that he shouldn't be terribly surprised that they would ask him to document the message himself. Then again, there was a part of him that wondered if perhaps they would have not wanted him to do it himself, and that the postmaster would've wanted to be the one to send the full message. Still, it didn't matter to him all that much.

He was a good writer, and he took his notes, picking his words carefully as he documented a message to his mother.

Mother,

I'm writing to you to let you know that I had a good first term. My memories of the serpent stairs are vibrant, as is my memory of the testing. Megan has been most helpful in helping me understand the reason I am here. I have questions about some of your earliest lessons that I was hoping you might answer for me regarding innate essence.

We had some difficulty during the term with outsiders, but that seems to be taken care of. I met an old friend of yours who offers his greeting.

Yours,

Dax Nelson

As he handed the paper over, the woman looked down at it. "You can send more. The charge doesn't change based on the message length. It's all a single cost."

"That's all I need to say," Dax said.

"You could probably send this by carriage, and it would be cheaper."

"It's fine. Really."

She looked at the page again, and then her eyes widened slightly. "I suppose so. Nelson."

He tried to suppress his irritation at one more person commenting on his family.

"How do you want to pay?"

"Can you charge it to my Academy account?" Dax asked.

He hadn't even considered that he would need to pay for it. The Academy hadn't been an issue before, as he had simply been billed, but now that the trunk of coins was missing, he wasn't sure how he was going to afford to pay for things.

"I suppose I can charge it. I can get it there faster, if you want to pay extra."

Was that a bribe? He didn't realize there were two layers of speed from the Post.

"You can charge that to the account as well," he said.

"Excellent," she said with a smile.

She leaned back, closed her eyes, and he watched as wind began to swirl around her. It was subtle, but the effect of it was obvious to him. There was a thick band of essence that stretched from her before disappearing beyond the building.

When she opened her eyes, she looked over at Dax. "It's done." She glanced at the paper. "I know it doesn't look like much, and most people are concerned that it's not being sent, but I can assure you—"

"I have some experience with Post."

"I suppose you do," she said, looking down at the paper before flicking her gaze back up at him. She pushed her glasses up on her nose, and then smoothed her hair again. "Nelson."

She smiled a toothy smile at him.

"Thank you," he said, and he took the paper, folded it up, and stuffed it into his pocket. He could have left it behind, but he didn't want the possibility that somebody might see what he had sent. There was enough danger with him having transmitted that to his mother.

He debated sending another message. He wanted to get word to Megan about what had happened and fill her in, but if she had done what she had claimed she was going to do, she would be dealing with her own issues and trying to get through to the Emperor. He didn't need to intervene in that. She needed to have her opportunity to reach the Emperor and prove herself as a Whisper.

"Come back anytime," the woman said, "either here or somewhere else, Dax Nelson."

He frowned, then headed away, not saying anything more.

Chapter Eleven

ROCHELLE HAD BEEN QUITE ANNOYED TO LEARN THAT HIS room had been tossed over. She had offered to let him stay in her room—on the floor of course—but Dax had declined. He didn't think that would be considered proper, and more than that, he had more than a little concern about whether Rochelle would suddenly become a target if he did that. He wasn't sure what he was going to do though.

Rochelle had wanted to see the room, so he brought her down and unlocked it, curious at what he might find looking through a second time. The chair was slightly at an angle, as was the bed, and the wardrobe door remained cracked. He looked around, noticing his sister's Whisper.

He closed the door. "Megan, if you're there, I sent word to Mother. And something happened in my room. I don't know if you have anything to do with it, but I don't think that you did, and I want you to be aware of what's going on at the Academy."

When he was done, he turned his attention back to Rochelle.

"You didn't do that before?" Rochelle asked.

"I was a little too concerned about the fact that my room had been targeted to be thinking about anything else. And then I went to send my mother a coded message."

"What did you send her, exactly?"

He took the piece of paper out of his pocket, and she unfolded it, looking down at it.

She smirked. "An old friend? Really? You don't think that's going to raise questions? She might not realize which old friend you're talking about."

"Probably not," he agreed, "but if nothing else, it might give her reason to look into what happened. When she does, I have little doubt that she's going to learn a bit about Desmond, and what I have been involved in. And now I just have to find some place to stay. I'm not terribly eager to spend too much time in Cedrick's basement."

"I told you that you could stay here. At least for now and until we figure out if the Order is responsible for it."

"It has to be them," Dax said.

"Maybe," she said. "But I still think we need to be careful. We can set up a few different runic traps to test. We don't even know how many members of the Order are still at the Academy."

"Maybe we should keep tabs on that."

She started to laugh at him. "You have to be kidding me. You want to get a sense for how many instructors might be a part of the Order?"

"We were doing something similar to that already," Dax said. "We were looking for members of the Cult of the Dragon, though we probably weren't looking in the right direction. We can figure out how many instructors stay here during the break and decide who looks suspicious."

"You know how to have a good time, don't you?"

He chuckled. "If you don't want to have any part of it..."

By the time they finished checking the three floors of offices, they headed out, and made their way over to the administrative building, where they paused for a moment.

"It's strange coming over here now," Dax said.

"It doesn't need to be," she said. "Your sister isn't—"

"This isn't about my sister," he said. "This is about... Well, it's about what else we dealt with."

He had to be careful. He had no idea how many other Whispers might be around the campus, especially here. Given that they knew there were already spies set up within the Academy, he knew that they needed to be extra cautious now.

They made their way along the hall, with Rochelle making notes while they made small talk about classes, their tests, and what the two of them thought that the second term might look like. They tried to be as inconspicuous as possible. When they reached the end of the hall and started up the stairs, they saw the registrar.

"Mr. Nelson. Ms. Alson. Can I help you with anything?"

"Oh," Rochelle said, smiling and carefully sliding her notepad up the sleeve of her robes. "We were just looking to speak with the headmaster."

"The headmaster?" She frowned, glancing between the two of them. "If you have an issue with your class assignments, you should come to me and not go to the headmaster. Or if it is an issue with something in your classes, you should actually go to your professor. Too many students think to bypass the professors, especially at this time in the term. I know testing can be quite difficult, and—"

"It has nothing to do with the testing," Dax said, carefully interrupting her. "I had been working with headmaster privately. I told him last time that I worked with him that I would bring Rochelle with me. She's trying to help me with my essence."

The registrar frowned. "Well, the headmaster isn't there."

"Do you know when he might return?" Rochelle asked.

They needed to be careful, as it was possible that the registrar had been working closely with Headmaster Ames and might even have been working with him and the Order.

"He has not sent word. That is not uncommon," she said, waving her hand dismissively.

"Can we leave a note for him?" Dax asked. That wouldn't be such an unusual request, especially not for Dax, who had been studying with the headmaster during the last term.

The registrar smiled. "Of course. If you'd like to leave something with me…"

"I'd really rather leave a note for him myself," Dax said, and he smiled again, trying to look as charming as possible. He wasn't sure that he accomplished it, but he needed to try something. "It's something of a more personal matter."

"Of course," the registrar said, waving her hand. "Be quick. We don't need students wandering the halls of the administrative building."

When they reached the top of the stairs, Dax paused, listening. He extended his awareness of essence, curious whether there was going to be any sign of the registrar having followed them, but he didn't feel anything. Then again, it was possible that he wouldn't feel anything. He didn't know what type of essence the registrar had, and more than that, he didn't know if she had some way of concealing her essence. Either was possible.

As they made their way along the hall, Dax noticed that most of the offices were empty. Rochelle made a few comments, and notes in her notebook, before Dax hesitated. He looked behind him, noticing a bit of essence that was moving.

"I think she's following us. We should move quickly."

Rochelle nodded, and they raced up the stairs.

The top floor was quiet. The administrative building was only three stories, with each story containing a series of halls and offices, though Dax had never been to the third story. His sister had offices on the main level, and the headmaster on the second level. He was surprised to find that the third story was an open space.

Rochelle had stopped and was looking around. "I can feel something here," she said.

"Because there is ambient essence," Dax said.

He could feel it, but he could also see it. It seemed to swirl around him. It was odd, as ambient essence was rare. He wondered why there would be some here.

Dax found a door that blocked them from going any further.

He pressed his hand up against it, and he paused for a moment, focusing on what he could feel. He wasn't sure what it was, but even as he focused on it, he could feel that there was some sort of ambient essence on the other side of the door.

He looked over at Rochelle, who shook her head.

"You shouldn't—"

Dax didn't give her an opportunity to finish, and he began to transfer the essence that was in the door.

He had no idea if it was going to work, but he had done

something similar once before, and as he pulled the essence off, holding it inside of himself, the lock suddenly clicked.

He pushed the door open.

A small, clear cylinder rested on a pedestal inside of the room. It was the only item there.

He looked over at Rochelle, frowning at her. "It's a flare."

"And it's glowing the way you described the crystal."

Dax frowned at it for a moment before realizing that she was right.

What was it doing here?

Desmond had said something about a primary essence flare.

Did that mean that he had found it?

"What do we do with it?" Rochelle asked.

Dax looked around. "I don't think *we* do anything with it. Desmond brought it here."

"Are you sure? What if this was here from before?"

"Had it been here before, I'm sure that Ames would've used it."

He backed away, closing the door before replacing the essence that he had used to open it.

They hurried toward the stairs, listened for a moment, and Dax began to feel a bit of essence coming up the stairs. He didn't recognize it, but he suspected that it was the registrar. She was probably looking to make sure that they left. Now that he knew about the essence flare, he didn't want to be caught here. It would raise questions, and he wasn't sure that he had any good answer as to how they had found this in the first place.

They hurried to the other end of the hall, where there was no sign of a door, no sign of a staircase, no sign of any way out. He searched. He didn't want to be caught up here, as he didn't like the idea of the registrar knowing that they had snuck in someplace that they weren't supposed to go. Rochelle's eyes widened, and she began to search all around, as if to try to find some way out, but there was no other way.

He didn't have to rely only on searching with his eyes, did he? He could focus on trails of essence.

And there had been ambient essence here.

Dax thought that he might be able to use that, probe outward with it, and test whether there was an opening that he could follow.

He pushed. When he did, he recognized that the ambient essence flowed.

"There," he said, motioning toward a space along the back of the wall. It was dark, and he couldn't see much to it, but Rochelle didn't argue. They hurried over toward it, and he found another door.

It was locked, much like the one with the crystal had been locked, and Dax hurriedly transferred the essence out of the door, into himself, and then unlocked it before stepping inside.

Once they were inside, he pulled the door closed behind him and let out a heavy breath.

They were in a narrow hall. Stone walls seem to squeeze in upon them.

"What did you get us into?" Rochelle asked.

"I don't know," Dax said, smiling at her. "But at least we aren't out there."

"Right, we aren't out there, but now where are we?"

"Inside of the administrative building. Somewhere."

They began to walk through the hall, and as they went, Dax began to feel the essence that was pressing upon him, and though he couldn't tell whether that essence was focused in any sort of way, he recognized that there was some sort of a power to it, and he focused on that, letting it draw them through the halls. By the time they reached the end of the hall, what he suspected was the end of the administrative building itself, they still hadn't found anything else.

Rochelle kept close to him, pushing up on him.

She frowned as he turned her around, and though he couldn't squeeze past her, she tried to allow him to.

"You have to go," he said.

"Go where? Back to the door? That's where we should go, you know. We go back, we find our way out, and—"

A scraping sound came.

Dax cupped his hand over her mouth, quieting her.

He constricted his essence as tightly as he could to look for anything else that he might have missed before. Other than the ambient essence, he saw nothing.

They paused.

The sound didn't come again.

Dax breathed out a sigh of relief.

He focused on tightening his essence down into a tight ball, and as he did, some of the darkness around him began to clear. He realized why. Everything dark here was essence. Dax didn't recognize the type of it, but it seemed to form a sort of a buffer around them.

He noticed a pale trail they could follow and motioned for Rochelle to follow him until they reached a ladder set into the wall, which they climbed.

It let them onto the roof of the building.

They stood there in the fading daylight. Rochelle looked over at him. "Well, now what?"

Chapter Twelve

THEY STAYED UP ON TOP OF THE ROOF OF THE BUILDING until it was dark. They watched people leaving the building and were satisfied when the registrar left, which told him that they were safe to go back into the building. Then they hurriedly made their way through the strange narrow hall once more until they reached the door, which Dax once again triggered by transference, then headed down the stairs to the main door of the administrative building.

Dax could feel just how complicated the lock was as he transferred essence through it until the door opened and allowed them to step out and into the darkness.

"If we missed dinner…" she said, growling at him.

"We won't have missed dinner."

She looked toward the window, her gaze heading toward the administrative building. "Somebody is going to know that we were there. Especially if the headmaster knew that it was there. Others in the Order are going to get involved."

She was probably right. "Let's get some food, and then we can decide what we are going to do about it."

They headed to the cafeteria, which was not as busy as it often was. The juxtaposition of different scents of food was almost overwhelming. It was one of the unique features of the Academy—how there were different types of food that represented different areas of the Empire. He went to the section that kept the kind of fruits and breads and meats that he was familiar with, scooped them onto his tray, and then took a seat while waiting for Rochelle to join him. When she did, she simply sat for a moment, staring at her tray.

"What is it?"

"None of this is quite like I was expecting my Academy experience to be. I really just wanted to learn how to be a healer. That's how I was going to help my family and make money for them."

"That's what you are mostly concerned about?"

"Mostly," she said. "We don't have the Nelson money."

"That's not what I was getting at," he said.

She shrugged. "I'm not trying to imply anything, Dax. We just don't have your kind of money. We need all of our family to be productive. It's the only way that we can keep..." She shook her head. "It doesn't matter. I just thought that I was going to take my seminars, learn what I needed to learn, and then return home. Now I'm not even sure what I'm going to be able to do. And I don't know that my family is going to be happy that I stay here over the break."

"You were going to go back home?"

"After testing is done, we have ten days or so. That's what I was going to do. Now we need to stay to investigate the Order—unless you intend to hire a wagon to get home. I'm sure your family has the funds to pay for that."

He leaned back, crossing his arms over his chest, and he breathed out heavily.

"What? I'm sorry. I know that you get a little touchy about being referred to as a Nelson, even though that is your name, and that your family is so well known within the Empire, but—"

"That is not it," Dax said. He leaned forward. "I had something in my room. I had mostly forgotten about it until now, but it was something that my mother gave me when she sent me off to the Academy."

"What?"

"I'm not sure that I want to tell you." That earned him a scowl. "Fine. My mother sent me with some gold coins. I assume it was for my tuition, but it seems like she sent me with much more than I would've needed."

"How much more?"

"A trunkful."

Her eyes widened. "A trunk?"

Dax hurried with his response. "I realize how that sounds, and I know that it makes me sound like I am spoiled, but again, I thought it was all for the Academy, because I had no idea how much things were going to cost here."

She started to laugh, before she leaned forward, trailing off. "It's really doesn't cost a trunk full of gold," she said. "If it did, how many people would be able to afford tuition at the Academy?"

Dax shrugged. "I don't know. Somebody made it sound like they adjusted their tuition based on your capability of paying."

Rochelle frowned. "Right. I might've been the one to say that."

Dax started to smile, but the smile faded quickly as he thought about the missing coins. "Anyway, when I didn't get charged, I didn't think much of it. I stuffed the trunk under my bed and left it there. I had intended to talk to Megan about it, but then when Megan started being all questionable with her behaviors, I decided against that as well. And with everything that we have been dealing with, I sort of forgot about it."

"You know, Dax, I know that you don't like to talk about your family, and your wealth, but not a lot of people would have simply forgotten about a trunk full of gold."

He looked around, and was thankful that the cafeteria was relatively empty, so he didn't have to worry about too many people listening in and hearing what she was saying.

"I get that," he said, whispering. "But *somebody* has it now."

"Maybe it's your sister," she said. When Dax frowned, Rochelle took another bite and finished chewing before she went on. "You said it yourself. She'd been into your room several times, right? And given everything that she was a part of, and all the things that she had been involved in, wouldn't it be somewhat likely that she had a hand in that?"

"I doubt that my sister would've broken into my room and taken the coin."

"What if she thought that was for her?"

Dax opened his mouth to argue, but then he closed it again.

What if she had?

"See?" Rochelle said. "Now you're thinking. Maybe your mother planned for you to get that coin to your sister."

"But why?"

"I don't know. Desmond made it sound like he knew my mother."

Dax sat quietly for a few moments. "What happens if they try to actually charge me for things here?"

Rochelle smirked at him. "You know, you still *do* have your family name. That matters to the Academy."

"Maybe," he said, reaching across and taking a hard candy from her tray, popping it into his mouth and sucking on it. It was grape flavored, and he didn't love it, as it had a bit of sourness to it as well. "I still would have much preferred to have had the money."

"Right," she said with a bit of a smile. "So would I. You know, I guess I'm disappointed that you didn't trust me enough to let me know that you had brought a"—she leaned forward, dropped her chin almost to the table, and lowered her voice to a whisper—"*trunk* full of money." She grinned at him, winking at him as well.

Dax gave her a little bit of a shove. "I was trying to be serious."

"Oh, I can tell that you're deathly serious. You know, if it was me who lost that," she went on, sitting back up and grabbing for one of the other hard candies on her tray and popping it into her mouth, "and me who had family members who were a part of some mysterious organization, I might start to track down what it might be spent on. And where would I start?"

"Desmond," Dax said.

Rochelle shrugged. "That's where I'd start."

"I probably should go to him, anyway," Dax said. "He might want to know about this crystal, though I'm not exactly sure I want to give it to him yet."

Rochelle clapped her hands together softly. "I love it. Now we have a case. We're like detectives. The case of the missing trunk. No. That doesn't sound good enough. That wouldn't be the kind of stories that are written. The case of the missing money? The case of the missing gold. That sounds better."

"I love that you're having so much fun with this."

"Why shouldn't I? It didn't affect you before now. You had all that coin, and you had no idea what was even there. You didn't know what it was for, nor did you need it, and now that it's gone, you care? We don't know why she sent it with you. Maybe she actually thought that you needed it for tuition. There are all sorts of explanations, and we don't have any clue what they might be. It doesn't matter. What matters is that we figure out what else we do with this."

Dax breathed out heavily, and he looked around the inside of the cafeteria. "When you're done, I'm ready to go."

"You get the floor," she said.

They went back to her room, and they sat up talking and reading while Dax shared with her some of the things that he had learned about different types of rare essence, which he was not at all surprised to learn that Rochelle was fascinated by. As they grew tired, a knock at the door caught their attention, and Cedrick stood there, frowning at them.

"Where have you been?"

Rochelle filled him in on what they had done, along with what they were planning with the instructors. Cedrick rubbed his eyes as he listened, shaking his head.

"We have professors doing that, and now we have the stories of Tarin getting caught using some rune-marked weapon—"

Tarin was one of their fellow first-year students. Dax had interacted with him a little, but he didn't know him that well. The only thing that he knew about him was that Tarin didn't get along well with Karelly and her crew, which he figured was a good thing.

"What do you mean?" Dax asked.

"Just what I said. I don't really know much more than that, so it's basically rumors."

Dax and Rochelle shared a look.

"What is it?"

"Well, you said 'rune-marked weapon.'"

"I did," was all Cedrick said.

"Well, it's about my room," Dax explained. They hurriedly filled him in on what happened, and Cedrick remained quiet for a moment before finally shaking his head.

"Not him. Tarin isn't any good with runes. He was in basic runes with me."

"Maybe whoever gave him a weapon, then?" Rochelle suggested.

"You think this was a student?" Cedrick asked.

"I don't know," Dax said. "Maybe. But it's probably more likely the Order."

"Somebody turned your room over? Do you think it is tied to the Order?"

Rochelle brought a finger up to her lips, shushing him. "We don't know who is listening. And given what we know about Dax's sister, it's quite likely that somebody is."

"Right," Cedrick said. "So what are you doing? Do need a place to crash? You can stay in my room. It's a bit of a mess, but I'm happy to welcome you in there."

"I'm going to stay here tonight," Dax said.

Cedrick smirked at them, but Rochelle just glowered at him.

"Nothing's going to happen like that," Dax said.

"He's been quite concerned about how this might be perceived," Rochelle said.

"I'm sure he is." He winked. "Well, I'll leave the two of you alone."

He stepped out, closed the door, and Dax heard Cedrick laughing as he made his way down the hall.

"What do you think about Tarin?" Rochelle asked.

"I don't know. Probably nothing, but we should look into it a little bit."

"I agree."

When morning came, Dax's neck was stiff, and he got up to see Rochelle still sleeping on her strange bed in the middle of the pond in the center of her room. She was curled up, facing the wall. He leaned over the edge of the water and shifted the covers over her, making sure that she was decent. He even tucked her in a little bit. She whispered something under her breath, then quickly fell back asleep. He didn't say anything more to her, just slipped out of her room, thankful that it didn't seem like there was anybody in the hall with them.

He wasn't sure what to do. It was morning, and he still was curious.

Dax went back to his room, unlocking it and slipping inside. When he did, he paused for a moment.

Somebody had been here again.

The chair was tilted. He was certain of it. Everything else looked as if it had been untouched though. The cabinet was just as ajar as it had been before. The bed was angled ever so slightly. But the chair...

Why the chair?

He dropped down to his knees, looking underneath his desk, but he didn't see anything. He focused on essence, concentrating it down into a tight ball, but even then, there was nothing.

He looked underneath his bed again, and as he had suspected, the trunk was still missing. There was no sign of where it had gone, no sign that it had ever been there at all.

He crouched for a few moments, thinking about what his mother would say if she found out that he lost that much money. He knew exactly what his father would've said. He would've received a severe punishment. Punishment with his father could take many forms. Often it was shunning, silence that Dax had learned was not really as bad as his father liked to believe that it was, but sometimes it was isolation. He had been locked into quiet rooms many times and left there for several days at a time, given only water to subsist on. Other times, his father could be harsh with his words, but that was usually meant for smaller infractions. The worst times, the times that Dax hated most, were when his father used fire on him.

It had forced Dax to learn to control the innate essence that he possessed inside of himself when he was younger. He didn't have much, and certainly not enough to counter anything that his father might have done to him, but it had been enough to prevent him from experiencing the worst of his father's punishments. That, combined with what his mother had done to help him when he had been punished, had gotten Dax through it.

It was part of the reason that he didn't want to go to his father, and part of the reason that he was perfectly content not having a fiery essence where he was going to have to learn from his father.

Between his father and Thomlin, there were plenty of reasons not to go home.

And if his father were to learn about how much gold

he'd lost, Dax had a strong suspicion of what his punishment might look like, and worse, he had a strong suspicion of how it might feel.

Transference essence might help, and it might permit Dax to draw some of that essence inside of himself, perhaps even shielding himself, but it wouldn't protect him entirely from a master of fiery essence.

He turned, looking back toward his desk. When he did, he noticed something on the chair itself. He tilted it back.

There was a marking.

He hadn't even noticed that before, but then again, he been more concerned about the floor itself, looking for something in the stone. He hadn't paid any attention to the underside of the chair. It was a rune. Well, more than one rune, as it looked to be a series of them. And those runes created a pattern.

He focused on it. Somebody had been here and had placed that pattern on the chair.

The question Dax had was *why?*

Chapter Thirteen

"I DON'T RECOGNIZE IT," ROCHELLE SAID.

He had carried the chair back to her room but left it outside in case there was something to the runes that might be transmissible. He thought about leaving it in his room, but he didn't want to do that either.

"I don't recognize it either," he said. He didn't have that much experience with runes in general, but this one looked to be particularly complex. And he had no idea why it would be on his chair.

"I've never seen anything like this in the unclaimed lands, and I don't know anybody who has. This is beyond my capability."

"Even though you did so well on your test?"

"Just because I mastered what I needed to know on Alibard's test doesn't mean that I'm a rune master."

"And you did have some bit of transference that helped. Right?"

He had forgotten about that, but obviously Rochelle had

not. She wasn't wrong, though. Transference had given him an advantage. Runes were useful, even when someone had considerable power. They allowed for a storage of essence, and with the right form, they could concentrate it. He had no idea what purpose these runes had, only that they did look fairly complex.

"Let's take a tracing," he said, changing the topic.

"You said it was too complicated to make."

"But there are ways that we can make a tracing," Dax said, "especially with something like this that is a bit more complicated than what we are able to copy."

He grabbed a sheet of paper and a piece of chalk, and placed the paper up against the chair, then began to work the chalk over it to create a rubbing. When he was done, he held it up to her.

"That's better than I would've done." She leaned back, resting against her bed. "It just doesn't make sense. I don't get why you would be targeted."

"Thanks," he said.

"Oh, don't be like that. I just mean that it doesn't make sense that you would be targeted in a dorm in the Academy, as a first-year student. You're a Nelson, after all, so maybe that's the reason. It's just... Well, it doesn't make a lot of sense."

"When has anything that we've done so far over the time that we've been in the Academy made a lot of sense to you?"

"That's a fair question."

Dax carried the chair back to his room before setting it down and angling it so that he could keep track of how he had set it. He wished for some rune that might prevent anyone else from getting into his room. At least he could track whether somebody was coming in and doing anything here, though what he really needed was to catch somebody in the act.

He finished his survey of his room and headed out, closing the door. He traced a quick rune, mostly to see if anybody would trigger it, then met Rochelle outside of the dorm. She looked toward one of the distant buildings. "Research."

"I thought you said you didn't want to take the time to do that. Somebody has a transference exam that they have to be worried about."

She gave him a soft shove. "I do have to worry about it. Not all of us are transference experts like you, so all of us have different needs for studying. I don't want to fail transference just because I don't like it. But in the meantime, let's study these runes."

"I'd like to look into whether we can make any of them traceable."

"What you mean?"

"I want to know if there's any way of identifying if somebody comes through. Actually, what I'd really like would be to figure out who came through and keep tabs on that."

"We could see if runes have a certain signature." When he frowned, she shrugged. "By going to Professor Alibard."

"You trust him enough?"

"I don't know, and I'm not thrilled with bringing professors into things, but I think we need answers. Or at least you do. We just have to ask questions about the complexity of the different runes and leave it at that. You don't have to tell him where you found it or why, or anything else. We haven't looked into him yet."

"I don't think we have to worry about him," Dax said.

"Just like you didn't think that we had to deal with the

headmaster." She shook her head. "Let's be smart about this."

"And what if we have to be smart about Desmond?"

Her face fell for a moment, and she looked around before settling her gaze back on him. "I *was* smart about Desmond. And I was right about him as well."

They headed into the faculty building and made their way to Alibard's room. There was no guarantee that he was even going to be there—Dax didn't know what his office hours were, as he hadn't spent much time with Alibard. And although his classes' exams were done, he probably had other responsibilities within the Academy at this point that Dax and others couldn't even know about.

Alibard surprised them by being there.

He looked up when they knocked, though his door had been cracked already, letting them see that he was seated at his desk. He had a pile of books stacked around his room, and others were stacked haphazardly on shelves all around. A portrait behind him looked like a painting of the Great Serpent, though it was a fantastical version, one that was all serpentine, with massive spread wings that Dax couldn't even imagine were functional.

"Mr. Nelson," he said, sitting up and smiling at him. "And Ms. Alson. To what do I owe this honor?"

"We have a rune question," Dax said.

Alibard chuckled. He flicked his finger, and the door closed behind them. Dax had barely noticed the stream of wind essence that came from him. And as soon as he noticed that it was wind, there was a bit of concern that flushed through him.

Another Whisper?

"The exam is already finished. You both did well," he said, smiling tightly, glancing down at his page for a moment before looking back up at them. "Quite well, in fact. Especially given everything that we have gone through this term with the cultists attacking the Academy. Such nasty work."

"Well, I just wanted to show you a rune that we found. We wanted to get your opinion on it," Dax said. He glanced over at Rochelle, who was quiet. "We don't know if there's anything here, but it was complicated enough we thought we should ask an expert."

Alibard smiled. "I generally direct students to the library, as when you find a unique rune, the best strategy for learning is to research such things. Unless you have something particularly intriguing."

Dax smiled. He thought that this was particularly intriguing, but…

Another thought came to him. How many rune masters were there at the Academy?

He knew of Alibard, and he knew that there were probably a few others, but what if it had been Alibard who had placed the marker on his chair? The idea seemed ridiculous, but so too did the idea that somebody would come into his room the way that they had.

Dax stirred himself from his thinking. "Anyway," he said, stepping forward and unfolding the piece paper that he had made the rubbing on. "I found this. I took a rubbing because I wanted to look into it, but I was hopeful that maybe you could steer us in the right direction about how to start. I don't recognize some of the symbols here."

Alibard took it from him and set it on the table, and then he looked down at it. He said nothing for a few long moments. After another moment, he pulled out a magnifying glass, and then began to sweep it over the surface.

"Intricate work," Professor Alibard said. "Very detailed.

Not the kind of thing that we see very often these days. And you said you *found* this?"

"We did."

"On a bookcase," Rochelle offered.

Dax looked over at her, but he didn't contradict her.

"In the library. While we were studying for trans-ference."

"Ah. Well, then, I suppose it is a little bit surprising. There are many items in the library that have been made over the years. Some of them are a bit more intriguing than others, though this one does catch my eye. I haven't seen anything quite this complicated in quite a while. Would you mind if I borrowed this?"

"It's the only one we have," Rochelle said. "We could make you another rubbing, if you don't mind."

Alibard smiled, nodding carefully, then looking up at them. "Of course. Well, you can see the basis of each of the primary essences within this pattern. There are five primary essences that we typically attribute to things, but in this case, there is a working of different markers around the perimeter. I don't know if it is representative of additional primary essences, or if these are secondary sources." He looked down again, frowning. "The rubbing isn't as perfect as it could otherwise be. Maybe if I had an opportunity to review it more directly."

"I could show it to you sometime," Rochelle said.

Alibard nodded. "Excellent. Well, I guess if you were to look into this, I would start with the primary essences, and some of the older rune patterns for them."

"Older?" Dax asked, getting closer to the desk.

"They are ancient patterns," Alibard said. "We have newer patterns that are considered more efficient, though there are some who believe that the older patterns are just as effective, if not more so. I don't have a strong opinion one way or the other, as I do feel that all such patterns are equally effective for such uses."

Dax took the piece of paper from Alibard when he held it up for him. He folded it, sticking it back into his pocket.

"Is there anything else?"

"That's it," Dax said. "Thank you."

Alibard turned his attention back to his book, or to whatever it was he was working on, leaving Dax and Rochelle in silence for a moment. She looked at him, then urged him toward the door, where Dax hurried out, closing the door behind them even though Alibard hadn't had the door closed before. They said nothing until they were outside again. Then Rochelle looked up at the building.

"He's going to find out that we were not telling him the truth," Dax said.

"Maybe, but he might not even remember that we were here."

"He's going to remember. You just gave him something intriguing."

"Well, we know where to start."

"I will start. You need to work on transference."

"And I believe that you promised to work with me."

Chapter Fourteen

THEY SPENT MUCH OF THE NEXT DAY WORKING ON transference. Rochelle had gotten herself worked up about the test, believing that it was going to involve draining creatures through transference and attempting to make comments to him about what exactly that might mean for the creatures.

"You do realize that the professors have no interest in us taking too much essence from any creature. And I would know if we were."

She shook her head. "It's just what I was always told about the class."

"Well, unless you can see it like I can, you don't have any way of knowing just what it is that others are doing with transference. I suspect all they are going to have us do is draw it and manipulate it."

They were seated outside, near enough to the transference pens that they were able to get up and practice periodically, but far enough away that they didn't have to smell the animals too often. Mostly, she worked with cattle. It was easiest for her, as the cattle didn't have any difficulty with releasing their essence, and they were domesticated to a certain extent so that they were practically pleasant about it.

"I don't know that we have to pull the essence in at all," she said.

"Maybe not you," Dax said. "That's the way that my essence works. I have to pull some part of it inside."

Rochelle watched him. "So what does it feel like?" She was resting her elbows on her knees as she looked at him.

Before Dax could answer, Karelly and several of her friends came through the transference grounds.

"When my uncle gets here, you'll get to see *real* transference. He has a gift. Most gifted with transference in generations." She glanced in Dax's direction. "And I think he'll be most disappointed in how transference is taught these days."

Karelly moved past before Dax could hear what else she was going to say.

Dax let out a frustrated sigh. "I really have to get past her," he muttered.

"I just can't stand the fact that she's always wearing new clothes," Rochelle said.

"What?"

"Oh, I know that she has money, and that my family doesn't have what she does, but it's like she has to flaunt her wealth."

Dax frowned. "I hadn't even realized."

"That's not the sort of thing that you would have realized."

"Well, I'm sorry, nonetheless," Dax said.

Rochelle's essence was flowing through her, a bit of bluish energy that was surging. It was almost as if she were readying to unleash it at Karelly, though he knew her better than that and doubted that she would ever attempt anything like that. Finally, Rochelle let out a long sigh.

"We both have to get past her. I think it's going to get harder, though," she said. "Once the second term begins, there's going to be fewer students."

"I guess I hadn't given that much thought."

"Maybe it's time that you do. She's probably going to be here. I mean, Karelly obviously has enough favoritism within the Academy to stay, and unfortunately, she has enough influence here, so we will have to do our best to just get along with her."

"I can try," Dax muttered. If it weren't for her personality, Karelly would actually be a lovely woman.

"I just hope we don't get assigned to work on a project with her." Rochelle leaned forward, glowering at Karelly. "Some of the second-term assignments require that we work together with others. I really don't want to work with her."

"I'm sure you're not alone in that," Dax said.

"I like to keep our group together."

"Well, then we have to try to be in as many of the same classes as possible. That would make it easier, right?"

She nodded.

"And I can help you, and the others, with what I can see of essence. Like how you're holding on to water as tightly as you are right now."

She looked down at her hands. "You can see that?"

"Well, it's faint, and I have to really constrict my essence in order for me to see it, but it's there."

She shook her head again. "And that's the other thing, Dax. The way that you are able to see essence is strange to me. You talk about needing to pull essence down inside of you, while I need to push it out." She sat up. "What if, when you gain mastery over the other essence that the Great Serpent gave you, you are going to need to push it rather than pull it?"

Dax shrugged. "I had thought about that myself. I spent so much time trying to push on essence the way that Professor Jamesh was teaching that I do have a pretty good concept of it. And to be honest, once I constrict it down, I do have to push it through me, but I push it in a different way. I tighten it, and then I send it out through my limbs, into my heart and into my head."

"And I do none of those things," she said. "Why do you think it's so different?"

"I don't know. Maybe the type of essence, or maybe it's just the way that my mother trained me? When I was younger, she had me working on essence, trying to help me understand how to use and manipulate certain aspects of essence, so that I could use it as soon as I had my own essence."

"Very few people can work with their own natural essence before they are gifted from the Great Serpent," she said.

"I know that," Dax said.

"And you're saying that you can?"

"I'm saying that what my mother taught me was a little different," he said. "So…"

So maybe what he needed to do, and what he had already started to do, was to reach out to his mother, and see what she might have known.

He was at the Academy, but if he could really find a way to get word to her, and could share with her what he had experienced, and what he had been dealing with, it was possible she might be able to help explain more to him. Given everything that he had come to learn about his mother, and what he had come to learn about his sister, Dax couldn't help but feel as if maybe having his mother and her contacts with the Cult of the Dragon on hand might be beneficial, anyway.

"Anyway," he said, getting back to the topic, "we were talking about transference. So like I was saying, I don't think that we need to worry about you doing anything with that essence other than just drawing it out. I think that's the first test."

"And if it's more than that?"

"If it's more than that, then I suppose I could help."

Rochelle shook her head. "No. I'm doing this on my own. I'm going to learn what I'm supposed to learn, and I'm going to become the essence wielder that I'm supposed to be. And even if you do have the underlying control over essence that you have, that doesn't make it right for you to help somebody else like that."

"I didn't say I would help you cheat," Dax said.

"Good, because that's the way it sounded."

"I just thought I would give you a little more strength."

She frowned at him. "Strength?"

"Well, depending upon what the test involves, I think that's something my essence might provide. I'm going to have to keep working with it so that I can make sure that I have the right control over it, but I might be able to add something to you. To all of us."

Rochelle was quiet for a few moments. "I think it's time to go. I don't like sitting so close to the cattle."

"You don't think they are cute?"

She wrinkled her nose. "Maybe, but they smell."

"Maybe it's just me that smells," Dax said.

"Oh, you definitely smell. I'm going to have to fumigate my room."

Dax frowned. "I can't keep staying in your room."

"And I don't see what the issue is. Well, other than sleeping on the floor."

"I've been starting to think about ways that I could protect my own room," Dax said. "If I can find protective runes, I might be able to place them and—"

"You are talking about placing protective runes around your room when whoever placed that inside of your room obviously knows more about runes than we ever will."

"Then we need to go to Desmond," Dax said. "Not just for that, though maybe that would be enough reason. But we need to go to Desmond to understand the flare too."

"You're probably right," Rochelle said. "It's time that we got help."

"You know, it was easier when my sister was still here. Actually, it was easier when we trusted the headmaster."

"Now we don't know who to trust," Rochelle said.

"And I don't know if there's going to be any way for us to find anybody that we can trust. Not with the Order active."

Dax wished that it were simpler. But unfortunately, there was nothing simple about this.

They started off, heading out of the Academy grounds, and when they reached the edge of the Academy grounds, heading toward the artisan district, Dax paused, turning and looking behind him. He constricted his essence down tightly, looking for the possibility that someone might be out there, watching him.

They wandered the artisan district, and when Rochelle looked as if she wanted to head directly toward Desmond's home, Dax shook his head and guided her away so they were less conspicuous. They passed a blacksmith shop, though it was run by an unusual sort of blacksmith, one who used fire essence in his forgings. Dax looked in the window, noticing several different items with rune marks on them. They continued on, and they passed a florist, a baker, even a gardener, though the items that the gardener seemed to grow looked like glass flowers rather than real, living ones.

"You know, it's really quite peaceful out here," he said.

"I've been trying to tell you that from the very beginning," Rochelle said.

"I don't listen so well," Dax said.

She started to laugh. "That is the understatement of the year."

Dax watched the essence around him, looking for anything that might be moving, but he didn't find anything obvious. That suggested they weren't being followed, which was reassuring. They weaved through an alleyway, and then onto a side street, the buildings pressing close together, almost precariously so. Most of them were brightly painted wooden structures, though some were older stonework that looked more like the rest of the city, or at least closer to the Academy design.

"I never asked you, but do you have some sort of a map on how to get through here?"

She snorted. "No. I can follow the markers."

"There are no street markers."

"Not street markers. Building markers." She pointed. Dax looked up, and he saw a massive rune etched on one of the buildings. "You just have to follow them. It is a bit more confusing, at least, until you start to see it."

But as Dax looked at the rune, he did see a faint trace of power within it.

Maybe that was what only he was supposed to see. Or maybe others could see it as well. Regardless, the energy that was within that room, the energy that he could see coming from it, struck him as…

It struck him as significant.

As they headed through the streets, he saw the familiar figure of Karelly. He motioned toward her, and Rochelle frowned.

"What is she doing out here?"

"Probably meeting that transference uncle of hers. Maybe we should follow," he said.

She pressed her lips together. "We don't need to create more drama. We have enough the way that it is."

"But this is Karelly. I'm certain that she's involved in something that she shouldn't be."

"Oh, almost certainly," she said. "But we don't need to deal with it."

Karelly disappeared into a storefront just down the road, and Dax hesitated.

"That's an awfully expensive shop," he said.

It was primarily a jeweler, though Dax had never been inside himself. He wouldn't have the funds—or at least, he would never be willing to use the funds—to go and shop there. He'd known she was wealthy, but he had not realized just how much money Karelly had so that she could spend it *that* casually.

"Guess it's not her uncle. Maybe she's picking up some extra work," Rochelle said, shrugging.

"Maybe."

"Let's just get going. We need to get in to see Desmond."

That was probably for the best. He didn't want to wait around here too much longer, partly because he didn't know if it was going to be safe for them. And they needed to get answers. All of this was taking far too long otherwise.

They made their way toward Desmond's home, where they stopped in front of the door, then knocked. Dax waited.

When he started to knock again, Rochelle looked over at him. "I don't think that he's here. We can return later."

He had questions about what they had found. Desmond would have to know more about the flare, but where was he?

Dax took a step back, and he stared at the door for a moment, and debated whether he should try transference on the door, wondering if there would be any way for him to pull upon the essence within it. Even if he tried to do that, he didn't know if it would work.

He decided against it. Doing so might destabilize something for Desmond, and that was not something he had any interest in doing, especially if he thought that Desmond might be able to help them in the future.

"Let's get back," Rochelle said. "I do have a transference test to deal with."

"We both do."

Chapter Fifteen

DAX WATCHED THE STUDENTS LINING UP FOR THE transference test. He had considered volunteering to go first before deciding against it. There was no advantage in going early. And with everyone that went before him, Dax could observe. Most of the students worked relatively well with transference, drawing just a little bit. When it was Rochelle's turn, she did the same, and she released it just as skillfully.

By the time she came over to him, she was grinning. "I remembered what you said about not holding onto it too long. It worked for me."

Dax didn't have the feeling that the professor wanted anybody to fail, as she gave even those who struggled a few chances to get through their exam. By the time it was his turn, he was ready, and stepped up confidently and began to pull upon the essence. He held onto it, and he noticed that it felt like he was trapping some of that essence.

He had never done that before, and he certainly didn't intend to hold onto that essence this long now. He could feel it inside of him. Dax tried pushing it back, but even as he attempted that, it seemed as if some part of the essence linked to him. It was like he was communicating with him —or merging with his own essence.

He panicked and pushed.

The cow bellowed as if pained. That stripped some of the connection, and he was able to push the essence back.

"Mr. Nelson?"

Dax turned his attention to Professor Madenil. "I'm sorry," Dax said. He began to push the essence out, and then triggered the small seesaw resting on the table, which was the way that they were supposed to prove that they were drawing upon essence from somebody else. He used that, and as soon as he finished pouring that power out of him, the seesaw began to teeter wildly.

He withdrew, but not before looking over at the cow. Dax couldn't help but feel as if there was some sort of a connection there, and he wasn't sure what it was, or why he would feel it, only that the connection lingered. Even once he withdrew his hand from the cow—even though his hand wasn't even necessary for making that connection or having that transference—he began to feel something else: some part of that essence, or perhaps some part of that essence that had lingered within him.

When he went back to his seat, Rochelle looked at him.

"I can tell you when we leave," Dax whispered.

Professor Madenil motioned to the class and smiled. "Everybody did quite well today. Transference can be a difficult topic, especially in the first term, when you are working on your own manipulation. The first term is primarily familiarization with concepts. Very few are expected to have mastered anything more than the basics. A few of you have done quite a bit more than I would've expected this term, and so I will be speaking to you separately, and inviting you to focus your studies on transference. As you get further in the Academy, you will be given an opportunity to concentrate your studies on one aspect of essence wielding or another."

What would Dax choose to focus on? Would it be valor? That would be what his family would want from him. Would it be essence manipulation? He could see some advantages in that, but he didn't know whether there was going to be anything useful to that given that his form of essence manipulation was quite a bit different than what Professor Jamesh taught. What about runes? They certainly were useful, and he wanted to continue his study in them, especially as he had started to gain a greater insight as to how those runes could be used. But even with that, Dax didn't know whether it was someplace that he wanted to focus his efforts.

Then there was transference. He didn't think that he needed additional study, but maybe what he needed was to better understand how to manipulate essence the way that he would learn in transference. By the time they left, he no longer felt the same anxiety about what had happened.

Rochelle was watching him. "Do you want to talk about what happened?"

"Not particularly," he said.

"Then do you want to celebrate?"

He considered. "Actually, I'd like to see if we can't find Desmond. I still have questions for him."

"Does this have to do with the Order, or does it have to do with what just happened?"

"Maybe a little bit of both."

Rochelle nodded, not pushing for him to tell her anything more.

They headed through to the artisan district, before finding Desmond's door and knocking. But once again, there was no answer.

At this point, Dax was starting to question whether Desmond was even going to come back. He had no idea how to reach him otherwise. When they had last seen Desmond, he had told them that if he they needed him, that all he had to do was to send word to him, but if he was going to be absent like this...

"I really wish he would've given us some way to try to contact him," Dax said.

"Maybe you should try your transference on the door."

He arched a brow at her. "I didn't think that you wanted me to do that."

"Well," she said, looking around before turning back to him, "I don't know that we want to do that, but I doubt that Desmond will be too upset. Besides, I don't want you carrying that thing around."

"You probably are right," he said.

He focused on the door. The runes that were placed here were quite a bit more complicated than other runes that he had dealt with before, but at this point, Dax had started to realize that he could use his transference essence in ways that would allow him to withdraw any power from a rune lock. And so he drew power out.

It happened slowly, almost as if there was some sort of resistance against him, and a series of lines began to form in the door. The essence strained against him as he drew it in, almost as if the door itself were fighting him. But then he heard a lock snick open.

He glanced over at Rochelle, who nodded.

They pulled the door open.

"Does it feel different to you?"

"It feels the same as it always feels," she said.

"There's something not quite right here," Dax said.

"Why?"

"I don't know. Maybe it's protected? I think we need to be careful before we just go lunging inside," he said. "I don't really know what this is, or what it is that I feel, but I can tell that there is something here."

She shrugged. "Be my guest."

Dax reached into his pocket, and he fumbled, feeling for something to toss inside, before realizing that he didn't have anything other than the crystal with him. And he wasn't about to throw the crystal inside the room.

Instead he grabbed a cobblestone off the street nearby and tossed it into the home. It shattered immediately, looking like it went through some barrier of power before getting ripped apart.

Rochelle took a step back.

"Could that have been *us*?" she asked.

Dax shook his head. "I doubt that he would've been able to do anything like that to us. There is probably some sort of a security measure on the door that activates protections in here."

"So we aren't going into his room, are we?"

She frowned, leaning forward. Dax felt the urge to pull her back, not wanting her to get too close, not wanting anything to happen to her, but at the same time knowing she would probably be fine as she leaned forward and peered into the darkness of his home.

"Do you think we could send a message to him?" she asked.

"How do you intend to send a message to him?"

"I don't know. I thought about just yelling inside, but

he's got that strange hallway that would make it difficult, anyway. Maybe we go through the Whisper network."

"Or maybe we just do something more traditional. We use the Post."

"Sure, because the Post is going to be able to get to Desmond without any difficulty."

"I doubt they're going to have that much trouble," Dax said. "Besides, what other way would we have of getting to him?"

She frowned, seemingly irritated. "Fine." She waved for him to follow, and they took a roundabout way back toward the Academy. They worked through the artisan district at first, then veered out to the main part of the city. When he looked over at Rochelle, she shrugged. "I just want to stretch my legs a bit. With everything that's been happening inside of the Academy grounds, it feels too cramped."

"I understand," he said.

"Good. I was a little worried that you would object."

They paused at a few food carts, and Rochelle paid, which Dax felt guilty about, if only for a little bit. They stopped and looked at a few murals that had been painted, and he pointed to a few different runes before a strange strand of essence caught his attention. He wasn't exactly sure why, but he saw something moving.

He motioned to Rochelle, and she followed him.

"What do you think it is?"

"Don't know," he said. "Probably nothing." He shrugged. "But it's stronger than some of the other essence that I have seen."

"That could mean many things."

He nodded. "I know."

"So long as you know." She followed him.

The essence moved almost languidly, changing directions, and then veering off before disappearing altogether. At one point, he could have sworn he caught a flash of fur. Were they following some escaped transference creature?

Then he lost the trail.

He breathed out a frustrated sigh. "Well, so much for that," he said.

"Lost it?"

He nodded. "It's gone."

"Good. Then we can get back."

"Back to what? Your room? Exploring mine? Searching for answers?"

"Yes," Rochelle said. "To all of it. Just because we don't know how we're going to search, we can't stop. In fact, I would argue that because we don't know, we have to keep going."

"I just wish we knew more about all of this."

"Well, it's up to us to keep searching, then."

Chapter Sixteen

"WHERE HAVE YOU BEEN?"

Dax looked over at Cedrick, who had met them at the cafeteria. He hurriedly filled Cedrick in on what they been doing, and Cedrick whistled softly.

"That's... something. And here I figured that you were more concerned about how you did on your exams. I passed mine, by the way. I know mine weren't nearly as difficult as your advanced classes, but I passed them, and that's all that matters."

Dax nodded. "That is all that matters. And congratulations are in order."

"Congratulations? I'd like to *celebrate*. We're done with our exams."

"So what happens now?" Dax asked.

Rochelle frowned. "What do you mean?"

"You know, I hadn't even considered it," Dax said as he started toward the cafeteria, as they really did need to eat, "but what happens in between terms? We knew that the tests were one part of the transition, but after that..."

"After that, we have a break, but it's brief," she said. "Ten days, which isn't a whole lot."

"Some people go home," Cedrick said. "But only if they live close enough to the Academy that it makes the journey worthwhile. I live far enough away that it would be difficult, and I really don't know that it makes much sense, anyway. Since you're along the unclaimed lands, I don't know that it makes much sense for you to do that, either."

It was too far for him to go home to the unclaimed lands. And he didn't necessarily want to see his family. At least, he didn't want to see his father or his brother. He would be open to seeing his mother.

"I've got to finish testing first," Dax said.

"You only have valor left," Cedrick said, waving a hand. "And you already passed it."

"I still have to show up," Dax said.

There was a bit of a commotion as Aidan came into the cafeteria, pushing past a pair of first-year students. Rochelle had been upset before about Karelly wearing all sorts of new clothing, but now Aidan did as well, sporting a deep blue jacket with heavy embroidery on it. How much would that have cost?

Dax was never one to really care about money, but then again, from what Rochelle had suggested, he didn't have to because he had it. What would it have been like for him to have not come from money? Would he have been different?

Could Karelly be responsible for his missing trunk?

As much as she annoyed him, that seemed even beyond her.

"Maybe he won't pass," Cedrick said.

"We could be so lucky."

He looked around, and he realized that Gia was already in the cafeteria, but she was seated by herself. He frowned.

Getting to his feet, he started toward her, but she moved her tray away and headed out of the cafeteria.

"Is everything all right with her?" Dax asked.

Cedrick shrugged. "Some people get a little uptight around exams."

He looked over at Rochelle, who frowned at him.

"I didn't say you."

"She doesn't have to take the valor exam either," Dax said. "So I don't know why she would be like that."

He gathered his food, and once he was done, he took a seat at one of the tables. Rochelle took a seat across from him, and Cedrick sat next to her. Dax fell into a quiet rhythm, eating.

"Well," Cedrick began, interrupting the silence, as he often did. "What have you been doing?"

"Dax has been helping me make sure that I was prepared for transference," she said.

"Tutoring? And here I thought that maybe there was something more exciting going on between the two of you."

Dax looked up and glowered at him before turning his attention back to his food. That was part of the reason that he didn't want to spend so much time at Rochelle's room, but at this point, given that Desmond had disappeared, there wasn't going be any way for Dax to get the help that he needed, and he didn't think that he was going to be able to find the answers that he wanted. So he just turned to eating.

When he finished, he got up and said his goodbyes, heading back to his room. Rochelle caught up to him. She didn't say anything, and they trudged back into her room, where he crashed on the floor. The next morning, he got up early and made his way toward the valor grounds.

He really did have to attend valor, even though he didn't have any testing to do.

He thought that he might be early, but Professor Garrison was already there, and he was talking to Gia.

Dax stood off to the side, near the rack of the essence blades, trying not to listen. A few of the other students came in, and they gave Gia and Professor Garrison space.

When they were done, she looked in his direction.

Dax decided that he'd had enough of that.

He stormed over to her. "What is your issue?"

"I..." She looked down. "I don't know. I've just been unsettled since we got back. I feel like... Well, I feel like I can't do nearly as much as the rest of you can with essence. I mean, I'm only in basic classes, other than this. And this is valor, and I'm a Stonewall, so I'm supposed to be good at this."

"What does that matter?"

"It matters because basic essence wielders are... well, we end up as fighters."

Dax frowned. "That's the only thing that you're worried about?" He and Rochelle had already talked about trying to figure out a way to help Gia and Cedrick get into more advanced classes—but they hadn't said anything to either of them yet.

"Isn't that why you brought me along in the first place?"

"I brought you because I thought that you could be useful in a scrap, but that's not the entire reason that I asked for you to come along. I trusted you. I don't know a lot of other people at the Academy who I'm willing to say the same."

She frowned at him. "You brought me because you could trust me? Not because I'm a Stonewall?"

"That's not really why I wanted you along. Well, not

that it wasn't a factor. You are nearly as good at valor as I am."

She glowered at him. "Nearly? And that's not what's bothering me. It's that all of you are going off into your advanced classes. I'm the only one in all these basic classes."

Dax blinked. "And that's what's bothering you?" She nodded. "We can help you. You've got enough friends now who are more than happy to help you figure out what you might need to know to keep progressing."

He hadn't even considered the possibility that would be a problem for her, but maybe he should've. The only reason that he didn't have her in other classes was because she was in basic classes, and Dax had been assigned to only advanced classes. Some of that was because of his sister—well, all that was because of his sister, thinking that she was going to be able to protect him—but Dax had done well in his advanced classes, anyway.

"Manipulation, transference, runes, politics. I suppose all of it."

Dax smiled.

"It's not funny," she said.

"And I didn't say that it was funny; I was just smiling. You do realize that you have control over what classes you take? The registrar offers suggestions, but you don't have to stick with them. Especially if it's a particular area of interest for you."

"What if it's too much for me?"

"Well, if it's too much for you, then you go back to basic classes. I don't see the issue."

"You don't see the issue because you'll never have to do that," she said softly.

"And neither will you. You have friends who will work with you."

She took a deep breath, and then she nodded. When she did, something of her demeanor began to shift, and she smiled at him. "Thank you, Dax."

"Did you really think that we weren't going to try to help you?"

"I didn't know. And… well, I thought that you just wanted me because of my fighting ability."

He chuckled. "Well, I'm the better fighter."

Professor Garrison raised a hand, and everybody fell into silence.

"The testing today will begin with some basic forms. Everybody has been working on this for the term, and while I know that we have been working at a breathtaking pace, we are going to ask that all of you demonstrate what you have learned through this term, so you can demonstrate the skill that you have acquired, and we can prove that you are worthy of advancement into further advanced valor classes. The testing will be straightforward, but it is not going to be today."

Everyone started to talk quietly.

That surprised Dax. He had thought that today would be the testing for valor because they were very nearly done with all the other exams, and he would've expected that they would've needed to finish with valor so that the term could end.

"As I'm sure you're all disappointed, the reason is quite simple. We don't have our usual cadre of instructors." Dax and Gia shared a look, though neither of them said anything. "But I have a plan for alternative arrangements for appropriate testing regardless of having the necessary professors there." He smiled. "And in exchange, I thought that we would ask a pair of our more advanced students to demonstrate what they know, and what valor can teach in the next term."

He turned to look at Dax and Gia.

Dax knew what the professor was getting at.

Professor Garrison strode over to them. "I apologize," Professor Garrison said, "but I did need the students to see something. I was hoping you could walk them through a sparring session demonstrating some of the movements you were teaching them this term."

"Just what they were learning this term?" Gia asked. "Would you have something else in mind?"

Gia shrugged. "Well, Dax and I haven't had an opportunity to *fully* test each other."

Professor Garrison grinned. "Oh. Wonderful. A Stonewall and a Nelson sparring." He turned back to the class. "I will ask them to demonstrate some of the basic forms, but then we will allow them to break into a full-blown sparring session. Once this is over, we will talk about testing terms when you return for tomorrow."

He snorted, and then they took steps apart as they positioned themselves into their stances.

Dax started with the udin style and began to move into gauhr. He slipped from one to the other, changing positions as he twisted and turned, flowing through some of the movements that he had been asked to demonstrate to the students throughout the term. Gia met him, and they went through attack and defense. Neither of them spoke, but neither of them really needed to, as this was really more of a demonstration than anything else.

As they went, both began to pick up the pace.

Gia lunged forward, dropping down, sliding her fist

toward his belly, but Dax twisted to the side, and he grabbed her, flipping her over.

She managed to spin out of that, then landed with her back facing him, but he darted away, spinning in a kick.

It was a combination of styles, and as soon as he recognized that, Dax knew the demonstration was over, and the sparring had begun in earnest.

He smiled to himself.

Gia was quick and strong, and she was incredibly skilled.

But he had his own skill. Dax didn't have his father's technique or fire ability, but he'd trained daily, and he had pushed himself for many years. In that time, it had been unusual for him to spar with somebody her size. Often, his father would have him spar with somebody much larger than him, because his father believed that was the only way that he was going to get better. But Gia challenged him in a different way.

Dax let her make the first move.

She darted at him, and he slipped his foot off to the side, catching her leg and hooking it. She reacted, yanking her foot up and nearly upending him.

He was forced to release the hook, and he spun around, grabbing her around the waist, but she slammed her elbows down on his arms, breaking the grip.

She looked up at him, grinning. "Not bad for a Nelson."

"I was just going to say it's not bad for a Stonewall," he said.

"Essence, or no?"

"What do you think?"

As soon as he said it, earth exploded near him and sent him staggering back.

He reacted, drawing on transference and summoning

some of the earth essence out of her, reflecting it back. He landed near the essence blades, though they were makeshift essence blades, nothing more than practice swords.

Could he use them similarly to an essence blade?

It might be fun to spar with them.

He grabbed a pair, tossing one to her, and then he used a bit of earth essence with his transference to explode upward.

Dax felt her bursting toward him.

He braced, readying for the impact. It would be significant.

Some part of his mind screamed a warning, and in that moment, he knew where the impact would strike. It was as if he could anticipate the flow of essence, even though he couldn't yet see it.

He twisted, and while he was in the air, he felt a bit of wind essence somewhere near him, and he drew on that. As soon as he did, he sent that out through him, creating a gust of wind that directed him a in a different path, and then landed.

Immediately, he turned back to Gia, and he drew upon earth once more, creating a reflection of her essence.

It wouldn't last.

His reflection was not nearly enough to counter anything that she did, especially with her level of control and his inexperience.

But he was in a place with other students who all had different types of essence.

As he turned, feeling the essence all around them, Dax began to notice different patterns that were here, and he began to pull upon fire. He sent that streaking through a burst of stone.

She froze, looking at him. "Not fair."

Dax turned and slammed into stone. He couldn't see it, as she had solidified a thin, almost translucent wall in front of him.

He drew upon transference, drew upon what she was using, and shattered the stone.

Another blast, and he staggered backward.

He popped up, using wind to go sliding off to the side, when…

When he felt another warning in the back of his mind.

As soon as he felt that, the ground began to tremble.

The warning alerted him, even though he hadn't known what was coming.

Almost too late, he jumped.

A blast struck him from behind.

He drew upon wind, wondering briefly if whoever he summoned the wind from realized what he was doing, or if it was too much. He darted toward Gia, punching through the stone, but her blade caught his.

Gia grinned at him.

They stood facing each other, blade to blade, neither of them moving.

Professor Garrison clapped his hands.

"Wonderful," he said, turning to them. "And such dramatic skill. I must say, I didn't realize that Mr. Nelson had his father's fire connection, though I shouldn't be terribly surprised. He must have some aspect of it." He watched Dax for a moment, the question lingering in his gaze, despite the amusement in his tone. "And as you see, this is the height of valor at somebody this level." He turned to the class. "All of you will get to a semblance of this skill by the end of your time at the Academy. Next term will involve you using actual transference blades, which will grant you more of what you saw here."

He and Gia bowed politely, the same way that they would've if they were sparring back home, and then they carried their blades back to the rack.

"You think that it was wise for you to reveal so much of your transference like that?"

"I wasn't really thinking about it so much," Dax admitted.

"Obviously," Gia said, laughing at him. "But I think I had you that time."

"I think you did, too. I was running out of strength."

She frowned. "You were just *starting* to run out of strength?"

"Why?"

"Because you punched through the last of mine."

Dax chuckled. "Well, I guess we won't know which of us would win, will we?"

"I say rematch."

They returned to the class, and others there were starting to look at them with a different expression. They had been treated differently throughout the term, partly because they had been helping to instruct, but now…

"And now you see why I will be asking Mr. Nelson and Ms. Stonewall to participate in the testing." He turned to them. "You will be evaluating your fellow students' performance."

All they could do was nod.

"Excellent," Professor Garrison said again, clapping his hands together and turning back to class. "You are all dismissed. Be ready. Testing begins tomorrow."

Chapter Seventeen

DAX WAITED OUTSIDE OF THE VALOR CLASS FOR PROFESSOR Garrison, but he never came out.

Gia waited with him, tapping her foot and frowning, every so often looking back toward the training ground as if wishing that she could return. And given that they had just completed a quick spar, he suspected that was exactly what she wanted, because he suspected that she believed that she truly could take him. At this point, given how tired he was, he thought that it was possible that she actually could take him.

"You don't seem all that thrilled that we are going to be a part of the testing," Gia said.

"You are?"

She shrugged. "We've been teaching with him the entire term, so I suppose it's not terribly surprising he would ask this of us."

"Are you going to feel comfortable telling one of our classmates that they didn't pass?"

She frowned. "He wouldn't make us do that, would he?"

Dax shrugged. "To be honest, I don't know. It's possible. Garrison did take us outside of the Academy and use us to search for the Cult of the Dragon, so I honestly have no idea what he's willing to do. Maybe he would force us to test and fail students."

"We don't actually have to be the ones to fail them," Gia said. "We can just tell him how they perform. Maybe we suggest that he retest them if we don't think they've done as well as they need to."

"That's actually a pretty good idea."

"I'm due for one every now and again." She shrugged for a moment before looking over. "Were you planning on going home?"

"I didn't realize that was an option until recently. So no. How about you?"

It felt like they had not talked to each other in a long time, even though it had only been a few days.

"No. My family doesn't think that it's necessary for me to return, as the return journey is just too expensive. We don't all have Nelson wealth."

"That's my mother," Dax said.

"Your mother, not your father?"

Dax shrugged. "Well, most people think that is my father, because of the things that he sells along the unclaimed lands, given the creatures that try to cross near our holdings. But most of it comes from my mother. She's figured a way to monetize pretty much everything that happens and comes through our holding."

"Impressive," she said. "Maybe my mother could learn a thing or two from yours. Mine never really talked about much. She sort of lets my father deal with everything. And he trained me to fight, which I think my mother wasn't thrilled with. If it were up to her, I would be more like her, and…"

"And what?"

"Oh, it would be more of me just learning to be the perfect housewife."

"So you're glad you're at the Academy."

"I don't know what I would do if I wasn't at the Academy. So yes, I suppose that I'm glad."

He let out a heavy sigh, and they caught up with Rochelle, who was waiting outside of the dorm.

"Does it feel nice to be over with all of that?" Rochelle asked.

"It's not exactly over," Dax said, then he filled her in on the testing, and what they were going to have to do.

"So you just sparred?"

"Well, I think he wanted us to demonstrate what valor could be like," Dax said, looking over at Gia. "And it might've gotten a little out of hand for the two of us."

"Was it out of hand?"

"Not for me, but I think you were," he said.

He was still tired, and more than that, he was a little bit troubled about what he had experienced during the sparring session. There had been that strange awareness of what Gia was preparing to do.

That was the only way that he could think to describe it. An awareness. It had come unbidden. It had come when he had been distracted, drawing upon his transference and attempting to fight. It had given him an alert that something was amiss, even before he would've noticed it through his ability to see and feel other types of essence. If this was the understanding that he had asked for—and possibly been given—by the Great Serpent, then why would it have manifested in that way?

The better question, and one that Dax didn't have an answer to, was whether there was any way that he would be able to control it. The only time that he had noticed it was when his life seemed like it was in danger.

Then again, he had never really been in danger in the sparring session. Gia wasn't going to harm him. She might have been trying to, and she might've been sparring with as much as strength as she had, but he'd never really worried that she was going to actually do something that would hurt him. This was Gia, after all, and Dax didn't think that she was willing to take a sparring match to such extremes.

"I have something to tell you both," Rochelle said, interrupting his line of thinking.

"What is it?" Dax asked.

"It's about the headmaster," she said, lowering her voice as she looked around the inside of the yard. "Not that people want to talk about it, but I think it's important for us, especially, to speak of. He's not coming back. The job has been posted."

"What?" Gia asked.

Rochelle nodded. "My mother sent word. She wanted to make sure that everything was going okay at the Academy. She said it wasn't surprising, because the headmaster had long been looking to retire, or some such nonsense, and so she wasn't surprised by that."

"So I guess that means he's really not coming back," Dax said. He took a seat on the bench that Rochelle had been on, and Gia took a seat on the other side of him.

"I've been hearing a few rumors about students not doing so well on their exams," Gia said, looking over at Dax and Rochelle. "Mostly basic students."

"What are you trying to tell us?" Dax asked.

Gia hurriedly shook her head. "Oh. I didn't think about

it like that. Not me. I'm doing fine, I think. And if I were to fail my exams, I don't know that my parents would welcome me home."

"Why not?" Rochelle asked. She glanced from Gia to Dax. "Don't you two both have parents who are happy to train you in whatever essence you have?"

"I think happy is a bit of a stretch," Dax said. "And it's not so much that they are happy to do it as they feel as if they don't have any choice but to do so. Only I don't have fire, so they weren't willing to teach."

"I think mine would," Gia said. "But I don't want to end up there."

"Why not? I think if my parents had been able to teach me, I probably would have stayed—no. That's not true," she went on. "I still would have wanted to come to the Academy, because I would've wanted to see if there was anything here that I could learn that they wouldn't be able to teach. My grandfather wanted me to come to the Academy as well. He always told me that there was much more that I could learn at the Academy than what I could from staying home. And he always liked how there was a breadth of knowledge found at the Academy that couldn't be found elsewhere." She smiled. "I miss him."

"If I failed out of the Academy, I'm not exactly sure what I would do," Dax said.

"Well, I have a hard time thinking that you have much to worry about."

"Maybe Dax doesn't," Gia said, "but others are worried. Like I said, there are some who aren't doing quite as well as they thought they would." She started to laugh. "Including Aidan. I don't think he's in any danger of failing, but he's not doing as well as I think he intended."

"You seem almost excited about that," Rochelle said.

"It's not that I'm excited," she said. "Well, maybe I'm excited. He could be awful. So I wouldn't mind him having a little comeuppance. Just a little. Nothing too mean."

Dax snorted.

"Anyway. It's probably all because of the pace they were pushing us. I kept thinking that maybe we would be given a bit of reprieve, especially considering what we know—"

Rochelle cut her off with a slight shake of her head.

"Anyway," she went on. That doesn't seem to be the case."

Other students began to arrive, and Gia frowned. She got to her feet and waved as she headed away.

"Something is bothering you," Rochelle said. "I don't think that you have to worry about failing."

"It's not that," Dax said.

"Then what is it?"

"Well, something happened during valor."

He filled her in on what had happened when he had been working with Gia, the way that he had felt that strange warning. She studied him, and for a moment, she said nothing. Then he began to feel a bit of energy washing through him. He didn't know what she was doing, but he recognized her essence as it swirled through him. It was soft, gentle, and not unpleasant. When it cleared, there was nothing remaining. He didn't expect for her to leave any permanent essence behind, and he thought that he might've been able to pull on her essence if he really wanted to do so, in order for him to try to test whether or not there was anything there that he was going to be concerned about, but he didn't need to.

"I don't feel anything amiss," she said.

"Would you have?"

"Maybe," she said. "I think that we need to start testing

you more regularly. Maybe we need to start testing others more regularly as well. I didn't think about this, but what if something happens, and we don't even know it because we haven't been checking on it? All it takes is you being put into some sort of a life-threatening situation?"

"Well, I don't know if I would say that was life-threatening," he said, looking ahead at Gia. She was laughing at something that Cedrick had said.

"Or what your essence at least perceived as life-threatening," she corrected. "We could test that, if you want to. Sort of see what this can do."

"I don't like the sound of that," he said.

"Just because I intend to hurt you doesn't mean that you need to be worried about it," she said, grinning at him.

"I *definitely* don't like the sound of that," he said.

She laughed. "Oh, I think our break is going to be quite fun."

Chapter Eighteen

THE VALOR TEST WENT SMOOTHLY. DAX'S FEARS ABOUT NOT being able to pass any of the students proved unfounded. All of the students that he tested proved capable. Dax put them through a series of movements, and though they were basic, everyone succeeded. It eased his mind.

Gia had seemed pleased as well, and as soon as the testing was done, the students were dismissed to go about their day.

He had tried to approach Professor Garrison again, but the professor had disappeared before they had an opportunity to speak to him. He didn't even know what he was going to ask him, but he had questions about the professor's previous experience with Ames given a photo of the two of them they had found in the library at the start of term.

So with that, valor was done. His last class was done.

And the term had ended.

It was sort of unceremonious.

Dax hadn't exactly known what to expect, but when all the tests were done, students began to disperse. The dorms began to empty. Classrooms were empty, and professors became unavailable. The only part of the Academy experience that hadn't changed was that the cafeteria was still open, though there were far fewer people at the cafeteria when they would go for their meals.

The rest of the city remained active, which was a stark contrast to the Academy grounds. The artisan district was particularly vibrant, something he'd noticed when he had gone to Desmond's door looking for the man, still finding him gone.

He hadn't received any word from his mother, though he wasn't sure whether she would get back to him. Even if she did, he had no idea what she might say to him.

So he stayed busy with his friends.

Most other students had left for the break, which left him and his friends in relative quiet. It was nice not running into Karelly or some of the others who trailed after her like some sort of lost puppy, and not having to worry about who he might run into on the grounds. Gia had been working diligently with all of them, and she was far better with essence manipulation than she gave herself credit for, so he wasn't surprised that she had that gift. Runes required a bit of prodding, and he thought that she was going to need some help there. She was very early on with transference, and he felt as if there were going to be some techniques that he might be able to teach her that would help bring her along there as well.

Dax was preparing to head toward the transference grounds when he felt a strange stirring of essence and a tingling working at the back of his neck.

Dax spun. His heart hammered in his chest as he prepared transference. He didn't know which member of the Order was coming at him, but he was certain that was what it was. He was outside of his dorm entrance, and there was a rumbling of earth.

A *familiar* rumbling of earth.

Gia.

That essence struck, catching him. Had he not been alerted to it, he might have been caught even worse. Dax tumbled off to the side, hopping to his feet, and began to draw upon transference. Gia held her hands out in a placating gesture.

"Only doing what Rochelle asked that I do," she said.

"She asked you just to attack me randomly?" he said.

"Something like that," she said, grinning at him. "She said that we were supposed to test your awareness. I figured that it was probably for the best, anyway, because I want to know about your awareness as well. Anything that will help me get an advantage with you."

A tingling began to work upon Dax's neck again, and he rolled off to the side.

Cedrick popped out from around the doorway, grinning at him.

"Nope," he said. "I didn't hit him. I don't know what would happen if I did, especially since I have life essence," he said, sounding much more at ease with his essence than he ever had before, "but he probably wouldn't have been very happy with me."

Dax got up, dusting himself off. "And I'm still not very happy with you."

Eventually, Rochelle came around the front of the building. She glanced at him, but she shrugged, almost nonchalantly. "You need to know."

"I don't need our friends to attack me."

"Better your friends than strangers. You need to know how you are able to react. And you need to control it."

"He can't even control transference," Gia said.

Dax drew upon a bit of earth essence, summoning some from her. He appreciated the fact that he no longer had to be up close to somebody in order for him to use it, and as he did, he slammed into the ground right at her feet.

She barely reacted. She caused the stone to flatten and then sent another burst at him, which caused Dax to go staggering back a step. He tried to draw upon transference, but Rochelle stepped between them.

"I didn't do this as a chance for the two of you to spar again. Then again, maybe you should." She looked over at Dax. "That is how you are going to be able to find what you need to feel."

"We could go to the valor grounds," Gia said helpfully.

"Great," Dax said.

"That afraid of sparring with me?"

"No," he said, and he breathed out a heavy sigh. "I'm not afraid, and I think that you and Rochelle are right. It's just that I don't like being a spectacle."

"You aren't going to be the spectacle, but you are going to help us have a spectacle," Rochelle said, clapping him on the shoulder.

They headed toward the valor grounds, but he stopped in his tracks when he noticed Karelly talking with Professor Alibard. He motioned to the others, who just shrugged. He hadn't seen much of her—thankfully.

"You really have to let it go," Cedrick said.

"I know, but…" He frowned. There was a flash of light in the sky.

The last time that he had seen something like that had been when the Cult of the Dragon had attacked.

He pointed, but nobody else could see it.

When he described what he saw, little more than a

bloom of power, he had stared, looking for any evidence that there might be something else out there, but nothing else came.

He focused on essence, tightening it into a tight ball inside of him, and he began to focus even more, considering what he had seen and whether there was anything more that he might be able to observe about it. But nothing more came.

"Come on," Rochelle urged. "We don't know that there is anything even out there. It could be just a simple flare."

"I doubt that it is a simple flare," he said, wondering if that was an intentional reference to the two they had already found before.

He thought of the crystal—the flare—they'd seen. He wasn't sure what to make of it, though it was different than the Great Serpent flare he'd found. Why would the headmaster—and Dax was convinced that it had been the headmaster—have kept it in the administrative building? And why wouldn't they have used it? Desmond had made it sound like it was useful for anyone.

He turned and continued to make his way toward the valor grounds when he felt a strange tingling along his neck. It was the same tingling that he had felt before.

He ducked, spinning, but Rochelle was standing to one side of him, Cedrick off to the other, and Gia was a few paces in front of him. There was another attack coming in his direction.

"What did you feel?" Rochelle asked, crouching down next to him.

Dax found himself looking up at the sky, focusing on it, trying to see if he might be able to answer her question. But he did not uncover anything. There was energy, he was certain of it, but what else?

Nothing. Nothing that Dax could put into words.

He straightened, and then he tilted his head up, closing his eyes. He started to constrict his essence. What he needed now, more than anything else, was to have a matter of control over his essence so that he could try to see something.

But he didn't need to constrict it quite as much as he once did in order for him to see essence. Ever since returning to the Academy, he'd been able to see it more clearly than before. Now, as he opened his eyes once more, he noticed a flare of light flashing. It wasn't the same as what he had seen near the swamp when drawn by the Great Serpent. This was a band of pale white, and little more than a flicker. He started after it when Rochelle called after him.

Gia caught up to him, and he felt her through the earth essence that she was rumbling upon, practically gliding on it as she hurried over to him. But she didn't challenge him.

"I saw something in the cloud," Dax said, motioning toward it. "And I don't know what it was."

"Order?"

"I don't know. Order or the Cult of the Dragon. Either way, I wonder if they waited until the term was over, when there weren't going to be as many students here."

"That implies that they are concerned about people's safety," she said.

Rochelle caught up to him. "We shouldn't go over there without any sort of protection," she said.

"You want to go and attack something?" Cedrick asked. "We don't even know what they are. If there is something there, shouldn't we have others with us?"

"But who do you trust?" Rochelle asked.

Cedrick opened his mouth, looking as if he was going

to argue with her, but then he clapped it shut again. "I suppose I don't trust a whole lot of people. You three, of course. But maybe you're right. I can't trust anybody. We're just so darn trustworthy."

They moved carefully, slowly, and when Dax reached the edge of the Academy, he passed into the outskirts of the town beyond, continuing to watch the sky. He found no other flicker of light, no other sense of power.

But he couldn't shake what he had felt.

He really wished he had his essence blade with him. Dax had stopped carrying it with him, instead leaving it behind in Rochelle's room. He didn't think that it looked all that great for a student to be carrying a weapon with him.

"I guess I haven't seen anything more."

"Good," Cedrick said. When Rochelle looked over at him, he shrugged. "Oh? I'm supposed to be disappointed that we aren't possibly running into some sort of dangerous situation again? Think about the last time. We certainly aren't strong enough to handle that ourselves. Without Desmond and his little tricks, we wouldn't be able to do it."

"Maybe we should go back. I haven't seen anything more. And even if there is, I don't know that I want to come out here unarmed. Besides, I might have this wrong."

"You didn't see anything, then?" Rochelle asked.

"Not that. What if this wasn't something coming, but something leaving?" Dax asked.

"What would have been leaving?" Gia asked.

Dax shrugged. "I don't know. But I suppose we have the term break to test and make sure that none of our professors are dangerous. Because when they get back, and classes resume, I don't know that we're going to have the time."

Chapter Nineteen

DAX ENJOYED THE EMPTINESS AROUND THE ACADEMY, EVEN if it was strange. They had been spending time in the library, looking at runes, though they had not found any additional markings inside of his own room. He had searched, and he knew that he should be thankful there wasn't anything else.

But he also still had not found Desmond.

That bothered Dax more than it probably should've, as he didn't know that it even mattered if Desmond was gone, but increasingly, Dax began to question whether Desmond's absence was tied to the Order or to the Cult of the Dragon. If it was the latter, then perhaps Desmond was off on some useful, and possibly essential, mission on behalf of the Cult of the Dragon, maybe even serving the Great Serpent itself.

Still, if that were true, it bothered him that Desmond hadn't told them where he was going or how long he was going to be gone. They needed Desmond's help, didn't they, especially with the Order still active? And he was convinced that the Order remained active. He couldn't do anything about it, other than try to visit Desmond's home—something that he did several times. Each time he went, he tested the lock, finding it easy enough to open with his transference essence, and then he would test whether there was any danger if he were to try to go inside. Rochelle often went with him, and Cedrick did another time, and each time that he went in, Dax found that the room was guarded in some fashion, though Dax wasn't entirely sure what it was.

The most recent time that he had gone to his home, Dax had stood in the doorway, focusing on the essence there, debating whether he would try to use some form of transference to pull the essence off. He never did.

"Are you going to go in?" Cedrick asked.

Dax had looked over at him. Gia and Rochelle were off together, presumably studying. Rochelle had taken Gia under her arm, wanting to help so Gia could take advanced classes as she'd intended over the next term.

"I don't know that it's safe for me to go in," Dax said, looking back at the door. Every time he turned his head, there was a bit of a shimmer, faint enough he wasn't even sure if he was seeing it correctly. It didn't have the same essence reflection that he saw from Desmond either. "You've seen what happens when I toss rocks inside."

Each time that he had returned, Dax had brought more rocks, some scraps of metal, some bits of wood, and other items try to test whether there was a danger inside for him. Each time that he threw one of the things inside of the room, they would shatter, or they would simply vanish.

"Why would he have placed protections like that?"

"Well, we know what he's dealing with," Dax said, not wanting to speak aloud the role Desmond had with the Cult of the Dragon.

"Still," Cedrick said.

Dax closed the door, releasing the transference essence back into it, and then stood in the street for a few moments.

"When he gets back, you should ask him how to better protect your room. Well, maybe we should ask him how to better protect all our rooms."

"That's not a terrible idea," Dax said.

They fell silent for a moment.

"What do you want to do?" Cedrick asked.

"Well, if I go back to the Academy too soon, Gia will want to spar, and Rochelle will try to test my essence. And I'm not exactly sure that I want to be threatened that way today."

So far, it seemed to work fairly consistently. Any time there was a danger to him—whether real or imagined—his essence seemed to react. It caused a tingling through him until all the hairs were standing up on the back of his neck, almost like an insect crawling there. It was an itch, but it was also not unpleasant. It had worked to help him find dangers, and he was optimistic that it would continue to work, but he didn't have any control over it. It happened regardless of what he did.

"You could please let us keep watching you with valor. Two skilled people battling like that is not something that most get a chance to observe."

"Just what we want to do: entertain you. And there is a limit to how far we can go. I haven't been able to beat her yet."

"But she hasn't been able to beat you either."

He and Gia had sparred a few more times since the Academy had let out for the term. Any time that they had, Dax had thought that he was going to get the best of Gia, but each time, Gia found some new trick, some new use of earth that Dax had not been able to counter. He kept trying to mirror her essence, and when he was around Cedrick and around Rochelle, he was able to draw upon some of their essences, something that had grown increasingly easy for him to do, but when it was just him and Gia…

He didn't have her ability with earth. He wouldn't be able to handle her directly. Transference was only as good as what he could reflect of another, and challenging anybody with their own type of essence meant that he was just a pale imitation. He needed to have portable essences, he thought, similar to what Desmond had on him.

He'd not found any other flashes of essence, though he did continue to look.

"Would you want to come with me to the edge of town?"

"Really?" Cedrick asked, looking around. "I was hoping that maybe we would get some food."

"We have several hours until the cafeteria opens again for mealtime," Dax said.

"I never mind the wait," Cedrick said.

"If you don't want to go, then I'll just go myself."

He actually understood why Cedrick wouldn't want to go. It could be dangerous. Dax had his essence blade hidden beneath his cloak, something that was easier to do now that the term was over. He wasn't sure what would happen once students returned to the Academy, as he had grown increasingly comfortable carrying his essence blade. If the Order were to come, he wanted to have a weapon.

"I can come," Cedrick said with a surge of irritation. "It's just that I don't like leaving the city. I'm not as much of a country person as you are. But if I'm going, should we gather the others?"

"I'm just taking a walk. That's all."

"You realize that if we take a walk, and we run into

trouble, they are going to be pretty upset with us. With you."

"I doubt that we are going to run into any problems," Dax said.

He agreed, and they headed out of town, where it became increasingly clear that Cedrick was uncomfortable. Dax looked over, and Cedrick shrugged.

"It's not the leaving of town. It's the forest."

Dax gaped at him. "What do you mean, 'the forest'?"

"Well, I suspect that along the borders of the unclaimed lands, you're accustomed to having all sorts of forest, and all sorts of dangerous creatures. But in my part of the world, everything is a bit more refined," he went on, looking back toward the city. "And I'm more accustomed to having some niceties."

"And you think that where I live is…"

"I didn't say what it was," Cedrick said. "Why did you want to come into the forest?"

"The last time that I was here, we came for valor," Dax said, looking over at him before turning his attention back to the forest itself, sweeping his gaze all around them. "I think that Professor Garrison knew about something here. And with a flash of essence, I am wondering if he might have known what it was."

Dax trekked through the woods, jumping over some logs, veering around the trees, and finding a trampled path through the forest undergrowth. It reminded him of what was near his homeland, near the unclaimed land, and reminded him of the freedom that he'd had when he was younger, when he had been back home. Maybe he shouldn't have been so intrigued by that, but he couldn't shake the familiarity, and the sense of relief at being away from the city.

At one point, he had to stop to wait for Cedrick to catch up, but when he did, he had his face wrinkled up, as if in disgust.

"It's life essence," Dax said. "Much like when we were in the forest when we had left the serpent stairs. Your essence reacted to that."

Cedrick frowned, and then he began to look around, snapping his fingers. The bubbles drifted upward, tangling with some of the branches. Much like what had happened in the other forest, the branches began to swell, reacting to Cedrick's essence.

"Maybe I *should* spend more time out here," Cedrick said. "It's just that…"

"It's just that you don't really care for it," Dax said with a bit of a smile.

"That is what it is. Why do you think that the Great Serpent gave me something that I don't care for?"

"I thought you liked your bubbles."

"I like the *idea* of the bubbles, or I did at first. And then I began to think that maybe they were just more decorative. Now that I know there's something useful to them, I suppose I should try to make better sense of it."

They continued through the forest, with Dax turning down a narrow trail, following the essence. At one point, Dax thought he heard something moving, but he turned and didn't see anything. He kept his own essence tamped tightly down, and he noticed a faint undercurrent of essence all around him coming from the trees, the undergrowth, all the plants. It was life essence, and it was more potent than what he had anticipated would be out here.

They reached a broader trail.

"Why is this path through here?" Cedrick asked.

Dax shook his head. "Well, some things do move through the forest."

"When they have perfectly good roads outside of the forest?"

Dax started to laugh, but he noticed something on one of the trees.

It glowed.

It was obviously essence, but it was a different sort of essence than what he had seen from some of the other trees. It wasn't the same greenish hue of the life essence that radiated throughout the forest. This was dense, and he recognized immediately that it was concentrated essence, coming from a runic marker placed on the tree.

"Look at this," he said, crouching in front of it.

Cedrick joined him, and then he crouched down. "You know I'm not that good with these sorts of runes. It looks sort of like the one on your chair... Oh. That's what you are thinking."

Dax withdrew a piece of paper and looked for some chalk to make a tracing, but he didn't have any. Instead he used some damp earth and smeared it over the marking to make the tracing of the rune, curious who would have placed it, and what it did. He needed to know more about it.

"I'm going to follow this," Dax said.

"Follow it where?"

"Wherever this takes me. You can go back, but I think I need to do this."

"Oh, I'm not going back. I can just imagine what Rochelle would say if she knew that I abandoned you when you found something like this and then started chasing it through the forest. So I guess it's just the two of us."

"I guess so," Dax said.

He hoped that he wasn't making a mistake.

Chapter Twenty

THE TRAIL LED THEM DEEPER INTO THE FOREST. HE HAD found another rune, linked with the one that he had found on the tree. Dax wondered if there were others like it that were outside of the forest, closer to the edge of the city. A trail of essence linked them, though Dax suspected he was the only one who would be able to see it. At least easily.

There was always the possibility that it was tied to the Order, but this felt different than what he would've expected from them. Dax wasn't sure why, but the runic pattern that was in his room, on his chair, hadn't seemed as if it was any sort of a threat. It was more like a marking, and probably had some connection to power that Dax still had yet to identify.

Maybe the Cult of the Dragon?

They paused at one point. They hadn't brought enough supplies for a long hike in the forest. They had to be careful, as there were some creatures in the forest, though he hadn't seen any so far. When he'd come out here with Professor Garrison, however, he had.

"Do you hear that?" Cedrick asked.

"I don't hear anything," he said. Then again, he had been so focused on the trail of essence linking the different runes that he wasn't even sure that he would've been able to hear anything if there was something out there.

"I think I saw something now," Cedrick said. "And if there's something here, we need to be careful. This is the forest, after all. We were told to be careful out here, Dax."

There was real worry in Cedrick's voice, and Dax straightened, turning to look over at him. His friend was staring, looking up at the trees, down at the undergrowth. He had a bit of nervousness to him.

Dax understood it.

When he had been younger, going out with his brother and his father into the unclaimed lands for the first time, he had felt much the same way. And they had been cautioned about the forest, for much the same reason. There were creatures here that could be dangerous.

"Just stay by me," Dax said.

"Because of what?" Now there was real panic rising in his voice.

Dax started to smile to himself, but he realized that was a mistake. "I have my essence blade."

"When we were in class the first week, we were warned to stay away from the forest."

Dax didn't remember that, but then again, he had been so tired from trying to deal with the different types of essence that he was suddenly able to see, and from trying to tamp down that ability so that he didn't get overwhelmed, he wasn't sure he would remember what had happened quite as well as he should. "I don't remember that."

"Yeah, well they were telling us that we needed to be

careful of dangers outside of the city. I think it was in valor."

"That fits. Then again, Gia and my valor instructor weren't particularly concerned about what we would find outside of the city."

He looked along the line, following the linked runes. He was tempted to go back, but there was something out there, something that he could feel, some sort of line that marked this place, and Dax felt compelled to keep moving along. He wondered if Cedrick would be upset if he kept going.

"I'm willing to go back if you want to, but I do feel like I need to keep moving here," Dax said. "And if you aren't comfortable with it, I will come back later with Gia."

"Oh, now you really know how to tweak my backside."

"What?"

"I'm not going to be the one who goes back so that you can go and get her. She's just going to try to torment me more—tease me about the fact I wasn't willing to stay with you. No. I'm going to stick with you."

Dax shrugged. "I don't know how much deeper we're going to have to go into the forest, but I can see this trail stretching ahead of me. I don't know what it is, but I feel like I need to follow it until I figure out what it is. It's tied to something in my room, and…"

"I get it," Cedrick said. "And like I said, I'm willing to go with you. But just make sure that you keep that blade of yours handy."

They kept moving.

The trees were denser in this part of the forest, towering high above them. They were a mixture of oak and pine, though an occasional birch tree rose. Dax focused on the essence within the trees, marveling at how much he could see. It created something of a pathway, leading him away from the trails worked through the undergrowth.

He reached a strange boulder.

When he did, Dax could feel something different about it.

He approached it carefully, tamping down his essence as tightly as he could. There was the green of the forest, the brown of earth, there was even a bit of translucent essence in the air. Dax could see it all. All of it swirled and glowed and illuminated for him, as if it were wanting him to notice that it was there. But when he crouched down in front of the stone, Dax noticed that there was another tracing, another rune, on the stone itself.

The complexity of the rune was beyond anything that he had ever seen before.

Dax wanted to take a tracing of it, but he doubted that it would be reflective of the true nature of the rune. Cedrick crouched down alongside him.

"I can almost feel something from it," he said.

"I can too," Dax said, tracing his finger along the rune. He could feel something, though wasn't exactly sure what it was. It seemed as if the rune was somehow concentrating essence. "I don't get what this is," Dax said, "but the others all felt like they were concentrating essence, and it leaves me wondering if maybe something here is using these markers to concentrate essence in the area."

"If there's something like that in your room, then what purpose would it have in trying to concentrate essence there?"

It was possible that it tried to draw the essence of the person who lived in the room, Dax realized. That was a more terrifying prospect.

He straightened, dusting his hands on his jacket for a moment, and then looked around. "Maybe we should go."

"Dax?"

He shook his head, turning and looking over at Cedrick. "Sorry. I'm taking too long. I just feel like we need to better understand these runes, but maybe we need to be better supplied to do that." He wanted to say that he wanted Rochelle with him, because she was more of the scholar than Cedrick, but that would only hurt Cedrick's feelings. He could make tracings, and they could use those to help figure out what was here, but even the tracings might not be enough.

"Dax," Cedrick said again.

Dax turned, looking over at him. "I said that I was ready to go."

Cedrick shook his head.

He pointed.

Dax followed the direction, and as he did, he saw something that stopped his heart.

In the shadows of the trees, there was a massive spider-like creature. He would've almost called it a spider, but the face that looked back at him was almost humanoid, fangs filling its mouth. It had eight tall, thick legs, with a hard carapace over its body.

All of it left Dax feeling cold.

"What is that?"

"It's a silk shatter," Dax said.

"I don't suppose you would want to tell me what exactly a silk shatter is?"

"Something that shouldn't be here in the forest," Dax said.

He'd heard of them, but he'd never seen them.

"Is it going to hurt us?"

"Probably," Dax said, deciding that it was better not to lie to him.

He brought his hand closer and closer to the hilt of his essence sword, careful to avoid doing anything too dangerous but at the same time recognizing that if the silk shatter got too close to them, it would attack.

They were known to be fast and powerful, but they were also known to...

Almost too late, Dax realized his mistake.

"We aren't alone," Dax said.

Chapter Twenty-One

DAX STAYED HIS HAND.

He knew better than to try to attack the silk shatter because he could already feel the essence around him from a second one of the creatures. He wasn't sure where it was, only that it was somewhere in the forest nearby. Instead, he kept his gaze focused on the silk shatter directly in front of him. He could feel something from it, a bit of power that seemed to echo and reverberate inside of them, but there was also a strange, earthy texture of essence, mixed with a bit of another essence, something that seemed to glow.

Fire and earth?

Could the silk shatters have multiple forms of essence?

There were only a few creatures along the unclaimed lands that had multiple types of essence, and none of them were particularly potent. The creatures were dangerous but not powerful.

This one had at least two powerful types of essence, possibly more.

He held his hands up, not moving.

Cedrick frowned, looking over at Dax briefly before turning his attention back to the silk shatter. "Do you care to tell me why you aren't going to attack?"

"Because the others are overhead," Dax said.

Cedrick jerked his head up.

Dax immediately wished that he hadn't said anything. Branches swayed overhead, and he heard movement chattering along the branches, as if the silk shatters were talking to one another.

That bothered him. The silk shatters couldn't speak, could they?

"Who are you?" the silk shatter said, striding toward them.

Dax felt everything within him go cold.

There were powerful creatures along the edge of the unclaimed lands, but none of them were sentient.

The silk shatter had an almost triangular face. As he got closer, he realized that what he had thought he had been able to see of his features was not quite accurate. The creature had five eyes, two on either side of his face and one in the center of his forehead, and all of them seemed to be focusing on Dax.

Reaching for his essence blade would be dangerous, so he resisted the urge.

It would be equally dangerous to use transference, but at least it would appear less threatening.

If it came down to that, Dax doubted they would be able to escape. This creature radiated considerable essence. He had no idea what level it was, but it was much higher than either he or Cedrick could claim.

Dax closed his eyes for a moment, and he focused on what he could feel of the essence around him. As he did, he began to recognize that there were other strands of essence, other aspects beginning to bloom around him. He could feel them. It was like a map that formed in his mind, one that illustrated where the other silk shatters were and how they were moving in the trees overhead.

There was something else that bothered him too.

He hadn't felt the strange tingling along the back of his neck.

They weren't in any danger. Either he didn't believe it, or his essence didn't believe it.

"We followed the essence trail," Dax said, speaking aloud, though he wasn't even sure if the silk shatter spoke aloud or if he did so in his mind.

"What essence trail do you think you followed?" The silk shatter stood on six legs, and he brought two of his forelegs together, as if clapping.

There was a clicking sound that Dax realized he'd been hearing throughout the forest. Now there seemed to be a pattern within it.

Could the silk shatter be speaking with the others, or was there something else?

Each time the silk shatter tapped his legs together, there was another bloom of essence that tunneled down into the ground.

"There is an essence trail that spreads through the forest," Dax said, bringing his hands down to his sides. The movement sparked a bit of a reaction from the other silk shatters around him, some in the trees dropping down, falling on what looked like thick greenish bindings.

Dax thought that it was like spiderwebs, until he realized that they were descending on essence. Green essence.

Life essence.

So he saw fire and earth inside of this primary silk shatter, but these others were using life. It left Dax thinking that this one was using life essence as well.

"You would not have seen this," the silk shatter said.

Dax shook his head. "I saw it. It stretches throughout the forest, creating a trail that leads here. I assume that is yours?"

"You are not the one," the silk shatter said.

"I'm not the one?" Dax frowned, and he looked over at Cedrick. He couldn't help but feel as if there was something odd about this. "We don't come to fight," he said.

The silk shatter tapped his legs again, and once again, there came a strange rhythmic sound and a burst of essence that radiated, spreading outward and down into the earth, as if the silk shatter were trying to reveal some of that power.

"You would not be able to harm," the silk shatter said.

That was probably true.

How many of their instructors knew about the silk shatter in the forest?

Given the movement of this creature, the power that he felt, Dax couldn't help but feel as if there had to be someone who was aware of it. He couldn't be the only one who would have found it.

Could he?

There weren't many people with the ability to see essence the way Dax did. And without that ability, Dax would not have been able to find it.

"You may take them," the silk shatter said.

Five of the smaller creatures, each nearly the size of a dog, began to surround him and Cedrick, greenish essence erupting from them.

He didn't know what would happen if it struck him.

Cedrick would probably be fine, as he suspected it was life essence, but what would it do to Dax?

He needed to do something.

Not fight, though.

"I saw the Great Serpent," Dax said.

The silk shatter stopped moving, and he dropped to all eight legs, crawling toward him. When he stood again, he was taller than Dax, but he still didn't try to attack. He began to tap his forelegs again, and there was another rhythm. He suspected the silk shatter was drawing on power in a way Dax couldn't even see, but he could feel it.

"Many who come to your Academy," the silk shatter said, his voice dripping with a bit of scorn as he mentioned the school, "claim to have seen the Great Serpent. None have recently."

"I have," Dax said. "I saw the flare. I held the crystal."

Dax didn't know if he was making a mistake here, but at the same time, he felt as if he needed to do try to do something. The gift that the Great Serpent had given him had been one of understanding, hadn't it?

That was what Dax needed to use now.

Cedrick had remained quiet, and Dax realized that he was somehow frozen in place. Some of that strange life essence that the other silk shatters had been using had started to swirl around Cedrick.

Dax reacted.

He did it without thinking, and he began to use transference, drawing that essence out and freeing Cedrick. He erupted it, sending it out in a similar band, striking the five silk shatters that had circled them. There was a strange, unpleasant shriek, and the others echoed the sound, scurrying closer to the larger silk shatter.

"There's no need for that," Dax said.

The silk shatter lowered himself and looked at Dax, now watching him with distrust.

How could Dax know that?

"I don't care for what you did to my friend. He has life essence, much like you do."

"Life?"

Dax still had a bit of that life essence in him, and even though he thought that he might draw upon more of the other essences that were descending from the trees around him, he decided not to do that, as he didn't want to draw the anger of the other silk shatters.

"You have earth. Fire. Life. All of it. I can see it."

"What do you mean that you can see it?"

"I can see it," Dax said. "That is the gift that the Great Serpent gave me. That is the *first* gift the Great Serpent gave me."

Maybe it wasn't even the gift that the Great Serpent had given him but the one that Dax had taken for himself.

"What else do you see?"

The silk shatter reared up and once again tapped his legs together.

Dax could feel the essence, and he realized there was more there.

Wind.

Water.

He couldn't believe it, but this silk shatter—and maybe all the silk shatters—had multiple essences.

"You're using wind, water, and earth right now. I can see most of it, and I can feel quite a bit of it," Dax said.

Cedrick gasped.

"Now, do you care to tell me why you are trying to attack us?"

"We only attack because you attacked first," the silk shatter said.

"We didn't attack," Dax said. "We were following the trail of essence. That is all that I did, because I wanted to understand the different rune patterns that I've been seeing."

"Where?" the silk shatter asked again.

"Behind you," Dax said. "I don't know who placed them, as I've been trying to determine the pattern, but this one…"

He stepped forward, and immediately the other silk shatters started to surround him, using life essence once more. Dax reacted the way that he had before, and now that he knew that life essence would cause a reaction from them, he pulled it off, then sent it out using a band, though he didn't have much control over it.

He managed to push the other silk shatters back, and he stepped around the larger one and pointed to the boulder. "Here," he said, and he crouched down, tracing his hand along it.

"I do not see this," the silk shatter said.

"What do you see?"

"Heat," the silk shatter said.

"I see." Dax understood the difficulty. If they were able to see heat, that meant that they probably were not able to see the contours of light around them and may not be able to see the markings on the boulder. If that were the case, then it was possible that they would not have known that there was anything here at all.

Dax pointed to it. "There is a complicated runic marker —I presume that you know what a runic marker is," Dax went on, waiting for the silk shatter to tap his legs together again, almost as an affirmation, "and it seems like it is drawing upon power here. I don't know what it is, only that it is concentrating something. We've seen several of these throughout the forest. They all seem to be linked together. I found more of them outside, and…"

Dax tried, but he didn't really have any good inclination as to what he had found. At the same time, he also didn't know if there was anything more that he needed to share with the silk shatter.

"Show me," the silk shatter said.

"I can't. I don't know how to show you anything."

The silk shatter began to push fire out.

And as he did, Dax realized what the silk shatter was asking of him.

Dax used transference.

He had no idea if it was going to work all that well, but he began to call that fire into him, and when he pushed it back out, he tried to form it in the same image of the runic pattern that he had seen on the boulder.

That wasn't going to work. It was too complicated for him.

Instead, he turned the fire and looped it around the boulder, then sent that fire out until it collapsed over top of the pattern. The fire seemed as if it were trying to consume it, but it didn't. Instead, it just blazed for a moment, and then it stopped.

When it reached the rune, it glowed for a moment before dissipating.

Dax wasn't sure what it had looked like to the silk shatter, but to him, it looked like the pattern had drawn in the essence, then swallowed it. There was a trailing of essence around it, but where that pattern had been remained a void of power.

"I see it," the silk shatter said.

And when he did, there was a bit of worry in his voice. Once again, Dax wondered how he was aware of that.

"What is it?"

"Something dangerous."

Dax smiled to himself, as he thought that the silk shatter was dangerous, and he couldn't imagine that the old creature would have something that he feared. As he smiled about that, though, he realized that might be a mistake.

"What do creatures like yourself find dangerous?"

The silk shatter didn't answer. Instead, he clapped his legs together again, and the others near him leapt from the ground and back into the trees. It wasn't that they jumped. It was more that the essence that they possessed trailed out of them and shot upward, spooling around branches and allowing the silk shatters to disappear.

And then there was only the large silk shatter left.

"Where are you going?"

"Away," the silk shatter said.

Then he disappeared.

He left Dax and Cedrick alone in the darkened forest.

Dax couldn't breathe.

He finally reached for his essence blade and unsheathed it, using that to help him feel for any additional essence, but he found nothing more than a remnant of power.

Finally, Cedrick broke the silence.

"What was *that*?"

Dax shook his head. He didn't have any answer.

The only thing he could think was that the silk shatter was afraid of something.

Which meant *they* should be afraid of something.

Chapter Twenty-Two

"I DON'T THINK THAT YOU SHOULD'VE GONE OFF INTO THE forest on your own," Rochelle said, sitting outside with them and staring toward the edge of the city. They were seated on the edge of the Academy grounds, near the lawn, so that they could look out toward the forest.

Dax concentrated his essence to see if there was any trail that he might have overlooked, but even as he looked out into the distance, he didn't see anything. "You're right," he finally said. "I really shouldn't have gone off on my own, and I should've turned around when I realized there was a danger."

Gia was quiet.

Dax looked over at her. "Have you ever experienced any silk shatters on the border?"

"Only heard about them," Gia said. "I'm surprised they would've come so close to the Academy. There are quite a few powerful creatures along the unclaimed lands, but they tend to avoid populated areas. I don't know why the silk shatter would've come so close."

"That's my concern as well. But it's more than that. Think about this," he said, looking from Rochelle to Gia and finally back to Cedrick. "We're talking about creatures that can speak. We are talking about sentient creatures. When I lived along the boundary of the unclaimed lands, we dealt with a lot of strange creatures, but we also never found anything that seemed sentient."

"Did you hear it?" Gia asked Cedrick.

Cedrick shrugged. "I heard talking, mostly from Dax, but I could hear something else. It was more like a chattering."

Dax hadn't even realized that Cedrick hadn't been aware of it, as they had been quiet during the walk back. Then again, Cedrick had seemed shocked by what they had encountered.

"You didn't hear anything?" Dax asked.

"I told you that I heard *something*," Cedrick said, and he shrugged again, "but I don't know what it was. But I trust you. If you say that the creatures were talking to you, then they were talking to you. I felt them do something to me." He shuddered, then rubbed his hands up and down his arms before looking out into the distance. "It felt cold. I felt like I couldn't move. It was like I was going numb."

"They were using life essence on you," Dax said. "I had to use transference to draw it off. And then I used it against them."

Rochelle sat quietly, but it was Gia who spoke.

"They attacked," Gia said. "And you still tried to talk to them."

"It was sentient," Dax said. "That's significant. And the silk shatter had considerable essence."

"You're the only one who saw it," she said.

"I'm the only one who *can* see essence," Dax countered.

And that was what bothered him as well. He was the only one who could see the essence, so he was the only one who would've known that the silk shatters had the abilities that they did, and that combination of essences. It might've just been the larger one who had multiple essences, as Dax had not seen anything but life essence from the smaller ones.

"We should look into them," Rochelle said, cutting the two of them off. "If there's anything that we can learn about the silk shatters, then we should dig into it. Besides, we still need to look into the runes. I agree with Dax; we don't know much, but it makes sense that there would be sentient creatures. Think about the Great Serpent. There's no reason that there shouldn't be other creatures that can take on enough essence to become sentient."

"Why would they need to take on essence to become sentient?" Dax asked.

"I suppose they wouldn't," she said. "But more essence might allow them to be able to communicate. I think that we need to dig into this more, and we can't reveal it to anybody else until we have a better sense of it."

"So we're just going to sort of forget that we have some giant, terrifying spider out in the forest beyond the Academy," Cedrick said.

"I don't think it makes sense to ignore it," Rochelle said. "I said that we were going to look into it, and we were going to see if we may be able to dig more information out and find out what was going on with it. There might be something that we can uncover about these creatures. And if they are sentient, or if anybody has suspicions about sentience, then we should be able to find something in the library. That's the best place that we could look into something like that."

Meeting the silk shatter had raised another series of questions that Dax didn't know if he was ready to ask—or have the answer to. Cedrick had been with him and hadn't even been aware that he had spoken to the silk shatter. Was that tied to what he had asked of the Great Serpent? And what if the silk shatters weren't the only sentient creatures?

Gia got to her feet. "I'm going to get some food."

"I'll join you," Cedrick said. "I think I'd like to get some food, take a bath, and get to bed early." He shivered again, running his hands up and down his arms before looking over at Dax. "Thanks for an interesting day."

Rochelle watched him. "I know you, Dax. You're thinking about something else," she finally said.

"I'm thinking about the silk shatter," Dax said, nodding to her. "Shouldn't I be?"

"Oh, I am quite certain that you should be thinking about the silk shatter, and I know that you are thinking about something else as well."

"You don't know what it's like along the border of the unclaimed lands," he said.

"And I don't see what that has to do with anything," she said.

"It has to do with the fact that we have some sentient creature, or what I know but no one else can prove is a sentient, near Academy grounds. And it makes me wonder how many other sentient creatures are out there. How many have my father, Gia's father, cut down over the years?"

Rochelle was quiet for a long moment. "Somebody would know if that were the case," she said. "They're probably just monsters."

"Monsters?" He frowned, and he shifted, turning to

look back toward the Academy. "We're a people who worship the Great Serpent. What is that but a monster?"

Rochelle fell silent.

"I don't like it," Dax said. "But I *did* ask the Great Serpent for understanding. When I was with the silk shatter, I didn't have that strange tingling on the back of my neck. It was like the Great Serpent wasn't trying to warn me."

Rochelle watched him. "Maybe because you haven't mastered that connection yet."

"Or maybe the Great Serpent doesn't want me to harm those creatures."

He sat quietly. He knew that he should go and get some food, and failing that, he should go to the library, because it was good advice for them to begin researching the silk shatters, especially if they were sentient creatures, even if Dax could find a way to prove that to the others. But at this point, he wanted nothing more than to just go back to his room and to rest.

If only he could go back to his room.

But it wasn't safe.

He sat quietly, staring off into the darkness.

When he did, he concentrated his essence down, trying to focus on whether there was anything around them that he might be able to detect. But the only thing that he saw was the way that Rochelle was using her bluish essence, and how that swirled through her, forming a band of power inside of her. He didn't try to interfere with that, but there was part of him that knew he might be able to draw that essence, transfer some of that into himself.

"May I try?" Rochelle asked softly, almost as if knowing his thoughts.

He nodded. When her essence washed through him, he was aware of it the moment that it touched him. It started slowly, building. There was a faint coolness to it, but it wasn't unpleasant. And it didn't hurt.

As it worked through him, he could feel her testing, probing, and he could tell that she was using some sort of water pattern, even though it was one that he wasn't familiar with. Unlike the rest of them, she'd had quite a bit of experience working with her primary essence thanks to the seminar she was taking.

He only wished he had some way of taking a transference seminar so that he could learn more about how to use his own essence. How was he supposed to learn what he could do if there was nobody around him who understood it?

Rochelle continued to send her essence through him, and when she was done, she sat back, clasping her hands in her lap, and watched him. "I don't feel anything. If you're concerned there's some lingering effect from the silk shatter, it's not there."

"Would you know?"

"It's possible I wouldn't," she admitted, "but I wasn't trying to heal anything. I was just trying to detect. That's one of the very first uses of water essence. At this point, I don't detect anything strange, which is what I was concerned about."

"I suppose I should be reassured," Dax said. "And now I just want to rest."

"How much did you exert yourself?"

"I don't know—maybe more than I realized."

He was tired, and perhaps was feeling the effect of everything that he had used essence for, including the conversation with the silk shatter. That exertion might've been too much for him.

He got up.

"I could go back with you," she said.

"That's not necessary," Dax said. "You should go have dinner. Stay with them. Do some research. I'm going to sleep."

He trudged up the stairs, making his way toward his room and unlocking the door before he realized what was that he was doing. When he stepped inside, he froze.

Something about the room was different.

It took him a moment to see, but then he found a rune on his floor.

And it was even more complicated than the others.

Chapter Twenty-Three

DAX SAT IN FRONT OF THE RUNE, STARING AT IT.

"What do you think caused this?" Rochelle asked, leaning over his shoulder.

He was surprised that she hadn't taken a seat across from him, as it would've been just as easy for her to do that, to study the rune from that angle rather than to sit behind him. But Rochelle seemed as if she were concerned about getting too close to it, probably because of what Dax had said about the power within the rune, and how it had the ability to absorb additional essence.

"I don't know," he said.

Cedrick sat on his bed, snapping his fingers, and forming pink bubbles that drifted. Gia remained in the doorway, almost unwilling to come inside. It was probably because of what Dax had said about the other runes that he'd seen outside of the city, but nothing here was obviously dangerous.

Unlike the one on his chair, which was no more than an inch in either direction, this one was nearly as large as his foot, and it had a series of patterns within it that Dax could feel and see. When he attempted to use his own transference essence on it, he could feel something pulling on him.

"I don't feel anything from it," Rochelle said, though she continued to trace her hand around it, every so often spilling a little bit of water essence into it. She didn't push too much out from herself, though Dax couldn't tell if she was testing the rune on purpose or if it was drawing power from her.

"Well, what are we going to do about it?" Cedrick asked. "Obviously, somebody placed these here to scare us. Or to scare you," he said, looking over at Dax. "And to be honest, it's working on me. I suppose you are a bit scared?"

Dax stared at the marking. "It's not that I'm scared of the pattern. It's the complexity of the rune. I don't know the purpose behind it, and that's what bothers me."

"But it's the same as you found in the forest?" Rochelle asked.

"I think so." He pulled out his paper, and he made another etching, though he had done that already. He would need to go to Professor Alibard eventually.

After getting to his feet, he paced for a moment. "We know that it absorbs essence, the same way the others did. But why?" He breathed out heavily, then turned his attention back to the others before looking out. "I want to go back to the library."

"I don't know that we're going to find much about it," Rochelle said. "When we looked for the other rune, we didn't find anything there."

"It's not just the runes, but also the silk shatter."

Dax felt as if all of this was connected.

He stepped out of his room, waiting for the others, and

Cedrick shuffled out quickly, followed by Rochelle, who glanced back, studying the floor.

"I think we should probably cover it up," she said.

"Why?" Gia asked. "You think that it's going to be less active if it is covered?"

"I don't even know if it's active. Until we figure out the purpose behind it, I feel like we need to do something more than just leaving it alone."

They grabbed his sheet off his bed and covered it up.

"You know, if you had a little bit more money, Nelson," Cedrick said, "you could have bought a rug. Maybe this wouldn't have been a problem then."

"Maybe," Dax said.

There was still the issue of the coin that had been stolen from his room, though that seemed to be the least of his worries.

They headed to the library. Rochelle grabbed a stack of different books on runes and a stack of different books on creatures before taking a seat. Gia and Cedrick sat off to the side and gave Rochelle and Dax space. At first, Dax thought it was only courteous, or that they were just not interested in the topic at hand, but then he realized that Cedrick was working with Gia on rune patterns. He smiled to himself. "I guess I wasn't expecting Cedrick to be the one to try to work with Gia," he said. Dax had been a tutor for Cedrick and others in his basic runes class during the previous term.

"He picked it up quite quickly," she said to him, leaning across the table and dropping her voice. "And he's going to take all advanced classes this next term as well. I think having all of us in the same classes might be helpful. At least that way we can all progress in the same way."

"Well, we aren't all going to be in the same classes," Dax said, looking at her. "You aren't taking valor."

Rochelle watched him. "About that," she said, and she glanced over at Gia, then at Cedrick, before turning her attention back to Dax. "I don't know if I should take a formal valor class, but I would like to learn a bit of valor. I probably need to, given what we have been through and that we might have to deal with even more."

"I can teach you as much as I can, but it's going to take time," Dax said. He agreed with Rochelle that it would be beneficial for her to be able to defend herself.

"I don't need to learn the hand-to-hand fighting. At least, not the way that you and Gia fight." She wrinkled her brow. "I want to learn about essence blades."

"That's just an extension of the rest of it."

"Not exactly," she said, and she turned her attention fully to him. "Essence blades can be used by those without any other fighting style. And they can be used for different purposes. If the Order comes again, I want to be able to protect myself, even if it means using an essence blade."

"We can work with that. You can even use my blade. I still have the one that we found." It had proven a little more useful to him than other essence blades, for some reason.

"Thanks. I really appreciate it, Dax," she said quietly. "All right. Now let's dig in."

"I wish it were easier to do this," he said.

"You mean finding information about the runes, or about the other thing?"

"Well, the other thing," he admitted.

"You aren't concerned about the runes?"

"I am, but we also need to know who is placing them and why."

"The 'who' is important," Rochelle said carefully, and

then she looked up, meeting his eyes, "and 'why' is probably tied to the 'who.' But if we can understand the 'what,' the reason behind the rune, then we might be able to find the rest of the answers we are looking for. And you are certainly capable of doing that. I have seen you finding things others can't. So I want *you* to dig into this. You and your ability, I suspect, give you the advantage. Use that transference. And," she went on, smiling tightly, "use whatever the Great Serpent has recently given you."

"I don't think it works like that," he said.

"You don't think it does, but you don't know. And until we better understand it, I think that you should take the time that you need so that you can find everything we want. Speaking of, I have another idea about the other little dilemma that we have."

"What idea is that?"

"Oh. I should've said that sooner. The transference pens."

Dax blinked. "What?"

"Most of those creatures are domesticated, but not all of them. Especially as we get closer to the start of term, I think that you should spend more time there, where you can use your newfound gift, if that's what it is, to see if you can uncover anything about your creature theory from the transference pens."

He hadn't even considered that, but it was a pretty good idea. If there was something that he wanted to learn about creatures, he needed to have exposure to creatures. And rather than going out into the forest—something that Dax had contemplated but hadn't been looking forward to—going to the transference pens, where there were other magical creatures, creatures with essence, might be the safer way to find something. Maybe not sentience, but at least an understanding.

"Now. Would you stop complaining and begin to read? I don't want to have to tell the others that you are shirking your duties here."

She smiled, and Dax turned his focus and began to read.

Chapter Twenty-Four

THEY SPENT SEVERAL DAYS IN THE LIBRARY. IT WAS NEARING the end of the term break, and Dax still hadn't found any information on the runes. He had wanted to go to the essence pens, but the one time that he had gone, there were only cattle there. He could feel the innate essence within the cattle, but Dax didn't feel any other sort of essence within them, and he certainly didn't feel any sort of connection to them that would make him think they were sentient creatures.

Instead, he had focused on the runes, pouring through dozens of books that Rochelle had found. She wasn't wrong about his ability.

Increasingly, Dax began to feel like some aspect of his transference ability related to what he could use within his mind. It was almost as if he could transfer knowledge, but it was slow. Working that way allowed him to puzzle together information that he wouldn't have been able to piece together otherwise.

Gia and Cedrick worked together, with Cedrick

helping her with advanced essence manipulation techniques. None of the librarians who remained on campus were bothered by the first-term students in the library, though perhaps they found it odd that they were here on their break.

"Now I just have to figure out transference," Gia was saying.

Dax looked up. He was tired. He had been looking at something about some ancient rune, something that predated the Empire, and had not been able to follow it. The writing was difficult, and the runes themselves were complicated enough that Dax couldn't follow them, but he found himself struggling through it anyway, hoping that some part of his mind might make sense of everything he was reading. It had happened before. He had read something, and the next morning he had awoken and pieced it together, as if understanding came while he was sleeping. He'd thought it was just his mind churning over things, but when he had said that to Rochelle, she had smiled at him knowingly, and implied that the Great Serpent had gifted him with knowledge.

"I can help you with transference," Dax said, trying not to sound too tired.

"But you have to be looking into this," she said.

"I need a break, and transference actually happens to be a specialty of mine," Dax said with a bit of a smile.

"Everything tends to be a specialty of yours," Cedrick said.

"And it's all because of transference," Rochelle said, elbowing him and taking a seat at the table. She had another stack of books, and she shoved half of them in Dax's direction.

"It's not as difficult as it seems."

"Maybe not for you, but I'm a Stonewall. My people don't do much with transference."

"Neither do mine. Anyway," he went on, "transference is merely a matter of focusing on the essence outside of you. And when it comes to some of the creatures they bring to us, they have highly concentrated essence, so it makes it easier for you to reach for it."

"So you just have to push it out?" Cedrick asked. "They make it sound like it's so much more difficult than that."

"It's really not. Once you have a handle on essence manipulation, it's really just a matter of using those same techniques. You feel the way that your essence flows inside of you and then direct it."

"Is that what it was like for you?" Cedrick asked Rochelle.

"I never managed to make a transference connection," she said. "And the professor made it sound like not everybody could. She said it was a gift—a blessing from the Great Serpent. Those who can make that transference can find a higher order of understanding and are better able to connect to the power in the world." She said it as if she were reciting something that she had heard in a lecture. Dax suspected that was exactly the case.

"That's terrible," he said.

"Well, it is what it is," Gia said. "I was resigned to the fact that I probably would never be able to be much of a transference expert. And maybe I won't. But maybe if I have somebody like you…"

"I need a break, anyway. Why don't we go to the transference pens?"

"I'll stay here," Rochelle said. "The three of you can go. Besides, I have already had Dax's lesson."

He got to his feet, and the others joined him. Gia and

Cedrick were debating how quickly they would learn transference as Dax guided them toward the transference yard,
and he was surprised when he got there to find a bit of
commotion.

He found Professor Madenil inside of the yard,
motioning to three others. He didn't recognize any of them.
They were burly, large men, and they radiated heavy earth
essence. One of them had fire essence. All of them had
creatures they were dragging from a wagon caravan and
putting into the pens. Dax didn't recognize the creatures,
but they were large, with massive antlers on their heads and
long, spindly tails.

"Oh, Mr. Nelson," Professor Madenil said, looking over
at him. "Did you bring some friends to the yard?"

"I was coming to practice," Dax said, shrugging. "They
both have intentions of taking advanced transference, and I
thought that I might help them before the term begins."

She smiled. "Excellent."

Dax blinked. "You don't mind?"

"Oh, why would I mind? We encourage anybody to try
to take advantage of the opportunities that the Academy
offers them. And one of the opportunities is learning from
your fellow students. You will not learn everything from
your instructors. Even when you eventually leave the Academy," she said, glancing over at Cedrick and then at Gia
before turning her attention back to Dax, "your learning
won't stop. You will find that you can learn from everyone
around you. Sometimes, *everything* around you."

From the way that she said it, Dax was left wondering
how much she knew about these creatures—and if she
knew whether any of them were sentient. It was something
he would have to ask her about later.

"And besides," Professor Madenil went on, looking over

at Dax with a broad smile curling her lips, "I was going to ask you about tutoring some of the basic students as well. It's wonderful you have already shown an interest."

"I don't know if I have time for additional tutoring," he said.

"I doubt you are going to benefit from advanced transference this term. You've already shown a measure of control greater than you would be expected to learn. I was hopeful that you might be inclined to work with me in the transference yard. It would give you a chance to spend more time with the creatures, and I can give you a bit of one-on-one tutoring. It won't be quite as direct as what you would get in class, but I think it will be far more applicable. You will likely find what I can teach in this setting to be much more useful to your future goals."

Dax had no idea what his future goals were. He hadn't even considered what he wanted to do once he left the Academy. He wanted to make sure that he survived the Academy first. Considering what he had encountered with the Cult of the Dragon and now with the Order, what else would he face on behalf of the Empire?

"That would be great," he said.

"Very good. I will talk to you more about it once the term starts, as I wasn't really expecting to see you today…" She glanced over. "Do you want to help with the frosthooves?"

"Those are frosthooves?" Dax hadn't seen anything like them before, as they were not typically found near his family's holdings, though they were known to live elsewhere in the unclaimed lands.

"Indeed," she said. "And they really were captured for second-year transference students. Once you get into the second year, you start to learn a bit more mastery over your own transference, and it's easier for you to control and manipulate another creature's essence. I wouldn't ever allow a first-year student—at least, not typically—to work with something like this, though..." She frowned, biting her lip, and then nodded, as if coming to a decision. "I am curious whether you, with your innate ability," she went on, studying Dax, and seemingly ignoring the fact that Cedrick and Gia had come with him to the yard, "might be able to do something more."

"Can I get my friends started first?"

"That would be for the best," she said. "I don't want anybody to get in the way."

It was a strange way of putting it, but Dax shrugged, and he guided Cedrick and Gia over to the cattle pens.

"What was that about?"

"It sounds like I'm going to be tutoring whether I like it or not," he said. "And she also said that I won't be taking advanced transference because she wants to give me some private tutoring instead."

Cedrick frowned. "Private? I don't know that I've heard of any instructor doing that before."

"She said I get to work with some of the other creatures."

"Like those things," Cedrick said, nodding to where they were dragging another of the frosthooves over toward the pens.

"They're violent," Gia said. "But their meat tastes delicious."

"Really?" Cedrick asked.

"Well, we don't have incursions that often, at least not out near my land, but it happens occasionally. When we do, it's considered a delicacy. My father has always enjoyed bringing them down."

"Well, apparently they are difficult and dangerous for somebody to use with transference, so I'm going to see what I can do with them." He turned to the cattle pen. "To start with, though, I want you to focus on these. The key for you, and for you," Dax said, nodding to Cedrick and then to Gia, "is to focus on the essence you can feel inside of yourself. Then I want you to touch them. Don't worry. They're domesticated, and they have plenty of experience with students using their essence, so for the most part, they don't mind it when you draw on it. What you need to do is feel the flow of essence. You want to connect what you have flowing through you to what is flowing within them, and then you need to push it out."

"So I just have to form a link?" Gia asked, making the connection right away.

"Exactly," Dax said.

"How do we do that with our essence, especially if it is not the same kind of essence as the animal has?"

"I don't think the essence type is what matters," Dax said. "Because you're not using their essence. At least, you're not using it directly. You're just guiding the way they use it and expressing it outside of them."

Cedrick shrugged, and he moved down and reached into one of the pens, touching one of the cattle on its head. He whispered something to it.

Gia looked back at Dax. "Does it work just like that?"

"Mostly. The hard part is pulling its essence, as you've been pushing yours. You can do this, though."

She rested her hand on the cattle nearest her, and he noticed how her essence shifted. It was slow, but he could see it drawing in a stuttering sort of movement. Had Dax not been as attuned as he was, maybe he wouldn't have noticed it.

She suddenly froze.

"Just like that," Dax said. "You're close."

"I can feel it," she said. "But it is hard to use."

Dax nodded. "It's going to be hard. It's not how you normally use essence. You usually push it, and this is a matter of pulling, then pushing. Does that make sense?"

"What about me?" Cedrick asked. "I mean, I get why you're helping Gia. She certainly is prettier than me, but I'd like you to help me with the pulling and pushing, and whatever it is I'm supposed to do here."

"Maybe you look too much like the cow." Gia grinned at Cedrick, then stuck her tongue out. But then she turned her focus back, and when she began to pull on the essence, Dax didn't even need to help her. The way that she pulled on it, the power that she was using, was stronger this time. She had learned.

And then he felt the stirring power coming from the cow.

"Oh," Gia said, her voice catching. "It's... so easy."

Dax smiled. "With these creatures, it is. Once you start to move it, it flows pretty easily. I was hoping you could feel that."

"Now that you've helped her, can you come over here and help me?" Cedrick asked.

Dax held Gia's gaze. "See? You can do advanced transference. You do belong here."

She turned her attention back to the cow, saying nothing.

Dax headed down to Cedrick, glancing over at Gia, then past her. Professor Madenil was watching, and there wasn't a smile on her face. Dax wasn't sure what she was thinking, but it looked as if she were concerned. That didn't seem right.

Once he finished with Cedrick, getting him to hold onto this type of essence, he would go over, learn about the frosthooves, learn about their essence, and see if he could transfer anything there. If he could, then he could begin the process of testing them for sentience. He didn't expect it with the frosthoof any more than he did with the cow, but maybe Professor Madenil knew about other creatures that might have sentience.

It was a question Dax was growing increasingly concerned with answering, as he needed to know just how many creatures were a real danger.

Chapter Twenty-Five

AFTER WORKING WITH HIS FRIENDS, DAX WAS PLEASED WITH himself. Gia had picked up on transference quickly, and even Cedrick, who had not been all that capable with transference before, had gained a measure of skill much more rapidly than Dax would've expected. He stood there for a while, watching the flow of their essence, then turned and made his way over to where Professor Madenil was working with the frosthooves.

She glanced over in his direction, and when she turned her attention back, Dax noticed that she was using a faint trail of essence as she did. "You will find that essence transference with frosthooves is going to take a little bit more strength than what you are accustomed to, Mr. Nelson. It involves drawing upon an aspect of essence that might be beyond a first-year student. I would be quite intrigued to know if you have the capacity to do this."

This was a test, he realized.

And perhaps when it came to the professors, everything was a test. He should've known better. Especially when it came to transference, and the fact that he obviously had some talent with it, Professor Madenil wanted to make sure that he was not permitted access to the transference yard, and the pens, without having the necessary capabilities.

"What's the primary problem with working with them?"

She paused, hands on the iron bars of the pen. She had put one of the frosthooves inside, and its massive antlers swung from side to side. Every so often, the creature would look over, and Dax couldn't shake the feeling that there was something almost aware in its eyes. He wasn't sure if that was his imagination or if that was something real, but regardless, when he watched the frosthoof watching him, he was left with the impression that there was something about it that understood.

"Resistance," Professor Madenil said. "These creatures are likely to resist, and you will need to overcome that."

"Is it dangerous?"

"It can be," she admitted. "There's always the possibility that you will overwhelm the creature itself when you begin to use a measure of transference against resistant essence. It takes a gentle touch to slide past it."

"I often feel a little bit of resistance."

Professor Madenil finished what she was doing— placing a runic marker on the pen, Dax realized—before turning and facing him. "There are different approaches to different creatures like this, Mr. Nelson." She looked along the row of pens. "With cattle, transference is very straightforward. You will find no resistance, as you have seen. The cattle practically *want* to share their essence with you. Some of that comes from the fact that they are domesticated, and in some regards, they live to serve, but in others, it is simply tied to the fact that their essence is poorly commanded by them, and they have a considerable amount of it, so they want to get rid of extra essence.

"Other animals hold onto their essence more tightly," Professor Madenil went on. "In the case of the frosthoof, I would say that it is of moderate difficulty to access that essence. Not as difficult as, say, the Great Serpent," she went on with the bird of a smirk, "but still challenging. And the more that you work with this, the more experience you get with testing yourself against different types of essences so that you can learn whether one requires a heavy touch or a lighter one."

"I see," he said, though he didn't, really. She had only had him practicing with cattle for the most part, and in that time, Dax had come to feel a measure of confidence in his skill, but... But he hadn't only worked transference on cattle, had he?

When he had been out dealing with the Order, traveling with his friends, he had learned that he had a measure of transference against other things, and with other people.

Maybe the resistance wouldn't be as significant for somebody like him.

"What do you mean, using transference on the Great Serpent?" Dax asked.

Madenil turned away from him. "It was just hyperbole. Nobody would actually try to draw upon the Great Serpent, Mr. Nelson. Such a thing would be dangerous."

It left Dax with a few more questions, none of which he felt comfortable asking at this point, especially not around Professor Madenil. He wasn't sure about her affiliations, nor did he know whether it had really been just a joke or whether it was something more than that. What if she was with the Cult of the Dragon? Worse yet, what if she was with the Order?

"Would you like to try connecting to the frosthoof?"

Dax frowned, staring at it for a moment. "You don't think that it's going to be dangerous for me?"

"We are talking about transference with wild creatures, Mr. Nelson. Anything at this point, anything beyond domestic creatures, poses a bit of danger. I will be here and will be able to help guide you, if you need it," she went on, though there was a tone to the way she said it that seemed to suggest perhaps she didn't think he would need it. "And if you have any difficulty, we will regroup, and we will see where that challenge comes from. What do you say?"

Dax looked over to where his friends were still practicing. Each of them was standing in front of a pen, and as he watched, he noticed that both of them were still appropriately drawing upon transference essence, with much more success—and much more skill—than they had before. "What is the typical progression for students in your class?" he found himself asking as he watched them.

She glanced over, and she chuckled. "Are you worried that you are not making appropriate progress?"

Dax shook his head hurriedly. "It isn't that. It's more about trying to understand what my friends need to do, so that when I talk with them, I can give them a bit of guidance."

She frowned, turning to look at Gia and Cedrick before she turned her attention back to Dax. "Noble of you, Mr. Nelson. And part of the reason that I think that you will make a wonderful instructor for some of your other classmates. At least, once you gain some mastery of additional basic skills. But you don't need to worry. We will continue to guide your friends, and the other students, through the elements of transference."

"I wasn't really worried," Dax said. "I guess I haven't

given the different applications of transference much thought."

"Ah. Now I see your question. Well, once we have people with more mastery of transference, there are quite a few different applications, especially as we begin to move into more advanced classwork. Many of the classes have overlap, as you have probably seen. You cannot work transference unless you have a measure of essence manipulation. And until you have ability in essence manipulation, you aren't able to truly power runic markers. But when you do have mastery over those things, then you are able to do far more than you would've been able to do before. There are still limits. It will not allow you to progress to the next tier in your training, if that's your question. It does allow you to use more power than you normally would, but until that time…"

"Until that time, transference is the key," Dax said, thinking that he was understanding some of what she was saying. But there had to be more reason for transference than just to make essence wielders stronger while they were still learning.

"Well, transference is beneficial when you are at this stage, or at their stage," she said, nodding to Cedrick and Gia. "But it is once you are even more advanced that transference becomes even more beneficial. Think about what type of essence you possess."

He didn't say it, but he suspected that she knew about his transference essence. He was beginning to think that most of his instructors knew about the kind of essence that he possessed, in fact, and were thinking of ways he could learn to use it.

"And think about what type of essence your friends possess. You have different types, most likely."

Dax looked over. From here, he could see the dark brown of earth flowing from Gia as she worked with the cattle. He could see the faint pink streamers of Cedrick's strange life essence. And he thought that he understood.

"You mean that there are ways of adding a different type of essence than what you traditionally can control."

"Exactly."

That had been Dax's experience as well. He had used his own transference connection, and he had drawn from some of the others around him, using that technique to borrow power so that he could fill himself with strength. It was still strange for him to be aware of it. And stranger still that they were talking about drawing it from animals.

"Are there limits to transference?"

"You are asking quite basic questions, Mr. Nelson. You would have known this had you been reading your books."

Dax flushed. "I'm sorry, Professor Madenil. It's just that with the last term going the way that it did, we were so preoccupied on making sure that we got through our exams that—"

"I understand what it was like," Professor Madenil said. "And we did require that you students perform far beyond what is typical for students of your age. Unfortunately. And I fear, as I expressed to the headmaster, that doing so will only have led to poorly trained students. Unfortunately." She shrugged. "I recognize there are some difficulties with what we asked of you, but if you are going to keep coming to the transference pens, you are going to need to have full understanding of the application, and the usefulness, of the type of essence we have been applying." She looked over at the frosthoof. "To begin, we will focus on this one."

He sensed her disapproval, and he vowed to himself that he was going to take steps to make sure that he was ready the next time that he worked with her so that he would have a better understanding of the types of things that he knew, and needed to know, about essence. Transference was fairly academic in certain regards, and there were countless books on the subject. Dax had even read quite a few of them, but mostly it had been about trying to gauge what kind of essence he had, and whether his own type of transference essence would be applicable for anything more. Now that he had Professor Madenil's frustration, Dax knew that he was going to have to work hard to ensure that he did not upset her any further.

"I would like you to extend your awareness out to the frosthoof's essence," she said.

Dax faced the pen. He had the distinct sense of energy from the runic marker worked into the pen.

The creature was watching him. It twisted its head, angling its antlers at him threateningly.

He needed to understand the essence from the creature, and he wondered if there was something he could identify from it. It did feel a little cool.

Not cool. Cold.

He jerked back.

Dax hadn't even realized that he had been probing, pushing outward and trying to strain and draw upon the connection of the frosthoof, but he had done so without even meaning to. The act of transference had become second nature to him, even though there were dangers to it, and there were aspects of drawing upon that essence that Dax needed to be more cautious about, as he could feel some parts of that building inside of him.

"Ice?"

"Very good, Mr. Nelson. This creature is connected to ice."

"Which must be connected to water as its primary essence?"

"Exactly," she said. "Water, but it might have variations within it, depending upon the person connected to ice. In the case of frosthooves, it is a variant of ice essence, and you will begin to feel a bit of wind essence mixed within it. A secondary feature, as it were."

Dax stared at the frosthoof and felt the creature looking at him again. Once again, he began to pull upon the essence, drawing it into himself. He could feel something of that essence as it started to flow through him, and this time, he was braced for the cold much better than he had been before. When he had dealt with that cold the last time, it had come upon him too suddenly, without him having the opportunity to prepare for it.

But ice was just ice.

Water.

He wondered what Rochelle would do with an essence like this. Water was healing, and that was her purpose with it, but there were other aspects of her own essence that he had seen her using, aspects he knew she had control over, that left him wondering if perhaps there was more to her connection with water than he'd thought. After all, she had made it clear that her essence had quite a bit of difference from her family's essence type, having diverged when she had connected to the Great Serpent.

Dax continue to pull upon the essence, letting his awareness of that fill him, and focusing only on the cold, only on the way that it flowed into him.

But as Professor Madenil had said, there was resistance.

He felt it as if the frosthoof were daring him to try to draw on that essence.

Dax hesitated.

And as soon as he hesitated, the essence connection shattered.

It felt as if an icicle broke around him.

He jerked back.

Professor Madenil watched him, and then she started to laugh.

"As I said," she went on, "these creatures are little bit more complicated than what you have already attempted before. I must say, Mr. Nelson, I am impressed that you have enough skill that you are able to connect to it in the first place. Most people aren't able to make any sort of connection to the frosthoof the very first time that they attempt to do so. And when they do, they don't much care for it."

"I'm not afraid of it," Dax said.

"It's not a matter of fear," she said.

"What is it a matter of?"

"It's a matter of understanding. Did you feel the cold?"

Dax nodded.

"And did you feel the frosthoof drawing away from you?"

He nodded again. That had been the other thing he had felt, and he thought that he understood what she was getting at. She had known that the frosthoof would resist.

"Is there a way to force the frosthoof to give up its essence?"

"That, Mr. Nelson, is the key to transference." She nodded to him, then she started down the pens.

The key to transference was *forcing* them?

What if it wasn't, though?

The cattle had seemed to willingly gift their essence, and there had to be other creatures who would give that essence just as willingly. But when he had sparred with Gia, and even battled with the Order, he had simply taken essence, hadn't he?

Gia hadn't even been fully aware of him taking essence from her. Others wouldn't have recognized it either. So he was left wondering if the same thing could be said for creatures. Could he use transference on them without actually harming them?

He felt like they were aware, but that shouldn't stop him from what he needed to do here and now. If he dealt with another attack—and Dax was confident that they would unfortunately face another attack, given the dangers they already knew were out there—he wanted to be ready for it. And in order to be ready for it, he was going to have to have a complete understanding of transference so that he could understand how to manipulate his own essence, and that of any others he might have to face.

Dax turned his attention back to the frosthoof, and he set to work.

Chapter Twenty-Six

The Academy grounds were quiet.

It had been peaceful, almost, though there was a part of Dax that began to wonder if perhaps that peacefulness was simply an illusion, and if it would shatter once the Academy filled with students once again. He still didn't know what it meant for him to have reached the second tier of his acolyte progression, though he did feel a greater awareness of essence. Perhaps that was all that it granted. He didn't know if what he had learned would help him as he struggled to reach the third tier, where he would supposedly learn how to quantify just how much essence he could use.

As far as he knew, the others had reached the second tier as well, but something about Dax's progression felt a little different than what they had gone through. Maybe it was just the fact that he had possibly added another essence form, or maybe it was that he had consumed direct essence from the Great Serpent more than once. Either way, he did not know why he was different. Only that he was.

The Academy would be quieter once students returned, from what Rochelle said. A small section of students would never come back because they were either not progressing as quickly as they were supposed to or because they had failed their exams.

"There are some people who simply don't pass their exams," she said to him one day when they were standing outside.

"I have a hard time thinking that they are going to expel anybody after this last term," Dax said. "I know that the professors—and the headmaster," he went on, glancing over at the administrative building, which he had not visited since they had taken the crystal they'd found there, "wanted us to progress and use essence in ways that we had never attempted to do so before, but they had to have understood that students simply did not have the necessary experience to be able to use essence in that way."

"I don't know," Rochelle answered, and she looked all around her. Gia and Cedrick had gone off to spar with valor blades, which Gia had been adamant that she needed to work on during the break. She kept asking Rochelle to go with her, but Rochelle had declined so far. Dax knew that she was going to need help, and that he was going to have to help her, but for now, she had declined his offers as well. "I think the professors understood the purpose behind it, and given the type of attack that we dealt with, and the ferocity of it, I can't see them backing down from what they ask of us."

"It just seems a bit much."

She shrugged. "Maybe it is a bit much. But there is a benefit. From what I can tell, more students advanced to the second tier this time than was typical."

"Which means we have to progress to the third tier before others."

"We don't know what that's going to involve," she said.

"Because they haven't told us anything about reaching the second tier."

She shrugged. "I think it's fine. Most people wouldn't have reached second-tier acolyte until the end of their first year. You're not even supposed to be a wielder before the end of your time at the Academy. And that's another few years."

"We might have to try to advance faster if the Order comes at us." Even becoming a wielder might not be enough, he realized. They were dealing with those who could claim to be masters—even headmasters.

Which meant pushing himself, struggling to understand the essence that he had, and all other forms. Maybe it was why he felt compelled to go to the forest, even though he knew that it was probably a mistake—a terrible one, at that.

But something drew him. Idiocy, probably, or perhaps a desire just to get outside of the boundaries of the city. There was something freeing about being away from the sights and the sounds and the smells and everything around him, something freeing about it, like the way he had felt when he had wandered his home near the unclaimed lands and searched for information. He had never known enough then—not nearly as much as what he wished he understood now. Dax couldn't help but think of all the opportunities he would've had then to have tested some of the other creatures he had encountered for any signs of sentience.

But so far, here, he had not uncovered anything other than the silk shatter.

Before he knew what he was doing, he reached the outskirts of the forest.

He paused, looking back at the city, and everything there was quiet. The main part of the city wasn't necessarily quiet, but the Academy, and the students within it, did serve as something of an engine for the rest of the city. In between terms, the city itself seemed to take a bit of a break. Dax wondered if that was normal, or if that was unique because of what they had been experiencing lately. At this point, he simply did not know, though he wasn't sure that it even mattered.

He turned his attention back to the forest, and he focused on his transference essence, tightening it down into a tight ball, focusing as much as he could. Finally, he saw something.

It took a moment to realize what it was. It was a faint glow in the trees up ahead. He hurried toward it, and then he saw something, though it took a moment to realize what it was. It was a marker.

This one was on a boulder. As he approached, Dax crouched down in front of it and began to run his fingers along the rune. It looked much like it had when he had been in the forest before, though he wasn't sure why it seemed familiar to him. Maybe that was another aspect of transference.

Dax constricted his essence down even more than before, looking around the forest. There were others. He hadn't paid attention when he had been here before, which probably had been a mistake. Now he was certain they were here.

He walked slowly and carefully, pausing every so often to listen to the sounds of the forest around him. It might have been a mistake to come out here on his own, as he was not equipped to handle any sort of dangerous creature he might encounter, especially if the silk shatter were to return.

As he moved along the western edge of the city and near the southern portion of the forest, he slowed. There had been several other markers, though none of them obvious. And none had any clear pattern that he could identify, though all looked highly advanced.

Would Professor Alibard recognize something about them?

He was the only one that Dax thought might be able to help him, though he didn't know if he would be willing to work with him. If he wasn't, then Dax would have to find the answers on his own, something he did not know if he was equipped to do.

He paused for a moment, noticing a faint trace of green in the trees.

It might just have been the life essence of the forest itself, but it might be something that was out there trying to draw his attention.

Dax unsheathed his valor blade and wondered if he should push essence into it. He didn't feel anything unusual, and certainly nothing that made him think that he was in any sort of danger. Dax thought that the essence warning that he'd gained from the Great Serpent should provide him with an alert if there was any danger here, and so far, he didn't feel anything. Which meant that he could be perfectly safe, or he could be in terrible danger.

As he held onto his essence blade, he started to creep through the trees, making his way carefully until he found the greenish trail. It was hazy, broad, and covered the ground in a blanket of essence. It all seemed to be life essence, which Dax drew upon and transferred into himself. There was an aspect of it that felt familiar, though he was unsure as to why. He held onto it, curious how long he would be able to maintain that connection as he followed the path in front of him.

He found it easy to do, and as the pale green began to intensify, the broad, hazy blanket of life essence that he had initially observed began to thin down into something that looked more like a tree trunk, and then into a tree branch, and finally into a dense, thick vine that pulled him along. He stopped trying to use transference on it, recognizing that it seemed to be more of a path for him to follow than anything else. By the time he noticed it thinning down into something like a rope, he started to feel like he was getting close.

Not a rope. A spiderweb.

Or at least, something akin to a spiderweb.

When he noticed a rustling around him, Dax stopped.

He had reached a dense part of the forest, dense enough that he couldn't see more than ten feet in front of them. Lush grasses, shrubs, and trees grew all around him, though Dax had no idea how the light could filter down deep enough for the grasses to grow as rapidly as they did. He paused, keeping his essence constricted but also holding onto his essence blade, worried about the possibility that he might come across something more dangerous. When he heard—and honestly, felt—movement near him, he refused to look up. He suspected that it was the silk shatter trying to scare him.

Then a shadowy form emerged from the shadows in front of him. Dax braced himself, constricting his essence tightly, and studied the massive silk shatter that he had seen before. Dax was certain that this was the same one. There was earth and fire and wind essence all throughout it. Probably water as well, though he didn't see it as clearly.

And the silk shatter had used life essence for him to find him.

"You returned," the silk shatter said.

"I had a feeling that you wanted me to return," Dax said, and he motioned to the path that he had been following. "Either this was a trail to find you or some sort of trap."

The silk shatter stepped forward, rising up on six legs and tapping the front two together once again. A rhythmic sound echoed in the earth and left Dax trembling for just a moment before he tamped down his fear. He had to get control over himself, and control over his emotions. He had no idea if the silk shatter meant him any harm, but at this point, he had to stay calm until he could better understand nonetheless.

"If you intend to attack me, go ahead." Dax brought the valor sword up, but he held it carefully, point angled slightly downward but with a grip that would allow him to point it at the silk shatter if he needed. It wasn't much of a threat, at least not from somebody like Dax, but the silk shatter darted back, dancing on his six legs before he reached the edge of the trees. When he did, he tapped his forelegs together once again, the steady drumming building.

"Did you call me?"

"I sensed your presence in the forest."

"So then you called me?"

Dax had been following the trail rather than the runic markers, which was a mistake. Had he been paying attention, he might have seen the silk shatter.

"You spoke to the Great Serpent?"

There was almost an eagerness to the question.

"I saw the Great Serpent," Dax said. "All people like

myself, who come from the Academy, go for a testing. When I was there, I had an opportunity to see the Great Serpent."

The silk shatter tapped his legs together again. "Lies," the silk shatter said.

"For some people," Dax said, taken aback. How could the creature know that some people were not actually given an actual vision?

"Did you see him?"

Dax looked around. This time, he truly looked around.

He had an awareness of the silk shatter in front of him, but as he swept his gaze around him, he became aware of even more. Hundreds upon hundreds of these creatures were surrounding him. Hundreds upon hundreds of them were there, all of them watching, waiting, almost expectantly, as if they needed to know the truth.

Dax, for his part, wasn't even sure what he was supposed to do or say, only that he felt like what he said next, and how he reacted to this, was going to be pivotal.

"I don't know. Not at that time, I don't think, but later. After I left. There was a beam of light. A flare is what my people call it. I went to it, and I was given a series of visions. Each of them with the Great Serpent, at different times in its life, until..." Dax shrugged. "Then I took on essence."

"What did you ask for?" the silk shatter asked.

Now there was an even greater intensity than there had been before, almost as if the silk shatter were daring Dax to answer, or perhaps daring him not to answer correctly. Either way, Dax felt an unease about what he might do or say, and he felt a bit of fear about how to handle it. He wanted to say and do the right thing, but he wasn't sure what that might be.

He knew what he had asked the Great Serpent for, but

he also didn't know if that mattered to the silk shatter. As he focused, though, he didn't feel any sort of danger. He should've felt the tingle on the back of his neck, the same sensation he had detected when he had been sparring with his friends or anytime that there was an unusual essence nearby. But around the silk shatter, Dax felt nothing. It might only have been that he could not feel anything, or perhaps there was no danger here and his essence, and the Great Serpent's gift, was telling him as much. Perhaps these creatures were not going to harm him. Dax had to hope that was the case.

"I asked for understanding," he said.

The silk shatter hesitated, then tapped his legs together again, which caused the ground to thunder. The other creatures all around him began to scatter. "Then you shall have it."

Chapter Twenty-Seven

THE SUDDENNESS OF IT ALL LEFT DAX STANDING ALONE with the silk shatter, without any idea about what was going on. He felt a bit of fear but wasn't sure if he was in any danger. He didn't think the silk shatter wanted to harm him, as Dax had a strong suspicion that the creature would've been able to do so. Even with his essence blade, and powered with transference essence, Dax doubted that he was strong enough to handle something like the silk shatter. There was a combination of different essences within the creature, and with them blended together, it would've been far too difficult for Dax to do anything useful against him.

"What happens now?" Dax asked.

"You wanted understanding, human," the silk shatter said. "And I will provide it for you, assuming you are willing to take a journey."

"I was willing to come out here in the first place, so obviously I am willing to take a journey. I just don't want you to attack—or eat me." He added the last as little more than a whisper before immediately regretting it.

"Your flesh would not taste good," the silk shatter said.

He started to turn, and Dax hesitated.

Was that a joke, or was the silk shatter serious? Given the way he had said it, he certainly sounded like he was serious, and Dax didn't much care for that. His flesh wouldn't taste good?

"How many humans have you eaten?"

"None," the silk shatter said.

He heard a faint, stonelike scratching sound, and Dax took that as laughter, of all things. "A joke?" Dax asked.

"Do humans not have humor?"

"We have humor, just not in situations like this."

"When do you have humor, then?"

"I suppose… Well, anytime," Dax said, and he frowned. "Anyway. What is this? What do you want to show me?"

"You will come."

"I am coming," he said, "but what am I supposed to be doing?"

"You will come; otherwise I will need to eat your flesh."

The scratching came again, more strange laughter.

Instead of arguing, he followed the silk shatter. The forest became thicker and denser, with strange, dangling vines beginning to drape down from branches so that he had to push his way through the forest to make his way after the silk shatter. The silk shatter seem to be moving much easier, though it took Dax a moment to realize why.

The silk shatter used earth to make sure that he didn't sink into the ground, and he used a bit of wind to guide the dangling vines out of the way. When that didn't work, Dax recognized that the silk shatter was using life essence to impact the vines, causing them to either shrink or simply flow out of the way. The entire effect of it was quite impressive.

Would he even be able to use transference on the silk shatter?

He thought about what Professor Madenil had said, and how he was going to have to force the essence from some creatures, but at this point, he didn't know if he would've been able to do that, nor did he know if he would've been strong enough to draw upon the silk shatter. Of course, there was also a possibility that if he were to try to draw upon the silk shatter that it would be viewed as an attack.

Instead, he simply followed close behind the creature, making a path and keeping his essence tamped down tightly for the possibility that he might need to use it. When he did, he was able to see the shifting of essence all around him.

At first it was a slow, steady buildup of ambient essence around him, but the deeper that he went into the forest around the silk shatter, the more that Dax could feel this ambient essence growing. There was a power to it, and an energy that struck him as significant. The only other time that he had felt anything quite like this was when he had been in the tower near the Great Serpent. The deeper he went, the denser the forest became, and the more of that ambient essence began to flow around him.

"How is this even possible?" Dax asked, unable to keep the question inside any longer.

"What part of it?"

"All of it," Dax said. "The essence. You being here. This place."

He noticed that the trees had started to shift so that branches mingled together, some of them creating small caves in the upper parts of the trees. When he stared, using his tightly bound essence, Dax noticed that eyes peered out at him, and there were strange streams of the essence he had seen before. Those were the places the silk shatters lived.

How could they live in the air?

The better question, though, was how they could have managed to control the essence so tightly here, and how they had avoided the attention of the Academy so long.

"This place is our home," the silk shatter said, "but the fringe of it. If I were to bring you to the heart of it, you would not survive."

"Why?"

"The Queen would destroy," he said.

"Is that another sort of joke?"

The silk shatter turned to him, and the long forelegs tapped together again, causing the stone sound to emanate deeply, practically reverberating through Dax's chest. It left him feeling as if some part of him were reacting to it.

"The Queen would destroy," he said again. Then he kept moving.

Not a joke, Dax realized.

As he followed, Dax could feel the essence all around him, and he noticed that there was more than just life essence within it. That was the predominant essence, though in the forest, that wasn't surprising to him. But there was also earth, and wind, and vaguely, Dax was aware of a bit of water essence as well. The only of the primary essences he didn't see, but he could distantly feel, was fire. Given that he knew that the silk shatter in front of him had fire essence, Dax was not at all surprised by that detection.

"So if I can't go into the heart of your city, what am I supposed to do here?"

"You follow," he said.

Dax had no idea where he was, but he didn't feel the tingling that indicated danger. That had to be a good sign. Didn't it? Increasingly, he began to ignore his own worries of danger around him. These creatures were more than just intelligent. They were civilized.

And they were startlingly close to the city.

Had the Academy known?

"Do others know that you live here?"

"Others know but choose not to know," he said. "And we prefer it that way. They prefer it that way as well."

"But if others knew that you had so much ambient essence here, they would want it for themselves."

Ambient essence was valuable for many reasons, but it allowed for a much more rapid progression. He could imagine students at the Academy coming out here to try to take advantage of the ambient essence so that they could reach higher tiers faster than they would just through training and testing.

But he didn't see anything here that would suggest that anybody had been using ambient essence, nor runic patterns—though he wasn't sure that he had an opportunity to truly test that or explore. If there was power here—and obviously, there *was* power here—Dax thought that he was going to have to try to keep track of how to reach it so that he might be able to return.

"They would not be able to find this place," the silk shatter said, far more confident than Dax would've expected. "They are not capable of such things."

"How are they not capable?"

"Your people do not see." He turned, and when he did, there was something in his eyes. It seemed as if he recognized what Dax was able to do.

The silk shatter had already known that Dax could see essence and follow it.

And he could do more than just see it.

"You said that I might come here to try to find understanding, and that there was something here that would help me understand what it was the Great Serpent wanted from me."

That last wasn't exactly true, but Dax thought that it had to at least align with what the silk shatter had wanted in bringing him here. If Dax could understand that, maybe he could learn more about his own essence, and he could learn more about how to control it.

But it was more than that. He also had the other aspect of essence to consider. Understanding.

And unfortunately, even though he had been trying to make sense of it, trying to understand whether there was anything in the Great Serpent's gift that might help him know more about his own essence, Dax couldn't say it had been much use to him so far.

"I can see essence," Dax said, "and I think that's what you wanted me to do. He wanted me to know that your people were here. Why?"

The silk shatters continued to make a circuit through the trees. They never went any farther than the perimeter, or what Dax suspected was the perimeter, of the silk shatter city—just remained in the strange homes worked into the tree overhead. But even that might not even have been homes, Dax realized. What if they were some sort of fortress, a way for the silk shatters to scout? From there, they could hide, and anybody who came through unsuspecting might be either attacked—and the idea of silk shatters attacking unsuspecting people seemed horrifying to

Dax—or deterred in some way. Either way, the positioning seemed to be intentional.

"You needed to know that we were here."

"I needed to?"

"You wanted understanding, did you not?"

"I suppose," Dax said. "But you obviously know the Great Serpent."

"The Queen knows," the silk shatter said.

"How does the Queen know the Great Serpent?"

"She was there when he rose," he said, his voice soft, almost reverential.

"She was... *there?*"

Dax thought about the visions he'd had when he had taken on essence, and the amount of power that he had felt as he had been gifted it. The Great Serpent was impossibly old. Everybody agreed on that. And with the Great Serpent's age came power and experience, and most people knew that the Great Serpent had lived in these lands for longer than the Empire had even existed. The Great Serpent had watched cities and nations rise and fall, only to rise again.

But if the Queen was there...

The idea seemed impossible, but as Dax turned, looking toward the city, he could feel something else coming from it, some bubbling of energy, something that struck him as familiar. It was what he had felt when he had gone to the tower, to the place of the Great Serpent.

"How was she there?"

"There are many great powers in the world," the silk shatter said.

"Like you?"

There was a strange scraping of stone once again, the

laughter coming from the silk shatter. "Not me. Not compared to the Queen or the Great One."

"And the Queen and the Great Serpent…"

"Have long looked out for each other's best interests."

"I see," Dax said, but he didn't. "What does this mean?"

"Mankind goes to the Great Serpent looking for answers, looking for understanding, and looking for power. Others come to the Queen."

The silk shatter tapped his legs together again, and when he did, there was another thundering of earth, another echo that left Dax trembling with it. If others went to the Queen, it suggested a far more potent power than Dax would have imagined—something greater than that of the Emperor, and possibly even rivaling that of the Great Serpent.

"And the markers that I found?"

"You should not have seen them."

"Because I'm human."

The silk shatter turned to him, and Dax realized that they had been gradually making their way away from the silk shatter city, putting more and more space between it and them. That had to be intentional, as he believed that the silk shatter was trying to keep Dax from finding it. Even though he might have had his essence concentrated and could see essence from everything around him, he still didn't think that he would be able to find the silk shatter city on his own.

"They were not for you."

"Somebody wanted me to see them," Dax said. "And whether it was the Great Serpent or another, they were placed in such a way that I was meant to find them."

"Not you."

"Then who?"

"Do not return," the silk shatter said.

"Or what will happen?"

The silk shatter tapped his legs together again. "Do not return."

Dax felt the threat this time. There was no joke, no hint of mirth, though he wasn't even sure if he would've recognized it if the silk shatter had tried to tell another joke. He wasn't sure what to say. "Somebody wanted me to find that path, and the Great Serpent wanted me to have understanding."

"And you have understanding now. You see. One path for humans, one for others. You do not go where you do not belong."

"Who is to say where I belong?"

"The silk shatters say," he said. This time, he reared up on four legs and tapped his front four legs together in a single thunderous clap.

The ground trembled.

The amount of earth essence expended in that single movement left Dax speechless. He was pushed back, and even if he had wanted to fight against it, Dax doubted that he would've been able to. He didn't know if he had the necessary strength to do so. He feared what it meant, and more than that, he feared what the silk shatter might try to do if he were to challenge him.

"I just want understanding," Dax said.

"You will not find any more here."

With that, the silk shatter turned, and it seemed as if the forest swallowed him quickly.

As Dax watched, he couldn't help but wonder if the silk shatter was wrong. He hadn't thought that Dax would find understanding here, but Dax thought the opposite.

This was a place of essence. This was a place of power.

Maybe this was the kind of understanding that the Great Serpent had wanted him to gain, but he would need the silk shatter to permit it. Dax could feel essence all around him, and within it was a steady drumming of earth, along with the whispering of wind, a bit of warmth from fire, and possibly even a dampness of water. Essence was all around him.

What would these creatures do to him if he were to remain here?

And so he turned away. He wandered, following a faint trail of green that grew ever broader as he walked. He realized that the silk shatter had provided him with another path, one that guided him out of the forest. As he followed it, he looked for other markers, but he saw none.

If they were not for Dax, then who were they for?

That was the question that lingered with Dax as he made his way out of the forest and reached the perimeter. Here, he paused, turning his attention back and focusing. Even as he did, Dax could not feel anything. But he was left with questions, and he was left searching for understanding, the very thing that he had wanted from the Great Serpent.

The problem was that he wasn't sure what he needed to do to find that understanding. Maybe there would be nothing that Dax could do. Maybe it was simply about knowing that the world was larger—and stranger—than he had ever known.

Or maybe the Great Serpent had planned something else.

Dax would just have to figure out what it was.

Chapter Twenty-Eight

"I think we're going to have to talk about how you keep disappearing like that," Rochelle said while they sat over their meal.

The cafeteria was empty, as it had been throughout their break, and Dax was eating quietly, keeping mostly to himself. He had shared with her that he had gone back to the forest and found more of the markers, but he hadn't yet shared with her about the silk shatter, nor the threat that they had made to him. At this point, Dax wasn't sure that there was any point in doing so, as he didn't know if there was anything that he could do about the silk shatter that would change anything that he had already done. If they didn't want him to go there, then he wasn't going to be able to go there.

"I just needed to wander," he said.

"You could've wandered over to the valor yard," Cedrick said, chewing on a piece of hard candy. He'd finished his meal quickly and picked out a candy to keep eating. He looked tired, but he was also bruised in ways that

Rochelle's healing had not been able to fix. "I might've had a better chance with you than I did with Gia."

"Do you really think so?" Gia asked, sitting upright and eating slowly, deliberately, a satisfied look on her face. "Because that makes me feel good if you think Dax isn't as dangerous as me. Of course, him being a Nelson, I'm not surprised by that."

"I seem to remember our sparring coming to a draw," Dax said.

"You remember, but is that really what happened?" She glanced over at Rochelle, and she flashed a smile. "Boys. They always think they can win. Sometimes they are led to believe certain things as well."

"Don't do that," Dax said.

"What's she doing?" Cedrick asked. He crunched down on his candy, then winced. He rubbed at his jaw for a moment.

"Oh, she's trying to make it sound like she let me win."

"The truth can be painful," she said, grinning at him. "And I would never want you to think that you aren't a strong enough boy," she went on, leaning forward and reaching for him, as if to take his hands, "because we know that boys can be so sensitive at times."

"They really can," Rochelle said.

"Well, my jaw feels sensitive, but that's because she punched me. I mean, she actually punched me, Dax. Who does that?"

"You asked for valor training," Gia said. "I wasn't going to give you substandard training. That would not do anything for you when you try to take advanced valor."

"If it's like that, I don't know if I want to take advanced valor," Cedrick said.

"There really isn't anything quite like that in advanced

valor," she said, shaking her head. "That was more for my benefit."

"You want to beat up your friends?"

"I don't *want* to beat anything up," she said. "I just thought that I would give you an opportunity to experience what it's like to face somebody who knows true valor."

"And there is an element of sparring when you go to advanced valor," Dax said, chewing slowly. He was thankful for this diversion. He still didn't know what he was going to do about the silk shatter nor about the power that he knew was out there. He felt as if he needed to take advantage of the ambient essence that he had detected in order for him to reach the third—or even maybe the fourth—tier so that he could be ready for when he dealt with the Order again. He just had to ensure that he didn't anger the silk shatter when he did. "When you take advanced valor, depending on what Professor Garrison wants of you, he will likely have you learn different fighting styles. If you work with Gia and me over the rest of the break, and even after break is over, we can help make sure that you know enough about the different fighting styles that you should be well equipped for the basics."

"That wasn't at all like what I took in basic valor," he said.

"What did you take in basic valor?" Rochelle asked.

She seemed genuinely interested, though she had never been interested in valor before—she had said she didn't believe there was any purpose in fighting. Then again, she was a healer, and healers almost universally never served as fighters. That didn't mean that they didn't serve on the battlefield, as Dax had heard stories about soldiers needing the services of healers, but they were never asked to do the actual killing.

"It was a lot of standing and postures and moving from one place to the next," Cedrick said, waving his hands dismissively. "It felt like I was learning dance moves, but I never really knew the dance."

"It is like dancing," Gia said, grinning at him. "The most beautiful kind of dance. And once you become skilled at it, you can dance with anyone."

"Great," he said.

"Perhaps Dax would like to demonstrate a dance?"

"I'm eating," Dax said.

"You look like you're moping," Rochelle said.

Dax looked up, and Gia had already stood. She grinned at him, and Dax realized that he wasn't going to get out of this. At this point, though, he wasn't sure he really wanted to get out of it. If it was going to help his friends, then shouldn't he do it? That was the one thing that he was coming to learn during his time at the Academy—that in anything that he might do, any fight he might be in, he was going to need his friends to get through it. At this point, Dax thought that the only way that he was going to be able to handle anything he had yet to face would be by working with the people who knew him the best.

He pushed his tray away and got to his feet. "I don't know that we really should do this in the cafeteria."

"There's nobody here," Gia said. "And besides, we just want to show Cedrick the purpose behind the movements and dances that he learned. I think I was probably too advanced for him earlier."

"Fine," Dax said, shaking his head.

He took up a position, and then he bowed to Gia.

"Look," Cedrick said, waving his hand at them, "they even start like they are dancing."

"Careful," Gia said, "or I'm going to require that you get up here and dance with us when this is over."

Cedrick grinned, then snapped his fingers, and but a few bubbles began to pop from his fingertips.

He and Gia faced each other, and Dax took up a jain style stance. It was one of the very first styles that he had learned, and probably one of the first that Gia would've taught Cedrick, as it was incredibly basic but also fairly useful. Gia recognized it, and Dax started, making a few slow strikes in the air. As he did, Gia countered, blocking each strike in the appropriate technique. They moved slowly, steadily, their feet shifting as they moved across the stone.

"See," Gia called, without looking back over at Cedrick, "it *is* like a dance. If you know where your partner is going, you will know how to move. That is basic valor."

"Too basic," Cedrick said.

"Well, it starts out very basic, but the more you memorize of the styles, the faster the dance gets."

She began to increase the pace. Dax picked it up, following her.

But there was no malicious intent here. There was no real sparring at this point, either. This was merely a show of forms.

When Dax had been learning how to fight, learning basic valor at home, he had needed to demonstrate forms many times. It had been in a bit more formal setting than this, and he had needed to impress his father in order to advance to increasingly complicated patterns, but it had been no different than a demonstration. He was pitted against somebody who could counter, and he was forced to go through each of the attack moves while somebody else blocked. Once he had finished, he had been expected to go through the counter, taking on Gia's role in this dance. They would go through all the advanced fighting techniques until Dax was cleared to move on.

It was more of a test than anything else.

With Gia, there was a bit more fluidity to it than what he had done when he was with his family. She was very skilled with this fighting style, so as Dax moved, twisting and darting, striking and kicking, he found her there. Each time that he brought his fist up, she would block his arm, then a kick from his leg, and then she would step back, press her hands together, and bow for a moment before she darted forward.

"Wait, now she gets to lead?" Cedrick asked. "Okay. This is not at all like dancing."

"It can be if you're not so selfish," Rochelle said.

Dax was on the defensive side now, and with each movement that Gia made, he stepped through the patterns, feeling the flow. It was almost reassuring to be back moving like this. Then again, it served no purpose. There were very few times when he would ever have to fight like this, especially now that he had access to an essence blade and, more importantly, to his own essence.

They kept moving.

Gia was quick, steady, and she hurried through the movements, picking up the pace until they reached a crescendo. Then she took a step back and bowed again.

Finally, she went and took a seat at the table, looking over at Cedrick.

"See? A dance. It's the kind of dance that everybody should learn to do."

"I might even like that," Rochelle said.

"I thought you didn't want to fight?"

"Well, I didn't realize it was like that. I thought it was

going to be more about stabbing and poking and killing, and I wanted to learn how to use the essence blade so that I could know what I was going to have to do if I had to deal with anything. But I also didn't think that I was ever going to want to actually use it," she said. She looked over at Gia. "Will you teach me to 'dance'?"

"You don't want me to help you?" Dax asked.

"I think she has a much better technique than you do," Rochelle said.

Gia barked out a laugh, and she nodded. "I can teach you. And Cedrick. I suppose that it's only fair. We have Dax teaching all of us so many different things, and it's not fair for him to be asked to demonstrate all these things at the same time."

"Thanks," he said.

He started picking at his food again, his mind turning back to the silk shatter and everything he had encountered in the forest earlier in the day. He still wasn't quite sure what he was going to do about it if anything. He wanted understanding, though. And he wanted the opportunity to draw on the essence that he had detected out there. More than anything, that seemed to be what the Great Serpent had been prodding him toward. Power and progression.

Dax finished his meal in silence while the others continued to talk about valor. They didn't have much time before the rest of the students would return to the Academy, but they made up a plan for how Rochelle and Cedrick and Gia would all keep working, learning different training techniques, so that they could all eventually be able to spar.

"What now?" Cedrick asked after they were all finished with their meals. "I mean, we've had such an exciting day." He looked over at Gia. "Or painful day, I should say."

"How about going to the artisan district?" Rochelle suggested.

"Why there?"

"I don't know," she said, shrugging. "It's a bit livelier, and we haven't been dealing with anything quite exciting all that often lately, but…"

"You want to see if *he* is there, don't you?" Gia asked.

Dax had many questions for Desmond. Out of everyone, he was the one person who might be able to provide him with more information on the silk shatter and the power that was found in the forest near the city. "I think it's probably a good idea to talk to him," he said.

"The two of you go," Gia said to him. "I'm getting tired."

"I am as well," Cedrick said.

They waved goodbye before heading to their dorms, leaving Dax and Rochelle alone.

"Do you think the two of them are…" he started, thinking about the possibility of Cedrick and Gia going back to a singular room, and the rumors that might spread about them. He had been concerned about himself and Rochelle, but he had overlooked Cedrick and Gia.

"I don't know," Rochelle asked. "It's possible. Cedrick tends to get excited about different things, and well, you know how he can be."

There was a transition of essence once he reached the artisan district, where not only did the buildings shift, adding color to the drab stone of the Academy grounds, but the different variations and striations of color to the essence around them began to change, practically assaulting him the moment he stepped into the artisan district.

"Are you going to tell me what you really did earlier today?"

Dax looked over at her. "What's that supposed to mean?"

"You don't have to act like it's some sort of secret. I can see it in your eyes. You're keeping something from us. I don't know what it is, and I don't care, to be honest—only if it is going to cause problems for us. What did you do?"

Dax breathed out heavily, as this wasn't the place where he wanted to talk, and if he'd had his choice, he thought that he would've wanted to go someplace where others wouldn't be able to hear them. He wasn't sure what to make of the silk shatters, nor was he sure what to make of the kind of power they possessed.

"I just found a few more of those markers are along the perimeter of the forest," Dax said. "I was trying to understand what they were, and so I walked along the edge of the forest for most of the day and kept testing for different things. That was pretty much it."

"And you don't see any sort of pattern to it?"

"No pattern," he said.

No pattern. If the patterns and the runic markers that he had seen were tied to something for the silk shatter, wouldn't there be a pattern to them? If they were some sort of trail, there should've been a way for somebody to be able to find the trail and follow it.

"I didn't see a pattern. But they're incredibly complex, far more so than anything else I've ever seen before. I don't know if that means anything—"

"It means something," she said. "It means that there are types of runic patterns that we don't understand. Which isn't surprising, even if you've progressed to third-tier acolyte."

"I never said that I had."

"You didn't have to say it. You were advanced the way it was, and then you had the flare, which probably helped more. Plus there's the way your transference skills seem to be increasing. The only way that would be the case would be if you had progressed again. But that still doesn't mean these runes are anything to worry about."

"Oh, I don't know about that. One of them appeared on a chair in my room."

"And your floor," she said with a bit of a smile.

"Fine. My floor, and my chair. So we just leave them alone?"

"No. We don't leave them alone. We keep looking. And maybe your transference talent will help with that."

"If I can figure out how to harness it. If not, maybe Desmond knows something," Dax said. "I just hope he's there this time."

Chapter Twenty-Nine

DESMOND HAD NOT BEEN THERE THIS TIME.

They had wandered the streets of the artisan district for a while, but they had not found any sign of him, nor had they found anything that suggested to them where he might've gone. They wandered through the district for a little while, buying some food, looking at some paintings, listening to some performers, generally enjoying themselves and the quiet of the night around them. It was a nice, and uneventful, evening. By the time they headed back to the dorm—where Dax slept on Rochelle's floor again—they were both tired.

When he woke up, he did so to a strange drumming sensation.

Dax had thought that it was in his dreams, and when he had been drifting, there had been a part of him that felt as if he were back in the forest, talking to the silk shatter, feeling the earth essence coming off the creature as it drummed its massive legs together. But this time, it seemed to attack him.

When he sat up, he did so slowly, rubbing at his eyes.

There had been something that awoke him, though Dax wasn't sure what it was. Maybe it was just a memory of what he had been through, but he couldn't shake the feeling that it hadn't been a dream.

Earth essence. He was certain of it.

He sat for a moment, looking over to where Rochelle was laying on her strange bed in the middle of the pool, her hair dangling off the side of it and nearly into the water. If he had rolled any closer to the bed, her hair would've tickled his nose. Getting to his feet slowly, he slipped his essence blade into his belt and headed toward the door to the room.

As he pulled it open, Rochelle stirred, looking over at him. "What are you doing?"

She rubbed her eyes, looking as if she wanted nothing more than to roll over and go back to sleep.

"I felt something and can't really sleep, so I'm going to take a walk."

"You know what time it is?"

"Not really," he said.

She let out a sigh, and she rolled to the edge of the bed, sitting up for a moment. "I don't either. But you said you felt something?"

"It was probably just a dream," he said.

"Probably. But this being you, and with your attunement to essence, I don't want to just let 'probably' be the answer," she said. She looked over at the pile of clothes she'd left in the corner from the day before. "Turn away."

He did as she asked and gave her a few moments, and then she cleared her throat, giving him a chance to turn back around. She now stood completely dressed, carrying an essence blade of her own.

"You don't even know how to use that," he said.

"Well, I know that, and you know that, but anybody else we might encounter won't know that. So if nothing else, it might be helpful to have another weapon."

"There's not going to be anything out there," he said.

"You don't know that, and while we both hope that's the case, we should be prepared for the possibility that there is."

Just then, Dax felt another thundering. It was fainter this time, but this time, he was awake, and he was certain of what it was.

He looked over at Rochelle, but she didn't seem as if she recognized it.

Then again, she might not. Water essence probably wasn't enough for her to detect what he suspected was earth.

"There was a trembling again."

"I will come with you, and I'm going to bring your old friend." She rested her hand on the blade's hilt.

"You've been spending too much time with Gia," he said.

"I think I need to spend *more* time with Gia so that I can learn to dance like she does."

"Fighting like that doesn't really make you a good essence blade wielder," he said. "They have some overlap, but not a lot."

"Are you such an expert?" Rochelle asked with a bit of a smile.

He ignored her, heading out of the dorm and then stopping just outside to look at the early morning light. It was not quite dawn, but a few streaks of color were starting to show in the sky. He could feel the crispness in the air, and he breathed it in. He appreciated the quiet, the solitude of this time of day. It reminded him of his lessons with Headmaster Ames.

They had only been outside for a moment when another thundering echoed. This time, it was close.

"What was that?" Rochelle asked.

"Wait, you felt that?"

"I don't know how I couldn't."

Dax turned, tamping down his essence, looking for the source of what he had felt.

Then he saw something.

A light blazed against the early morning sky.

"Fire," Rochelle said.

"We need to wake up the professors," he said.

"I see that," she said. "Don't do anything stupid."

Dax nodded, then raced directly toward the fire.

Not do anything stupid… well, that was difficult for him, as most of the time, he found himself drawn toward danger. This was a bit different. This time, he raced toward it, before he realized where it was coming from.

The administrative building.

The third story was blazing.

Somehow, the rest of the building seemed to be intact.

He wasn't the only one here. There were several of their professors, including some he didn't know, that had surrounded the building. Some of them were working with wind, and Dax could see the faint, translucent swirls of the essence that they were wielding as it worked toward the building and tamped down the essence there.

He didn't see any fire wielders though. That was what they needed. A skilled fire wielder would be able to draw the flames off fairly easily.

No one was paying attention to him, so Dax simply focused on the fire. He could transfer it, couldn't he?

It was possible that it would be dangerous, and that if he were to summon it the wrong way, it might burn through him, but he had been around fire his entire life. Anyone who saw him might even assume that he was a fire wielder himself.

He was nothing more than a first-year student, and he was still learning how to handle his essence, how to handle his transference. But they didn't have a fire essence wielder.

And that made this all the more dangerous.

Unless they had somebody who could wield the fire and move the flames around, there wasn't going to be any way for them to stop it. The wind essence wielders could draw the air out and tamp it down, but essence-driven fire could continue to burn. Earth could counter it—Dax had plenty of experience with people who had that connection to essence—but even that might not be enough. Water was useful in more than just healing, and he could see how the right type of water essence wielder could be helpful. He doubted that there would be anything useful a life essence wielder could do.

Which meant that a fire wielder needed to be here.

He found Professor Alibard among the others.

"Mr. Nelson," Professor Alibard said, looking over at him. His face was locked in a look of concentration. "I am afraid that I'm a little bit busy. There is nothing that you need to be doing. This is quite well in hand."

"My father is a fire essence wielder," he said, "and I know about fiery essence. I know that it can't be put out by wind or water or earth or life. You need fire essence. So is there a fire essence wielder I can get, or who might be here?"

Alibard finally looked at him, and this time, he frowned. "No, unfortunately. We don't have any fire wielders here at this time, as we are in between terms. And we are holding the fire in check, but it is all that we can do to keep it here."

"I could help," he said.

"I don't believe you have fire."

Dax shook his head quickly. "Not exactly, but my essence should help with this."

"You are merely a student, Mr. Nelson. Go back to your dorm. This will be dealt with."

Dax backed away when he collided with Rochelle.

"They were already up," she said, looking at him, "as you can see."

"They don't have a fire wielder," he said.

"So?"

"So this is fire essence," Dax said.

Even as he looked, he could see the essence glowing within it. It was intense, and it blazed more brightly than most fiery essence that he had seen before. He could imagine his father here and what he might do were he to focus on this kind of flame and try to draw it away. Maybe it would've been too much for even his father.

"Don't," Rochelle said.

"What?" he said, slipping around the side of the building. There was a gap in the essence wielders here, and up ahead, Dax noticed a door, and he thought that if he were to run for it, he might be able to get inside.

Once there, what did he really think that he was going to be able to do?

Draw essence, he decided.

"I can see that look in your eye, and it's the one that tells me that you are going to try to do something that you shouldn't be doing. And knowing you, you're going to ignore me regardless, and... Dax!"

He had run forward, focusing on the flames.

The wind continued to swirl, and while there was considerable essence power within it, it wasn't doing much. From where he stood, he could see the fire spreading, the flames starting to drag along the surface of the rooftop. It wouldn't take long before it bounced out into the city, perhaps even into the artisan district, where the effect of the fire would be far greater.

"Somebody needs to do something, and there are no fire wielders here. I'm not one, either, but I have something almost as good."

"It is not almost as good," Rochelle said, running over to him and grabbing his arm. "You have already said that your essence doesn't transfer nearly as effectively as somebody who has natural essence."

He was nearly to the door. Behind him, he could hear the shouts of some of the professors. They were focusing on the fire above and didn't seem to be paying any attention to somebody down here.

"Let them work."

"If we had a fire wielder, then maybe. But we don't, so I can't just stand back, Rochelle."

He reached for the door.

It was locked, he could see that, and he could feel that there was some essence within it, so he was going have to transfer that out as well. He hoped the runes on it were damaged too much at this point to be effective.

"That's not the reason that you are doing this, Dax. I know you better than that."

"It's the crystal," he said. "We left it. We don't know what it is, and we don't know why it's up there, but it's a Great Serpent flare. Shouldn't we make sure that it's safe?"

"Oh," she said, looking behind her. "The others probably know about it."

"Maybe," Dax said, though he wasn't even sure if that was the case. It was possible that no one other than the headmaster would know about the crystal. "If it burns, think of what will be lost."

"Nothing," she said. "We don't know that anything is going to change if the crystal burns. We don't know anything about the Great Serpent, and the gifts that it provides, and whether this is anything that will matter. All we know is… What are you doing?"

Dax had stepped forward, and he rested his hand on the door, feeling for runes. He could feel some energy and started to draw it inside of himself. The transference happened slowly—far more slowly than Dax preferred—but he could feel it building as it flowed through him.

Heat blazed in the door. It was uncomfortable.

"I'm just testing," he said. "Just give me a moment."

"Testing. You mean you're going to go in. After all that. I can't convince you."

He shrugged. "After all that, you made me realize that I really need to go inside. So good work, Rochelle."

"Fine. Then I'm going with you."

"You don't have transference," he said.

She patted the essence blade at her side. "I have this. And I have something better."

"What is that?" Dax asked.

There was a heavy crack, and it sounded as if some of the stone of the Academy building was going to crumble. Dax didn't like the idea of heading inside, but he also didn't like the idea of not heading inside either.

"Water."

"How is water going to help us? I've already told you

that this is fire essence, and fire essence needs more fire essence to tamp it down."

"Water is going to help if you get yourself hurt, Dax. Water can heal. Now, if you are going inside, let's just get this over with. I want to go back to bed."

Chapter Thirty

THE HEAT WAS OUTSTANDING.

The hall side was filled with smoke. Dax left the door cracked so that some of the wind from the wind essence wielders would be drawn through the hall and back outside, hopefully summoning the smoke and distributing it away from them. From outside, it seemed obvious the flames were concentrated on the upper levels of the building, but inside, there were occasional fires elsewhere.

"There's something I didn't consider," he said.

"Only one thing?"

"Well, more than one thing, probably, but I don't know what I'm supposed to do with the fire once I transfer it into myself."

Rochelle paused, and she looked along the hallway. From here, Dax could see where the registrar's office was, and he was hopeful that nobody was in here. This was just an office building, after all, and not a place that anyone stayed.

"Runes," she said.

"What?"

"We can place runes, and you can place fire into them. They'll be temporary, at least until they can get a fire wielder here, and then you can hold it. Do you know any runes that will hold fire? I mean, besides the basic ones that we learned in Alibard's class last term."

"Well, there are a few that I can think of, and most of them are relatively easy to make, but I've never actually tried to place anything into them before."

That was part of the problem. He had experience with transference, and he had studied runic markers, but he had no experience in actually using the knowledge he had. That meant anything he might do, and any kind of power he might use, could go poorly.

"Let's get going," she said.

They reached a trail of flames along the ground. It looked as if somebody had tried to burn doors here. The doors had their own protections placed upon them and were obviously designed to withstand other types of essence, so thankfully they had held back the attack.

He crouched down in front of the fingers of flame. If nothing else, he could test whether he could transfer the fire away. If he couldn't, then there was no point in him going up further into the building, as all that would do was put them in more danger.

He focused on the flame, and he began to draw upon it.

"What are you doing?" Rochelle asked.

"I'm starting to transfer," Dax said.

"Not before you make other preparations," she said.

He cursed himself. She was right. He needed something to write with.

"I don't have anything to make the rune."

"You have your sword."

It was a good idea, though not one that he was eager to attempt.

He wouldn't be able to do it otherwise, though. Unsheathing the blade, he scratched the point of it into the stone, feeling as if the stone attempted to fight him. Dax was forced to use the valor blade and transfer essence into it as he went. In doing so, he drew some of the earth essence out of the stone—something that he hadn't even realized was there when he had begun—and formed the pattern. It was basic, but basic didn't mean that it would be ineffective. Then he spilled the rest of the earth essence out and slammed it into the wall nearby.

"I had to use transference," he said, looking over at Rochelle.

She nodded. "I suspected. I wasn't going to say it to you, but I figured that the stone would be enhanced."

Now that he had his essence blade unsheathed, he decided to draw through it. He pulled the flame into it. It glowed, and then flames began to crackle along the surface.

More importantly, the flames that had been along the floor sputtered out.

Dax dropped the point of his sword down to the rune and then reversed the effect. He pushed. Essence flowed out of the blade and into the floor.

"It seems like it's holding. Now we have to hope it continues to hold," Dax said.

They reached the end of the hall, toward the stairs, and started up. The smoke was heavier here. Dax shifted his cloak, pulling it up and around his nose, and Rochelle did the same thing. He wished that there were some way he could move the smoke away.

Wasn't there?

It would've been embedded with essence, as well, so

there didn't seem to be any reason that he wouldn't be able to use transference on it. He held out the essence blade, then pulled.

It was slow, slower than it had been with the flame, but gradually the smoke started to drift into the blade. Dax pointed it behind him, then expelled the smoke. They continued up the stairs and got to the next landing, where he hesitated. He didn't feel any flames, didn't feel anything coming along the hall that made him think he was in any sort of danger. But he was worried he wasn't going to be able to draw all the fire off.

He made a quick fire containment rune at the top of the stairs. "In case I need it."

"Good idea," Rochelle said.

She rested a hand on his arm. A wave of water essence worked through him, and for a moment, he felt that power flood through him. He hadn't realized it, but he had been getting tired, and he had been feeling the effect of the smoke and everything else starting to build. He hadn't been paying attention to it as much as he should've been, but as she cleared that from him, he felt… better.

"Thanks," he said.

"Just keep me alive."

"That's my plan."

He darted forward, and there were a few more tracks of flame, which Dax drew into the sword. He was aware of how easy it was becoming to draw on some of this essence. He would not have been able to do this before going up the serpent stairs the second time and consuming additional essence. This was tied to reaching second-tier acolyte.

Or was he even higher than that?

Until classes resumed, he didn't know if he could determine whether he had somehow reached a higher level.

Searching through the forest, seeing the essence around the silk shatter, and simply experiencing some of the ambient essence may have changed something for him, even without him realizing what was happening.

Rochelle looked along the hallway.

"Somebody used the fire to ransack these offices." She pointed to one of the offices. "Look. That was the head-master's. That one was his undersecretary's. That one…" She shrugged. "I don't know. But all the doors are open."

"Then somebody had the key," Dax said.

"Maybe, or maybe they just knew how to break in. You don't have any key, and you could break in."

"So you're saying that somebody else has my kind of essence?"

"It doesn't even have to be your type of essence. It could be the Order or even just a random fire. We don't even know."

Nothing about this felt random.

He reached the end of the hall, and from there, he made three fire containment runes.

He wasn't sure if they were going to be strong enough, but he wanted to have enough ready so he could place essence into the runes, especially depending upon what they encountered when they went up the stairs.

He started up, Rochelle staying behind him. There was a distant cracking, and Dax worried the stone would crumble, but it held. Somebody had placed essence, and runic markers, skillfully within the building.

Then he reached the top of the stairs.

Fire raged in front of him.

Dax held out the essence blade, and he began to pull fire into it. This time, the fire essence was considerable. It was just a matter of transference, though, and he continued to call it into his blade, filling it with energy. Fire burned inside the blade, making the metal glow brightly.

Dax raced down the stairs, passing Rochelle and dumping the essence into one of the runes that he had formed. This wasn't going to be fast enough.

He darted back up the stairs. The flames continued to blaze in front of him.

"It doesn't even feel as if I did anything," he said.

"The heat isn't quite as bad," she said.

She was holding onto her essence and radiating it from her, using water to keep her safe. He was thankful she had that measure of control and worried what would happen if she were to lose it.

"Be careful," he said.

"Not all of this is mine. I'm just mixing with some of what the professors are doing. I don't have their skill or control over water, but since there is some here, I can guide it to us."

He nodded, turning his attention back to what he was doing. Why risk himself? Would the building collapse? Did it matter if he let it?

He couldn't shake the feeling that it did matter, that there was something else here. Not only that, but anything that he could do to keep ahead of the Order was the right thing to do.

He drew more fire.

He filled his blade with the essence once more, transferring as much as he could. As he did, he began to feel the heat blazing inside of the sword.

It was almost too much.

His hand throbbed.

Rochelle was there, touching him, and a wave of healing energy washed over him.

He raced down the stairs, dumping the fire into the containment rune that he had made before racing back up. Once again, Rochelle rested her hand on him. He felt her healing wash over him.

"I'm going to have to place some runes here," he said.

"Or there might be another way you could do this," she said. "You can express it."

"I don't know where I could do it, though. Maybe if I could take some stone out, it might work, but there's no guarantee."

"Just try," Rochelle urged.

He focused on the stone.

It had power within it. Essence within it.

And probably runes etched in the stone that he wasn't going able to overpower.

He had to get past those runes somehow. There was essence all around him, and he drew it into his blade. Earth flowed, and he turned, expressing it behind him. Then he tried something different, driving the blade into the wall, cracking it.

He pulled more essence into the blade, into the wall, and through, creating an opening in the stone. Hopefully it would be enough.

Rochelle looked at him. "What are you doing?"

"If I start to burn up, just make sure you heal me."

"Oh, Dax."

"Just pull me away if I'm starting to get burned," he said softly.

Then he held his hand up behind him, focusing on the essence behind him, not the flames themselves. He held his other hand on the hilt of the essence blade.

And then he drew it into himself.

Fire essence didn't necessarily burn. It was just essence.

He was just transferring essence. But there were already flames.

He summoned the flames, the fire, and the essence through himself, letting himself be something of a conduit, and poured it out into the essence blade, where he expressed it beyond the building.

If he could get the fire outside of the building, the others would be able to contain it more effectively.

Rochelle kept a hand on him.

At first, Dax worried about what that would do, and how her water essence might inhibit him, but it didn't seem to be doing that at all. Instead, whatever she was doing, the way that she was using her water essence and letting it flow into him, healed the injuries that he received as he pulled fire through him. And there *were* injuries. He was surprised, as he wouldn't have expected to get hurt by what he was doing, but he could feel the fire flowing through him, leaving it feeling as if his insides had been scalded. It was almost as if he could feel the effect of the flames, and he could feel something of the fire itself dancing inside of him.

He tried a different approach.

He could pinch some of that essence off, and he could absorb it into himself. Sometimes when he used transference, it felt as if part of that transference lingered inside of him, however unintentionally. He never intended to keep essence he'd transferred trapped inside of himself, but it happened nonetheless. And some part of him changed when that happened, he knew. Regardless of what his professors might claim, he did wonder if transference could help him more rapidly advance. And if so…

And if so, he wondered, could he reach wielder level even faster?

The pain inside of him began to ease, and essence flowed more easily.

It was almost as if he had become a part of that fire essence, as if by transferring a part of it into himself, he allowed himself an easier opportunity to manipulate and hold it.

Dax continued pouring fire out of himself until the essence faded to nothing.

Only then did he stop.

Once he did, he kept his hand on the hilt of the essence blade, feeling the strange energy along with what Rochelle was doing to him.

He started to pull the essence blade out of the wall. It left a small gap in the stone, and it was enough for Dax to feel the energy that was there. As he withdrew the blade, there was a sputtering of power. His transference didn't work. Dax looked at Rochelle, confused.

"Rochelle?"

He blinked, trying to clear the fatigue from his eyes, but it didn't work. More than that, he realized something else. The essence that he had been trying to draw resisted him.

It took him a moment to realize why.

Somebody was here with them.

Chapter Thirty-One

DAX CONTINUED TO ATTEMPT TO TRANSFER ESSENCE, BUT IT grew increasingly difficult.

He felt heat building inside of him, but more than that, it felt as if it were merging with him in a painful way, like what had happened during the transference exam when he had drawn on the cattle's essence. He had to be careful and not hold it too long, as he had no idea what would happen otherwise.

Rochelle stayed close behind him, pushing up against his back. He felt some of her essence flowing from her, powerfully enough that he thought he might even be able to use some of it, if it were to come down to that.

"Dax, I don't know what to tell you, but I feel something up there. And it seems like the heat around us is starting to build again."

He had been straining to make sense of what he felt and hadn't even noticed.

"I'm trying to transfer it," he said. "But I'm having a problem here, and I don't know how to draw it off. I'm trying to pull on the heat and the fire, and I can feel something there, but I don't know if it's enough for me to draw it away." He glanced over her shoulder at her briefly before turning his attention back to the flames. "Just be ready to run."

"What are you planning?"

All around him were flames, making it difficult to see anything more. Heat and ash and smoke lingered from the attack.

None of it seemed as if it were trying to target him. There was a bit of fiery essence that lingered, but not so much that he thought it would overpower him. Surprisingly, he could still draw upon some of it, and he thought that he might be able to send it away from himself if he were to try, though he didn't know where he could expel it.

Maybe out of the crack in the wall, but the only way he'd been able to do that before had been by driving his essence blade into the stone. He worried that he might have reached some limit to how much essence he could draw inside of himself. There had to be one. He could make more containment runes, but there was always a danger that they would fade or fail.

The sound of something up ahead caught his attention.

Dax reacted.

He began to pull upon essence in the air and into himself, holding it down as tightly as he could. As he did, he noticed something about the fire. It wasn't just pure fire. He hadn't noticed it before, or maybe he hadn't been paying attention to it, but there was a bit of shadow to it.

There were variants of fire. When he was younger, his father had wanted him to know those variants, as he had wanted Dax to be prepared for the various types of fire he might receive when he went to his testing with the Great

Serpent. His father had always assumed that he would receive a form of pure fire, but that wasn't necessarily a given.

"It's shadow flame," he said.

She frowned. "I've never heard of it."

"It's rare."

He didn't say it, but shadow flames were almost never found within the Empire. Shadow flame essence mostly came from some of the wild creatures they encountered along the unclaimed land, and never from any human.

Given what he had experienced with the silk shatters, and what they had said about essence and going to the silk shatter queen for essence gifts, Dax wondered if maybe it was all connected.

He paused for a moment, taking his essence blade and scratching a containment rune into the stone, and he dumped all the dark shadow essence that he was holding into it, wanting to release as much as possible. He didn't want to hold onto it any longer than he needed to. Then he approached the box.

"Move quickly," Rochelle said.

Dax knew that he needed to move quickly. He didn't know if he had the strength, though.

He started to pull on the essence, feeling the flows there. It seemed as if it reacted to his touch, and he transferred essence out of it and into himself more easily than before. Had he not dumped the shadow flame essence into the containment rune, he might not have had the necessary strength.

There was a strange stirring of movement not far from them. What was here with them? Dax didn't know, but he did know that he had to get to whatever was inside.

He pulled the door open. Rochelle stayed with him, and then he darted toward the crystal.

"I will take that," a voice said.

It was deep and booming, and it seemed somewhat rough at the same time, as if it were used to yelling... or tied to the fire in some way.

The figure that approached reminded him of the headmaster, but his essence wasn't right. Not only that, but the shape wasn't right, either. He was solid and more muscular. He carried a singular essence blade, rather than a pair. And he couldn't tell what kind of essence he had, but he could tell it was different, even though it radiated from him with a similar energy as what he had felt from the headmaster.

It was probably shadow fire. And given what he felt from the essence all around him, and the power that he had just experienced while trying to defend everything that was here, the amount of shadow fire—of fire essence in general —that this person possessed was considerable.

Much more than my father.

And that was saying something. Dax's father was incredibly powerful with fire essence and gifted in a way very few within the Empire were.

"What you decided to go for—I must admit, I didn't think I was going to be able to burn it out. I thought that I would have to bring the entire box with me to keep them from knowing that it was gone." The man shrugged, as if unconcerned about that. "But you... Well, you..." He took a step toward Dax, frowning as he did. "You don't look like anybody who should be here in the first place."

The voice was right; he and Rochelle weren't supposed to be here.

"We just wanted to put out the fire," Dax said.

"An interesting technique. What was it? Wind? Not any

sort of wind that I've seen before, but perhaps the Academy has finally learned a few things. And you," he said, looking at Rochelle, "have water, but a strange version of it." He frowned, and then he took a step toward Dax.

Dax held onto the power inside of himself, the power that he had drawn off the lock for the small box. He didn't know what he was going to do with that power, but at this point, he was loath to release it.

"What are you doing here?" Dax asked instead.

The man started to smile. "Just me?"

Dax frowned at him, but then he tamped down his own essence as tightly as he could, using that to try to catch glimpses of the other essence that was all around him. As he did, he noticed that there were faint stirrings of other essences nearby. What he felt was not as bright as this man's shadow fire essence, but there had to be a dozen of them around him. And they were all powerful.

They had truly made a mistake.

He should have listened to Professor Alibard.

"Not just you," Dax said, flicking his gaze from side to side before turning his attention back to the man. "But there are more than just us here as well."

That brought a better reaction.

"No? I believe the rest are outside thinking they can handle these flames."

"Shadow fire," Dax said.

The man turned back to him, and his grin faltered. "It is. How is it that you know this?"

"I know quite a few things," Dax said. The man leaned forward. Rochelle grabbed Dax from behind, squeezing his arm. "What are you doing?" Rochelle hissed.

Dax didn't even really know. He shouldn't antagonize

this man, but he wanted answers. Not only that, but he had to try to find a way for them to escape.

The man took another step.

Dax raised his essence blade. He pushed with his free hand, touching Rochelle, squeezing her wrist.

"Look at you. A little valor. Do you really think that weapon scares me?"

The man drew his own blade.

Not for the first time, Dax wished that he had a greater control over essence rather than just transference. Any of the primary essences would be useful here. Anything he did would be secondary—and would involve power Dax didn't —and couldn't—fully control.

He frowned as he drew up even more essence, focusing on the fire around him, and pushed it into his blade.

The man glanced at Dax's blade.

"Fire essence. Interesting."

The man's own blade began to glow.

That was all Dax needed. He darted forward.

He was quick, trained by his father, and he knew valor, so he wasn't afraid of fighting with an essence blade. But the man didn't try to fight with a blade. Instead, his flames began to expand from the end of it, the glow carrying a strange darkness that mixed with the fire.

It was impressive, and it was something that Dax had never seen firsthand.

The man brought his blade up to parry Dax.

He doubted he could win in a fight like this, certainly not while drawing on someone else's primary essence. But he wasn't exactly trying to win.

Rochelle seemed to realize what he was doing, and then she began to build water, tracing it in a pattern around him.

It was nothing more than a way to try to disguise the

attack, but thankfully, Rochelle understood what it was Dax was attempting to do, and she had her own essence she could use. The man darted toward them, but as soon as he saw the water, he backed away for a moment, giving Dax another opportunity. He darted forward, driving his blade at the man.

The man lunged, but Dax darted off to the side, feigning one direction before drawing fire around him and through his blade. The end of it glowed with more intensity, which caused the man to pause.

It gave him the opening he needed.

Dax jabbed at him, then pressed outward with borrowed water essence from Rochelle. The man jumped back.

And into the box.

Rochelle slammed the door while Dax poured essence out of him, everything that he had drawn around him, into the door to lock it. Rochelle surprised him by adding a ring of water essence around the box, even though Dax had no idea whether it was going to make a difference.

He stood for a moment, panting, still holding onto the glowing sword.

"Now what?" Rochelle asked.

"Now we have to deal with whoever else is here," Dax said, turning and looking at the rest of the room. As he did, he had the distinct sense of movement, and of the fire that was building.

And within it, there was something else entirely. Something dangerous.

More shadow flame.

But this didn't feel quite like Dax would've expected.

Chapter Thirty-Two

DAX CLENCHED HIS SWORD. HE HAD NO IDEA WHAT MORE he could do here.

He looked at Rochelle, and then at the box, where he felt essence building from whoever it was they had trapped inside. So far, it was holding.

But how much longer would it hold?

He held the crystal in hand, worried about what would happen.

Protect the flare.

The stairs were one possibility, but were they the only one?

He could go to the back wall. He and Rochelle knew about the secret passageway, but if they were to go there, and they were to get trapped, there was a very real possibility that they would end up burned alive.

He was growing tired. He had been drawing upon essence, and given that it was not his own essence—though Dax wasn't sure if that made much of a difference—he wasn't sure how much more he was going able to transfer.

Even if he could continue to transfer essence, there was a possibility that he wouldn't be able to draw that essence out as effectively as he wanted, and it would lead him to failure.

"Suggestions?" Rochelle asked.

"I think we have to head back down the stairs," he said. "I thought about going back into the wall, but—"

"I don't want to get burned on my way down," Rochelle said.

"That was my concern as well," Dax said.

"I'm glad we're on the same page," Rochelle said. "But what are we dealing with here?"

"I have no idea. Something is moving. And we have to be careful that they—or we—don't free whoever is in the box."

They had gotten lucky. He knew it was nothing more than that. And whoever was there was obviously a powerful shadow fire wielder. Probably headmaster level.

They couldn't wait.

"Down," he said, starting toward the stairs.

Shadows moved near him, and flames danced even more. Dax tried to call the fire, summoning more of it into himself, but he didn't know if he was strong enough. Every time that he attempted to do so, he could feel some of that flame working against him, and it felt as if there was some part of it that was burning him. Changing him, possibly.

Finally, he noticed a tingle on the back of his neck.

"That's too bad," he muttered.

"What is too bad?" Rochelle asked.

He tapped on the back of his neck. "I'm starting to feel that warning again."

"Only now?"

"It's strange that it took until now. Apparently, the

Great Serpent doesn't think I'm in any sort of danger of burning up."

"Or maybe the Great Serpent knows that you have enough transference essence that you can handle fire?"

It was possible, but even if that was the case, why did he feel it now?

What was it? Was it the pressure coming at him?

He turned his attention back to the box where he had trapped the man, but it seemed as if it were holding. The box was glowing, and Dax had no idea how long it could withstand the power they'd trapped inside it.

"Someone's coming," Rochelle said.

Dax realized she was right. There was movement. Sounds of shouts. And of essence.

Fire essence, primarily. Dax could see it glowing. There had to be at least three fire essence wielders, all of them with a blazing orange essence, and they strode up the stairs, drawing away the flames.

The shadowy movement around them continued to build. Others were coming for the crystal.

And Dax had no idea whether he could trust anyone with it.

He had been holding onto quite a bit of power but could no longer do so. He released it. It created a band of fire around them, and Rochelle added water, almost as if she were aware of what he was doing. Then the fire started to sputter.

All around him, everything began to fail. It happened rapidly.

The flames that he had been holding, the flames that he had been pushing away from him, suddenly vanished.

The heat disappeared as well. A gust of wind burst through, and Dax could feel the torrent as it flowed. There was nothing else that he was going to do with it, as the strength behind that, and the control of the essence, was more than what he possessed. He was tempted to try to pull upon it, but even if he were to try, he didn't know if he had the strength.

Rochelle took his hand and squeezed.

Dax decided then that he needed to sheathe his essence blade. Rochelle looked over at him and frowned.

"I don't want the Academy to know what I did," he said softly.

"That's not going to be the only question we're going to get."

He shrugged, knowing that was probably true, and not at all sure what else they were going to be able to do about it. Maybe nothing. The inside of the room blazed with light, and Dax hoped they were safe.

But then he saw the colors of the three that strode for them.

They were dressed in dark black robes. Dax had seen them before. The last time he had seen them had been when he had been inside the testing tower, trying to get to the Great Serpent.

He didn't recognize these Guardians, but that was what they were.

One of them broke off and turned toward Dax and Rochelle.

This person blazed with a fiery essence that was connected to wind and earth—more essences in any one person than Dax had ever seen before.

"What did you do here?"

"They are students," a voice said from behind the man. Dax flicked his gaze past, he was thankful that Professor Alibard was there, commanding the wind as he strode forward. He looked at both Dax and Rochelle, frowning at them. "Perhaps in the wrong place, and doing something they should not have, but they are students nonetheless."

"Why would students be here with the Cult of the Dragon?"

Dax shared a look with Rochelle.

This was not the Cult of the Dragon. He wasn't even sure if it was the Order. He didn't know what it was.

"We were trying to help with the fire," Dax said. "We saw the instructors were having a hard time putting it out, so—"

"So a pair of students decided that they would run into a burning Academy building and put out flames their professors struggled with?"

Dax had nodded. "I have some experience with fire. My name is Dax Nelson—"

The man stepped forward, and the suddenness of his movement, and the overwhelming aura of essence coming off him, made Dax hesitate. He tried not to move any further, but he also had to try to resist drawing upon his essence, transferring it from the man and into himself. As he looked at him, the man glowered.

"Nelson?"

"His father is Gerand Nelson," one of the others said, and Dax bobbed his head in a quick nod.

"I suppose you would have some experience with fire," the man said.

Dax let out a sigh, though he did not relax. Not yet. He wasn't sure that he could relax until the other Guardians allowed them to leave.

"And you still thought that you would come up here and deal with the Cult yourself?"

"We didn't want the building to burn," Dax said. "She

has water, so we thought that with my connection to fire and hers to water, we might help. We didn't know what we were going to find."

"Foolish," the Guardian said.

"Quite foolish," Professor Alibard said, joining Dax and frowning. "Apparently we have foolish students, but then our headmaster encouraged students to train aggressively because of the Cult of the Dragon."

Dax stayed quiet.

Was Professor Alibard helping them, or was he just trying to minimize the fact that they had come in, and that the professors had failed to put out the flames?

The three Guardians watched Dax for a few moments before they headed over to the box. Dax didn't have an opportunity to see what they were doing, as Professor Alibard stepped in front of him.

"What were you two thinking?"

"I told you," Dax said, looking over at Professor Alibard. "We wanted to put the fire out. We thought that we had the ability to do so and didn't realize it was going to be so difficult."

"You don't have that much of a connection to flame. Certainly not like your father, Mr. Nelson."

"Not quite like my father," Dax agreed.

Professor Alibard frowned at Dax. "And it looks like somebody has developed a better control over their essence manipulation. Interesting. Well, the two of you should go back to your dorms. We will take care of this, and then we will talk more."

Dax needed to get away from here before they were asked more questions that he wouldn't have answers to.

"Something's inside this," one of the Guardians said.

Dax looked at Rochelle, who shook her head.

"I think he broke inside, but he got trapped," Dax said.

Rochelle squeezed her eyes shut, and he could sense her frustration with him. He wasn't going to stay silent. But then again, he wasn't sure that anything that he could say would be all that beneficial.

"He?" One of the Guardians turned to Dax. "Did you see who it was?"

"We didn't. Just fire. That was it."

"That's not all it was," Rochelle said. "You thought it was shadow fire."

Dax shot her a look, but she just shrugged.

"It might be Raisor," one of the men said.

"He wouldn't be here."

"You don't know that," the other said.

Professor Alibard started to push them toward the door. "Get some rest, and we will talk later."

As they crossed the lawn, Dax turned his attention back, and he couldn't help but feel as if there were glimmers of flame that he saw throughout the sky, something that seemed as if it were moving, but shadowed, nonetheless.

By the time they reached their dorm building, he was tired, and he wanted nothing more than to lie down, take a break, and rest. But he wasn't sure that he could. They had drawn the attention of the Guardians.

But what else had come to the Academy?

Chapter Thirty-Three

As he sat outside, the smoke lingered in the air, though without the same potency as the night before. They needed to know more about this Raisor, but without Desmond in the city, he didn't know who to ask.

Which meant looking through the library.

Dax looked over at Rochelle, who had been quiet. After returning to the room and crashing, he had awoken to try to work some of the smoke smell out of his cloak, only for Rochelle to attempt to use water on it. It had worked to a certain extent, muting the odor, but it had not been as effective as he would have liked.

"Do you want to tell us why the two of you didn't wake us up?" Cedrick asked.

"Probably because Dax decided that he was going to go running into the building himself," Gia said.

"There wasn't so much a *plan*," Dax said. "It was more about just trying to help. And we wanted to make sure they didn't get the crystal."

"That's right," Cedrick said, leaning back and glancing at Gia. "The mysterious flare. The one that he claims they were able to find but nobody else knew was even there."

"We told you what we saw the last time we went in there where we saw the Guardians," he said.

They looked over at Rochelle, who nodded blankly.

"So Guardians showed up?" Gia asked, leaning forward and resting her elbows on her knees. "How are we supposed to feel about that?"

"They protected the Academy," Rochelle said.

"So they made it seem," Cedrick said. "What if they are a part of the Order?"

Dax couldn't ignore that possibility. There had been the strange creatures that were there. And given what he'd seen in the forest of the silk shatter, he was worried. What if they were working with the Order?

Why would they be?

The only thought he had was that it was tied to the Empire, and some desire to overthrow it, but that seemed awful.

"Maybe it was the Order," he said, but Rochelle looked at him, watching him as if she knew that he was not convinced. "But the Guardians believe it was the Cult of the Dragon."

"You don't think so," Gia said.

"I don't think so," Dax admitted. "We know they wouldn't do that."

"They would if they were talking about a flare," Gia said.

"We need to be careful," Rochelle said. "We don't know who else might be listening. But yes. It's possible that even they might be interested in that."

Dax looked at her, surprised. He hadn't expected that she would feel that way, but she wasn't necessarily wrong. It was possible that the Cult would want to know more about that, and possible that they would try to use it. Anything to serve the Great Serpent.

It was even possible that this had all been orchestrated by Desmond.

But if so, where was he?

"We need to find a place to talk more openly."

"You could place more runes like you used last night."

"You made runes?" Cedrick asked.

"Well, I tried to use containment runes, partly because I was only able to transfer so much fire."

"What will happen when Professor Alibard sees those?" Rochelle asked.

Dax hadn't given it much thought.

Somebody was going to notice that he had done that. The only way that he would have been able to etch into the stone would've been stone essence. He had done it with transference, but now he worried that it might have revealed too much about him.

"We need to find some other way to talk more openly. And we have to look into Raisor."

"Why do we need to be doing this?" Cedrick asked.

"Because it has to do with the Order," Rochelle said.

"So you agree with Dax."

"About this?" She shrugged. "I do."

"What about your sister?" Gia asked. "She has ties to the Emperor. Maybe she could help us."

Dax had been giving that some thought, but so far, he hadn't been able to figure out how he would be able to reach her. At this point, Dax didn't even know if he could get in touch with his sister. There had to be some way, but so far, any attempt that he had made to try to speak to her using the Whispers he thought she might have set up had failed. There had to be something interrupting them, as Dax had not been certain that he was even talking to Megan when he'd tried.

"I can keep trying," Dax said. "Maybe the registrar would know some way of getting in touch with her. At least, assuming that I'm willing to reveal that she is my sister."

"She might not be too thrilled with us," Rochelle said.

"Because you wandered the building?" Cedrick asked, winking at Dax. "Apologize. Tell her that you got lost."

By the time he made his way to the administration building, there were two people standing watch.

One of them was a thin older man who emanated earth essence, and the other was a younger woman with black hair and severe features. They both carried essence blades, and they both were staring straight ahead.

Guardians that Dax had seen had multiple types of essence. Maybe they were not full Guardians yet.

When he stepped forward, they both looked in his direction. "It is closed," the man said, his voice harsh.

"I'm a student, and I'm trying to reach the registrar," Dax said.

"You can find her in the office building," the man said.

"What happened here?" Dax asked. He might as well try to get some information, though he wasn't sure that these two would offer him anything.

"Fire," the woman said.

"It must've been bad," Dax said, trying to sound as innocent as he could, and knowing he was probably failing.

The woman eyed him up and down before seeming to take in his essence blade. "A student?"

Dax shrugged, and he realized that he was going to have to acknowledge the essence blade, but that was an easy enough thing for him to do. "We're in between terms. I'm working on valor. I'm Dax Nelson," he said.

As soon as the words were out of his mouth, he wished that he had not said it. He didn't need more people questioning his family connection.

"I don't care who you are. Get moving."

He didn't hesitate and hurried toward the office building, quickly finding the registrar. Her office was on the main level, in the second room. There was a large, makeshift sign on the door that said "Registrar".

Dax paused in front of the door, then knocked.

It was close enough to the start of the next term he would've expected other students to soon be filtering in, asking about classes for the next term, so the fact that the registrar was here wasn't unusual. What was unusual was who was behind the door.

This was an older, mousy-looking woman seated at a desk. She was different than the usual registrar.

"Can I help you, young man?"

"I was looking for the registrar," Dax said.

"Yes. That is me. Newly assigned to this post," she said, sitting upright and pushing her glasses up on her nose. "Can I help you? The term doesn't start for a few more days, so you have time to make adjustments to your schedule."

"I am Dax Nelson—"

The woman looked down, and she pulled out a large leatherbound notebook and began to flip through the pages.

"Oh, of course. Mr. Nelson. First-year student. Advanced classes, all of them. Passed them, which is surprising, given that you didn't have advanced scores previously."

Dax resisted the urge to say anything, especially as he hadn't known that little detail. Given that his sister had been the one to push him toward his classes, he supposed he shouldn't have been terribly surprised.

"I like to think I did pretty well," Dax said.

"You did just fine," the woman said. "Not all students did, unfortunately. But I suppose that with the difficulties we have seen thanks to the Cult of the Dragon, that is to be expected."

Dax wanted to correct her and tell her that it wasn't just the Cult but the Order and the headmaster as well, but he decided that would probably be a mistake.

"And the Emperor has determined that more supervision of the Academy is necessary," she went on. "Regardless, given that there have been some unfortunate circumstances regarding the administration over the last few months, I will, of course, begin looking into it. Anything unusual needs to be investigated."

"I didn't realize there was anything to look into," he said.

"Oh, very much so. Considering what we have been seeing of those involved around the Academy, we must be diligent, Mr. Nelson. We must be cautious that those who want to do harm to the Academy and the Empire are not allowed to run free."

Dax held her gaze for as long as he could before backing away.

He couldn't help feeling as if this new registrar was dangerous.

Anything unusual needs to be investigated.

Like strange runes in his room. That could be a problem for him—if he couldn't figure out who was responsible for them.

He felt as if there was far too much going on that he could not understand.

Chapter Thirty-Four

THE POST STATION WAS QUIET.

It was still early, still before the start of the term. As Dax headed inside, he flashed a smile, looking along the row of different postmasters, and wondered who he might be able to talk to, until he saw the same young woman whom he had spoken to the last time he had sent a message to his mother. She grinned at him, and he headed over to her.

"You again," she said, smiling. "Come to talk to your mother again?"

Dax shrugged. "Well, I was just hoping that my mother might have responded."

"You get along well with your mother?"

"I do. Shouldn't I?"

"I don't know. I like a young man who cares about his mother." She leaned forward, twirling her hair as she was watching him. "What is the message this time?"

Dax had prepared, and he slipped a piece of paper over. This one had more of the same, along with an attempt to try to get word to his sister. It was coded in a way that he hoped it wouldn't draw the wrong kind of attention, but Dax didn't know for sure.

"I can send this. Do you want to expedite it again?"

"Same cost?" Dax asked, this time feeling a little bit more sensitive about price, even though he had not struggled with money. Yet.

"Same, but I will expedite it for free." She grinned. "That is, if you would be interested in getting drinks later."

She was certainly cute enough. "I suppose I could do that sometime."

"Excellent. Drinks with Dax Nelson," she said under her breath before forming the essence that would convey the message. He watched as the swirl of wind essence streamed up and away.

"All done," she said, and winked at him. "You'll let me know when it works for you? I'm sure Dax Nelson is a busy man."

Dax wasn't sure that now was the best time to be making arrangements with someone else—nor was he sure how the others, including Rochelle, would react. Maybe they'd be upset with him. But it wasn't that he really wanted to do anything other than have a drink with her. They'd understand that, wouldn't they?

"A little, actually. But I'll let you know."

As he was making his way across the Academy grounds, Dax began to feel a bit of guilt. He shouldn't go out with the woman from the Post, especially because he had the feeling that she was taking advantage of him because he was a Nelson. He had enough of that at the Academy. Not with his friends. They didn't seem to care that he was a Nelson. But there were others who did.

He saw a pair of Guardians.

Dax had not seen many Guardians around campus. He knew they were there, and knew that they were still active, but he hadn't come across any. At least, not for a few days.

He was tempted to follow them, but he suspected that doing so would only draw the wrong kind of attention. The fact that they had been at the administrative building at the time of the fire was already the wrong kind of attention. Instead, he veered off, nearly colliding with the new registrar.

She was coming out of the building, and she looked up at him. "Mr. Nelson. Did you come to ask questions about your schedule?"

Dax blinked. "Well, not really. I was just…" Dax didn't know what to say about what he had been doing, or why he was here. He certainly didn't want to risk angering the registrar. "I was just heading back to my room."

She looked around. "This way?"

"I was taking a long way," he said.

She pressed her lips together. "Yes, well, you certainly aren't required to take any particular path around campus. I must say that it is unusual for so many students to have stayed behind after the first term. I suppose that traveling all the way back to our lands would've been difficult." She was watching him, and he couldn't help but feel as if there was something dangerous in her gaze. "Even for a Nelson."

"It's too far to make it quickly," Dax said. "My parents weren't expecting me to return."

"And what did your sister do when she came to the Academy?"

Dax froze. He shouldn't be terribly surprised that she had known about his sister, and yet he still was.

"My sister was a dedicated student."

"I didn't say that she wasn't."

"No," Dax said hurriedly, "what I mean is that my sister was a dedicated student and so she decided to stay behind at the Academy. Besides, she had a different kind of essence than what my father wanted to use to protect the border."

"Indeed. Well, given what I have heard about activity along the border, perhaps he wouldn't mind additional help these days." She tipped her head to him. "Good day, Mr. Nelson."

She left him, and Dax felt a wave of relief when she was gone.

He didn't like that interaction, and he was starting to realize there was something about her, and the way that she was watching him, that made him all too worried about what else she might ask.

He needed to go and check on Desmond.

He had gone every single day since the term break, and this was no different. As he made his way over to the artisan district, Dax picked his way through the streets, and then he found his way to Desmond's home. He was reminded of the very first time that he had come out here—how difficult it had been for him to find Desmond's home, and how he'd wondered whether he would ever be able to learn his way. Rochelle had needed to guide him. She had been keeping the street markers from him, though he wasn't really all that upset about it, as she hadn't deceived him about it. He just wished that he better understood how that power transmitted, and whether there was anything more to them than what he had learned so far.

When he reached Desmond's home, he paused for a moment in front of it. Something about the home felt different.

Dax wasn't sure what it was, but there was a distinct sense of happiness here, something that he had felt before but hadn't recognized until now. He could feel some energy that was here. He could feel...

Had Desmond come through here?

Desmond had a strange sort of power, reflective, mirrorlike power, and Dax didn't know if there was any way for him to follow that essence to figure out what Desmond was doing.

But if he was already here, then he might be able to get some questions answered—including why there was a flare at the Academy. It felt as if it was long past time that they get those questions answered.

When he knocked, there was no answer.

He waited, and then he knocked again.

Dax pulled on the lock essence, then pulled the door open.

He could feel the essence here. He found another loose cobblestone, and he tossed it inside. It shattered, much like it had before. But this time, Dax detected the flow of the essence strands there.

That was new—and it suggested a level of control that he hadn't possessed before. Which meant that his control over essence must've been improving.

He focused on the essence in front of him. Then he drew on it.

When he did, he felt the strands of essence there. They seemed like a spiderweb, crisscrossing, almost translucent. He was more aware of it now than he had been before, and he attempted to pull on the essence, separating it freely from the doorway.

He took a step forward, worried that he was going to feel some sort of pain, but there was nothing.

He took another step.

Dax looked down, and the silvery glowing border was

there. He reached back, closing the door behind him. And then he started to release the essence behind him as well. If this was some sort of a trap, he wasn't about to get caught in it.

Dax had not attempted to break into Desmond's home like this before. Would Desmond be angry?

As he took another step, there was no additional trap. He reached the edge of the silvery boundary.

And then he stepped onto a platform that seemed as if it created a distinct separation. He no longer felt the flow of essence behind him. It felt odd.

He looked out, and the boxes in the hallway were definitely different than they had been before. Some of them were stacked high and filled with a jumble of items, many of them reflecting a bit of pale light inside of the room. Others were filled with books and papers, and one had strange coins inside it. Moving on, he reached the end of the silvery hallway before stopping.

There was no room on his side. It just went to dark, empty space.

What is this?

He reached his hand out, but then he began to feel the strange tingling on the back of his neck. The feeling was subdued and had not happened often enough recently that he had come to trust it, but in this case, the fact that he was reaching out rather than trying to draw upon essence made the warning seem more important, and it forced him to jerk his hand back.

He focused on his essence, tightening it down until he could see the silvery lines around him. It had to be some part of the mirror conduit that Desmond had placed, but there was nothing here. It was like a void. There should've been a room here.

Could Desmond move it?

If so, the possibilities were incredible. He had known about mirror essence, but this suggested something else. Until he understood it, it was unsafe for him to linger. So he backed away.

He stopped and looked at one of the boxes, sorting through some of the books, but he found nothing useful to him. Most of them were on history. One of them was a story about the Great Serpent, which he thought was amusing, and several of them were on runes, which sparked his interest for a few moments until he realized that they were more about basic rune making, and not at all like what he was worried about. He didn't find anything else.

He checked another box and found one that was filled with different items, some of them small spheres, other statues, and one that looked vaguely like it was a sculpture of the Great Serpent, though the detail in that was not significant.

Finally, Dax reached into the hall, where he focused on the essence that he knew was there Again, he drew it into himself so that he could hold the trap at bay, then he shifted, pulling open the door and stepping back outside. He carefully reset the locks, and the trap, before closing it up once again.

Dax had learned nothing here, only that there was more strangeness to Desmond than ever before. There was no way of transmitting sound through that silver hallway. No way of notifying Desmond that they needed to reach him.

Maybe his removal of the locks, and the protective trap, might at least reveal that he had come here so that Desmond would know, and maybe he would return.

At least, that was what Dax hoped, though at this point,

he wasn't even sure that was going to accomplish that much. Instead, he turned, heading back into the street, back into the artisan district, and back toward his dorm— or, rather, toward Rochelle's dorm.

He didn't know what he was supposed to be doing.

And that, more than anything else, left him unsettled.

Chapter Thirty-Five

THE ACADEMY BEGAN TO BUSTLE WITH ACTIVITY AGAIN.

Students returned to the Academy slowly and steadily.

As they did, Dax found himself missing the quiet of the Academy during the break. The Guardians had seemingly left, having stayed for several days before dispersing. He had mostly avoided them, not wanting to get questioned about his presence in the building, though they had no apparent interest in him or Rochelle.

Before classes were set to start, Dax and Rochelle were waiting on Gia and Cedrick, who were working inside of the valor yard and talking quietly to each other.

"Isn't it strange that nobody has come to us to try to figure out what we knew, or what we were involved in?" Dax asked. "I thought they would ask more questions."

"We were just two students, Dax. Two inexperienced students who have no reason to be questioned."

"Still," he said.

Dax looked over at the valor grounds. Cedrick looked as if he were getting the upper hand as he darted toward Gia, lunging with a strike. Gia was quick, and she stepped off to the side. Dax noticed the way that she was using earth when she did, gliding on it. He doubted that Cedrick would even be aware that she was drawing upon earth as she was fighting him, but at the same time, it really probably didn't matter. Cedrick would occasionally draw upon his bubble power, using life essence in his attack, though Gia didn't seem to have any difficult countering that either. She battered it away, using a bit of her own earth essence to slap it out of the air.

They were all getting quite a bit more skilled.

Rochelle had even started to spar a little bit, though mostly with Dax, as they had been working through some of the basic forms to give her an opportunity to learn the earliest part of the dance, as Rochelle had taken to calling it. She didn't like to practice out here in the open, as she was embarrassed, but they would often practice at night in the dorm room, moving slowly and steadily, giving Rochelle a chance to absorb as much of the different attack types as possible, and Dax an opportunity to teach her as much as he could. She was growing more skilled, but it was slow and steady progress, not the rapid progress it seemed Cedrick was making.

"I don't know that Alibard wants to talk to us about it," she said. "He seemed awfully upset about the fact that we were there in the first place, and to be honest, I don't really want to upset Professor Alibard anymore than we have. I think we have him for our second term."

"We do," Dax said. When she frowned at him, he shrugged. "I told you that I went to the registrar's office."

"You told me that, and you told me that it was a different registrar, and that your sister didn't have any record of being there."

"Well, we have the same classes. She called me back, and she wanted to talk to me more about my sister."

"Do you think she could be working on behalf of the Order or for the Cult of the Dragon?"

Dax shrugged. "I don't know. She seemed a little odd. I don't know how else to describe it. At this point, I'm starting to question everything that we have dealt with, and I don't have any real answers. The only thing that I really know is that everything these days has me questioning things constantly."

"I don't like it," Rochelle said.

He hated the fact that he didn't have answers. He hated the fact that he didn't have his sister here now, and increasingly, he was starting to hate the fact that he didn't have somebody else to bounce questions off of the way that he'd had Desmond or the headmaster or Megan before.

There was something else that still plagued him too.

It was the attack.

There had been some kind of shadow fire, but it wasn't traditional essence. That bothered him, though he wasn't sure that it needed to, or that there was anything about it that he would be able to find—or even understand.

Finally, Cedrick and Gia finished their sparring, and they joined them. Cedrick wiped a bead of sweat off his forehead, grinning as he looked around before settling his gaze on Rochelle.

"You know, I'm getting good enough that I should be able to teach you soon."

Gia snorted. "He's not, so don't let him tell you that."

"Don't worry. He doesn't look like he knows how to dance. Besides, Dax has been practicing with me."

"Oh?" Cedrick asked, looking over at Dax and winking.

"And what sort of things has he been demonstrating? More dancing?"

Dax borrowed earth from Gia, sending a rumbling streak toward Cedrick that toppled him.

Cedrick got up with a grin. "Somebody's awfully sensitive about these things," he said.

"Why don't you go and get your class schedules?" Rochelle said. "We have class tomorrow, and we need to be ready, especially because…"

Dax wasn't even sure there was an answer to her "especially because."

Because they had to get back to classes? Because they had to get back to a sense of normalcy? Or because they still didn't know what they were dealing with or whether there were any other dangers inside of the city?

He followed the others as they made their way to the temporary office building and collected their schedules. Everybody was quiet as they checked their lists. For the most part, they had the same classes, other than Rochelle, who did not have valor and instead had multiple water seminars.

"More seminars?" Dax asked.

She shrugged. "They are simple. Or at least, they are supposed to be simple. They aren't always. But they give me a chance to learn more about healing. And if I prove myself, by the time I reach my second year, I can take more advanced healing." She looked at the others. "So what should we do today? We only have today left before classes kick off again."

"I'd rather spend it *out* of the library," Cedrick said.

He still needed to find information about Raisor, but he hadn't learned anything in the library. Neither had Rochelle, and the two of them were both capable researchers. The fact that neither of them had come up with anything was a little worrisome for Dax.

They ended up wandering the streets of the city, stopping at a few stores and a few street vendors, where the others bought things, though Dax did not. At one point, Cedrick made a joke about it, but Dax just shrugged. He hadn't needed any money inside of the Academy, but outside of the Academy, he was in short supply of funds, and it felt awfully strange for him to even consider borrowing from anybody given the fact that he was a Nelson and was expected to be able to handle his own finances. He was embarrassed to tell the others about what had happened with the trunk.

At one point, he thought he caught sight of the familiar flash of Karelly's hair, but when he hurried forward, he realized it wasn't her. He hadn't seen her at the Academy since break.

He went back to Rochelle's room.

He and Rochelle sat up, talking into the night, her sharing stories of her childhood and Dax talking about his parents, something that he rarely shared with much of anybody. He focused mostly on the stories about his mother, and at one point, Rochelle called him out on it.

"Why don't you talk about your father?"

"I was never really somebody he was proud of."

"Does he know the kinds of things you can do?"

"When he thought I was going to take on a fire essence, he wanted to make sure that I was skilled with valor. I did as good as I could, but even in that, I was never as capable as my brother Thomlin."

Dax thought about his brother, and how skilled he was with the valor blade, much better than Dax ever had been. His father had made a point of telling him that over and over again, reminding Dax of just how little he could do compared with his brother. There had been a time that had bothered him, that Dax had wanted nothing more than to be like his brother, as he had been proud of Thomlin. These days, he viewed his brother quite differently.

"Does it hurt you?"

Dax frowned, and he shook his head. "I suppose I'm disappointed I couldn't be what my father wanted, but maybe it doesn't matter. I'm going to have to find my own way and figure out my own essence, and..." He shrugged. "When I first gained this essence, I didn't know what to make of it, and I thought that it was a weakness. Now I see that it's something more. It has its own sort of strength. I don't necessarily have the kind of essence I could use if I were battling with somebody, but I can borrow on those around me."

"Well, you can use your own kind of essence through the essence blade, can't you?"

"I can, but it isn't as effective."

"Maybe you need to try to figure out a way to make it more effective."

Dax didn't know what that was going to entail, but at this point, it didn't even matter to him. It might matter to Rochelle, but to him, the only thing that really mattered was that he keep gaining control over his transference essence so that he could understand just how to use it, and so that he might be able to draw on it when he needed to.

"Let's get some rest," he said. "We have classes tomorrow. Essence manipulation. What a fun way to start."

"Oh, it won't be as bad as last term, will it?"

Dax shrugged. "I don't know. I don't see how it could be."

Chapter Thirty-Six

As they sat the next morning in Professor Jamesh's class, he began the term by sharing with them that they were going to have to have complete control over their essence before their next tests, and they were going to have to use it in a series of targeted attacks in order to pass.

Rochelle leaned over to Dax, and she dropped her voice. "This is really aggressive pacing. I think this is second-year stuff he wants us to do."

"So maybe it's still tied to the earlier attack?"

"Or maybe it's because of the most recent attack," she went on.

Professor Jamesh talked to them about essence and manipulation.

"The next step of what you will need to learn for this term is how to express your own essence. It is going to involve universal techniques. Each essence type can radiate essence in a specific pattern. Not all essence can be expressed the same way, but most can be. We are going to work on various techniques that will help you figure out what you need to do."

Dax wasn't exactly sure if he was going to be able to express his essence.

He had used an essence blade to do something similar, and had a measure of control with that method, but that wasn't what the professor was talking about.

He didn't know what, in particular, he was going to need to do once he expressed his essence.

Could he even do anything? The way that he used essence was different. Transference didn't really have anything that Dax thought he could express, not in particular.

"You will feel the essence inside of yourself, and you will be able to feel the way that it courses through you. Once you begin to master that, the next step is for you to work on pushing it through yourself."

"You need to pay attention," Gia said, elbowing him.

Dax looked over. "I'm paying attention."

"Are you? You don't really seem like you're paying attention. And this is something that you need to get down."

"I can express essence."

Professor Jamesh hadn't said anything about needing to use his own essence, had he? What did it matter if Dax was drawing upon other types of essence, after all? The only thing that mattered was that he express essence. He could draw water from Rochelle sitting next to him, he could use life from Cedrick—though Cedrick's life essence was a little unusual—and he could use earth from Gia.

What he really wanted was to try to work on fire.

He focused on the different types of essence that were available in class. Everybody was murmuring to each other, as they were all working on their essence types and practicing various forms of manipulation, and so as Dax expressed a little bit of fire, he could feel it drawing off one of the students nearby.

And they jumped.

Maybe Dax had drawn too much.

Gia shot him a look. "Like I said," she mouthed at him. "You shouldn't be doing that."

"You just worry about you," Dax said.

She shook her head.

Professor Jamesh remained oblivious, standing in front of the board and continuing to expand upon the aspects of essence manipulation that they were going to need to know for this term.

"This will be how those of you who have reached second-tier acolyte will be able to progress to the third tier. Once you do that, you will find your appreciation, and your understanding, of essence has magnified. It is imperative that you have that opportunity because otherwise you will not be able to continue on toward wielder status."

It was the professor's way of saying they would fail out of the Academy. Dax recognized that.

But what would it mean for him? What did it mean for any of them?

He still wasn't sure how to quantify essence.

When class was over, he hesitated a moment before heading up to the professor. "How do we determine our essence level?" he asked.

He frowned at him. "It is a series of tests that happen prior to graduation. But then, each test that you take at the Academy is a test of progression."

"What about last term, when we were taking more advanced testing?"

He frowned. "I suppose that would complicate things. But I doubt that anyone here at the Academy has moved beyond second tier. It is theoretically possible, but we will see as the term progresses if you are advancing more rapidly than we would have expected. If so, it is a simple matter to challenge you, if that is your concern."

He hadn't been concerned about it, but at least it made a little bit of sense. He nodded. "Thank you, Professor."

Then he headed out, where he found Gia frowning at him.

"Why did you use hers?"

"What?" Cedrick asked.

"He used her essence. I saw it."

"Because I can't express transference essence like that," Dax said.

"I think it's because you haven't tried. You need to learn how to use transference the same way that other people use their essence. You can't rely on someone else's essence all the time."

"Why are you so upset about it?" Cedrick asked.

"Because he is training with a crutch," Gia said, turning to look at Dax. "And I don't want him to. I want him to train with his own essence so that he can use it the way he's capable of doing."

"I don't understand the anger," Rochelle said.

Gia shot her a look. "Don't you start in on me too. You're helping him. Let him practice and learn what he needs to control his essence. If we keep helping him, and letting him draw on us, he never will master what he needs to know. If something were to happen—"

"Easy," Cedrick said. "We'll work with him. He's been working with us, so maybe it's time that we return the favor."

He hadn't even considered the fact that he wasn't using his own essence. He was, but he wasn't at the same time.

"Thanks for the reminder. I will work on it."

"You had better," Gia said. "And if you need help, you can just ask us. We ask enough of you the way that it is already."

She turned and spun away, leaving Dax staring after her.

"She's just full of contradictions," Cedrick said.

"She's a Stonewall," Rochelle said.

Cedrick frowned at her. "What's that supposed to mean?"

"It just means that you can't know a lady," Rochelle said, and she looked over at Dax before following Gia.

Dax stood, wondering if maybe Gia was right in what she had said to him. There were times when he agreed that he needed to use other essence around him, and would have to draw on what was there; otherwise, he would be limited. Ever since going to the serpent stairs a second time, he had a greater ability to use and manipulate that essence.

But he did need to understand his own essence better.

While standing there next to Cedrick, he noticed Karelly carrying several books.

And a strange tingling on the back of his neck provided a warning.

"Why is the Great Serpent warning me about her?" Dax murmured.

"What was that?"

He shook his head. "Probably nothing. Or maybe not nothing. Maybe it's just my imagination. But it seems like the Great Serpent is warning me about Karelly. I just don't know why."

Chapter Thirty-Seven

TRANSFERENCE CLASS WAS QUIET.

At least, it was quiet for Dax.

The class was a large one—it seemed more than just Gia had decided to join advanced transference. It was easily the same size as his essence manipulation class, which was his largest class.

Dax stood off to the side, near the frosthoof pen, while the others gathered. He had come out to transference on the first day of classes hoping that he might be able to participate, but Professor Madenil had waved him away.

"You just standing there?"

Dax turned to see one of the other students, though he didn't think she was a first-year student. Dax knew most of the first-year students, at least by sight. This one was an older brown-haired girl with an easy smile. She stood in front of the frosthoof pen, her hand resting in front of the bars. But that wasn't the only thing that Dax noticed about her. What he noticed more was the way essence flowed from her, flowing from the frosthoof into her, where she then sent it circling before she released it.

She was *quite* skilled with transference.

But he didn't think that she had a transference essence like he did. He didn't know what kind of essence she had, but from the way that she was standing, it seemed as if…

She had water. But not just water. Something about what she did suggested cold.

Ice?

"I'm just standing here," he said, frowning and shrugging at her. "Professor Madenil decided I don't get to spend much time in class these days."

She turned to him, and she seemed to regard him in a way that she had not before. Finally, she nodded slowly. "You're that first-year student. Some sort of prodigy?"

"I wouldn't say I was a prodigy," Dax said, "just that my essence seems to lend itself to transference."

She turned back to the frosthoof. "Did she tell you anything about these? They're dangerous and more troublesome than the cattle that we have most first-years work with. I can feel something familiar about their essence, but I can't quite get it."

"Ice," Dax said, approaching.

From up close, Dax could feel the essence radiating from the creature, though he wasn't willing to attempt to draw on it, or to even hold it. He didn't know if the frosthoof would allow him to.

"Right," she said. "Ice. Can you feel it?"

Dax shook his head. "Not really, but I can transfer some of it." He shrugged. "I don't know if that makes any sense."

"Well, when you start to transfer essence, you get to

know the nature of it. Bessie here is perfectly content with me transferring her essence, but not all of them like that."

Dax started to smile at her before he turned his attention to her frosthoof. "Bessie? You named it?"

"Oh, I didn't name her. She gave me her name."

For a moment, Dax felt his breathing slow, and his heart stopped. The frosthoof had given a name? He had known about sentient creatures, and he wanted to know more about them, but...

But he realized the girl was playing with him.

"Is that right? Well, this one gave me his name," Dax said. "Marcus."

"Oh, yeah? Marcus is a pretty good name for a frosthoof, but not as good as Bessie."

Dax chuckled. He focused on the frosthoof that he had named Marcus, trying to draw its essence out, and as he did, he could feel some of its resistance to him. It was cold, and in this case, it was requiring him to try to trap some essence inside of himself. For a moment, it lingered. It was faint, cold, and then he began to pull some of the essence down inside of himself, thinking that if nothing else, he might be able to use that blurring of essence in order for him to pull on some other aspect of it. But as he did, the frosthoof—Marcus—started to resist him in a way that Dax wasn't sure he could overpower.

There was a part of him that didn't know if he even wanted to try to overwhelm an essence like this. He had to get a better understanding of what it involved to transfer. There had to be some technique he might learn.

"What are you doing with him?"

Dax looked up. He thought that maybe Professor Madenil had come over, but she was still talking to the first-year students, working with them on transference with the cattle. From what he could overhear, it was mostly review. His friends would have little difficulty with it.

"I'm just showing him Bessie," the girl said.

A taller boy with a ragged-looking cloak strode over. He smelled of hay, and he had a bit of dirt on his jacket and a long, slender stick in hand. "Don't let her harass you too much," he said. He thrust out one hand. "I'm Wiloph." He nodded to the girl. "And she's Alex. She can be a bit of a pain, especially with new students. Professor Madenil told me we were getting a first-year student here. Didn't think you would be able to do so much transference already though."

Wiloph was looking at Dax, and it occurred to him that Wiloph must be aware of what Dax was doing. He had been transferring essence from the creature near him, not even paying much attention to what he was doing. And as he did, he felt something flowing from the frosthoof, cold and comfortable. He sent it out, and then he left it swirling in the air. That must've been what Wiloph was identifying, especially because Dax hadn't been confining it at all.

"I have a bit of a skill with transference," Dax explained.

"We don't get too many second-year students who want to spend much time with transference."

"Why not?" Dax asked, looking over at the cluster of first-year students. There were quite a few.

"Well, assuming you pass advanced transference, you don't need to take it in your second year. It's an elective."

Dax hadn't known. "So everybody here is—"

"Trying not to take this class next time," Wiloph said, shrugging. "By the time you get to your second year, the class size is *much* smaller."

"And a little bit more open ended," Alex said.

"What you mean, 'open ended'?"

"It means that we don't have structured class time," Wiloph said. "She lets us come in here, work with the animals, as long as we provide some care for them. And as long as we do a good job, work with her at least twice a week, we'll almost always pass."

"Almost always?" Dax asked.

"Oh, don't scare him," Alex said, waving her hand and turning her attention back to Bessie. "He's just saying that some people get into second-year transference, and they seem to think that they don't need to spend nearly as much time as they should. They tend to drop off. So Professor Madenil simply dismisses them. They're failed out."

"Does failing an elective have the same consequences as failing a regular class?"

"I don't know," she said, turning her attention back to the frosthoof. "I don't intend to fail."

"I doubt you will. You're here constantly," Wiloph said. He shook his head. "She really likes animals."

"I figured that people would be here because they were really good at transference," Dax said.

"Oh, that's some of it," Wiloph said. He joined Dax at the pen, and he looked in at the frosthoof, stretching his finger out. He wiggled it, and it seemed as if the frosthoof nibbled at it before withdrawing. "But not all of it. Some of it is just people's interest in animals, and how much they want to spend time with them. To be honest, that's a big part of it. We get pretty interesting animals once you get into the second year. Not just the frosthooves, though these are the most visible. Professor Madenil has an entire barn filled with strange creatures."

That was what the professor had suggested he was

going to need to be a part of. Dax had thought he was going to work with her there though. "What do you do there?"

"Mostly we feed them," Alex said. "That's part of the responsibility, at least for a second-year student. Occasionally we get to work with them—especially with some of the easier animals to practice transference. Some of the harder ones are reserved for third tier or higher."

"Fat lot of that," Wiloph said, shaking his head. "We have two third-tiers and one fourth-tier. Not too many people interested in transference. Most people like animals," he explained, "but it's a lot of work the further that you get, especially because you have to pull some strange hours."

"I just figured that people would enjoy transference because of the way you get to work with different types of essence."

"Well, once you get past advanced transference, the amount of essence that you can actually use starts to go down." Wiloph glanced over to where the other first-year students were working with the cattle. "You get into working with some harder creatures, and while they do have useful essence, it's really difficult to draw anything out. You can spend entire months working with their essence and still not manage to draw that much out of them."

"Months?" Dax asked.

"Sometimes," he said. "And I think the professors like to keep some of the more obscure animals here because they want to test whether you can do anything with them. It's really more of an educational situation, not so much that you are going to ever really be able to use it, nor do I think they intend for you to be able to use anything that you're learning here."

"That's not true," Alex challenged. "If you can manipulate essence and function with transference on some of these creatures, the chances are quite high that you will be able to transfer essence from anything you encounter." She looked over at Dax, and she shrugged at him. "They assume that people who are interested in transference will spend more time along the unclaimed lands and then beyond, exploring on behalf of the Emperor."

"Is that what you intend?" Wiloph asked.

Dax frowned. He hadn't realized that about transference, but truth be told, he didn't really know much about it, nor about what it might mean for him and his future. He had never really intended to specialize in it, as he had sort of just fallen into it, but it did make sense to him.

"I guess I hadn't thought about it," Dax said. "My family lives along the border, so we're near the unclaimed lands, but my father mostly hunts the creatures that come through, and he doesn't try to use any transference on them."

"Hunts?" Alex asked.

"Right," Dax said. He mimed using an essence blade to carve through one of the creatures. When he did, the frosthoof nearest him—Marcus—reared back, pulling away.

Dax reacted and pulled on essence, trying to soothe the creature.

He could feel the essence reacting to him. The frosthoof had known what he was doing.

Had it known that?

"I see," Alex said, and she reached out, patting Bessie on head. "It seems as if they don't really care for that, do they?"

She strode away, leaving Dax with Wiloph.

Wiloph snorted. "Don't mind her. She gets a little touchy. She's *definitely* here because of the animals, but she does have a way with them. Some of them are a little more insightful than others, so I think your little frosthoof friend didn't care much for your movement."

"Are any of the animals smarter than others?"

Wiloph frowned, regarding Dax. "What do you mean?"

"I don't know," Dax said. "I guess I'm just trying to get at if any of the animals seem more aware, like this frosthoof was when I made that movement."

Wiloph nodded slowly. "Most are like the frosthoof, but sometimes you get a sense that they know what you're attempting to do with their essence. I stopped really thinking about it much early on in my second year. I just want to learn how to draw that essence, and once I get control over it, then I can use it. That's my plan. I don't have much experience beyond the unclaimed lands, but I'm hopeful that I'll get assigned to it because the people who do are able to bring back some pretty impressive things. When you do that, the Emperor favors you." He grinned, then reached in, and he smacked the frosthoof on the snout before withdrawing his hand. The frosthoof jerked its antlers toward him. "Although if you already have experience along the unclaimed land, you know this."

Wiloph wasn't going to be somebody that he could learn from, but maybe Alex would be. Dax found himself watching her as she stood off to the side, leaning down and touching something that was just hidden behind the pen. Dax separated from Wiloph, and he hurried around, but by the time he got there, he couldn't see what it was that Alex was doing, but could only sense the essence she'd been using.

She glowered at him and then strode away.

There had to be answers here. Dax just needed to figure out where to find them.

Chapter Thirty-Eight

DAX FELL INTO A RHYTHM OVER THE NEXT FEW DAYS.

After the strangeness of the attack on the Academy last term, along with whatever was happening out in the forest, he'd wanted normalcy. Classes made everything better. He enjoyed the time studying, as he felt as if it gave him a sense of purpose, but it also gave him a distraction. He had visited his room a few times, checking to see if there were any other disturbances or signs of anybody else who might've attacked his room, but Dax hadn't found anything. It didn't seem as if there were any new runes made, and the items that he had left in the room so that he could tell if there were any other disturbances had been left untouched. At least, as far as he had been able to tell. He still tried to reach his sister, but if Megan was listening, she gave no sign of it, and she made no attempt to reach him either.

Dax wasn't uncomfortable sleeping on Rochelle's floor, but eventually he would need to clear out his room and secure it so that he could get back to a sense of normalcy within the

Academy. If Desmond were around, he could ask him how to do that and whether there were any protective runes that he might know of that Dax could use. He was tempted to speak to Alibard, though Dax didn't know if he would even be open to his questioning. And if he mentioned what had happened, there was a possibility that he would take a more active role in the situation, which Dax didn't want.

"I don't mind if you stay on my floor," Rochelle said when he mentioned it to her.

"I know you don't mind," Dax said, and he held her gaze for a moment before turning away. "But I can't imagine that you really like me spending so much time there. A person needs their own space."

She chuckled. "Maybe *you* do, but I grew up sharing a room. It's really not that bad. Well, it can be a pain when I have to change, but I just do that in the bath anyway."

"I'd really like to get back into my room, but I would also like to know what someone was trying to do to me."

"Maybe they weren't trying to do anything to you. Maybe it was just a way of trying to communicate with you."

"We've been through this," he said.

And they had. They had kicked around different ideas about what had happened, and the purpose behind the markings, both of them theorizing about the reasons that they were there, and none of them having any clear idea about what it might be.

"I know we have," she said. "Then go back to Alibard. See what he can offer. Maybe he would be willing to share with you more about what he and the others learned about the attack."

"I doubt he's going to be that thrilled to share anything

with me about the attack. You saw how he looked when we were there. He didn't like that at all."

"Because we *were* foolish," she said, shrugging. "I mean, we're students. We shouldn't be rushing into a burning Academy building, especially one that has some sort of essence-manipulated fire causing the flames. We should've been smarter than that."

"But because of us—"

"Because of us, we managed to put the fire out," she said, holding his gaze for a moment. "And we managed to secure the flare."

"Fine," he said. "We didn't know what we needed to do, and we didn't know if there was anything that we needed to be concerned about, but that doesn't change—"

"It changes everything," Rochelle said. "And don't pretend like it doesn't. Go to Alibard, see if there's anything that he might be able to help us with, or you with, if that's what you're so concerned about. I know that you want answers, and I know that you think that you should—and could—uncover something more about all of this, but I just don't know what to tell you about it."

Dax looked toward the office building, which he had been avoiding. "You're probably right," he said.

She chuckled. "Probably?"

"Fine. You're right. Is that what you want to hear?"

"I want you to acknowledge my brilliance." She spread her hands off to either side of her, then grinned at him. "And I want you to use the resources we have. It doesn't have to be just the four of us. Well five, at least when Desmond is around. We need to take advantage of others. We can use their help. In fact, I think that we *need* to use their help. We don't even know what danger we are in."

As they headed inside of the building, he hurried past

the registrar's office, but he had the distinct sense that she knew he was there and might even have sat up as he passed. Maybe that was just his imagination. Then they reached Alibard's office.

Alibard generally liked him. Ever since Dax had shown predilection for the runes, Alibard had wanted Dax to help work with other students who needed assistance, something that he had come to find about many of his instructors. It was obviously the feeling of the Academy that somebody with some skill in a particular area would use that skill to help others who had a detriment in that same area. Dax didn't mind that, generally. If somebody had skills, he agreed they should share them. It was just that there were times when he didn't necessarily want to be treated differently, not only with runes but also with valor, and now with transference. It seemed as if there were so many different areas where he was set aside as an example.

Not essence manipulation though. Or politics.

He knocked, waiting for a moment. When Professor Alibard called him inside, Dax entered. The professor was seated at his desk with a large piece of paper stretched out in front of him. He didn't look up. "My office hours are not until... Oh, Mr. Nelson." He frowned, and with a flick of his wrist, the door closed behind him. Dax couldn't be certain, but he thought that he placed a wind essence shield around him as well. It would be a faint, little more than a translucent shift of essence, and as he tightened down his own essence, looking at the band of essence that Professor Alibard had used, he could see something about it, only what he could see was different than what he would've expected. It wasn't just wind. There was a trace of something else within it. A bit of darkness.

Earth, perhaps?

He had always seen variations in essence before, but lately, Dax had begun to notice distinct characteristics of each type of essence, enough so that he could see the striations that bound one essence to another.

When he had followed what Professor Alibard had done before, he had never noticed any earth essence within it. He had only noticed wind.

"I wanted to talk to you about the runes that I brought you before."

Professor Alibard sat up, and he clasped his hands in front of him, looking across the desk at Dax. "Only those? Not what happened to the administration building?"

Dax shrugged. "I didn't get the sense anybody wanted to talk about what happened at the administration building. Anybody that I have asked has brushed it off, as if there were nothing dangerous that happened."

"Oh, we only do that to those who didn't actually see it themselves. Well, and experience it themselves."

He motioned to a chair, and with a burst of wind, he dragged it closer to Dax. Once again, Dax had the distinct sense of a hint of earth essence within it, though he wasn't exactly sure what that essence was doing, nor did he know whether there was anything there that he might be able to transfer. He was tempted to try, but then again, he knew better than to randomly begin to transfer essence from others, especially professors, when he didn't know how they might react if he were to do so.

"It's good that you came, Mr. Nelson. I do think that we need to discuss your presence there that evening."

"I told you—"

Professor Alibard waved his hand, and he leaned forward. "You told me that you needed to have some sort of fire essence to tamp down what was happening. And given that you have shown no predilection for fire, I think that we should revisit that topic."

Dax's heart hammered for a moment, and he debated how much he wanted to share. Then again, it might not even matter. When the headmaster had been here, there had been others who had known about his essence. Now, with the headmaster missing, he didn't even know if there was anybody who he could keep that information from. Perhaps the professors, but eventually, Dax suspected that he was going to need to share with someone that they might help him understand his essence, and help him learn how to best utilize it.

"I have a bit of an affinity for fire," Dax admitted.

"Only fire?"

The question was soft, subtle, and Dax breathed out. He focused on Professor Alibard, and as he did, he began to use transference.

He started with wind, before realizing that he could feel the other element within him, something of a bit of earth, though it was faint, and not tethered to him the way he would've expected it to be. He held onto it, and he could feel the energy. There was a strain there, but it wasn't a strain that Dax couldn't overpower. It was just something that he felt within him. He began to draw wind, and then turned it, siphoning it outward.

As soon as he did, Professor Alibard sat up straighter.

"Wind?"

"Not exactly," Dax said. "I have what I have taken to calling transference essence. I can use essence around me. While I have my own sort of essence, it's not quite as functional as others. At least, not as functional unless I use another type of essence with it."

Alibard pressed his hands over the page that he had

been working on, smearing ink as he did, seeming unmindful of it. "You can draw other essence. And that is why you went into the building, because you thought that you might be able to do that with fire."

Dax nodded. "I did it with fire. I had to transfer some of the fire into an essence blade, but then I drew it into the runes that I placed, and then outside of the building itself."

Alibard was silent for a few moments. "You placed those containment runes?"

Dax flushed. "I'm sorry. I didn't mean to damage anything. I was just trying to trap some of the fire and did the only thing that I could think of."

"Do I give you the impression I am angry with you, Mr. Nelson?"

"I suppose not."

He shook his head. "No. I am not angry. It was just that I had not expected that any student would've been responsible for placing those containment runes. For one, the substrate would've been quite difficult, but you having the ability to transfer, as you say, would have solved that piece of the dilemma. So I suppose that makes sense. But the complexity of the rune is what surprises me. No first-year student should have been able to draw anything quite like that."

"I was just copying what you had demonstrated in class," Dax said.

Hadn't he?

In the heat of the moment, Dax had been so focused on the containment rune, about finding some way to secure the fire so that it didn't escape and about trying to save him and Rochelle, that he hadn't paid attention to what he was creating.

What if he had done something more?

There was the possibility that his essence allowed him to transfer knowledge that he hadn't even been aware that he was doing. That was one aspect that he needed to try to investigate.

"I demonstrated some basic containment runes," he said, nodding to him, "but little more than that. The type of rune that was placed had a measure of complexity to it that was surprising, even to me. Had you seen those before?"

"I… Well, I don't know."

"Interesting," Professor Alibard said. "Well. That explains one question that I had, and one that the Guardians were not able to satisfactorily answer for me, though they continue to search."

"They're still here?"

"They will be here for quite some time," he said. "At least, I suspect so. We probably will not even know that they are here. But that is not what you came to ask."

"It's about the rune."

"I've already told you that I haven't seen anything quite that complex. Even your rune, Mr. Nelson, wasn't nearly as complex as that. You may have access to some of my older works, if you want to research it yourself. Otherwise, I'm happy to work privately with you, if you think that you may be able to find something."

He had no idea how working with Professor Alibard was going to help him, especially if Professor Alibard didn't have the answers, but the offer of books did sound like it might be more beneficial.

"You have some books that might be helpful?"

"Mostly older works," Professor Alibard said, turning toward a bookshelf that was cluttered with piles of books. He motioned toward it. "Take what you want. Borrow it, I should say, and return when you've studied what you need. These are advanced, Mr. Nelson. And generally I hold them for postgraduate students who are interested in mastering runes. But in your case, given your predilection and your obvious intrigue, I will permit you to access them. Do not damage them."

"Thank you."

Dax gathered the books, and then he stacked them, taking a few more than what he had intended before heading out of the office. He held the books under his arm and smiled to himself.

At least this was a start. He had no idea what he might find, but at least it felt like he was heading toward something rather than waiting for something to happen to him. Maybe he could understand the runes that had been placed in his room. And if he could find something in these books to secure the flare until Desmond arrived—or somebody else who could keep it safe from the Order—it would be time well spent.

He just hoped he could do it in time.

Chapter Thirty-Nine

"I'M SURPRISED THAT HE ALLOWED YOU TO TAKE THESE books," Rochelle said, looking at the stack that Dax had piled on the table in the library.

He had found her seated at their typical table, positioned toward one of the back walls on the third sublevel. They tended to go deeper into the library these days, partly because it was a bit quieter there and had been somewhat peaceful during the term break, but now that school was back in session, Dax wasn't sure how long that would last. There might be other students interested in spending time in this sublevel. Neither of them really understood how many of the upper-level students were interested in taking that space, but they, as first-year students, would by necessity not have priority.

"I think he's curious about what I did inside of the administrative building. I thought it was just placing a containment rune that he had taught us."

"It was similar, but it wasn't the same," Rochelle said.

"You knew?"

She shrugged. "To be honest, I wasn't really paying that much attention to them. When you said that it was a containment rune, I assumed that was something you'd learned from Professor Alibard's class, but I struggled with those. It takes me a few days of really reading everything that we go through for me to master it. So if there was something that you picked up on in class, who was I to challenge it?" She smiled. "Can you imagine what they were thinking?"

"What who were thinking?"

"The others. The people who were looking into all of this. They might have thought that there was some significant rune master, and given that you were using fire in it as a containment pattern, maybe they were trying to figure out what you intended to do with that."

Dax took the first of the books, and he opened it up, beginning to work through it. There were depictions of each of the runes, along with a detailed description of the intent behind it. But they were not exactly straightforward. Even if Dax knew what a particular rune would do, it was a matter of making it that presented the challenge. There was a skill involved.

Dax certainly had experience with rune making, as he had been doing it from a young age, even while growing up on his manor house. But he didn't have experience with the complexity of some of the runes that he saw here. If he could learn something by studying—or using transference —then maybe he would understand what the runes were for.

By the end of the afternoon, Dax was tired.

When they'd finished studying, Dax was tempted just to

go back to his room—well, Rochelle's room—but he felt this strange tension building within him, and he wanted nothing more than to try to get out of the city, if only to wander and stretch his legs. When he said as much to the others, Rochelle looked at him, frowning. "You aren't going alone."

"You don't have to babysit me," he said. "I don't intend to go out into the forest, especially not at night."

Cedrick grinned. "I'm not sure that we can trust him. Look at him. He's got that look in his eyes, one that tells me that he probably wants to go running off, maybe after those strange creatures. I bet he's trying to worship them."

"Would you stop?" he said.

"Fine, fine," Cedrick said. "Let's get out so that we don't end up returning too late."

They headed into the city. After they passed the threshold of the Academy grounds, there was a strange sort of energy in the air that Dax was aware of. Maybe it was just his imagination, or maybe it was his growing sense of essence that alerted him to everything. Whatever it was, Dax felt much more attuned to these things than he had been before.

Rochelle noticed him looking toward the artisan district at one point, and she nudged him. "He's not there. We will know when he returns. Just... relax, I guess."

"It's difficult to relax when we are responsible for something as valuable as what we have," he said.

"Right, but you need to relax. Otherwise it just looks suspicious."

He started off, letting himself get drawn toward a more vibrant part of the city, where there was a street market. Even at this time of the day, the market was active. There were street performers, acrobats, minstrels, and a few story-tellers, all spread throughout the plaza. Street carts and vendors were scattered along the street, and people mingled. It created a cacophony of noise, a chaotic energy, and to Dax's eyes, it showed off different types of essence. There were quite a few people with essence control within the city, partly because of its proximity to the Academy, but mostly because everybody had some measure of essence, whether or not they gained control over it.

As they were heading through the city, he caught sight of a familiar student.

"Isn't that Tarin?" Dax asked.

He was a tall, slender young man, with deep-set eyes. He was walking with a pair of people who Dax didn't recognize.

"I think so," Rochelle said. "What's he doing here? I thought he got expelled?"

"I thought that I'd heard the same. Because of some rune-marked weapon."

Dax followed him, though he wasn't sure what he was going to find. As he hurried toward the other man, Dax weaved through the crowd until Tarin caught a glimpse of him. He said something to the others who were with him before waiting.

Dax glanced at his friends. "Just wait here for a moment."

"Dax," Rochelle said.

"It's fine." He hurried forward, over to Tarin.

"What are you doing following me?" Tarin asked.

Dax breathed out heavily. "I just wanted to ask you about—"

"I don't want to talk about my expulsion. Nobody really seems to care that I didn't have what they claimed I did."

"You didn't have a rune-marked weapon? That's what the rumors are."

"I know what the rumors are," he said.

"I'm only asking because I've been seeing strange runes."

"And you think I'm responsible? I was in basic runes, Dax."

"No," Dax said. "I just wanted to know if you could tell me more about where you got the weapon."

"I didn't get it. Someone put in my room."

"Somebody just put it in your room?"

"Well, they must have. And then my room was turned over, and they thought that I was responsible for part of the attack on the Academy. I was branded a member of the Cult of the Dragon. You know how hard that is to move past, Dax?"

Dax flicked his gaze up ahead to where the other two were waiting. One was a tall man with a hooded cloak covering his features. The other was a blonde-haired woman with dark skin and eyes that seemed to take in everything.

Members of the Order? Or were they with the Cult?

Or maybe they were with neither. Maybe Dax was just reading into all of it unnecessarily.

"I know how hard it is to move past. I—"

"Just let me be. We were fairly friendly," he said.

He spun, leaving Dax.

When Dax headed back to the others, he shook his head.

"Somebody placed the rune-marked weapon in his room," Dax said. "They did it to make it look like the Cult was responsible."

Rochelle's eyes widened.

"So you're thinking…"

Dax shrugged. "I don't know. I guess I hadn't really given it a lot of thought. I thought that maybe something strange was happening that was tied to the Order, but what if this was just somebody playing some dangerous prank?"

"That's awful," Gia said.

"It's the kind of thing Karelly would do," Cedrick shrugged. "That's what we're talking about, right? It is the kind of thing she would do. I don't know what sort of issues she had with Tarin, but maybe she's trying to make it look like you were a part of the same thing."

Dax thought about all the times that he had seen Karelly since the return.

And she had seemed as if she had more money.

Maybe she had *his* money.

Rochelle pressed her hand onto his shoulder. "You can't do anything about it now. You can't prove anything."

"I know. It doesn't make it right."

"No. But we can look into it. All of us. And if she had something to do with it, then…" She shrugged. "Well, maybe we can make it right."

Making it right. Dax wasn't sure if there was going to be any way to make it right, though he could think of one thing that would help: get Tarin reinstated. He didn't know the boy all that well, but if Karelly was responsible, then helping him would help Dax and his irritation with her.

They started toward the market when Dax noticed something overhead. It was on a building, situated near the second story, beside a narrow glowing light.

He found his attention drawn to it, and he hurried over while the others watched, waiting to see what it was that Dax was doing. At least they were accustomed to some of his quirks at this point.

Rochelle followed him, and as he looked up at it, she leaned close.

"Is it a street marker?"

It didn't look anything like what he had seen in the artisan district that marked the locations there.

"It's a runic marker," Dax said, and he frowned at it. "And I can't tell what, but something about it strikes me as similar to what I found in my room and…" He lowered his voice, turning to Rochelle. "And similar to what I found in the forest."

"So you think this is one of those complex runes. Out here, near the market, and up there?"

He nodded, feeling like that was exactly what it was. But why? These runes seemed as if they were activated, unlike the ones in his room. Otherwise, there were similarities to them.

Dax set off, chasing the runes, trying to make sense of what was there and what he could find out about it.

Rochelle stayed a step behind him, though she didn't speak. Dax appreciated that.

"He did this when we were in the forest as well," Cedrick said. "So am I right in assuming that he found something?"

"Looks like it," Gia said. "But what was it?"

"He says it was runes like what he found in the forest, and similar to the one that was in his room, but…" He could almost sense Rochelle shrugging behind him, and he was thankful that she didn't say anything more than that.

Dax followed the faint connection, and it brought him to a small temple to the Great Serpent, made of solid gray stone with what looked like ancient runes that had faded over time marked into it. It had been a long time since anyone had truly worshipped the Great Serpent, though there were always those who viewed that power as something to celebrate. These days, the old temples were held in high regard simply because of their craftsmanship—and the runes used to create them. The runes on it glowed, not even the simple one that caught his attention. That was what drew him.

When he motioned to it, Rochelle crouched down, and she waved her hand over it. Dax had the distinct sense of her essence flowing inside of her, and then washing outward. She was probing with water. She sat back, looking up at him.

"I can't really tell what's here. I can feel something, and I think that must be what you followed. How did you do that?"

"I can see it," Dax said.

"This one is different," she said, and she got to her feet, motioning to Gia. "See if earth tells you anything."

Gia frowned, but then she moved forward, beginning to probe. Dax wasn't sure if her use of earth was going to be destructive at all, as he had seen her use it in that way before, but as she probed, he noticed that there was no destruction. Earth simply flowed out of her, and she pushed some of that connection into the door. She paused for a moment, then she stood up.

"It's an earth-based rune, but not one I've felt before."

"How old do you think it is?"

"I don't know. It looks like the others," Rochelle said.

"Maybe older," Cedrick offered. He snapped his fingers, though it seemed to be more of a nervous tick than anything else. A few of his pink bubbles began to drift upward.

Dax frowned and looked at the runes again, then began to constrict his essence down until he noticed pale white lines. There was a subtlety to it. He could follow it. He let the trail guide him.

He hadn't gone very far before the essence flared again. He found another rune, this one on the ground. It was new, much like the others had been, and just as complicated.

"Does it mean anything that you have one on the ground, one close to the ground, and then one higher up?" Cedrick asked.

"Why would that matter?" Gia asked.

"I don't know. I'm just commenting on it."

Dax had no idea. The markers had to be connected, but he didn't know the purpose behind it. He needed a true rune master, and Dax was not one.

"Let's keep following," Dax said, "because I want as complete a picture as possible before I go to somebody else with this."

"Who are you going to with it?" Rochelle asked.

"There's nobody here that we can go to about this other than Alibard," Dax said.

"Does that worry you?"

He nodded. "A little bit. It feels like we are getting forced in a specific direction, and I don't know what to make of it."

Rochelle sighed. "I was hoping that it was just me who felt that way. Well, let's get going. We need to do this as quickly as we can and see if we can't figure anything out. Well, maybe if *you* can't figure anything out. You are the one with the transference cheat, after all."

"It's not a cheat," he said.

"It is for tests, not that I'm blaming you for taking advantage of it. But for this… Let's not call it a cheat. Let's call it our advantage. And let's take advantage of everything that we can."

So he set off, thinking about what it all could mean—
the different markers situated all around the city, and how
his findings might all be related. And more than that, he
wanted to know why the markers seemed as if they were
activated.

Chapter Forty

DAX HAD STAYED UP TOO LATE THE NIGHT BEFORE. HE HAD been following the markers throughout the city and found they created a zigzag pattern throughout the city, nothing at all symmetric or circular as he had first imagined. There had to have been two dozen of them in all, and for the most part, they were connected one to another. But not all of them were. Some of them seemed as if they connected to more than one, and there was one singular pattern that Dax had stumbled upon that didn't seem as if it was connected to anything.

Cedrick and Gia quickly grew bored of the search. They would lag behind, visiting with vendors, grabbing food and drink, or listening to musicians. Only Rochelle stayed with him, almost as if she feared him wandering off on his own. By the end of the evening, he had been more concerned than before, but the others had seemed less concerned.

In the morning, he woke up still sleepy. His head pounded, though he wasn't sure why. Maybe from keeping his essence constricted for as long as he had. It had been necessary, as otherwise Dax wasn't sure that he would've been able to see anything. The threads of essence around him had not provided any greater answers.

"You're already up?" Rochelle said.

"I have transference this morning," he said.

"What?" She laid staring straight up, and she squeezed her eyes shut. "It's too early for transference."

"It's my private lessons," he said.

She groaned. "That's right. Advanced transference, but *private* advanced transference."

Dax nodded. "I have no idea what that's going to entail, but today I get to go to the transference barn."

"I would've thought there was a fancier title for it."

Dax shrugged. "Apparently there are other creatures that Professor Madenil and some of the other transference professors keep there—more than just cattle or frosthooves."

"Just be nice to them," she said.

Dax sat up, rubbing the sleep from his eyes as he did. "Why would I *not* be nice to them?"

"Because you have this feeling that you don't mind using animals for transference, so I just want you to be nice."

"I've been nothing but good to those animals," Dax said.

"Anyway," she said, turning away from him and rolling back onto her side. "I'm going to get more sleep. I can meet with you later."

"The library?"

"I suppose."

He finished getting dressed, pulling on his boots and then deciding once again to bring his essence blade with him. Although there was the possibility that a first-year student with an essence blade might start drawing attention, he decided he wanted it with him anyway. He headed out, slipping out of the dorm in the early morning light. He wished that it weren't so early. After a night like the one before, where he had spent it wandering and testing for different strands of essence, he wanted nothing more than to get a good night of sleep. These days, Dax wasn't even sure what that looked like. A good night's sleep might be beyond him, at least until he could go back to his room, sleep on an actual bed rather than the floor, and have a chance to not fear the possibility of somebody breaking into his room and attacking him while he slept. Even inside of Rochelle's room, there was a bit of concern that something might happen. He was the target, wasn't he?

Although he wasn't sure whether that target was anything that he had to be afraid of, Dax wanted to be cautious. Given everything that had happened to him since he had come to the Academy, there was part of him that was on edge, worried about the types of things he had encountered, the types of things he still had yet to encounter. If only his sister would respond to him, whether because she was listening or because his mother had sent word to her. But she had not.

He followed the directions that he'd been given on how to find the transference barn. The building, situated at the edge of the Academy and closer to the edge of the city, was long and low ceilinged. Dax had passed the building a few times, and he had noticed that there were runic markers placed along the walls, but he had not given it much thought. He had thought that it was an old building, and possibly abandoned, as he never saw any students going inside of it. Shrubs grew along the walls, many of them a bit wild and unkempt. The ceiling itself was slightly sloped, as if to shed some of the rain, but it looked almost casually placed together. Some markings along the upper pitch of the roof suggested ancient writing, but Dax couldn't read it, so he stopped trying.

He picked his way forward, and once he reached the door, he hesitated in front of it, wondering if he was going to be welcomed. Professor Madenil had instructed him to join the other students, but he didn't have the sense that Professor Madenil was going to be there.

Maybe this was a mistake.

Why would it be though?

Dax was invited here, and as far as he knew, Professor Madenil wanted him to continue working with some of the other animals, and with other students. She wanted him to continue to understand how to use transference. And that was something that he wanted too, wasn't it?

He tested the door, found that it was locked, and was tempted to use transference on it to see if he might be able to unlock it, when he saw a cord near the door. A bell.

Dax pulled on it, and he waited.

He didn't have to wait long.

The door came rumbling open, sliding on some invisible track he couldn't see, and then a face looked out at him. It was one he remembered from the day before.

"I wasn't sure if you would make it," Alex said.

She turned, heading back into the building, not even giving Dax a chance to answer.

He stepped inside, and the smell struck him first.

It was a mixture of damp earth, dung, and something almost spicy, which Dax thought was strange. He pulled the door closed and looked for some way to lock it before realizing there was no need. As the door closed, an essence bar crossed it. He hadn't seen it from the outside, but once inside, he could easily follow the track of that essence band where it worked its way around the inside of the building.

The inside of the building was as low as it looked from the outside. There was an energy here that struck him as strange. He constricted his essence and saw flows of essence from all around him. A row of cages along one wall had one color of essence—this one a sickly green—while tables with small cages on it had other essences—this one a deep purple, so dark it was almost black. All around the room were other cages or partitions, and in the center of the room was a tall post that, even from here, Dax could feel the amount of earth worked into it, as if somebody had placed dozens upon dozens of essence runes into it in order to ensure it didn't shatter.

He stood transfixed.

"Are you just going to stand there?" Alex asked.

"I'm sorry," Dax said. "But I don't know what I'm supposed to do."

"Well, you're here to help, aren't you?" she asked. He nodded. "So help."

"How many people are here?"

She looked around before turning her attention back to him. "I see just the two of us."

"This is it?"

"Sometimes the professors help, but they have been a little preoccupied. There have been some transference hunters prowling about, and you know how Madenil feels about that."

"I have no idea," Dax said. He had no idea what a transference hunter was, for that matter.

Alex just shrugged.

"Where do I start?"

"Seeing as this is your first day, I will walk you through it. We have to feed the animals. Provide water. And if we have time," she said, glancing in his direction, "only then can you practice. Not until all the chores are done."

"I guess I was under the impression I would be working with the creatures."

"Oh, you will," she said, shrugging, "but again, only once everything is done. Not until then."

They started toward the row of holding cells near one side. It looked almost like a prison, as there were sections of stone with bars of metal that stretched from floor to ceiling. On the inside were strange-looking creatures, all about half Dax's size. They had massive heads and long arms with strange hooks on the ends of them. They were covered in a grayish fur, and their eyes carried a malevolence to them. Dax had never seen them, but he recognized what they were.

"Soilclaws?"

She nodded. "So you know about them."

"They come through the boundary of the unclaimed lands from time to time," he said.

"That's right," she said, her voice turning dark. "You're Dax Nelson."

"I didn't say I went hunting through the unclaimed land," Dax said hurriedly, realizing the source of her irritation. He didn't want to anger her, but at the same time, he also didn't know that there was any point in denying his family's responsibility for what they did. They served the Emperor, after all. Dax wasn't going to be ashamed of that.

"They have earth essence," he said, staring at them and realizing that it was a dense kind of earth essence. It seemed to be constricted tightly inside of their bodies, and it didn't go out into their limbs.

"Obviously," she said, glancing over at him.

Why was that obvious?

"What do they eat?"

"Well, that's actually surprising," she said, the question seeming to distract her from the irritation she'd had before, "as they like fruit and vegetables most of all. They'll eat some meat, but they prefer it to be rancid, which is disgusting. They have a predilection for such things." She shrugged. "Anyway. I like to give them fruits and vegetables because it makes them happy. And when they are happy, I am happier," she said, smiling to herself.

She crouched down and reached into a satchel that she was carrying over one shoulder, and tossed some apples, grapes, and tomatoes inside the enclosure. The soilclaw nearest them came scurrying forward, grabbing them off the ground. But he looked up at Dax the entire time, watching him with intensity. As the soilclaw moved, the earth essence within it seemed to move as well. It flowed from the central part of its body out into its arms, then its legs, before retreating.

"Like I said, they like fruits and vegetables. It's a treat."

The soilclaw put its back up against the wall. As soon as it did, Dax noticed the earth essence within the soilclaw starting to flow, as if it were going into the wall. There, it met some resistance. There was a flash, something that Dax suspected was only visible to him because of his connection to essence, but as soon as he saw it, he noticed the way that essences surged, and the soilclaw darted forward a step, almost as if shocked.

"What happened?"

She shrugged. "We haven't been able to tell. They probably use essence against the walls. The walls are protected, so if anything, they're testing the boundaries."

Dax was curious. Before moving on, he tried a small bit of transference, attempting to draw some earth from the creature. It was difficult to do so, as the soilclaw seemed to resist him. From the way the soilclaw was looking at him, the darkness in his eyes glowering at him, it seemed to Dax that it did realize that.

He hurried on, catching up to Alex as she fed treats to the next of the creatures. It was another soilclaw, and she tossed more fruits and vegetables inside. Much like the last time, the soilclaw scooped it up before backing away. This one didn't test the wall. Either it had already learned, or maybe the neighbor had communicated to it.

"It's not reacting the same as the last one," he said.

Alex shrugged. "Again, they all tend to be a little bit different. Soilclaws can be difficult to understand, but trust me when I tell you they are intriguing creatures."

"I'm sure they are," Dax said.

He could take his time here and question, he realized. Finish rounds with Alex, feeding the creatures, then he could work with transference. Maybe he could apply it to what he had experienced with the silk shatter.

"Come along," she said.

Dax followed her. They finished with the soilclaws before they moved on to a table with small cages, each of them containing tiny white-furred creatures. At the nearest one, Dax started to reach toward it, when she slapped his hand away.

"You want to lose a finger?"

Dax frowned. "It looks like a rabbit."

"Some rabbits," she said, and she grabbed a pair of tongs underneath the counter, dipping them into her satchel. She scooped out some raw meat with the tongs and held it toward the cage.

The small rabbit-like creature suddenly elongated, and an enormous mouth opened, with fangs that seemed much larger than its body should have. It darted toward the tongs, grabbing the meat out of them and yanking it away. There was a strange guttural grunt as the creature devoured the meat, faster than he would've expected.

He really would've lost a finger.

"What are those?"

"Oh," she started, "you don't have those along the unclaimed lands?"

"Nothing like that," Dax said.

"Weroxen. Feisty, almost violent. If you find them in the wild, you are better off just walking away."

"Walking?"

"They seem to notice movement," she said. "So if you walk, or stand still, they'll leave you alone. But if you have the right kind of essence, you can just smack them a little bit," she said, though she didn't demonstrate anything. "But not too much. You don't want to hurt them."

He could easily imagine his father's reaction to a comment like that, and the way he would react to somebody challenging him on attacking any of the creatures that were found along the unclaimed lands. In his father's eyes, those creatures were meant to be hunted, not just because they needed to be but also because that served the Emperor.

Alex continued grabbing meat and fed it to the creatures carefully.

While she worked, Dax focused on the creatures to get a sense of their essence. This one seemed to have something of life, but maybe a little fire. That was an odd combination.

"Are you coming?"

"Sorry," Dax said. "I was just studying them."

"Avoid their essence. At least, avoid it until you have a better handle on transference. That's what Professor Madenil said. These little guys really don't like it when we try to draw their essence. It angers them something fierce. They start to scream, and when one of them starts to scream, they all start to scream. The sound is like nothing you've ever heard before, and to be honest, I just do not care for it."

"They recognize when one of the others is getting targeted?"

"Is that what I said?" She shook her head. "Honestly. It's not like they're talking to each other. It's more like they're reacting to something happening to the other."

That sounded suspiciously like they were talking to each other, but Dax wasn't going to say that.

They finished with the weroxen, then moved onto small gray-furred creatures in a row of crates.

"Let me guess: something terrifying," he said.

"Sproutsels," she said.

Dax frowned, and she shrugged.

"These are just common gray sproutsels. They have quite a bit of essence in them, so it gives students a chance to practice with transferring. They're feisty but not necessarily dangerous."

Dax studied one of them. She was right. As he focused on it, he could feel quite a bit of wind essence, of all things, inside the gray sproutsel. It seemed to be concentrated, almost as if it were stirring up a torrent of power inside of the sproutsel that looked as if it wanted to be released.

"How long does it take you to go through and feed them?"

"On my own? Usually I can get done in less than two hours."

"How often are you on your own?"

She frowned. "Most days."

"What about Wiloph?"

"Wiloph handles later in the day. At least, that's what he tells me. But now that you're here, maybe you can handle the mornings. You didn't seem to have too much difficulty getting up early."

Dax wasn't going to argue with that, but it had been harder than he would've liked to admit. Still, if it gave him a chance to work with these different creatures, and an opportunity to try to understand their essence, maybe it would be worth it.

"Come on. We still have quite a bit of work to do. If you're lucky, we might have a little time to practice."

Chapter Forty-One

DAX HAD NOT HAD THAT MUCH TIME TO PRACTICE.

They had talked more than he had anticipated, while she was showing him all the different creatures and the feeding preferences for all of them. She seemed to know quite a bit about each of the creatures, and she obviously had an affinity for them. Dax appreciated that about her.

The soilclaws and the weroxen weren't even the most dangerous creatures that were there. They had one fire mudtusk, which Dax had been a bit leery to get too close to, though she had said that he didn't have to worry given the runes that were surrounding it, and a gibalt, which had a single horn in the center of its head, stunted wings, and a horse-like body, though it was only about knee-high. That creature had considerable earth and a variant of life essence, though Dax hadn't had an opportunity to test whether he might be able to draw on any of it. Still, there was a part of him that wanted to. There were so many strange creatures within the transference barn—he found himself fascinated by it.

When they were done, Alex had looked at him, crossing her arms in front of her chest. "Well?" she asked.

"Well, what?"

"Well, do you intend to return? Don't be like some of the others and waste my time. I spent plenty of time with you this morning talking you through all of this. You're going to disappoint Professor Madenil if you don't come back."

"I didn't realize that was an option."

"This would be an elective for you."

Dax thought about it. "I still haven't actually passed advanced transference. So I think this is actually part of my class."

Alex nodded. "Good. Maybe they need to do that more often so we can make sure that we have enough students working here." She shook her head. "It would be easier. Well, most of the time. I can't imagine what would happen if too many students were here. They might lose fingers." She started to smile, as if the idea of people losing fingers appealed to her. "Or they might be mean to the creatures."

"I won't be mean to the creatures. I will take everything that you told me to heart, and I will make sure that when I return, I'm ready to be useful."

"If we get done quickly, I can show you different types of transference," she said.

Dax had no idea how powerful she was with transference, but she obviously had an understanding of the animals and an interest in transference. If nothing else, that was the kind of person that he thought that he wanted to learn from, not somebody like Wiloph, who didn't necessarily care about the animals. More than that, as Dax had made his way through the transference barn, he had found himself questioning more and more the possibility of sentience with some of these creatures. Maybe it wasn't high-level sentience, certainly not like what humans had, or like what it seemed like the silk shatter had. But an awareness, and perhaps even some low-level planning? The soilclaws had made him feel that way the most. Every so often, he would look over at them, and it would seem as if they were watching him.

And he could see some earth essence coming from them.

The first time that he had noticed it, it had been a subtle effect. There had been a streamer of essence that had flowed from one of the soilclaws, heading to the wall before withdrawing. Then the soilclaw in the next cell over had used a bit of earth essence, and it had drawn it through, moving it from one enclosure to the next. It was as if they were using earth to try to communicate. That might have been what they were doing, though if that was the case, it suggested a higher level of communication, and a higher level of essence use, then what he had ever heard about when dealing with soilclaws.

He didn't see the same with anything else, but there weren't quite as many creatures that were the same in the barn. Only with the weroxen, from what Alex had said about them, was there a possibility that they already had their own type of communication, as they were able to chat amongst each other, sharing dangers.

When he was done, he was tired. It was a physical tiredness, not an essence-wielding fatigue. Worse, he still had class later today. One of his classes for the day was essence manipulation, and he worried that he was going to be too tired for it. He needed to focus during that class, as Gia had suggested, and learn to express his essence like a true essence wielder.

But if he needed to cheat, he had transference.

It did leave him wondering if it was really cheating though. It was his essence, after all. Why not use what gifts he had been given? Gia may not approve, but he was still commanding his essence.

He made his way to the library, and when he headed down to the third sublevel, he found Rochelle seated at the table like he had expected. She had a pile of books in front of her, and she looked up at him as he approached.

"You look awful," she said, and then she wrinkled her nose. "And you *smell* awful."

"The transference barn," he reminded her.

"I suppose. I wouldn't have expected you to stink so much. You're going to need to bathe after you come out of there."

"Great," he said. "One more thing."

He shared with her his experience and observations, talking about the soilclaws and other creatures, and the possibility that they might be communicating with one another.

She frowned. "I suppose it's possible. Wolves hunt in packs, and even things like dogs tend to understand simple commands, but what you saw with the soilclaws suggests something else, doesn't it?"

Dax nodded. "That's my feeling."

"So they're intelligent?"

"It seems that way. I don't know how intelligent, but more so than I think most people give them credit for."

"Then they shouldn't be held prisoner," she said.

"It's really just a testing. I don't think they're doing anything harmful to them."

"Other than holding them against their will, Dax."

"Other than that," he nodded.

"Well?"

"Well, what?"

"What are you going to do about it?"

"I'm not so sure there's anything that I can do about it. I'm just a student. And they are a part of the transference barn, and a part of the Academy."

"I think it's because of where you grew up," she said, as if coming to a decision. "You have a cavalier attitude about these creatures."

"I think you and Alex would get along quite well."

"Who's Alex?"

"A second-year student. Transference student, primarily. She loves the animals and seems to have an affinity for them in a way very few other people do. She made a point of telling me that I needed be nice to them, so…"

"So she cares," she said. "That's good."

"I don't have the sense that Professor Madenil doesn't care," he said.

"Unless she knows that the animals are sentient and doesn't care about it. Then that would be a problem, wouldn't it?"

"You know," Dax began, "there is another possibility. Maybe she knows what's going on with the creatures in the forest."

"Or maybe she doesn't," Rochelle suggested.

"That could be dangerous if true."

"I didn't think you were concerned about them."

"There's a difference between being aware of the danger and wanting to send somebody into it," he said. "And to be honest, there are certain factors about the silk shatters that I'm concerned about."

Dax rested his head in his hands for a while, and thought that he might've slept for a few minutes, but when he woke up, Rochelle was still poring over her books. Dax got up and began to wander through the bookshelves, until he found a section that he hadn't really been planning to go to but which seemed nevertheless to draw his attention. By the time he stopped in front of the section on different creatures, he found one book focused only on essence-infused creatures. This was what he had been looking for all along.

Dax turned the pages in the book, wondering if his transference ability might help, or if he would actually have to read. He skimmed the pages but didn't find anything useful, so he moved on to another book that reminded him of what Professor Alibard had given him. When he took a seat, Rochelle looked over at the book.

"Those don't look like books on essence runes," she said.

"Creatures," he said.

She nodded, then turned her attention back to what she was studying. "That's probably a good idea. The creatures, the runes, and the attack on the Academy are all somehow tied together. I just don't know how." She pulled a piece of paper out of her pocket. It looked like a tracing of the city —it was rudimentary, but Dax could immediately tell what she had done. She marked a location for each of the places where they had found the runes, then connected them with a line.

"You made me think about this," she said.

"I did?"

"Well, not directly, and perhaps not exactly this time. But you suggested something when you mentioned how the runes were connected, and you also said something about that when we were looking at the rune in your room. You said that it seemed to be made up of smaller runes."

"It seemed like that, but I'm not exactly sure how."

"So we have some powerful rune master who is making these."

"But these didn't look that way," Dax said, pointing at the drawing. That had been the difference between what was found outside of the city and on the streets and what was found inside of his room.

"Not exactly, but what if they are a part of some sort of larger pattern?"

"I think the idea is compelling. I just don't recognize anything from it."

"Well, maybe because we're just students. I've been thinking about how it feels like we've been forced to go to Professor Alibard because there really isn't anybody else who can help, but what if there is?" she asked.

He looked over at her. "What about Agatasha?"

"Oh," Rochelle said, sighing. "I don't necessarily know how I feel about that."

"Why?"

She stared down for a long moment. "She makes me uncomfortable. I don't know why. It's probably just a me thing, but that's how I feel."

"I understand, but we need answers, right? And she had answers about the Great Serpent."

Rochelle sighed. "Let's sit on it for now."

She turned back to her studies while Dax focused, beginning to work through the books, looking for anything that might help him with some of the creatures. He hoped that he could use his transference, and that he could find answers, but so far, nothing had come to him. He didn't know if—or when—it would.

Increasingly, he started to think that going to someone who had much better knowledge than they could find at the Academy, and somebody who knew what they had been involved in before, might be for the best. Even if Agatasha worried them.

Without Desmond, who else could they go to?

He needed answers. They needed answers.

And he couldn't shake the feeling that they were running out of time to get them.

Chapter Forty-Two

THEY STOPPED INSIDE OF ROCHELLE'S ROOM BEFORE heading over to Professor Alibard's office, depositing some notes that they had taken. Dax looked down at the floor. Somebody had been there.

"What is that?" Rochelle asked, stopping short inside of the room and staring at a folded piece of paper with a wax seal on it. On the wax seal was a dense wind rune, but there was also a bit of fire mixed in with it.

"It looks like a letter," Dax said.

"It means that somebody has come in *here*, now," she said, shaking her head and looking around. She started to pick her way around the room, lifting items off her desk, opening up her wardrobe, and even looking under her bed. Eventually, she sat down on the bed and stared at the letter. "I don't see anything else missing, but again, how would I even know?"

Dax had placed different protective runes around her room, as had Rochelle, but increasingly they were both aware of how inexperienced they were. It might not have been enough. He took a seat on a chair and reached for the letter. He suspected he knew where it was from, and who it was from, but he was surprised that it would be here.

When he traced his finger over the wax, he felt a strangeness within it, something familiar. There was fire and ice, connections that reminded him of when he was younger. Connections that reminded him of his mother.

"I sent word to her twice, and I kept waiting for her to respond, but I didn't expect for her to take this long. And… Well, I also expected her to send a response in a different way."

"Not breaking into my room," she said.

"Well, there's that," he said.

"Are you going to open it, or do you need me to?"

Dax chuckled. "If you want to, you are more than welcome to open it."

She shook her head. "I don't think I should be the one opening mail directed to you, especially when it has that marker on it. I have no idea what that's going to do to me, if anything, but I'll be honest, I have no interest in having the Nelson family angry with me because I opened their mail."

"Nobody in my family is going to be angry with you," he said.

He carefully tore open the letter and waited for a moment, thinking that maybe she was right, that there would be some sort of reaction from the wax seal, especially the moment that he broke it. But there was nothing.

That wasn't exactly true. He did feel a bit of essence spill out, and it washed through him. As it did, he was left with a question about whether she had been right. Maybe his mother had placed something on the letter that had made it so that only he could be the one to open it.

What would've happened if somebody else would've attempted to?

He sat back, and he looked at the contents of the letter.

"Well?" she asked.

"It's from my mother. She received my notification and wants me to be careful." He looked up. "And it says she's disappointed that I 'displaced my supplies.'" He shook his head.

"You told her about that?"

"I thought she needed to know that I lost it."

"You didn't lose it; it was just taken out of the room, where you had it just stuffed underneath your bed. You know, like somebody does. Honestly, Dax. If I were given a trunk full of gold, the very first thing that I would've done would've been to find a bank in the city—either that or some other secure location. I wouldn't have left it under my bed."

"I didn't think about it," he said.

"Of course not," Rochelle said.

He read the letter. His mother didn't offer him anything else. No help. No money. No mention of the Cult of the Dragon—though he hadn't really expected that. No comment about Megan.

There was a comment about the unclaimed lands. He had skipped over that.

"She's talking about my father being busier here," he said, looking up at Rochelle.

"So?"

"Well, she knows I don't really care about that, so why would she have included that in here?"

"I don't know. Maybe your mother thought that you wanted to know about your father and what he was doing, so you could decide whether the two of you have anything in common? I mean, honestly, Dax. It's almost like you've never received any mail from your family before."

"I haven't," he said.

"In the entire time that you've been at the Academy, you haven't gotten any letters from them?"

Dax shrugged. "Well, I didn't really expect to get anything, and with my sister here, I guess I had the only family connection I thought I needed."

She shook her head. "Wow. I really didn't expect that, but maybe I should have. You are Dax Nelson, after all."

"Would you stop?"

She started to grin, and then she cut off and looked at him. "I'm sorry. You don't deserve that. I know that your experience outside of the Academy is different than most, and quite different than my own, so let me apologize. Sincerely. But you shouldn't be surprised your family is giving you information about what's happening at home. Aren't you going to be expected to return and work with your family?"

"If I had fire essence, maybe."

"Once they know what you can do, they're going to have you come home, Dax."

He hadn't considered that.

Would they?

And would he want to?

There had been a time where working in the unclaimed lands was the only thing he would've been able to see himself doing. Now… now he didn't know. There were so many other things that he could imagine being a part of that working with his father along the unclaimed lands was very low on the list.

He folded the letter up and stuffed it into his pocket.

"What now?" he said.

"Well, we were going to go to Professor Alibard, and I still think that we need to do that. I redrew the rune, and we have the places throughout the city that we want him to explore so that he might be able to see them. Maybe he could help us identify what is going on. That is, if you still want to do that."

They headed over to the professor's office, with Dax pausing a moment as they passed the registrar's office. He made a point of looking in, only to see her sitting upright, watching him as he passed.

Once they were past, he shook his head, looking over at Rochelle.

"She makes me uncomfortable," she said to him.

"Me too, and I don't know why."

"She is the registrar," she said. "And in the absence of headmaster, she's probably one of the most important people at the Academy. She probably has some sort of incredibly potent essence that allows her to know who is coming. Besides, how many times have you come into this building in the time that she has been serving as a registrar?"

"I don't know. Three or four," he said.

"Exactly. And how many times do you think other students have come in here?"

Dax frowned, scratching at his chin. "I don't know. Probably not as many, but there have to be other students who have come and talked to the professors."

"This soon into the term? I doubt it. Other people are probably taking their time, but you, Dax Nelson," she said, her voice taking on a bit of mock seriousness, "have come here three or four times. And typically to see Professor Alibard. Given that he was the professor that was there the night of the fire, and that you are well known to have been there—"

"So are you," he said.

"Fine, given that we are *both* well known to have been there," she went on, shaking her head, "I am not at all surprised that there would be some suspicious eyes. Maybe about both of us."

"And that doesn't bother you?"

She shrugged. "I don't see why it should."

They headed up to Professor Alibard's office. The door was closed. That wasn't uncommon, as every other time that Dax had come to see Professor Alibard, the door had been closed. He knocked, and he expected that the professor would say something immediately, but there was no response. He knocked again, and then he hesitated a moment before attempting to use a bit of transference essence to test the lock. When he did, he felt resistance.

He was tempted to keep pushing, wondering if he might overpower that resistance, but Dax didn't know if it was safe to do that. So he stepped back rather than damage the lock.

"That's probably a good idea," Rochelle said.

"You don't even know what I was thinking," he said.

"You have a look about you that says that you were thinking about trying to force your way inside. If he's not there, we're not going to find anything. We need the professor, not his office."

She was right, and he had to get out of the habit of trying to break into offices, especially as doing so would only draw undue attention to him and the others. He had to be careful with that, as that wasn't what he wanted.

It didn't take long for them to make their way out to

Agatasha's house. It was situated just at the border of the city, and Dax looked over to Rochelle, realizing that they probably should have come over here sooner. The fact that they had waited until now to come out here was probably a mistake.

"We've been looking for Desmond all this time, and neither of us thought about coming out here?" Rochelle said.

"I know," he said. "It's a little ridiculous, isn't it?"

"A little bit."

"Do you want to knock, or do you want me to?"

"Oh, I think this should be you."

"Great," he muttered. He approached the door slowly, but before he had a chance to knock, the door came open.

Agatasha was a lovely woman with inky black hair. She looked much younger than Dax suspected she actually was.

"You," she said. "Students. Again? Although look at you —it seems as if you have raised yourselves to the fourth tier. Or perhaps I'm wrong."

Dax blinked. She could tell what progression he had reached just by looking?

"That's not why we're here."

"Let me guess. You need some help with the Great Serpent."

"Actually, we need help with Desmond."

"I'm sorry," she said, stepping back and closing the door.

"We don't know where he is," Dax said. "There has been an essence flare, and—"

She stepped forward, bringing a finger to her lips. "We don't talk about those things here."

"What things?"

"Essence flares," she said, her eyes darting around. "Such things can be dangerous. If you speak about them too loudly, those who are hungry for essence will come crawling toward you. Where did you see this flare?"

"Outside of the serpent stairs," Dax said.

She cocked her head to the side, watching him. "I'm afraid that is not surprising."

"It isn't?"

"Well, considering how much essence is found there, I would argue that it is not surprising whatsoever. I wonder why you feel the need to bring it to me."

"It's just that there was a flare here too," Dax said.

"That's not outside of the serpent stairs," she said.

"But that is what we found," he said. "And—"

She started to close the door again.

"We just need help finding Desmond, so we can ask him about it. We think the Order is after it."

She hesitated a moment. "I will send word through whatever channels are still open to me."

"That's it?"

"That is all I will offer."

"Even though there might be something happening in the—"

Agatasha closed the door on them.

Dax didn't even get a chance to tell her about what he thought was happening in the forest. Or about the runes. Or about anything.

All he could do was...

Nothing.

"She's really an odd one," Rochelle said.

"I know, but she obviously knows things."

"She knows things about the Great Serpent. And she's tied in with the Cult, but that doesn't mean that she wants to be a part of anything that we are doing. And we can't expect her to."

Dax breathed out a frustrated sigh. "I just feel like there should be something."

"Oh, you can feel like that all you want. But there isn't. How about we head back?"

"I suppose," he said. "Besides, I am curious about whether I really did progress the way that she said."

"She couldn't just see your level."

"Maybe she can. We don't know what kind of essence she has."

"There's testing involved, Dax. It's not that easy."

He focused on his own essence, wishing that it were. But Rochelle was probably right. As they headed back, Dax looked toward Agatasha's house, and he had a distinct feeling that she was looking out at them. He couldn't see her essence, though he couldn't remember if he could see it before.

He looked around before he settled his gaze back on Rochelle. "Well?"

"Well, what?"

"We can go and look at the runes throughout the city again, if you want."

"We have class later," she said.

"That's right. Anyway, I might need to go and talk to Professor Madenil."

"About what? Were you really that distraught about what you saw this morning?"

"Not exactly," he said, "but I do want to see if she might be able to help me understand more about what my mother referenced."

Rochelle crossed her arms over her chest, and then she shrugged. "I'll go with you."

"She's not going to be here," he said.

"I didn't think she would."

They headed out of the office building, with Dax taking a different route away, out the back door, so that he didn't have to pass the registrar. He knew that he was being a bit ridiculous about that, but he still didn't like the idea of her watching him, as it left him uncomfortable. He made his way over to the transference yard, where there were rows of plants. He hadn't been sure Professor Madenil was going to be here or in the animal holding pen, or if she was going to be somewhere else entirely, but he found Professor Madenil talking with a pair of older students. He didn't recognize either of them, but they were dressed in the robes of the Academy, with sigils on their left shoulder suggesting that they were third-year students.

When he pointed to them, Rochelle nodded.

"We don't see too many third-year students these days," she said, "because by the time people reach that level in their training, most want to leave the Academy and move on to some sort of paying job."

"There are some."

"Some, but they don't really spend much time in the Academy. By the time you get to be a third-year, you get to pick what you study, where you study, and..." She shrugged. "And I suppose that is my goal as well."

He smiled. He could easily imagine Rochelle spending her entire life inside of the Academy, but at the same time, he also had the sense that she wanted to graduate and help her family, using what she knew of healing, and of essence, so that she might serve her people. He thought it was one of the more endearing things about her.

When Professor Madenil turned, she saw Dax, and she started to smile, before trailing off as she realized that Rochelle was there.

"I don't need you demonstrating transference to any

first-year students," she said. "Anything that you do should be done in the presence of other students."

"That's not why I'm here," he said.

"You didn't come to demonstrate to your girlfriend?"

Dax shook his head quickly. "This is Rochelle—"

"I know her quite well, Mr. Nelson. She's in my class. But if you intend to strain the animals with a transference demonstration, I would appreciate it if you have a minimum of five students with you. Is that acceptable?"

There was quite a bit about the exchange that Dax wasn't quite sure how to take, not least of which was the idea that he was straining the animals in some way. When he had used transference on them, especially on the cattle, he hadn't noticed any sort of strain. And there had never been a restriction like that before. Why now?

"That is perfectly acceptable," he said. "And if you have any students who want to work on transference, I am happy to be available for them."

Professor Madenil waved a hand. "Very well. I know you went to the transference barn this morning. Hadn't been sure if you were going to be willing to do so. Ms. Darinas told me and said that you were 'functional.' I suppose that is high praise, coming from her." She started to smile. "Is that why you came, or was there another reason? Were you hoping to work with someone else? The morning is the busiest time and when we need the most help right now."

"I don't mind the mornings," he said.

That wasn't exactly true, as Dax didn't want to necessarily get up early every morning to help Alex, but at the same time, the idea that he would have free access to the animals there did make him feel like he was getting something out of it. More than that, if there was anybody he was going to work with, he appreciated working with Alex.

"I just wanted to know if you've heard about anything happening along the border of the unclaimed lands," Dax said hurriedly. "My family sent word about increased movement, and—"

"And you were wondering if you needed to leave the university to help your family. A commendable thought, Mr. Nelson. Especially for somebody like yourself. I suppose our own Ms. Stonewall would also feel the same way. It is true. The unclaimed lands have been more active than usual, but the Emperor has sent additional troops to handle that, so there's nothing to be alarmed by."

"What you mean by more active?" Rochelle asked.

Professor Madenil looked over at her, then turned her attention back to Dax. "Creatures often come through the unclaimed lands. Oftentimes they do so and create a bit of violence. It is why the Emperor values those who serve along the unclaimed lands as much as he does. They have kept a measure of peace and stability for a long time. Other times, however, some creatures have managed to sneak through, despite every effort those who are on the border make. We need to understand how they're able to do so and study them."

"You would bring creatures from the unclaimed lands to the Academy?"

"Many of the creatures that you have seen here have once been beyond the borders," she said. "And there is little danger in having them here with us."

"Other than—" Rochelle started, but Professor Madenil cut her off.

"Little danger," she said. "Now, if you don't mind, I need to get back to working and making preparations."

She hurried away, and it left Dax standing with Rochelle, who was staring after Professor Madenil.

"Maybe it was a good thing that we came here," she said.

"Why?"

"Because look at the preparations she's making. I think it has to do with what your mother sent. Something is happening along the border of the unclaimed lands, and whatever it is seems to be more dangerous than Professor Madenil wants to reveal."

Dax couldn't help but feel that she was right. But if that was the case, then what was happening? Whatever it was, his mother had made a point of sending it in the letter, of warning him.

But warning him about what?

Chapter Forty-Three

THE NEXT WEEK PASSED QUICKLY.

At least as quickly as time could pass at the Academy. Dax had gotten up early every day to head to the transference barn, where he and Alex would feed the animals—with him getting far more efficient with doing so. He kept observing the animals, primarily the soilclaws, hoping that he might find something that would help him know whether they were communicating with one another, and continued to feel as if the essence they were wielding between each other was some form of communication, though Dax wasn't entirely certain if that was true.

Dax had been studying the animals, but he hadn't been able to determine what the flow of essence did. He had hoped that he could learn something from the creatures about the type of essence they possessed, but he hadn't been able to identify anything. Without testing them—and Dax wasn't sure what that would look like—he wasn't sure that he could identify anything.

The other animals in the transference barn were relatively straightforward. They were terrifying, at times, but not dangerous to him. Some of them seemed as if they came to look forward to his visits. Surprisingly, the weroxen were among those that seemed like that. He had gotten accustomed to feeding them, making sure to use the tongs when he handed them the meat, but there was no longer a ferocity as they took it. By the end of the week, it seemed as if the creatures were taking it almost carefully.

Dax had begun feeling for their essence, probing them, trying to see if there was anything he might be able to detect, more so than what he could simply see. But he had not yet attempted to draw on it. Alex's warning about the dangers in doing so had stuck with him.

Then there were the smaller creatures. The sproutsels were pleasant enough, and Dax had practiced using wind with them, until he realized that he could easily draw it from them. After a while, he'd stopped trying to draw it from them and had started to focus on what he could feel inside of them, the way that they were utilizing wind. There was something compelling about it.

"Where did you learn to do that?" Alex asked on the fourth morning that he had come. Dax had taken a seat in front of the sproutsels, and he was focusing on the wind, letting it swirl in his hand, a small torrent of power spilling out. He was careful that he didn't release too much of it, but he was more fascinated by the way that he had drawn the wind out of it, and that the creature did not resist him.

"Oh, this? It's just a bit of the wind that I can feel inside of the sproutsel."

"What do you mean that you feel it?"

There was no accusation in Alex's tone, more a curiosity. She had taken a seat next to him, and she looked forward, studying the sproutsels.

"You can tell that the sproutsels use wind essence," Dax said.

She nodded. "That's obvious."

"Well, I can feel the way they're swirling it. I think it's their way of trying to escape," he said, though he wasn't entirely sure if that were true. It was just a sense that he had from them. The more that he had focused on the essence that they were wielding, the more he'd thought that, if nothing else, he might be able to find how the sproutsels were drawing upon that essence. And he might even be able to replicate the way they were drawing it.

He had not managed to control it quite as tightly as the sproutsels did, as the power that they were using, the way that they were spinning that wind inside of themselves, required far more control than what Dax could manage, but he still felt as if he might learn something from them.

"You can *feel* it?"

"It's subtle," Dax said. "But if you focus on their essence before you begin to draw it, you can continue the pattern."

That was the only way that he could describe it without revealing to her that he was doing something more than that. But it was, in fact, what he was doing. He could feel the essence inside of the sproutsels and the way they were using it. Maybe the animals could teach him about each of their particular forms of essence.

"Let me try," she said.

She closed her eyes, and she reached toward the bars of the cage.

She was far more fearless with the sproutsels than Dax was. He didn't need to touch them for him to pull wind off the sproutsels, so he didn't have to worry about them scratching or biting at his fingers, not the way that she would. Still, it didn't seem as if the sproutsels minded.

The wind was there. The sproutsels tended to be feisty, but they were kind enough to Alex, and probably for good reason. She came to them every day, and she fed them, treated them kindly, and made sure they had plenty of water. So they didn't bother her. Dax wondered what they might do to somebody else, though. If somebody wasn't familiar to them, would they permit them to draw on their essence quite as easily?

"I *can* feel it," she said, opening her eyes. "Why have I never noticed that before?"

"It's always been there," he said.

"Obviously," she said.

He shrugged. "I don't know. I think the tendency is to just transfer essence, but I've been trying to focus on what type of essence each animal has, and what I feel, before attempting the transference. I think there might be something that the animals could teach us about each of their types of essence."

She stared at him for a moment, and Dax began to flush.

He had said too much; he realized that, and he regretted it.

"I know how that sounds, and I know how foolish it—"

"No... I feel the same way. I've been trying to tell Wiloph that, but he just thinks that the animals are meant to be drained. 'A means to an end,' he likes to say."

"I suppose some people would feel that way," Dax said. "Some creatures simply want us to borrow their essence. But others..." As he looked around her, he couldn't help but feel as if some of these creatures wanted them to learn essence from them. The sproutsels, in particular, were more content when he was focusing on the way they were using wind. The one that he was now drawing upon seemed almost amused by his weakness with the pattern, though Dax wasn't sure if that was real amusement, or if he was trying to apply too much emotion to a creature.

"It's a pattern of wind that I've not seen before. I've never even attempted it like this," Alex said.

"I haven't tried the same with anybody else," he said. "The rest of these creatures are... well, some of them are little bit more irritable with us."

"That's an understatement," she said, though she smiled as she did. "But if you convinced the sproutsels to let you draw on this, maybe you can convince some of the others."

"Like the soilclaws?"

She turned to him, frowning. "The soilclaws take more than that, I think. I keep spoiling them with fruits and vegetables, but that hasn't convinced them to let me draw on their essence."

"You have to convince them?"

"I think that some who use transference would claim that you need to be able to overpower it, but that hasn't been my experience. There is a way of using essence so you can draw on them but so it isn't harmful to the creature. At least, that's how I feel." It was her turn to flush. "Anyway." She got to her feet, and she looked around. "I think we've spent enough time here for the day, and it's probably time that you get off to class."

"I should bathe before class, anyway," Dax said with a shrug.

"You know, the easy solution for that is to just change clothes. That's what I do. I know that it doesn't wash everything off, but it takes most of it."

"Thanks for the advice."

"Thanks for showing me something that I hadn't known before," Alex said. And it sounded as if she meant it.

He went about his day, taking time in valor the way that he had over the last week and working with Gia. In the evenings, he worked with Cedrick and Rochelle, trying to help both of them progress with their valor techniques.

Rochelle had pushed. She claimed to have wanted "dancing" lessons. At first, she had only been interested in doing them in her room, but as she had begun to gain some skill—and Rochelle had quickly progressed, despite her protestations that she didn't have any technique with it— she had been willing to step outside, and to even try practicing in the valor grounds. Gia claimed that Rochelle was a natural, at least with some of the basics of valor patterns. Once she learned how to use an essence sword, that would be a different matter. Dax and Gia had moved on to a more advanced section of valor, which involved them learning how to wield the essence blade.

The rest of valor had been going relatively smoothly.

Essence manipulation had been much of the same. Dax had done as he had promised to Gia, and he had been focusing only on transference essence, rather than drawing upon any of the other essences, to try to accomplish the goals Professor Jamesh wanted of them. He had found it difficult, though maybe that shouldn't have been too much of a surprise. He was forced to use his own essence and express it outward. His essence was designed to be constricted, allowing him to draw essence in rather than to express it outward.

Any time Professor Jamesh expected a demonstration out of Dax, he found himself using transference again. He always stuck to water, as he could crystallize it and send it shooting out of him. Rochelle never minded him doing it. But every time that he defaulted to using water for his demonstration, he noticed Gia looking at him with disappointment in her eyes.

Politics was the usual class, with the same dragged-out lessons about the nature of the Empire and its relationships with some of the surrounding nations. Dax listened half-heartedly, though he tried to pay more attention, especially once they were learning a little bit more about the boundary with the unclaimed lands. The lands beyond the unclaimed lands were typically known to be wild, with roaming bands of hunters that tended to be found there. The Empire had never expanded beyond the unclaimed lands, partly because it was too dangerous for them to do so, and partly because every time that the Emperor sent significant weapons through those lands, the soldiers were met with too much resistance, and his people were sent back bloodied and defeated.

It was part of the reason that the boundary of the Empire had stayed the way it was. Most agreed that it was the will of the Great Serpent, that without that, the Empire would have shrunk anyway. So the Emperor, using what the Great Serpent required of him, kept the boundary abutted to the unclaimed lands but no further.

Dax wasn't sure if that was true, as he had wandered the unclaimed lands himself. They were wild, and there were plenty of strange creatures that ventured through there, though he'd never had the sense that there was anything particularly dangerous about them, only the creatures that existed there. He was tempted to comment that in the politics class, but he'd decided against it, as he didn't want to draw any undue attention to himself, especially there. It was the one class where he could be quiet, simply absorb the lessons, and, when it came time to the test, regurgitate that out. It was relatively straightforward.

Runes class was much the same. They had opportunities to work through a series of runes each class, but any time that he attempted to talk to Professor Alibard following class, the professor dismissed them. Dax knew better than to push him.

Karelly was doing quite well in runes, something that she made a point of reminding people, making comments about how she was going to become the next rune master and even an instructor. At one point, Dax overheard her talking about how she had been getting private instruction on runes, which did nothing more than raise his suspicions about her role with what had happened to his room and to Tarin.

Dax couldn't prove it though.

At least, he couldn't prove it easily.

Somehow, he was going to have to find a way to talk to her.

He still didn't know why she would've done that—at least to Tarin. It was easier to know why she would have done that with him. She just didn't like Dax.

"I don't think that you're going to find a way to get through to her," Rochelle said. "She's not going to reveal anything to you." They were heading out of essence manipulation, trailing after Karelly and her friends, who were acting as if they were not at all involved in what had been taking place. Dax had a hard time believing that.

"I know that we're not," he said. "It's just that I feel like—"

"You feel like she's responsible. You showed Professor Alibard the runes found in your room. He didn't recognize them."

"What if she's learning them from him?"

"And now you're suggesting that a professor would be responsible for such a thing?"

"Not exactly," Dax said. "It's just…"

He looked over. Professor Alibard was heading into the office building. Something didn't seem quite right, though Dax wasn't exactly sure what it was. He motioned for Rochelle to follow, and she joined him as they hurried to catch up. When they did, he saw a large gash on the professor's cheek.

He looked at Dax, then Rochelle, and frowned. "What are you…?"

Professor Alibard wasn't able to finish.

He collapsed. It was only by luck that Dax and Rochelle caught him, keeping him from falling back down the stairs, toppling, and hurting himself worse than he already was.

Chapter Forty-Four

DAX AND ROCHELLE HELPED ALIBARD UP THE STAIRS, neither of them speaking as they dragged him along the hallway to his office. He still hadn't gotten to his feet, but as they helped him, Dax could tell that there was something wrong with him, even if he wasn't exactly sure what it was.

When they reached his office, Rochelle looked over at him. "Do whatever you have to do," she said.

"It's going to reveal to him the full extent of what I can do."

She looked down. "Maybe not. He might just think he did it."

Dax shrugged, and after a moment, he used transference to unlock the door. As essence rapidly began to stream out, Dax held onto it, then pushed the door open so that he and Rochelle could bring Alibard inside. Once inside his office, they set him down, then both leaned against the door.

"Well?" Dax asked.

"I suppose you're going to want me to try to heal him."

"I think that you need to. Unless we want to go and find somebody else."

"You want answers, don't you?" Rochelle crouched down next to Professor Alibard, and she held her hands in front of him. Dax had watched her using her essence many times, but this was something very intentional. He knew that she had grown with her healing skill, and he had seen her using her essence before, letting it flow out from her. But this was some different technique. He wasn't even sure if he would be able to demonstrate it with transference, though he doubted he would ever need to do such a thing.

"It may not even make a difference," Rochelle said. "I don't know that I'm helping him all that much."

"Just so long as you don't harm him."

She glanced in his direction and arched a brow at him before turning her focus back to Professor Alibard. As she worked, she continued to let water seep into him.

"It's a matter of letting his body do most of the work," she said. "But in this case, it seems as if there is something else. I... well, I'm not exactly sure what it is. Whatever happened to him might be more than I can handle. I can feel his obvious physical injuries, but something else is inside of him that I don't like, Dax."

He crouched down across from Professor Alibard, and as he watched Rochelle working, Dax didn't have any idea what it was that she detected, but if there was something there, and if it had impacted Professor Alibard, then he understood why she would be concerned about it.

She sent her bluish water essence flowing through him, and as that wave of power continued to work, building as it swept throughout him, there was part of Dax that understood what else was wrong with Professor Alibard. And it was something that he thought he might be able to do something about.

Dax started to use transference. When he did, Rochelle looked over, shooting him a harsh, frustrated stare. "I'm using transference on him," Dax said, "because I feel some sort of essence impacting him. I don't know what it is, but I can feel it layering inside of him. Just give me a moment."

"You think he's had some sort of essence attack?"

"To be honest, I don't really know. It feels like…"

It felt strange. That was the only way he could describe it. He drew upon the essence to try to pull it out of the professor, but it was difficult, and he didn't want to hold onto it.

And he realized that he didn't have to. He quickly withdrew his essence blade and carved a containment rune—this one a vague, nondescript rune that was designed to hold anything—and began to pour the essence he was transferring out of Professor Alibard and into the rune instead.

He breathed a sigh of relief as he didn't have to hold onto it any longer.

"What was that about?" Rochelle asked.

"I can feel some of the power that is within him, and I can tell that it is too much for me to hold. I am trying, but it hurts when I try to do so."

"Why do you think he had that attack him?"

"I don't have any idea. I can feel some of that power in him and draw it off, but there is resistance when I try."

"Even being able to feel that is progress for you, isn't it?"

Dax nodded. "I think so. It's more than I would've been able to do before."

Rochelle turned her attention back to the professor, using water essence to sweep through him. As she did, it felt as if some other bit of essence was dislodged. Dax could see it.

"It's working," he said.

"I can feel it."

Dax poured the dislodged essence into the containment rune that he had made. It held, thankfully. Dax didn't know what he would've done if it hadn't worked.

Finally, Rochelle breathed out heavily. "That's all I can do. I think I helped his physical injuries, and whatever you were doing seemed to help as well. I just don't know what you were doing."

"I was pulling the essence away from him," he said. "Something had attacked him with essence."

She leaned back on her heels, and then Rochelle shivered. "I don't like the way that sounds."

"I don't either," he admitted. "If something can attack us like that, somebody else might not even know about it. It would take somebody like…"

"Like you," she said. "And there aren't that many people like you within the Empire, I don't think."

Dax didn't think that there were there many people like him either. And the fact that something had targeted Professor Alibard…

They needed him to come around so that they could talk to him. Once he woke, they had to hope that he knew what had happened to him—if he didn't, Dax wasn't sure where they would go.

It felt like things were building, but at this point, Dax didn't even know what they were building toward, and he didn't know what sort of things they were going to have to deal with. The only thing he really knew was that he didn't care for the kind of attack they seemed to have sustained so far.

He helped move Professor Alibard, gliding him along the floor, and he and Rochelle took a seat at his feet, both of them sitting quietly, neither of them speaking.

At this point, Dax wasn't sure if there was anything to say, as he felt as if the issues they were dealing with were beyond him. Everything felt…

It felt off, though Dax wasn't sure what to make of it.

"What you think happened to him?" Rochelle asked.

"Runes," Professor Alibard said, and both of them jerked.

Dax leaned forward, and Professor Alibard propped himself up on his elbows to look around his room. "Mr. Nelson. Ms. Alson. Care to tell me why you are here?"

Dax met Rochelle's gaze, and they turned and focused on Professor Alibard. "We were coming up the stairs when you collapsed. We brought you here. We…"

"You removed something from me," Professor Alibard said, leaning forward again and locking eyes with Dax. "Do not deny it."

"What do you mean, 'runes'?" Rochelle asked, taking the attention from Dax.

Professor Alibard rubbed at his eyes, and he leaned forward, sitting fully upright. He swept his gaze around the inside of his office before his gaze settled on Rochelle for a long moment. "I was following the story of runes. I found some that were similar to what Mr. Nelson described."

"In the city?"

Would he have been injured in that search? Dax had seen runes throughout the city, but there had been nothing dangerous about them.

Unless they had gotten lucky.

"Not in the city," he said, and then he frowned, rubbing a knuckle into his eyes again. "Why?"

"It's nothing," Dax said.

"Obviously, there is something, and you are trying to keep it from me. You think you need to protect me from it. Why is that?"

Dax and Rochelle shared a look, before he shrugged and turned to him. "We came across some runes in the city. That's why we came to your office, in fact. We wanted to show them to you, to see if you might be able to identify them. They were scattered all throughout the city, and Rochelle seems to think that they form a runic pattern."

She gave him a look that suggested that she did not care for the fact that he had revealed that part of her theory, but she pulled out a slip of paper, and she held it out for Professor Alibard. He took it and studied it for a long moment.

"It looks runic in shape," he said. "But to be honest, I cannot tell you what it might do, as there is some irregularity to it."

"I did my best," Rochelle said.

Professor Alibard looked at her. "And I did not accuse you of doing a poor job, Ms. Alson. In fact, I think that you did a marvelous job, especially considering what I suspect were limitations in your ability to track these patterns."

"I think we picked up on the pattern, but I don't think we got all of them. It would impact the shape of the rune." And as he studied it, he wondered if maybe they should have searched for something else. Or maybe he should have been looking through the books that the professor had given him to study unique runes.

"Where did you get hurt?" Rochelle asked.

"Outside of the city," Alibard said. He started to get to his feet and wobbled for a moment, but Rochelle was there.

She grabbed him and guided him to his chair, where he sunk down.

He shook his head. "I forget how a healing feels. It has been many years since I have needed something like that."

"I'm sorry. I'm inexperienced," Rochelle said.

"And again, I am not disappointed in what you did, Ms. Alson. In fact, I doubt I would've been able to survive had you not done what you did."

"I had a little help," she said, glancing at Dax.

"What did you do there?"

He leaned forward suddenly, and he pointed, motioning to the runic marker that Dax had made on the ground.

"Oh, that? It is a—"

"I can see what it is, Mr. Nelson. Why would you have placed a nonspecific containment rune on the floor of my office?"

"Well," Dax began, glancing over at Rochelle, "because of what was inside of you. It seemed as if there was some sort of essence infesting you, or something along those lines. Rochelle wasn't sure what it was, so I drew it off."

"You drew it off?" He steepled his hands together, and he looked at the two of them.

Dax still had his essence blade unsheathed, though it was resting on the ground behind him. He felt strangely naked without it, which surprised him given that he was standing in front of Professor Alibard, somebody who would not cause any difficulty for him and whom he did not fear at all.

"I just drew it away. Was that a mistake?"

The professor was commanding wind and mixing it with a bit of earth before releasing it. It seemed to flow inside of himself, swirling, as if he were attempting to determine whether they had harmed him permanently. Dax probably would've done the same thing with the situation reversed.

"You did not drain anything, did you?"

Dax shook his head. "We didn't. We were just trying to help."

"Interesting. Well, I don't know exactly what it was that you did, but I thank you for it nonetheless."

"What are you going to do about the runes?" Dax asked.

"You don't need to worry about them, Mr. Nelson. The city is safe. The Guardians will ensure that it is."

He waved a hand, and Dax and Rochelle shared a look. Neither of them said anything, but they headed out of the office, realizing that was what Professor Alibard wanted of them.

The city was safe. But what was it safe from?

Chapter Forty-Five

ROCHELLE SAT AT THE TABLE IN THE CAFETERIA, LEANING toward Dax. He didn't like having conversations here, but there was enough ambient noise around them that it was a little easier here than some of the other places that they talked, partly because they were able to have conversations and not worry about somebody listening in. She chewed slowly, looking around the cafeteria, glancing at several of the other tables. There were only a few other students here at this time, as they had come early, though they had sent word to Cedrick and Gia, wanting their friends to know that they were doing so.

The walls of the cafeteria were bare, all plain stone, and the floor was a gleaming pale marble. It was spotless most of the time. There was an energy here, though it seemed to come from some of the runic markers that were buried inside the walls. Dax could feel those markers, even if he couldn't see them. Then again, when he focused his essence down tightly enough, he could see something more in those markers, could begin to see some of the essence trailing within them. The room was protected, like most places within the Academy were protected.

"Are we going to talk about what happened?" Rochelle asked.

"What are we supposed to talk about?" Dax asked, frowning as he turned his attention to his plate. It was a slab of meat, slightly overcooked, with all the vegetables. The food had been better during the term break, when there weren't as many students around to take the choice servings and fewer people for the cooks to prepare for.

"You don't want to talk about what happened to Professor Alibard?" She lowered her voice even more, and now it was barely more than a whisper. Dax was curious how quiet she would get, whether she would drop it to even more of a hushed whisper or maybe pull him in and talk directly into his ear. Or, this being Rochelle, he wouldn't even be surprised if she were to pull out a piece of paper and start writing. Everything that they did could have some way for someone to overhear or eavesdrop if they wanted to. They were within the Academy, after all, and if a Whisper wanted to know what they were doing, Dax had little doubt that they would be able to find out—it was just that easy for somebody of that level of skill to do such things.

"I want to talk about it, but I also don't know that there's anything that we will be able to do, as I have no idea if there is any danger to what happened to him."

"No danger? You saw what happened, and you saw the way that he looked. And you know what you pulled off."

"Pulled off?" Cedrick asked, taking a seat across from Rochelle and next to Dax. Gia followed behind him, a sheen of sweat on her forehead. Cedrick didn't have the same coating of sweat on his, which left Dax wondering what she had been doing that he had not. "What were the two of you doing now?"

"Oh, nothing more than saving Professor Alibard," Dax said, turning his attention back to his tray and cutting off a bite of meat. "We don't know what happened to him, but we found him on the stairs of the office, and he had been attacked by something. Maybe runes. I don't know."

"More danger?" Gia said. She shook her head. "And here I thought growing up along the unclaimed lands was supposed to be dangerous. Ever since coming to the Academy, everything that I have encountered here has been far more dangerous than anything that I experienced when I was at home." She looked over at Dax.

"My home was actually mostly safe. We had a few incursions periodically, but my father and his men usually handled those without any difficulty."

"Hey," Rochelle said, sitting upright and interrupting, "did you hear anything about the unclaimed lands from your family?" She looked over at Gia, who was quiet, sitting down and moving her tray before shifting some food around. "Because Dax finally heard something from his mother, and she alluded to some activity along the unclaimed lands."

"We don't know if that's what it was about," Dax said.

"And you made it clear that your mother didn't say anything that was unintentional, so anything that she would've sent you would have implied something significant, right?"

She held his gaze, and there was an intensity to it that Dax couldn't turn away from. She was right. His mother wouldn't have sent anything unintentionally.

"I suppose," he said.

"Anyway," she said, turning her attention back to Gia.

"Have the Stonewalls encountered anything that the Nelsons might not know about?"

Gia looked over at Dax for a moment before shrugging. "I don't keep in contact with my family that closely."

Rochelle grunted. "You don't talk to your family, either? What is it with the two of you? I've been sending regular letters to my family."

"And have they been replying?" Cedrick asked.

"Of course they have been," she snapped at him.

"Well, I have told my family about the wonderful friends that I've made, and our incredible journey that we took before the end of the term, but…" Cedrick shrugged. "Not so sure that it makes that much difference what I tell my family though."

"These are your families," Rochelle said.

"I'm getting the sense that we don't all have the relationship you have with your family."

There was a quiet that lingered. "It wasn't always that way," Rochelle said. "And I am mostly closer to my grandfather. But it took work. I wasn't always close to him, and I guess I'm not as close to my parents as I was to him, but that doesn't mean I don't want to see them. And I do see other family from time to time…"

She trailed off, glancing over at Dax, who offered a bit of a smile. He hadn't heard what had happened with the fotara she had saved last term. He supposed that he shouldn't be terribly surprised that Rochelle, of all people, took his feelings about the different creatures as seriously as she did. She had snuck a dangerous creature into the Academy after all—then snuck it back out to keep it from being discovered.

"What did you detect from Professor Alibard?" Gia asked after the silence had stretched.

"Some strange essence," Dax said in between bites. He chewed slowly. "To be honest, I don't know what it was, as I couldn't feel anything other than the strangeness within it. But we had to pull it off and store it in a containment rune."

"You had to *store* essence?" Cedrick glanced over at Rochelle before turning his attention to Dax. "That's something very advanced, isn't it?"

"Traditionally," Rochelle admitted. "But seeing as how this is Dax, and I suspect that he was using some form of transference in order to take some of his essence—or whatever it was he was draining off Professor Alibard—I don't know how advanced that technique actually is. Probably still advanced, but it's not even the first time that I've seen him do it. He did it when the Academy was attacked. He pulled fire into fire containment runes."

"Why?" Dax asked. "What's the issue with it?"

"It's just rare," Cedrick said.

Rochelle glanced from one to the other. "Anyway. We know the professor was attacked, but we don't know if it was the Order or someone else."

"Who else would it be?" Gia asked. "We know the Cult wouldn't have done it."

"Unless he is with the Order," Cedrick offered.

"Cedrick," Rochelle said.

He shrugged. "I don't know. It's possible. That's all I'm saying."

Dax actually agreed with that. They didn't know.

"So we have to keep an eye on him and who he might be meeting with. That's a reasonable thing for us to do. We should probably have been doing it, anyway," Dax said.

"If only your mother would answer," Rochelle said.

Gia watched them both. "She hasn't answered?"

Dax shook his head.

"I've heard from my brother. Not my parents, but my brothers. Apparently, there has been something pushing creatures through the unclaimed lands. They've been dealing with more and more attacks, which is nearly over-whelming their ability to withstand them. My parents have considered calling me back, but my brother has been standing up for me and telling them that I needed to continue my studies at the Academy so that I could be more useful." She rubbed her hand through her hair for a moment before looking up at them.

"And transference?" Rochelle asked.

"Of course, transference. I thought that maybe I could learn something there that might help us if we were dealing some of those creatures, and I thought that the more that I began to learn about the creatures, and kind of essence that they had, the more I'd be able to use some of that against them." She shrugged. "To be honest, I just don't know."

"I have a feeling that's probably the Order, but I don't know why," Dax said.

"For what purpose?" Cedrick asked.

"Distraction," Dax said. "That's about the only thing that I can come up with."

"So we need to keep closer tabs on everybody and their movements. That's not going to be difficult or anything," Rochelle said, "especially with all our obligations."

"We just need to watch everybody. If anything's strange, we let the others know."

The next few days went much the same, though every so often, Dax would go out into the city, looking for more information about the runes. He never found anything more. They were still there, the traces of essence linking them, but nothing seemed to have changed at all. At least, he didn't think that they had changed. He kept following them, searching for anything that might suggest that the runic energy was altered in some fashion, but so far, Dax had not uncovered anything that he found concerning.

Toward the end of the week, Dax found himself back in the transference barn once again. He had been working with the animals there for several weeks now, and he found himself drawn to the different types of essence. Alex no longer helped him in the morning, as she no longer needed to. Increasingly, Dax was able to function independently, working his way from cage to pen and onward, visiting with some of the creatures, testing their essence—and even drawing upon it. So far, only the soilclaws seemed to know what he was doing. They were far more alert than anyone had given them credit for before.

When he said something about that to Alex while she was watching him, she just shrugged. "They seem to be comfortable—more so lately than usual. I think it's because I've been giving them treats."

Dax wasn't sure if that was the case. The soilclaws were comfortable for perhaps a different reason. Increasingly, he thought that they were talking through their use of earth essence, but even if they were, Dax had no idea what it was that they were saying.

Dax went about his work.

As he did, he noticed trends in the barn's essence. Some of it was just how the creatures used it, and some of it was how the creatures interacted with the essence around them, as if they were more aware of essence than humans were. He couldn't help but feel as if there had to be some way he could learn from the creatures if he had an opportunity to study them better.

There were times when additional creatures would

show up, and Dax and Alex would be tasked with caring for them. Alex was familiar with them most of the time, and if she wasn't, one of the professors would introduce them to her—and occasionally to Dax—before instructing them on their care. It was simple work. And it was enjoyable.

He had gotten up early one morning and arrived at the transference barn before Alex got there. Everything was quiet. Almost too quiet. He had been standing in place and focusing on the essence all around him when Alex bumped into him.

"What are you doing just standing there?" Alex asked.

"I'm…"

He shook his head, and she frowned at him. "What did you trace on the ground?"

Dax frowned. He looked down, realizing that he had been tracing something with his toe: a rune.

He hadn't even known that he was doing it, but he recognized it. And he had pushed some of the essence that he had been drawing into that rune.

It was a holding rune, but a holding rune for what?

And how had he known to make it?

Chapter Forty-Six

DAX STOOD AT THE EDGE OF THE ACADEMY GROUNDS, looking off toward the forest. His classes had been going well—other than essence manipulation. Dax had not yet managed to expel any essence from himself as Gia had hoped he would attempt. The other classes had gone as well as could be expected. Valor was more of the same, with Dax and Gia training separately but getting more experience with the essence blades. He felt comfortable with it and was pleased that he was able to continue carrying his sword throughout the Academy without having to justify it. Politics was a boring subject, but one that Dax felt was simple memorization. He looked forward to when he no longer had to study the topic.

The one class that had been the most interesting—other than transference, which Dax had basically abandoned, essentially because he had his other transference assignments—was runes. Professor Alibard had been working with them and focusing more on some complicated patterns. Dax was getting better with them and more confident with his skills, but he was curious as to why they were being pushed the way they were.

And it did feel as if they were being pushed.

The classes consisted of the application of rune patterns. It was interesting, mostly because it did seem as if there were ways of merging rune patterns to provide more information. Many of those techniques were not any that Dax had considered before. The professor would have them demonstrate different series of runes to try to create something new. He pushed Dax, now that he knew of his nascent transference ability, to understand the runes better.

Outside of the class, however, they still had not been able to find more about what had happened to Professor Alibard.

Anytime Dax or Rochelle would approach him, he would dismiss them before they could ask questions. Dax had been tempted to follow him, but he had not left campus since the attack. At least, not that they had seen.

Now, Dax found himself at the edge of the city, staring out into the forest and wondering if the patterns he'd found there before might've been containment runes of some sort.

It was the middle of the day, and he had no classes the rest of the day. Rochelle anticipated that he would meet her at the library, the way they had the last few days, to study runes and look for answers on Raisor, the shadow fire wielder from the day the Academy had been attacked. He had evaded their ability to learn anything more, and Dax had instead switched to looking for information about strange creatures. He was always searching for information about sentient animals but finding nothing. He knew he should go join Rochelle at the library now, but the same time, he also wondered if he could find more information on his own. So he started out, heading toward the forest before he frowned, wishing that he had some way of communicating with the others.

There had to be some sort of essence rune, or perhaps a runic marker, they might place to help them communicate, but for now he was just going to go off on his own, the same way that he had the last time he had come out here. He didn't intend to do anything, and he was certain he didn't intend to get in any trouble, so coming here was just a matter of looking for information. That was what he told himself.

And maybe that was all that he would do.

He found the first of the runes the same as he had before. He concentrated his own essence down into a tight ball and could see the traces of power. He could see the way it was connected to another rune, flowing in three different directions.

When he had been here before, he had followed the trail two different directions. He didn't remember following a third direction. That was what he would do now.

The trail led north. As he stared at it, he had a distinct sense of where it was going: toward the unclaimed lands.

It was an easy enough trail for him to follow, though he wondered at the purpose behind it. It was made of essence, and the ease with which he saw it and was able to follow it suggested to Dax something about his own essence that he had started to suspect but had not been able to fully prove. Agatasha had commented on how he had reached a higher level of essence, but Dax had not really been able to determine anything for himself. Seeing the trail as easily as he could without having to constrict his essence down suggested a much higher level than he had thought before.

Was this what it was going to be like for him?

Essence power. The ability to see things.

All of that left him marveling at it.

He was moving steadily until he caught a flicker of crystalline legs.

He froze.

"You should not be here, human," the silk shatter said.

It was the same massive silk shatter that Dax had dealt with before, and his voice had grown deeper. Angrier, possibly.

Dax turned, looking around, and he noticed the guidepost didn't seem to progress any further from here. He had reached the last one. He had been following it for a while, and he knew that he was getting deeper into the forest.

Could the guidepost be leading him toward the city?

"What's the purpose of the boundary?"

The silk shatter glowered at him, as much as something with those eyes could be said to glower. He leaned back on his six legs, tapping his two forelegs in front of him, and there was a thundering of power.

Dax braced for what he knew was going to come and was not surprised when a dozen or more of the other, smaller silk shatters began to surround him.

All of them had the strange form of life essence within them. He was ready for the possibility that he might need use transference, but he also didn't want to have to do it, as he didn't want to attack them, and he certainly didn't want to cause any harm. Instead, he just stood.

"I'll ask you again," Dax said. "What is the purpose of the guidepost and the boundary?"

When one of the silk shatters tried to get closer to him, Dax began to transfer essence from it. The creature scurried away.

Dax turned his attention to the larger one, not wanting to attack but also not wanting them to attack him. "We don't need to make this difficult," Dax said. "We can speak. I serve the Great Serpent."

For whatever reason, Dax thought that was the most significant thing that he could say, as any time that he had interacted with the silk shatters, he'd had the distinct impression that they had wanted him to know that they also served the Great Serpent.

But what the silk shatters had told him about their queen suggested that there was something else, someone else, that they served even more than the Great Serpent. Perhaps this someone else was as powerful as the Great Serpent.

Dax had been raised to believe that the Great Serpent was the most powerful entity known. The silk shatters suggested otherwise.

"As you do," the silk shatter said.

"What is the purpose?"

"Safety," he said.

"Safety for you, or for others?" Dax asked, feeling as if that were the core of what he needed to learn.

"Safety," the creature said again. He raised up on his legs again, and he clapped the two forelegs together as he had each time he was trying to signal something. This time, there was a rumble in the earth. Dax was pushed back. He could do nothing about it.

He absorbed the force rather than using transference, and when it was done, he was standing several dozen paces from where he had been before.

The silk shatter was still in front of him. "Safety," he said again.

And then he clapped his legs together.

Each time he did, Dax was pushed back. He needed to learn something from this silk shatter, if possible, but he wasn't sure what that would entail. All around him were other silk shatters, smaller ones, and they were using life essence. Strands of it were working within them, and it slid along the ground, tiny, thin tendrils connecting them to branches overhead. It would be an easy thing for them to use those tendrils, Dax suspected, to launch themselves back into the trees. But that wasn't the only thing that he noticed. They also created a web like of greenish energy that connected all of them, one to another, as if their power were interconnected.

The silk shatter clapped his legs together again.

Dax followed the flow of the essence.

He tried to use the same technique that he did inside of the transference barn to learn what the silk shatter was doing. But he wasn't in time to follow the connection—or the explosion of power.

Some part of it reminded him of what he saw from the soilclaw essence. It was a pulse. Dax reacted, and he sent a similar pulse back. He had to draw power from the silk shatter, but he did so carefully, not wanting to risk angering the creature.

And then the silk shatter stopped.

"Where did you learn this?"

Dax blinked. He was near the edge of the forest. One more blast of power would be all it would take before the silk shatter would send him out of the forest. At that point, Dax suspected he would be able to barricade him from the forest itself.

"From soilclaws," Dax said simply.

He borrowed the essence from the silk shatter again, and he sent it out in a tapping pattern, the same one that he had seen from the soilclaws. The silk shatter froze, and the earth essence within it seemed to stop.

Then there was a powerful explosion, and Dax was tossed free of the forest, where he landed in a heap. When he got to his feet, the silk shatter was gone.

But Dax could feel something around the forest had changed.

The markings had solidified.

They had created a barricade. And, Dax suspected, that barricade would be something he could not overpower.

Chapter Forty-Seven

"I REALLY AM GETTING TIRED OF YOU GOING INTO THE forest on your own," Rochelle said, joining him at the edge of the forest the following evening.

It was nearly dark, though that didn't make a difference with Dax's ability to see essence.

"I'm glad that you went without me this time," Cedrick said. "I didn't like the last time that we went in there."

Gia frowned, squinting as she looked along the border. Dax wasn't sure if she was even able to see it, though he could. A certain power seemed to build and push against him—whether from the silk shatter or some other source, Dax couldn't tell.

"Are you sure about this?" Gia asked.

"I'm sure about what I felt. I told you, they threatened me, and tossed me out, and..." He took a deep breath, and then he shared with them what he had been seeing in the transference barn, including with the soilclaws. Nobody spoke, but when he mentioned how he had used a similar tapping pattern, Cedrick started to laugh.

"So you're concerned because this monster decided to attack after you used another attack on it?"

"I'm not convinced it's an attack," Dax said. "In fact, I'm pretty sure that it's *not* an attack. I think it's the way the soilclaws talk to each other. The silk shatter seemed to know, and it reacted the moment I used it."

"Of course it reacted," Cedrick said. "You were using something that it probably recognized as an attack. And," he went on, looking over to where Gia was standing, "you even said that you were transferring essence from it. It probably knew what you were doing and didn't like the way that you were taking essence from it."

It was possible. Dax had drawn upon the silk shatter quickly, and without thinking, but he had not met with any resistance. "I still didn't feel any danger from the Great Serpent."

"Fine," Rochelle said. "Then maybe they aren't dangerous. Let's go talk to them."

She started forward, and Dax reached for her, grabbing her arm.

"I don't know if that's safe or even possible."

"Shouldn't you know either way?"

She wasn't wrong. They strode along the edge of the forest and reached the nearest of the runes while Dax felt for the energy building. It was obvious to him, and it seemed to flow from some distant location. He grabbed a rock from the ground and tossed it.

It bounced off.

There was a crackling of pale white mixed with a few streaks of green, and the rock slammed backward.

Cedrick let out a large laugh, and then he grabbed the rock and tossed it as well. When it bounced away, Cedrick clapped his hands together, then began to throw rock after rock at the barrier.

"Enough," Rochelle said. She turned to Dax. "So. Obviously now we have established that there is a barrier here, and that whatever it is can hold objects back. We don't know if it would hold *you* back, though, do we?"

Dax shrugged. "I suppose we don't, but we have no reason to think it wouldn't."

"From what he is telling us, it doesn't sound like they are all that pleased by his presence," Gia said.

"Then we try to test it," Rochelle said, stepping forward and expressing some of her essence. When it struck, she was pushed back, though the essence seemed as if it joined the boundary itself.

But it didn't seem to harm her.

"Earth?" Rochelle asked.

Gia stepped forward, and she began to use her connection to earth, letting it flow out from her. It struck the barricade.

Dax was able to follow it more easily this time. He could see the way her earth essence struck the barrier's energy, then was pushed away.

Rochelle frowned. "I could feel that."

"So could I," Gia said.

"Maybe the power of my bubbles will be able to get past," Cedrick said, and then he snapped his fingers, allowing a massive bubble to form, before he sent it swirling toward the boundary. Once it struck, there was a faint shimmering, but then the bubble collapsed, allowing a bit of pink to flow into that boundary for just a moment before it dissipated altogether. "All right," he said. "So the bubbles can't get past either. Any ideas?"

"I don't know. Something is happening inside the forest." He looked over at Rochelle. "And I don't know if it's tied to what we've been dealing with at the Academy or if this is something else altogether."

"Not just something," Rochelle said. "Sentient creatures in the forest. I'm not sure we want anything to do with them." She turned, and she started back toward the city.

Cedrick hurried after her.

Gia stayed with Dax for a few moments. "I don't like this," she said, looking along the forest. "This forest runs all the way to the unclaimed lands. You're a Nelson. You have to know what would happen if creatures congregated." She nodded to the forest. "What if the Order is somehow coordinating with those creatures and driving them here? They could even use them to attack."

"It's possible," Dax said.

If that were the case, then could his mother have some interest in trying to get him to come home? He wouldn't have thought so, especially because he had a hard time thinking his parents would've cared all that much about what he was doing and how he was spending his time. But if there was an attack on the unclaimed lands, in his family holdings, that might be enough reason for his family to want him to return, especially if his parents knew his essence would actually be useful.

Dax would have suspected that they would not have known, but if his sister had been in communication with his mother, it was possible that she knew plenty about his essence, and about what he could do with it.

If they'd learned, what would happen? What would his father do? What would he expect of Dax?

He didn't want to return home. It was a strange thing to

realize, but Dax was content at the Academy, despite the dangers that were there for him. He was learning about things, experiencing things, that he wouldn't learn or experience back home. He could use the opportunity in the unclaimed lands to work on transference, but would he have as great an opportunity there?

He headed up to Rochelle's room. When he slipped inside, she was seated on the floor near the pool with her bed, staring at the floor. He looked down to see what had drawn her attention. And there, resting on the floor, was another letter.

"Well?" Rochelle said. "See what she has to say now."

Dax traced his finger over the wax symbol with the runes etched in it. He could feel some of the essence his mother had pushed into it. He couldn't tell what it was that she had done, only that it must have been from his mother, as there was a bit of ice inside of it, but it was mixed with bit of heat. His mother's essence signature.

Dax worked his thumb underneath the wax seal and flipped it open. He skimmed the letter.

"What does it say?"

"It says she's coming."

She frowned at him, leaning forward. "That's it? Two words. 'I'm coming.'" She looked up at Dax. "All that expense for this? You have to be kidding me."

"If my mother is coming to the Academy, then something has happened."

"And it has to do with the creatures around the unclaimed lands," she said.

Dax sank into the chair opposite the bed, holding the letter in his hands. If it was about the creatures, then who could be responsible for it? Maybe it really was the Order.

He wanted answers. The forest was the obvious place, but he had been banished from the forest by the creatures there.

So what now?

Chapter Forty-Eight

DAX WENT THROUGH THE MOTIONS OVER THE NEXT FEW days. He went to classes, trying to get a better handle on essence manipulation but not quite managing to express his essence as he wanted. Maybe that was the key to gaining progress to third tier or higher as an acolyte. He tried finding Professor Alibard, but he had not been able to, which meant that he and Rochelle had spent time in the library studying runes. They had not uncovered anything there either.

Politics had taken a slight turn. Lately, they had been learning more about the different border wars, though none of them had been recent. Dax wasn't sure why the politics instructor would take a turn from discussing the overall politics of the Empire and the Emperor's preferred delegations, but it was a welcome shift. Dax didn't mind learning about some of the border wars, though there were aspects of them that he had never heard about. There was one aspect of the Century Old War that had been compelling to him. Dax didn't remember hearing a lot about the war, at least not when he was younger and would've expected to have heard something from his family. He hadn't realized that even during the war, the creatures along the unclaimed lands had not been involved. At least, for the most part. That fascinated him.

After one of his classes, he had approached Professor Opan, and he had asked the question that had been bothering him.

"Yes, Mr. Nelson?"

Professor Opan was an older, reed-thin professor with graying hair. He had a bookish appearance, and he made Dax think of every scholar that he had ever met.

"I would ask you about the border wars," he said.

"Oh, something has interested you. That's good. I've noticed the attention has been waning in class lately, so I've been shifting the curriculum a bit."

At least Dax understood why that was the case, and he was thankful that it wasn't anything more intriguing. Although maybe some intrigue wouldn't have been the worst thing in the world.

"Have the creatures from the unclaimed lands ever been used in the border wars before?"

He frowned at the question and regarded Dax with a look that bordered on curiosity, but it was mixed with something else, something that Dax couldn't quite read. "Creatures?"

"Well, my family lives along the boundary of the unclaimed lands. We have difficulty with some of the creatures there from time to time. I was just curious if they had ever been used in the border wars before."

He wanted to keep the conversation vague.

"Ah. That's right. Nelson. Sometimes I forget who we have in the Academy this term. Between you and Ms.

Stonewall, we have a pair of students who deal with things different than most of the students. Most don't have such dangers in their day-to-day lives."

"It wasn't a danger," Dax said, before realizing that wasn't exactly what Professor Opan wanted to hear. "But it could be dangerous. When I was younger, I would go into the unclaimed lands with my father—"

"He would have an untrained and untested child go into the unclaimed lands? How barbaric."

"Well, he thought it was the best way for me to learn techniques of valor," he said. Barbaric? There was nothing barbaric about going into the unclaimed lands. Maybe if he'd had to deal with some of the creatures himself, but for the most part, Dax had never had to do that. His father—and his brother—had taken care of them.

"Still, I can't imagine what the Emperor must think. Well, seeing as how it is Gerand Nelson, perhaps the Emperor would fully approve. Any training technique that was necessary to defend the border." He shook his head, and Dax couldn't tell if there was a note of irritation, or perhaps something else, mixed within that.

"I just was wondering if the creatures in the unclaimed lands have ever been used to attack."

Dax had never heard of them being coordinated in such a way, but if they were sentient, maybe that was possible. And if so, could that be the Order's new plan?

The professor scratched at his chin. "It would be an intriguing concept. Something I've never even given much thought to, to be honest. But the creatures can't be commanded. They're wild. Essence mad, and often violent. Mostly violent, I should say."

"Essence mad?" There was so much about what the

professor had said that struck Dax as odd, but that was the part that caught him most off-guard.

"They have been trying to find ways to connect to essence. Most believe the creatures from the unclaimed lands are disconnected from essence, and they come into our lands to have a greater connection to it. The Great Serpent binds us, as you know."

Dax hadn't heard that before.

"What about the creatures we capture and bring into the Empire?"

"Eventually, they do stabilize," he said, waving his hand. "But not all of them do. I imagine that in your transference classes, you have seen simple creatures, unlikely to share anything more complex with you."

"So you don't think that they could be driven in any way?"

"I suppose they could be driven," he said, scratching at his chin again. "But again, it would take considerable effort, and you would have to have the kind of essence that might motivate them. Either that, or something that might draw them."

Could that have been what happened?

He kept coming back to the possibility that the silk shatters were somehow tied to what was going on. But he didn't know.

"Did I answer your question, Mr. Nelson?"

"Thank you, Professor. I think you've given me plenty to think about."

"Excellent. I am pleased to see you engaged."

Once he was out of class, Rochelle caught up to him and grabbed his arm, dragging him down the hall and outside. "What was that about?"

"I was just looking for information," he said. "He didn't tell me anything more than we already knew."

"So he doesn't think the creatures on the unclaimed lands could be commanded?" Dax shook his head. "Good. There were stories when I was younger about people like you and your family. Those who live along the unclaimed lands. You get referred to almost mythically. I guess."

"I really wish that you would have an opportunity to see what it was like when I lived along that border," Dax said, "because it isn't nearly as bad as what you would think."

"Not nearly as bad?" She arched a brow. "It's constant violence, isn't it?"

"Not really. Just from time to time. I actually like the peacefulness of it."

There were times when he missed it.

He closed his eyes, and he could almost feel it now. His mother had taught him to open himself to essence. Maybe he could do that now and come to better understand his own essence in ways that the Academy had not been able to teach him.

His mother had to have had some other motive for teaching him that. He just didn't know what it was. Maybe she had known more than she had ever let on.

Rochelle was watching him. "Library? Maybe we can find more about Raisor," she said.

They had been looking but had continually failed to find any answers. The Guardians had obviously known something about him, but Dax had not been able to find anything. That worried him.

"We really need to dig into it before something else happens," he said. "They are going to return."

They spent some time in the library but had no greater

success than they'd had before. Eventually, Dax went back to his studies, and the next few days were more of the same: spending time in the library, trying to understand more about the runes while also looking for information about sentient creatures and coming up short. Mornings were always spent in the transference barn, where he found himself focusing on the different essences of the creatures that were there.

Increasingly, Dax allowed himself to focus on the essence they had—not on using it but instead on trying to gain an understanding of it. Dax had asked the Great Serpent for understanding, hadn't he? He might not be able to know anything about their essence, but he could at least learn what they did with it. Some of it was obvious, like the torrent of power that the sproutsels used or even what the cattle did, as it seemed as if the essence allowed them to digest their food more capably. Maybe he could even learn how to control essence the same way they did so that when he drew it off others, he could use essence like that—something more natural.

Alex commented on that one morning. "You stare at them a lot."

"I'm just hoping to learn from them."

He knew how she felt about essence, and he knew how she felt about others trying to draw on that power, so he also understood that if anybody would appreciate him focusing, wanting to gain some understanding, it would be her.

"I suppose. Say, are you interested in seeing what Professor Madenil brought in?"

"What is it this time?"

The last morning they had gotten some more sproutsels, as they had released the others they'd been holding. Apparently there was a limit to how long Professor Madenil and the other transference instructors were willing to hold a creature. He didn't know how long that was, but it reassured him that she didn't hold them indefinitely.

"Something unique," she said.

She guided him through the end of the barn and through a set of rune-marked doors, to a part of the barn he had not spent much time in. He had been told during his first day that this was not a place that he was supposed to visit, and so he had not. Once through the doors, he felt power.

There was a large stone cell that took up much of the center of the room. Even from a distance, Dax could see that there were runes all around it, and he could feel some energy emanating from it. He wasn't sure what it was, other than the fact that the runes seemed to be containment runes, similar to some of the containment runes that he had placed.

"Are you sure it's safe for us to do this?" he asked.

She nodded, and she waved him forward. "It is. Just keep coming."

He followed her, and they reached the main part of the confinement cage. It was all stone. "How do we get inside?"

"This one is a bit unique," she said. "I didn't even get to see this until just recently. And," she went on, lowering her voice, almost conspiratorially, "I don't know if we're supposed to be here yet, but I did think that we should take a look, especially if we're going to be asked to care for it."

"Care for what?"

"You have to tap these three runes here," she said, ignoring the question and pointing to a section of the stone. Dax noticed the runes. They formed a triangular pattern, but they were simple—earth and life containment runes.

As she tapped them, he felt a faint shimmering of

power, and once she was done, there was a slight shift. And then it seemed as if the stone vanished. He knew that wasn't exactly true, as there was still a bit of shimmering energy, as if some of the essence had lingered.

Which was exactly what had happened. Essence had lingered, creating a transparent barrier that they could see through. He moved closer to her, looking through the essence, curious what was inside.

His breath caught. "A cindercrawl?"

The creature was enormous, with a slightly stooped back—though Dax wasn't exactly sure if that was from the stone that was keeping it inside or not—and wings that curled up on either side of it. A horned head swiveled around, looking at them, and it seemed to radiate fire, though of course it would—it was a creature of fire essence.

"Have you seen them before?"

"Only from a distance," he said.

They were creatures that even his father didn't want around, as his father warned him that they were far too dangerous for them to deal with. They would scare them away, using blasts of different types of essence from their essence blades, and would never actually confront them one on one.

"Who caught it?"

"Professor Madenil warned me that it's quite dangerous," she went on.

"It is," Dax said, "which is why I'm surprised they feel it's safe to have at the Academy."

"I think it was injured. And inside of this," she went on, pointing to the stone building, "it is relatively protected."

The creature was watching him—and not only him but Alex as well. There was an intensity to its gaze that reminded him of the way that the silk shatter would look at him. There was something to it that burned.

He could see the flow of fire within it. And maybe there was an injury, though Dax didn't see one. Would this enclosure even contain a creature like this if it weren't injured?

As he stared, he noticed a trail of fire.

Maybe there was something more he could learn from it.

He had asked the Great Serpent for understanding, and maybe this was how it was going to be given to him. In a cage, trapped, and forced to wait on people like Dax, like Alex, like other transference instructors, to free it.

Somehow, that didn't feel quite right.

Chapter Forty-Nine

"YOU LOOK TROUBLED," ROCHELLE SAID.

It was late the day after he had seen the cindercrawl, and Dax hadn't been able to get it out of his mind. He got back the next day, but the door leading to that secondary room had been warded with additional protections, and he hadn't been able to break through them—not without trying to drain the power, which he thought might be dangerous to do.

He kept coming back to the type of essence the cinder-crawl possessed. Fire. They had already been attacked by fire once, so why would there be a cindercrawl brought here now?

"Transference," Dax said, and he explained what he had seen.

Rochelle gasped. "They have that *here*?"

"Well, apparently, it's contained inside of incredibly heavy rune markers, and… Well, it probably is safe. I just don't like it."

"Because you think it's an intelligent creature?"

"I don't know," Dax said.

"Is that what it is?" Rochelle asked, turning to him and looking at him with a dark intensity. "I was just kidding at first, but it seems like—"

"I don't know. Maybe."

"You think many of them are now. Why?"

"It's because I dealt with them along the unclaimed lands. I want to know more about them. When I was there, when I was younger, I always wanted to understand. It drove my father nuts, because he thought I should just be interested in destroying, doing the same thing that he and my brother and all his men do. And maybe there's a part of me that wanted to, but there's also part of me that recognized that it was just violence for the sake of violence. To be honest, many of the things that they killed were valuable to the Empire, and the Emperor, which made my family wealthy, but…"

"But you wondered if they were killing them just because of their value."

"I think a little bit of me did." He shrugged. "I don't even know."

"You can ask your mother when she comes."

With everything going on, Dax hadn't been thinking much about his mother's arrival. He felt a little uncertain about what he would do and say when she came. So much for him had changed—not just about his essence but about his understanding of the world and his place in it as well. He shrugged. "I suppose I can. I don't know that she's going to tell me anything, but I can push her. She can be a bit stubborn."

"Must be a Nelson trait."

"Probably on my mother's side," he said, grinning at her. "But I don't mind taking after that."

They had reached the edge of town. It was time for Dax's usual journey out into the artisan district for Desmond. He motioned for Rochelle to follow, and they headed through town until they reached his door. He paused, and before unlocking it, he knocked, just as he had every other time.

When there was no answer, he began to pull upon the essence, but then he hesitated.

"Something's different here," he said.

"Is he here? You shouldn't unlock the door if he's already here."

"I don't think that he is."

But the essence felt off.

Could somebody else have come here?

Dax examined the door. It was fairly nondescript, with a few different runes marked on it, which would've been unique in other parts of the city but wasn't at all unique inside the artisan district. Runes were common, as were runes of significant power. Dax had become numb to them. So each time he had come to the door, he had not paid much attention to them, and he had found himself drawing on the power within them, holding it inside of himself and not at all bothering to test whether there was any danger to it. He had simply been accustomed to pulling on it, then releasing it. It had become almost second nature, given the way that he had been drawing it and the kind of power that he knew that was there.

This time, though, there was a new marking near the base of the door.

Dax crouched down, and he stared at it. For a moment, he was worried that it was a marking similar to what he had seen in other parts of the city, but this was a basic rune. A basic *containment* rune.

He traced it, and then stood, looking over at Rochelle and pointing. "Look at it."

She crouched down, and she ran her finger along it, and as she did often when she was trying to investigate different runes like this, she let a bit of water seep out of her and flow into the rune itself. She took a sharp breath, and then she stood, wiping her hands on her pants.

"I can't tell anything about it. It seems to be something quite basic, which means it's not tied to what we've been dealing with around the city."

Dax nodded. "I agree."

"Wonderful. We are in agreement." She snorted. "So what do you think?"

"Either it means that Desmond was here, and he was placing additional locks to try to see if somebody might trigger it—though if he was here, I would've expected that he would've realize it was me—or somebody else placed it. If someone else placed it, the question is who, and why."

"Unless they placed it because they didn't want him to go inside? You said it was some sort of containment rune."

"It's a containment rune, but it seems to be empty. So what I am left wondering is if there was something here that was placed so that anybody who might come would reveal themselves." He shrugged, shaking his head. "Again, I have no idea."

"What you want to do?"

"I want to see if Desmond is here."

"Then open it."

It was a simple matter, or at least, it should've been a simple matter, as he had done it plenty of times before. But there was something about that marking that left Dax on edge, and he had no idea whether it was going to cause any danger. So as he began to focus on the power from the other runes, he tried it to see if there was anything within this new one that felt wrong. Yet even as he began to pull upon it, he did not detect anything that felt particularly dangerous. He continued to pull on that power, focusing on it, and holding it inside of himself.

The empty rune at the bottom of the door…

It *was* a containment rune.

Dax pushed the power that he was pulling out and into that.

He felt it slide inside.

It was simple. Like a key going into a lock. And then the door came open.

"So nothing changed?" Rochelle asked.

"Oh, something definitely changed," Dax said, "and I wonder if it was Desmond, or somebody else who knows I've been coming here." He looked around, but even as he did, he couldn't tell if he had been observed. Dax hadn't been paying much attention to that possibility, which was probably a mistake given everything that they had been through. If they had been watched, what would the person have thought about him coming, breaking into Desmond's home as often as he had, and throwing stones inside? He started to laugh.

"What is it now?"

"I was just thinking about how ridiculous it must've looked for anybody who could've been watching."

"You mean the fact that we would open it and throw rocks inside?"

"Pretty much."

He drew upon the essence in front of him, and he took a careful step forward. He made sure he tested it first, but as soon as he moved forward, he could feel the emptiness around him again. He made his way into the silvery barrier, and then Rochelle took a tentative step after him, following him while looking around.

"Those boxes are different."

Dax looked into them. He hadn't taken inventory of what was here before, but he maybe should have. He wondered if Desmond was coming here, changing things, or if this was some sort of transient conduit that other people could have used.

"Where does it lead?"

Dax took her down the hall, where there was once again the blank emptiness. He didn't dare take a step forward, as he had no idea what was going to be out there and was afraid of the energy it gave off, afraid of what he might uncover if he did take a step beyond. But he motioned to it.

"It really is some sort of a conduit," Rochelle said, her voice quiet and a bit concerned.

"That's what I've been telling you. Desmond must have some secondary essence that lets him do this."

"It's more than just *his* essence, though," she said. "We shouldn't stay."

He took her back outside, where they stood in the street. He took the essence from the containment rune and poured it back into the door, locking it once more. Once done, they began their trek through the city, looking for runes. Dax held his essence tightly bound inside of himself as they searched.

They checked the locations of the ones that they knew about before moving on and searching for anything else that they had not yet uncovered. There was still nothing more to them. When he paused, he thought about the forest, and about the way the runes had suddenly been activated, forcing some sort of barricade.

"What if it's like that?" Dax asked, filling Rochelle in on his concern about the forest.

"You think that somebody—and these creatures, which is what you're particularly talking about—would create a protection inside of the city, where there are all sorts of professors, other rune masters, who should be able to counter it?"

An idea came to him, and it left him with a bit of worry.

"Do you have your map?"

She reached into her pocket, and she pulled out the marker. "I don't have any idea what you are getting at, Dax, but I can see that look on your face."

"What are they circling?"

The map was a reasonable depiction of the city, and it showed the Academy at the center of it. The runes surrounded it, and the Academy sat at the heart of it—not exactly in the *direct* center, but at least close enough.

"You think that somebody is creating some sort of a barrier to keep people from getting to the Academy?" Rochelle asked.

"What if it's not about keeping people from getting to the Academy?" Dax asked, looking over at her. "What if it's about keeping people from leaving?"

Chapter Fifty

DAX WAS TIRED OF TRYING TO FIGURE OUT WHAT KARELLY was after. He knew that she was involved in everything that was going on in some way. He knew that she was responsible for the runes that had been placed in his room. He wasn't at all sure why, or what she had hoped to accomplish, though he had his suspicions. He figured she was probably trying to get them expelled from the Academy, the same way that she had gotten Tarin expelled. He didn't know, however, why she would have been so upset about him.

Still, he had taken to following her to see if she had anything to do with some of the different runes that they had found throughout the city. He didn't think so. For all her bluster about being skilled with runes, any time that he'd actually seen her placing them, he had not been particularly impressed. He had been watching her during their different classes, thinking that maybe she would demonstrate something that would reveal what she was responsible for—and he'd also been watching Alibard's reaction to her rune making, but he had not seen anything to that end either. If she was some hidden rune master, then he had yet to see proof.

"Well," Cedrick said, sliding up to him. "I have a little bit of gossip for you."

Dax had been watching Karelly as she came out of the cafeteria. She had been visiting with several other students and watching him.

"What sort of gossip is it this time?"

"It's about our little friend there," he said.

"About this uncle of hers that she keeps going on about?" Dax asked.

"Him? I don't know anything that. Sounds like he just disappeared."

"Then what?"

"I think I know why she was not so pleased with Tarin."

"Why is that?"

"It's a bit complicated."

"How about you make it not so complicated?"

"Let's just say that it has to do with families, and old grudges, and..." He shrugged. "To be honest, the kind of thing I would've expected to cause problems at the Academy. I'm not even sure that she's ultimately responsible for what happened, or if she was just doing it because she felt like she had to for somebody else."

"What do you mean?"

"Well, from what I've been able to tell, her grandfather and Tarin's grandfather were once business partners. It was a long time ago, but apparently things didn't go so well, and the business dissolved, as things do, and his grandfather ended up keeping control of the business. It thrived, and her family had to start over."

"So this is all about some old business grudge?"

"Well, I think that's all it is for him." Cedrick shrugged. "You, on the other hand—well, I think it's just because you're a Nelson."

"Thanks," Dax said.

"Is that better than the alternative?"

"I'm not so sure," Dax said. "I think I would have liked to have not been the one responsible for angering her just because of who I am."

"Well, you didn't get expelled."

"Not yet," Dax muttered.

"I think it's because you placed protective runes on the door."

Dax had started to think that as well. He didn't have any proof, but with what she was doing, and what she was involved in, he wasn't exactly sure that he would get any proof. He couldn't shake that the protective runes had been far more effective than they had any right to be, especially given the measure of protection that he had used, and how he was almost certain that what he had done was not particularly impressive. Then again, Dax had made containment runes that had held fire from one of the Order, so perhaps he did have more talent with runes than he realized.

"Now you just have to prove it," Cedrick said.

"That's the problem," Dax said. "I don't know how we're going to prove it."

"Can't you just confront her? I mean, you're the great valor fighter, anyway."

"Sure," Dax said. When Cedrick's eyes widened, almost excitedly, Dax snorted. "I can go and confront her, threaten her with a valor battle. Knowing her, I have a hard time thinking that she's going to be thrilled to face me in direct confrontation."

"You're probably right," Cedrick said. "Which is a little bit ridiculous, isn't it?"

"A little bit?"

"A lot ridiculous? Well, I don't know. So this is all about letting her know that she can't challenge you anymore? I don't really know what you're going to do, Dax."

"To be honest, I don't really know what I'm going to do either."

"Are you going to challenge her?"

What would it accomplish? Somehow, he was going to have to find a way to help Tarin. Dax wasn't exactly sure what that was going to entail.

But an idea came to him.

"The runes have been keeping her out, right?"

"From what it seems."

"So if they've been keeping her out, what if I change things? What if I make it so that they *don't* keep her out?"

"So you're just going to welcome her into your room?"

"I'm not so sure that I'm going to welcome her in, but I'm thinking that if we were to maybe catch her in the act…"

"That's perfectly devious. I love it."

"The problem is that I'm not exactly sure I can prove she will be the one responsible." That was going to be the challenge, he knew. He would have to convince someone, somehow, that she was the one who had made the runes, not only on his room but on the weapon that had been taken from Tarin's room.

"So what's your plan?"

"I'm thinking."

"Is that a danger for you?"

Dax shot him a look.

The next few days were spent planning. Dax spent a

little time checking the city for other runes but didn't find anything. He could feel a little bit of a connection with them, however. The runes that were scattered around the city all seemed to have a particular feeling to them, and given what he was picking up, Dax was convinced that what he felt was probably tied to their purpose. He didn't know what the purpose was, but he thought that it had to be somehow designed to draw essence. It struck him as not terribly dissimilar to an essence trap, only a very unusual one. In this case, he wasn't exactly sure what it was nor was he sure why that essence trap would be so effective here.

When he said as much to Rochelle one day when they were wandering the streets, giving him an opportunity to look at the different types of essence surrounding them, she just shrugged.

"I think you're the only one who can pick up on it," she said.

"I doubt it's just me," he said. "I'm sure that others who are sensitive to essence would be able to."

"And what others are those?"

Dax had shrugged. "I don't know. Anybody who's tied to the Academy."

She started to laugh. "I don't think that's quite the way it works. But I love that you believe that the Academy is so attuned to essence. Nobody else is going to be able to pick up on the threads of essence here. Just you, Dax."

"And some of the creatures that are in the transference barn," he said.

"What?"

He shrugged again. "Well, it's been my experience that some of the creatures that are in the transference barn are attuned to essence. They seem almost supernaturally attuned to it."

"How so?" They stopped underneath one of the runes, and she stared up at it, frowning.

"Oh, it's just that whenever I am around, they will sometimes draw on their essence. It seems like they are working with the flow of essence, but then again, it's not a flow that I really know."

"So what is it?"

"Their own connections."

"You mean they're talking with essence?"

Dax shrugged. "Maybe that's part of it. Maybe that's all of it. I don't even know. I've been trying to figure it out, and trying to make sense of what it is that they do, and how they use their essence. But to be honest, I'm not really able to understand it at all. It just feels strange to me."

"So what if these different runes here aren't for us? What if they are for the creatures that you've been following outside of the city?"

Dax frowned. "I guess I hadn't given that a lot of thought."

"Maybe it's time that you do."

He snorted. "Maybe."

"Anyway. Let's keep searching."

"And planning."

"I think scheming would be a better word for what we are doing here, but anyway, I don't disagree with you. We need to make sense of what Karelly might be doing and how she's using that essence."

Dax had been trying to figure it out, but so far, wasn't entirely sure that he had done so effectively.

"I'm going to release the protections on my room," he said. "I know that it's probably dangerous to do so, and I'm thinking about what she might do the moment that she gets ahold of some of the contents of the room, but I

think if we can make her think that I'm not there, then
—"

"You intend to just draw her in, then attack her?"

"Maybe that's not the right idea," Dax said.

"I think it would be better to prove that she knows the kind of rune that is in your room."

"I don't even know if she will reveal that," Dax said.

"Oh, I'm almost certain that she won't," she said. "But I also think that you can't ignore the possibility that she will be drawn in in some way."

"What if we involve one of the professors?"

"You want to involve one of the professors in what is going on? Even more so than you already have?"

"I guess if we could time it in such a way…"

"It's just too dangerous," she said.

"Why?"

"Anything that you do is going to run the risk of her getting the best of you. And we know what she's willing to do. For that matter, we know what she wants to do. She wants to try to draw you out, to get you expelled. And if she does this the right way, it's going to work, Dax."

He wished that he could argue with her and tell Rochelle that Karelly's plan wasn't going to work, but he knew better. Karelly was nothing if not clever. And she had gotten away with other things at the Academy, so who was to say that she wasn't going to get away with this now?

"I'm going to be careful," he said.

They finished their survey around the city, and Dax didn't find anything else there, though he was curious as to whether he would be able to dig up anything more as he continued his circuit around the city. Without uncovering anything more, he couldn't help but feel as if there had to be some other answer to what he had seen.

He eventually returned, pausing in the stairway of the dorm before going to his room, however temporarily. Once there, he lingered for a moment.

"What are you doing?" Rochelle asked.

"I'm removing the protections."

"And then what?"

"And I'm going to remove the other runes. I'm going to scrub them free, and we are going to start fresh."

"You're not worried about disrupting anything dangerous?"

"Anything more than what's already there?"

"Right," she said. "Anything more than what is already there."

"No," Dax said. "I'm not worried."

She shrugged. "You do that, and I'm going to go back to my room. I'll wait for you."

He headed into his room. When he did, it was a simple matter for him to remove the protective runes that he had placed all around it. They had offered a measure of safety, but now they were no longer necessary. He stripped them free from the door, from around the door, and then once inside of his room, he searched for the larger runes that were here and began to disrupt them each. He started with the one that was on his floor. This one was a little bit larger, and it was a little more difficult for him to counter. But having spent as much time in the library as he had, and thanks to transference—even without knowing exactly what it was that he was doing—he had been able to learn more about how to disrupt such runes. He could wipe it away, though he did need to borrow a little of the earth essence from around him. Thankfully, there was some in the stone of his floor that he was able to borrow in order to etch the runes free. He worked on the chair, using a bit of fire to burn that away, and stripped away all the different markings in his room. There was no unfortunate reaction. He was thankful for that. There was a part of him that had worried that maybe there was going to be some danger to him, but nothing had happened.

Afterward, he returned to Rochelle's room. She looked at him, he shook his head, and then he settled onto the floor to get some rest.

He was awoken by a bell. He jumped to his feet and scrambled out of the room, following Rochelle.

"What was that?" she asked.

"It was a warning."

They raced down the stairs, and once he had gone down a second flight, he saw smoke.

His heart hammered. Another attack?

And it was on his floor.

"Go," he said.

"Dax," Rochelle said.

"Just go," he said.

He raced down the hall, fighting through the throngs of people and managing to avoid colliding with anybody, and once he got down the hallway, he saw smoke streaming along his door and flames crackling there. He hurriedly took out his essence blade and etched a containment rune on the floor outside of his door. He drew the fire off, working quickly. It was a simple matter, and easier than it had been when he had been inside of the administrative building, doing the same thing. Of course, at that time, he'd suspected that he had been actively fighting something—and maybe someone—who had been trying to fight him.

Once the flames were tamped down, he tested his door. It crumbled.

The inside of his room was completely destroyed.

The walls were coated with ash. The chair, his bed, his wardrobe, and his desk, had all been destroyed.

And on the floor was a different rune.

It was the only one that hadn't burned.

Dax didn't recognize it. There were levels of complexity to it. But he thought that he understood what it was for. Fire.

A dangerous type of fire, he suspected.

He saw movement along the hallway. Professors.

He debated. Should he leave the rune?

If he did, there was a possibility somebody would accuse him of experimenting with such things.

Even though he'd been targeted, he didn't know that he wanted that.

So he tried something else. He used earth from the hallway, mixed with a little bit of fire that he had drawn off into the containment rune, and burned through the rune. He disrupted it the moment that the first professor—Professor Jamesh—reached him.

"What happened here?" Jamesh asked.

Dax shook his head. "I don't know. My room."

"This is yours, Mr. Nelson?"

Dax nodded.

"And what were you doing?"

"I wasn't here," Dax said. "I was studying with Ms. Alson."

He frowned for a moment, as if trying to decide whether to believe him.

Rochelle came up the stairs behind them. He wasn't sure if he should be thankful that she had, or disappointed that she hadn't left.

"He was with me," she said. "I can vouch for him."

"Very well," Professor Jamesh said. "Did you leave a lantern glowing?"

"No lantern. I don't know what happened."

Professor Jamesh scrubbed a hand across his chin. "Considerable essence was wielded here," he muttered. "Probably some prank went awry. Well, if that is the case, then we will need to investigate."

"I'm happy to help."

"No," he said. "I think it would be best if you did *not* help. I believe you were also present at the fire at the administrative building during the term break?"

"I was," Dax answered carefully.

"That will arouse enough suspicion as it is. Go on. Finish the evacuation. We will take care of this. Once it is deemed safe to return, you may do so. I take it you will have a place you can stay?"

"I have a friend I can ask," Dax said.

"Very well."

As they slipped on the stairs, Rochelle looked at him. "Why didn't you say what you thought happened?"

"Leverage," Dax said.

Chapter Fifty-One

DAX APPROACHED KARELLY AFTER CLASS. HE KNEW HE still stunk of the transference barn but didn't really care. Given what she had done, he felt she deserved to deal with the stink.

She glowered at him. "You smell foul," she said.

"And you are foul," Dax said.

"Oh?"

"I know what you did," Dax said. "And I know what you did to Tarin."

She stood quietly.

"And you may think that I can't prove it, but you'd be mistaken. You see, you may think of yourself as something of a rune expert. But I have become one. You can ask Professor Alibard—if you think you can do so without getting caught for what you were doing." He glowered at her. "And I'm not going to say anything about what happened in my room. That is, if you fix what you did."

"I don't know what you're talking about," she said, turning away from him.

"I think you do. And I think that you have no reason to let to the grudge that your family had with his get in the way of his education. If you feel otherwise…" Dax shrugged. "Trust me when I say that I will share everything I know with Professor Alibard, including where you came up with the runes."

She hesitated.

"Because I know. If you do this, I won't even say anything about what *else* you took. And who you took it from. My father would be most displeased to learn how much your family stole from mine."

She stiffened. That threat had the desired effect. She walked away without saying anything else.

Rochelle came up behind Dax. "What was that about?"

"The leverage I was talking about," Dax said.

"What kind of leverage?"

"I've been trying to think about where she would've learned runes like that: runes for fire, but an unusual kind of fire. And then I thought about the other runes that were in my room. They were all sort of unusual, weren't they? The only way that I could make sense of it was if one person had knowledge of such things. One person who we have seen."

Her eyes widened. "No," she whispered.

"Raisor," he said. "She was grumbling earlier in the term about how her uncle was going to visit but didn't. And then there was something that Cedrick had said about her uncle having disappeared after having been upset with the Empire. Apparently, her uncle was quite powerful."

"That fits."

"I think so. Now, we just have to figure out what else he might know."

"Or what else she might have been involved in," she said.

"Maybe," Dax said. "But I don't have the feeling that she was doing anything to intentionally harm the Academy. I think that was just secondary. She was mostly interested in taking out her anger with me and Tarin."

She shook her head. "That's so devious."

"Sounds like her."

"Well, what are you going to do about your room?"

"It sounds like I'm going to be assigned another room. Hopefully in the same dorm."

"Good," she said.

"And I want to figure out more about the runes around the city. I noticed something when we were out there before. I'm wondering if Karelly had anything to do with them. We did see her out in the city—"

"Shopping, not placing runes. And besides, you said it yourself. The runes in your room didn't really do anything."

He shrugged. "Fine. I'll deal with her later. But I still think we should look. Will you just come with me?"

"Again?"

"Just humor me."

She breathed out heavily. "Just because it's you."

Dax checked on the runes all throughout town as he attempted to make sense of them. Rochelle stayed with him, and she was quiet, though she also seemed to have a bit of uncertainty as she followed him. Every so often she would look around before her gaze settled once more on Dax or on some of the markings he had been following.

"Well?"

"I don't think she'd be able to place these. They actually do something."

"But her uncle?"

That was a thought. Why would Raisor have placed the runes around the city? What purpose would there have been?

"The pattern doesn't surround the Academy," she said.

"It doesn't surround the Academy, but it does seem do something to it," Dax said. "And I can't help but feel as if that is the key to this."

"How is it all tied together?"

"To be honest, I just don't know." He paused at one point, and he was near the outskirts of the city, so that when he looked away, he looked toward the forest.

Dax began to collapse his essence down deeply, attempting to squeeze it as tightly as possible, wanting to control that flow of power. Dax didn't want to lose control over it, because it was too dangerous for him to do so. In this case, the only thing that Dax thought he might be able to do would be to hold onto that understanding, and to keep it tightly bound inside of him so that he could use it against whatever it was that he had to face. At this point, Dax did not know what he was going to have to deal with.

"So we have essence runes all throughout the city that you think are creating some sort of a band of danger near us." She looked at him, frowning. "Do I have that right?"

"Pretty much," he said, nodding. "But I don't know the purpose of them. And given what I have seen at the edge of the forest, I can't help but feel as if it is all linked together."

Dax took a moment, then tried something that he had done on the runes in his room. He wasn't sure that it would do anything, but as he traced a pattern, he felt a strange shifting of power. It was subtle, but maybe he could disrupt what had been placed here. And if Karelly—or Raisor, he had to admit—was responsible for this, then it would be useful.

He noticed more of the rune patterns nearby, and he hurried off, Rochelle following him. They finished their circuit, with Dax attempting to disrupt a few more of the runes. He wasn't sure if it worked on all of them, but he *felt* as if the strange power that had been there was different than before.

When they were done, Rochelle was just watching him. "What now?" she asked him.

"Alibard, and then…"

"Then rest?"

He shrugged. "I suppose we need to rest."

"Good. I'm tired, and you know that we have that project coming up."

Dax knew that they did, but the same time, he wasn't even sure that it mattered to him at this point. All that mattered was that they had to make sure that the city was safe. The Academy was safe.

After checking on Alibard—and not finding him again—they went back to Rochelle's room, where they slept. Neither of them was in much of a mood to talk, not like they often did for much of the night.

Dax had strange dreams that night that reminded him of his vision of the Great Serpent. There was a different power mixed in, one that felt like a drumming—that was then cut off. When morning came, Dax got up early and made his way toward the transference barn, where he began to make his rounds as he had every other morning since coming to take on these extra responsibilities. The early morning air felt different than usual, and there was a bit of a strange ambient essence in the air, though he couldn't fully identify the source of it. Maybe it came from the transference barn, though even that wasn't obvious.

He didn't see any sign of Alex, but that wasn't surprising, as Dax had come to the transference barn earlier than usual. By the time he reached the sproutsels, he rubbed a knuckle into his eyes as he started to feed them.

He continued focusing on the essence inside of the creatures. There was a pattern to it that he thought he could understand, and having been around the silk shatters, he thought he needed to understand.

Essence. Understanding. Transference.

Dax made his way toward the back of the transference barn, where he reached the doors. They were locked, but he began to question if they were locked to keep him out or to keep whatever was inside blocked from them. Alex had allowed him in here before, and he wanted to see what else was there.

Maybe what he really needed was to go to the cinder-crawl and see if he could understand the essence inside of that creature. Perhaps he could learn more about fire—and maybe even find a connection with what had happened at the Academy.

He made his way to the door at the back of the trans-ference barn, where he withdrew essence from the runes to open it. Once he stepped inside, he noticed a flow of power, along with more runes on the wall than had been there before.

And, surprisingly, there were more stone holding cells. Had those been there even the day before? He didn't remember such essence energy when he'd been through on his rounds yesterday. He realized that he was still holding onto the power that he had drawn off the door and hurried back over, releasing that back into it to lock it once more.

Dax approached the first of them.

When he did, he could feel something about the holding cell, and the essence within it, that troubled him. A series of markings along the surface of the stone caught his attention, but he couldn't tell their purpose other than containment.

He made his way around the first of the stone holding cells, which was situated in the middle of the room. There were other rune markers along the stone floor, and even more that seem to be targeting the center of the room itself.

Dax knew it was foolish, but he stepped across the runic markers and approached.

He realized that he was still holding onto the power that he had drawn off the door and hurried back over, releasing that back into it to lock it once more.

As he studied the boxes, he noticed something: a series of markers that weren't that different from what he'd seen around the city.

Could Madenil be involved?

He would never have believed her to be a part of it, but the runes *were* similar. Not the same, though—just familiar.

As he focused on them, he tried to make sense of what they were trying to show him, until he realized that they all were designed to hold whatever was inside of the holding cell. He found a set of markers at about chest height that did not seem to be tied to the rest. This one was for wind and water, nothing else. Dax frowned, and he focused on the runes, wondering if there might be something within it that he could detect. But even as he approached it, staring at it, there wasn't anything clear about it.

Tentatively, he used transference on it.

When he did, there was a faint stirring of power. It left Dax with a worry: what if he released whatever was inside of here? There was no guarantee that he would be able to put it back into the holding pen. Worse, there was the possibility that whatever was in here was incredibly dangerous, and that his mere presence here was a mistake.

But he had to know. At least, he *wanted* to know.

He pressed on the runes.

It seemed as if wind and water coalesced, creating a window in the stone.

Interesting.

He stood for a moment, and then he looked through.

He didn't recognize the creature on the other side. It had three legs, a massive torso, and an almost oblong head with something of a point to it. A dozen eyes twisted, turning to him. When they did, Dax felt a weight to that gaze. Not only that, but he had a sneaking suspicion that there was something within those eyes, something within that energy, that knew him.

He jerked back.

As soon as he did, the energy that he was holding began to withdraw, flowing back into the stone. The window closed. It did nothing to change the feeling that Dax had.

Whatever was inside was powerful. And possibly—probably—sentient.

Dax had been raised along the unclaimed lands, where he had experienced plenty of creatures, so there should've been no reason for him to be concerned about the ones they kept here. But with his rising concern about truly sentient creatures, he knew better than to overlook it. That was the consequence of what the Great Serpent had given him.

He approached another of the holding cells, and he realized that this was the same one that had been holding the cindercrawl before.

As he neared it, he tapped on the markers, and the window opened. This one was far more straightforward for him because he was anticipating what would happen, so as the window opened, he peered inside, curious as to what he might find.

The cindercrawl was there.

Dax had known that it would be, but he hadn't known that it would be crouched down, wings folded inward, looking as if it were fading.

What was wrong with it?

The cindercrawl looked up, blinked for a moment, and there was an intensity in its gaze that suddenly returned, surging as it stared at Dax. It started to stand, which forced Dax to take a step back.

The window closed, but he turned and looked at the others. He approached the next one.

He activated the window inside much like he had before. There was a large creature with pale white fur and massive paws resting inside. It looked something like a bear, only it had a narrower head and almost pointed ears. He wondered what kind of a creature this was.

The eyes that looked at him seemed knowing.

It was odd that there would be so many apparently powerful creatures. It struck him as significant, but he wondered how, and why, and whether there was anything that he could do about it. What had brought them here? Had something drawn them—or chased them?

Dax had feared that it was tied to the Order, tied to something and someone who had targeted them, wanting to hunt them. But that still didn't explain exactly how these creatures ended up here.

There were transference hunters, though Dax had never met any of them. He knew they were there, mostly because Professor Madenil had mentioned them as the method by which these creatures had been brought to the city in the first place. What sort of transference hunter would've been required to bring something like this here? Or the cindercrawl? Or whatever that first creature was?

He didn't care for any of this. He'd been so caught up in the idea of transference, the idea of these creatures and their power being something he could see and maybe learn from, that he hadn't even started to question why they were here.

There had been offhand comments starting from the beginning of the transference term. First there had been what Professor Madenil had said about the different dangerous creatures, like the frosthooves. And while they might generally have been more dangerous than the cattle, they certainly weren't dangerous. It wasn't until he had taken up transference in full, having come to the transference barn, that he had begun to see some of the other more exotic creatures. That was when Dax really should have been more curious.

Only he had been so caught up in what he had been doing, and trying to keep track of everything, that he had neglected it.

Now he started to wonder. They had animals here that were far too dangerous for the Academy. But no one had explained why they were here.

He stared at the bear, focusing on the creature's essence.

It was pale, white, and it seemed to be crisp.

Some sort of ice essence.

As he focused on it, Dax could actually see the flow of essence within the creature, and he could tell that the bear was preparing some sort of attack. It had looked as if it were attempting to layer ice around the inside of the stone cell, which, as Dax reflected upon it, he'd decided it probably was. Given the protections that were placed onto the stone itself, the containment runes that Dax had seen, he wouldn't have been surprised if it had been doing that for quite a while yet failing.

The creature sent a blast of ice at the window.

For a moment, the wind and water that formed the window started to crystallize.

Then the stone slid back into place.

Some sort of defense mechanism.

What about the others? He had seen the cindercrawl, and the flame power within it, but he wasn't even sure what that was. And the first creature?

Dax wasn't even sure what that was, nor was he sure what the creature's essence was, only that it was powerful.

There was still one more holding cell. He hadn't opened it yet, but now he was increasingly curious about what was here, so as he approached it, he was ready. He looked around, noticing the holding runes that were there, and he had a distinct belief they were relatively new.

But then he frowned.

Some of them were familiar to him.

Runes that he had seen. Runes that he had demonstrated.

The runes he had shown Professor Alibard.

And he thought about Professor Alibard's injury.

Along with his periodic disappearances.

He looked around the inside of this chamber. How many of these runes had been placed by Professor Alibard? Dax had been working with him, trying to gain understanding about the runes. What if Professor Alibard had been using what Dax had been showing him, taking that to apply to this?

He approached the holding cell, and as he did, he trembled as he touched the markers for the window. Now that he knew how to open it, he was fully prepared for anything that he might find inside.

So as he triggered it, he waited.

And then he froze.

The silk shatter that had escorted him through the forest was inside.

Chapter Fifty-Two

DAX COULDN'T MOVE. ANGER FLASHED IN THE SILK shatter's eyes.

"I didn't do this," Dax said. He had no idea how much the silk shatter could even hear him through the stone nor whether it would even make a difference, but he felt as if it were necessary to say something to him. "I don't know who is responsible, but I didn't do this."

There was still no answer.

The silk shatter looked at him. His five eyes seemed to focus on Dax entirely. Every other time that Dax had seen the creature in the forest, he had not had that same impression, so this was something altogether different, something that left him feeling uncomfortable.

But the silk shatter still had not spoken to him.

He leaned forward, and once again, he found the creature leaning back, careening up on his hind legs, as much as he could inside of the confines of the stone. He tried to tap his forelegs together. Dax braced, knowing that there would be a tremble in the earth that would follow, but there was nothing. Whatever the patterns were around this enclosure absorbed some of that, and they prevented the creature from causing the earth to shake.

He had no idea how the silk shatter would've gotten caught in the first place. He had been in the forest, hadn't it? And inside of an area that Dax couldn't penetrate.

But that didn't mean that others couldn't.

Then there was what Professor Madenil had said about the transference hunters.

That could be dangerous. If there were hunters using transference, maybe that was the reason they were moving. What if they were chasing the essence from the different creatures that were migrating?

But how had they found the silk shatter?

Dax frowned, and he stared at the markings. He was left with a dilemma. He had no idea who was responsible for this, but he didn't think the silk shatter should be held here.

If he released him, the silk shatter wouldn't harm him. *Would he?*

There was none of the irritation on the back of his neck to suggest the silk shatter intended to harm him. Which made him think it would be safe to remove the containment runes.

But even if the silk shatter didn't harm him, Professor Madenil might.

He could downplay it, Dax thought, trying to think of some way to blame the silk shatter on his escape, or perhaps one of the other creatures. He found himself looking back toward that holding cell, thinking about the silk shatter inside of it and thinking that he could not leave him there. It bothered him.

Dax breathed out.

This wasn't the reason that he had come here. He had

come because he had thought that he had needed to try to help take care of the creatures, but he had been compelled to come over here, which may have been a mistake. Now that he was here, Dax approached, and he focused on the containment runes for the silk shatter. He began to use transference.

He hadn't even drawn very much power before there was a clapping of stone, a buildup of power, something that thundered, and then...

Then the containment shattered.

The silk shatter burst free.

He pounced and landed atop Dax.

It was so startling and sudden that Dax could scarcely react.

And he couldn't breathe. The silk shatter was heavy, and the essence that he radiated outward and through him was incredible.

"I didn't have anything to do with this," Dax said.

"You would keep us from the key to the parlay?" the silk shatter demanded.

"I didn't keep you from anything," Dax said, mind racing to make sense of what was going on. He wasn't sure that he understood, but it had to be the reason he—and maybe some of the other powerful creatures—was even here.

The silk shatter continued to press down on him, and Dax was forced to use transference.

Having spent time around the silk shatter and recognizing his essence made it easier for him, but he also didn't want the creature to think he was going to harm him. Dax drew on earth and life and wind and water, even a bit of fire, transferring all of it. He had never attempted to do something quite like that before, but he simply drew the essence into himself. He held it and felt some part of himself beginning to shift. Then he turned it outward, and he let it explode upward, into the silk shatter.

The suddenness of the force of that explosion sent the silk shatter staggering backward. He started to pounce toward him again, but Dax held his hand out.

"I didn't have anything to do with this," he said. "I don't know what happened here, but I can help you. Please."

"You *are* with them."

"I don't know who you are talking about." He swept his gaze around, realizing where he was and how it would appear. "Well, I suppose you would say that I am with them, but I didn't do this."

The silk shatter stomped on the ground, and again, there came a steady trembling. "You have held us. You have held *it*."

Now he felt what was happening.

The silk shatter was disrupting the other containment runes.

"Please," he said. "I didn't have anything to do with this. I…"

"You are with them."

"I am a student at the Academy here. I'm trying to understand essence. That is what the Great Serpent asked of me."

Appealing to the Great Serpent had worked with the silk shatter before. Hopefully it would work now.

The creature tapped on the ground again, and another flare of earth went rumbling away from it.

Dax reacted, using transference, trying to draw some of the energy out of it. He could feel the containment runes starting to sputter. He worried about what would happen.

He feared the cindercrawl, the bear, and whatever the other strange creature was, and he feared what might happen if they were to escape.

He held his hand up, and once again, he spoke. "I didn't have anything to do with this, and I don't know what's happening here, but I can help you."

"You will release it to her."

Dax shook his head, and he looked around. "Who? The bear? The cindercrawl?"

Or worse, he thought, the strange creature at the other end. But none of them really made any sense to him. What would he free?

And how would he free them?

Dax could feel something here, but he didn't want to have any role in releasing anything. He was especially afraid of the cindercrawl, though each of these creatures had to be incredibly dangerous, given the fact that they were held in such tightly bound containment boxes.

Then the silk shatter began to tap his legs again.

Dax had to release the earth essence that he had already held, exploding it upward rather than at the silk shatter, using transference on the essence to disrupt the containments.

The essence continued to tremble, and then he realized something.

The silk shatter wasn't just trying to use essence to try to disrupt the containment, though that was part of it.

"Please," Dax said, "I can help you, but you have help me understand what happened here."

"You will release it to her," he said.

"If you tell me what we have, or what you think that I have, I will do whatever I can in order to release her."

"Release," he said again, then once again.

The creature waited, watching him. Increasingly, Dax could feel the energy coming off the silk shatter, the way that he was continuing to let all his different types of essence out.

"Help me understand…" Dax wanted nothing more than to try to understand what it was that the silk shatter wanted out of him so that he could get out of this alive. The silk shatter was powerful, and if he managed to disrupt the protective enclosures around him, then there was a very real possibility that he wouldn't.

One of the other stone containments began to crack.

Dax looked over, and he was not at all surprised to see that it was the bear's.

Cold began to erupt from the box. Dax drew upon that cold with transference, wishing that he had better control over it. As he drew on that cold, he sent it toward the silk shatter.

If nothing else, he would slow it, which might give Dax a chance to get free.

The ice crawled along the surface of stone until it crackled. Then, with a massive explosion of stone and ice, the pen shattered.

There was a strange drawing of energy, and Dax glanced over his shoulder, looking for a moment to see if some of the other containment crates had broken. He was relieved when they didn't, but instead, he saw the door to this holding pen starting to open.

Who—or what—was coming?

He moved closer to the silk shatter.

He tried to hold onto the ice essence, but the bear was raging, and Dax's attempt at containing its essence was growing increasingly difficult. As he pulled that essence, Dax stored it, and surprisingly felt it flowing inside of him

—and staying. He had felt that before, but he had never really known if it was a permanent change. This felt distinct in a way that other things had not. He felt a vibrant surge, and an awareness of the essence around him, that he hadn't noticed before. There were bands of color that flowed within each of the essences, including from inside of the bear—and the silk shatter.

Each type of essence had other striations of color.

What was this?

The only answer that came to mind was that he must have progressed in some way. He would need to test himself to see if he had, but for now, he was content knowing that he could at least temporarily progress by holding onto borrowed essence. That had to be significant.

And if he were to confront one of the Order...

Dax doubted that he could progress himself to a wielder level, but he might be able to make it seem as if he were.

Pushing those thoughts away, he neared the silk shatter.

"Please," Dax said again, "I want to help you, but for me to do so, I need to know more about what happened."

"Then return what was gifted to us."

The silk shatter roared, standing up on only two legs now, and there was a steady drumming. Each leg clapped together, two at a time, working down his body.

Thump. Thump. Thump.

There was a pressure with each one. It was painful.

Thump. Thump. Thump.

He felt the silk shatter's power.

He felt the energy. He felt the call.

Thump. Thump. Thump.

But a call for what?

Chapter Fifty-Three

THE DOOR BEHIND HIM OPENED, AND NOW FIGURES WERE framed in the doorway.

Dax couldn't see who they were, but he noticed flashes of essence—and slight variations within them—that he thought were significant. Each time he felt that strange thumping, pain echoed through him.

Thump. Thump. Thump.

Each one filled him; each one left him trembling.

Thump. Thump. Thump.

He tried to use transference, but transference on this scale?

Whatever it was that the silk shatter was doing, the way that he was pulling upon energy, was far more than Dax could counter. Maybe his progression, temporary or not, would allow him to use transference.

Thump. Thump.

A return cry.

Stone exploded behind him.

He spun, and he ducked just in time to avoid a piece of stone that came flying toward him.

It was the cindercrawl.

It shot upward, circling in the air above him, heat beginning to radiate along its body. Dax drew upon its fire, feeling a bit more comfortable with fire than he did with ice, as there was something familiar to that for him. As he drew on it, he immediately created a flame barrier in front of him. He couldn't hold onto it indefinitely, but he could use a rune to shoot flames upward and prevent the bear from rumbling toward him and destroying him.

Thump. Thump.

Then he felt wind.

At first, Dax thought it was coming from the silk shatter, as he did know that the creature had some wind essence. But he wasn't entirely sure that was the source, only that it was swirling, and building, and was more potent than what he had ever felt from the silk shatter before.

Dax stayed low, thinking that maybe it was coming from the cindercrawl, or perhaps from the remaining caged creature. But as he rolled to his side, looking over, he realized it didn't seem to be the case. The cindercrawl continued to circle, heat radiating along its body, but gradually, that heat started to fade. It seemed almost as if the flame and heat inside of it was getting tamped down. Dax had never seen anything quite like it before, but something was drawing essence away.

Transference?

Thump. Thump. Thump.

That wasn't diminishing though. The power continued to echo, rumbling through the room, and the more Dax could feel it, the more that he began to recognize that the silk shatter was calling to something.

Then the figures approached.

He noticed the dark robes. He noticed the essence blades held outward.

Guardians.

They were draining the essence from the cindercrawl.

There was one pointing at him. He could feel something drawing on him.

"I'm on your side," Dax cried out.

He began to call upon essence, and he pulled on it.

He had transference, didn't he?

Dax wouldn't let these Guardians drain him because he happened to be in the wrong place at the wrong time. He got to his feet and quickly withdrew his own essence blade, and he held it outward, pointing it at the Guardian.

It seemed as if the air crackled. Transference met transference.

Only Dax was aware of something different.

It seemed as if however the Guardian was using transference, it was not the kind of transference that Dax had.

It didn't seem to be transference, only runes.

That was what it was. Transference runes.

Could that have been what he'd seen?

He focused, and on a whim, he drew upon fire, and then on ice, wondering if he could draw upon both. He was surprised, pleasantly so, to realize that he could. Both creatures that were near him radiated power through him, through his blade, which erupted outward.

As he held onto the essence, Dax began to feel something strange. He was aware of how that Guardian's rune attempted to pull the essence that he was drawing upon, to transfer his essence into it.

It was a strange feeling, but it also guided him. He could

resist. It was a simple matter for him to do so. Dax had far more transference ability than these Guardians did.

He pushed his power into the room.

All the time that he'd spent in his classes involved learning how to make and place runes. What he wanted to do now was something different. What he wanted now was to overwhelm the rune.

And that was simple enough.

The rune shattered, erupting essence outward.

He heard a strangled cry. Something clattered.

The essence blade.

He smiled.

He darted forward, and he raced out through the open door.

There was a steady drumming behind him, and he could feel it.

Thump. Thump. Thump.

He practically collided with Alex.

She looked up at him, eyes wide. "Dax? What are you doing? Were you…?"

"Yes. I was in there, and the creatures escaped."

"They escaped? Wait. *Creatures?*"

"There was more than just the cindercrawl," Dax said. "And they are all escaping, and now we have Guardians in there, and apparently they can use some sort of transference rune to try to diminish them, but…"

He looked around. The animals inside of here were all agitated. There was a steady, wild sort of energy. A shrieking.

Thump. Thump. Thump.

"Something's going on," Dax said, "and they want something, but I don't know what it is. The silk shatter—the creature that looks something like a spider," Dax said, motioning toward the other room, where he could still see it, just drumming, calling, "is looking for something. Someone. I don't really know. He asked me to release her."

"He asked? They can *talk*?"

"The silk shatter can. I think the bear might be intelligent, as well, and the cindercrawl certainly is." Dax shivered at what he had felt, but he didn't want to repeat it, as there was nothing within him that thought he could deal with that. "Anyway, we need to find what they're after."

"Why?"

"Can you feel it?" Dax said, and he looked around. "Because these creatures can."

Thump. Thump.

Dax was going to have to do something, but he wasn't sure what it was.

Thump. Thump.

What if he could follow the silk shatter's call?

He had no idea if such a thing was possible, and he had no idea if there was any way that he would be able to understand anything at the end of it, but he had to try to find something. If he waited too much longer, he feared what was going to happen here, and he feared what might befall the city—and the Academy.

He braced for the power here.

Thump. Thump.

"Do you know any other place that they might have creatures held?"

"No place else," she said. "This is the only place."

There had to be some other place.

That was what was getting called to.

And maybe that was what this was all about. Not about the Order—not like he had believed. About movement. About creatures.

And now they were held.

"Oh, Great Serpent," Dax muttered.

"What is it?"

"Just something dangerous. I need to go."

"Go? With what's happening here, and with the creatures getting wild?"

"I'm going to come back, or at least, I intend to come back, but you need to get out of here."

"I'm not leaving them. Not when they're like this. I can calm them down."

He wanted to tell her that it was going to be difficult, and maybe impossible, but he also knew better than to tell her what he was going to do. So he said nothing about that. "Good luck," was all he said.

He raced toward the door.

Professor Madenil was there, standing in the doorway, frowning at him. "Where do you think you are going?"

"No time," he said. "Apparently you captured a silk shatter, and he wants something that's not here, and if we don't bring it to him, or bring him to it, he is going to destroy this entire place. So…"

He thought that she was going to try to stop him. Instead, he felt the pressure behind him.

Thump. Thump.

"But the Guardians—" she said.

"I don't know what the Guardians were doing bringing these creatures," he said, taking a risk to think that was who was responsible. "But it was a mistake."

"They did not bring them. They have captured them in the city. Alibard and others have been trying to secure the city to prevent additional ingress—"

"With runes?" Dax asked.

She frowned.

Could that have been what this was all about? The silk shatters were kept out of the city? But why?

The flare.

That was the only thing he could think of.

The fire in the building. The creatures that he'd seen there. And the Order—Raisor.

What if the creatures had been there to collect the flare, and Raisor had stopped them to take it for himself—and the Order?

There wasn't any time to waste. He had to try to do something—even if it didn't work.

"Well now we have all sorts of creatures angry at the Guardians. You may want to stay out of it until I get back."

"Back?" Professor Madenil asked, and she arched a brow at him. "What are you going on about, Mr. Nelson?"

"I think I can help. But you have to trust me."

She frowned. "You should not interfere with the Guardians."

"I'm not trusting the Guardians. Not with this. They don't know what they are doing."

He went racing across the campus.

By the time he reached his dorm, he heard his name shouted behind him. He spun, seeing Rochelle with Cedrick.

"No time," he said. "Meet me at the administrative building. We have to get inside, because the silk shatters want the flare."

"And you're just going to give it to them?" she asked.

"I think that's what we're supposed to do."

Rochelle gaped at him, but she didn't say anything.

"How do you intend to get past the Guardians?" Cedrick asked.

"Painfully," Dax muttered.

Now that he had progressed somewhat—though he wasn't certain if it was permanent yet—he could see the striations. It allowed him to use more of his power than he had before. That had to be the key to stopping this.

Not stopping. Freeing.

He went running. Rochelle stayed with him, and he looked over his shoulder to see Cedrick racing off in a different direction.

"He's getting Gia."

"Great," he said.

"Are you sure about this?"

"Not at all," Dax said.

Thump. Thump. Thump.

It seemed to be building.

Whatever it was that the silk shatter was doing, it was starting to rise in intensity. He needed to find whatever it was the creatures were after, get it to them, and keep them from destroying all of the Academy.

"I don't know if this is going to work, but there might be another way to get into the administrative building," Rochelle said.

"How? Did you find some back entrance? Or do you intend for us to climb up the way that we snuck out?"

"Different," she said. "I found something." He looked over, and she shrugged. "Well, while you've been off in the transference barn every morning, I've been spending time in the library. We've needed to know more about that member of the Order, haven't we? And though we haven't been able to find anything about him, I did find something else. I have to show you," she said.

"I don't know if we have time."

"We have to have time. At least, we have to have time for this."

He raced into the library, past the librarians, who shouted at him and Rochelle, and then down. He thought that she was going to take him to some sort of research section, but she took him deeper, into the fifth sublevel, and then she opened the door before motioning for him to head inside.

It was a dark, narrow hallway.

"What are you doing?" Dax asked.

"This connects," she said. "The library connects to each of the other buildings. It's an old way of getting around campus. I found it when I was studying one time."

"You found this door? Or you found—"

"Is now the time to ask?"

"I suppose not," Dax said.

They went hurrying forward, and deep in the ground, Dax could feel something more, something different than what he had felt before, to the point where the walls felt like they were beginning to shake around him.

Thump. Thump.

"Do you feel that?" Dax said. She nodded. "That's the silk shatter. At least, one of them. I don't know what he's doing, but he's calling to others so that…"

She rounded on him. "The silk shatter is calling to others?"

Dax nodded. "Calling. And they are answering."

Thump. Thump. Thump.

They hurried along the hall, and they reached a door at the end.

"This is as far as I was able to go," Rochelle said. "I figure that with your transference…"

Dax examined the door. It was old. The metal within it seemed slightly warm, and there were markers on it that he had not seen before, but there was a certain sort of energy within them. He frowned, and as he studied it for a moment, he began to transfer the essence.

Even as he did, he recognized something different about it.

"This doesn't lead where…"

The door came open.

Blackness greeted them. Blackness streaked with silver.

A conduit, like what he'd found in Desmond's home.

But a conduit to where?

Chapter Fifty-Four

ROCHELLE PUSHED HIM INTO THE DOORWAY.

"Look at it," Dax said. "I don't know if you can see the silver, but it's a conduit like in Desmond's home. But I don't know where it's taking us."

Thump. Thump. Thump.

He looked over at her. "Not this way, then."

She nodded, and they raced back out of the library, upstairs, then out. The Academy grounds were more chaotic now. Students had filed out of the dorms. Instructors were racing around.

And there were creatures.

Dozens of them.

Many of them were surrounded by instructors, all trying to subdue them, but from what Dax could see of the creatures' essence, they were all powerful.

And they were attacking.

"Oh, Great Serpent," Rochelle muttered.

"Come on," he said, grabbing her arm and dragging her with him. They raced toward the administrative building, where they paused. Two Guardians blocked the main entrance.

"Any thoughts?" Rochelle asked.

"None that are good," Dax muttered.

"Well, we could try to draw them off."

"I don't know if that's going to work. We need to over-power them."

Rochelle frowned, arching a brow at him. "You want to overpower the Guardians? Servants of the Emperor? Are you mad?"

"Well, they don't have to know we're doing it."

"Dax…"

Cedrick and Gia joined them then. He filled them in, and Gia frowned, turning toward the door. "I suppose that means you and me?"

"No," Cedrick said. "Too risky."

"Actually," Dax began, "I have a better idea. I'm going to use something Gia wanted me to focus on. But I'm going to need to borrow from all of you."

They all frowned at him.

"I need to focus my transference essence, but I'm going to need to borrow yours as well. I think the combined power should allow me to draw what I need and focus it outward. So," he said, filling them in on what he was think-ing, "here is what I propose."

As he shared, they each nodded. Then they took up places around him.

Dax could feel their essence more easily. It was easier surrounding him than it was in a line. And so he began to transfer their essence. He wouldn't have even considered this had he not been inside of the transference barn and drawing upon fire and ice at the same time. In this case, he wanted life, water, and earth. It was a strange combination, but it really wasn't meant to do anything other than provide a vessel for transference. And he didn't want to kill, just incapacitate.

From a distance, Dax hoped he had enough range.

Earth and life could help with that, and water would be able to wrap his essence burst in enough of a band to keep the range to what he needed.

Dax focused, and then he pushed.

When he did, he wrapped each of the other essences around his bolt of transference essence. It struck the Guardian. The man opened his eyes wide, and then he collapsed. As the other started to turn, Dax focused, then pushed, using everything in him to do so. It struck just as the man was bending over. It caught him in the forehead. He collapsed immediately and began to convulse.

"That might've been a little more than you needed," Rochelle said.

She raced toward them, and as soon as she got there, she sent a healing wave of water through them both. Dax didn't hesitate, though. He was already through the door and heading toward the stairs.

Cedrick and Gia were with him.

They darted up the stairs, and he had his essence blade in hand so that by the time he reached the second-floor landing, he was ready—but not ready for what he faced.

Three dark-cloaked men stood in the hall.

Dax thought he recognized one of them.

No. He did recognize him. It was the same man that he had seen in the forest outside of the Serpent Stairs. This *was* about the Order.

The man turned. Dax used transference, exploding it outward in a burst, but it faded when it struck.

Of course it would, because the Order had some sort of dissipating power.

He snorted. "Nice try, kid."

He raised his blade.

Gia surprised him.

She darted forward, driving her essence blade into the side of one of the others of the Order. She turned, kicking at the legs of another.

Gia was doing well.

She understood valor and was well trained.

These others might've been powerful essence wielders, but there was a difference between essence wielding and being skilled at valor. Perhaps that was one of the lessons that Professor Garrison had been hopeful they would learn. Maybe that was part of the reason he was comfortable letting the two of them just spar.

Dax approached Raisor. "You knew about these creatures."

"I knew," he said. "That is sort of my specialty within the Order." He smiled. "Once I realized there was a flare, I knew what was happening. I knew what to expect next. It would be an essence parlay."

Dax wasn't sure what to make of that, but maybe he didn't need to.

"And so you thought to take the flare."

"The flare, among others. It was easy enough to convince the transference hunters to gather the creatures. They are simple folk."

"The hunters or the creatures?"

He smiled tightly.

"Because the creatures are not simple."

"And you think that I should be concerned about the word of one student?"

"Not just one," Cedrick said.

"I'm here," Rochelle said, stepping forward.

"Three students," Raisor said, chuckling. "And fools at that."

Raisor raised his blade. Dax had fought him before and barely survived. This was a master essence wielder. He might've even been at headmaster level or higher. He had more power than Dax could wield. Even temporarily raising his essence level might not be enough.

He remembered something else. Having been in the transference barn, he had learned that he could shatter a rune.

He didn't have to be that powerful to break it. Just more powerful than he was.

He focused on the essence around him.

And there *was* essence around him.

Not only that of Rochelle, Cedrick, and Gia, none of which he wanted to harm, but only a pace in front of him was one of the fiery containment runes that he had used before.

He focused on transference. And *only* on transference.

Then he pushed through his blade, expressing his essence as Gia had wanted him to master. Power poured out and toward Raisor's sword.

Raisor tried to pull back, but Dax forced more into the sword. There was a loud, strange shriek, then a pop. The rune, transference of some sort, shattered.

He nodded to Cedrick. "Now you can attack."

Pink bubbles drifted out of his blade. Raisor frowned at them, but as soon as Cedrick's bubble struck the man, he started to scream.

"There's some life for you!" Cedrick yelled.

Gia was facing Raisor, and she nodded at Dax. "Go.

We can hold him."

Dax wasn't sure they could—but he needed to trust them. He couldn't stay here.

He darted to the top of the stairs.

Distantly, he was aware of the trembling.

Thump. Thump. Thump.

When he got to the top of the stairs, he saw five people. One of them had the door of the strange chamber open and was standing inside. The other four were mingling around.

What were so many from the Order doing here?

And how had they been hiding here all along?

He stood for a moment, realizing where he was standing, and then he released the containment rune. It was a simple thing, as he had placed it himself, but directing the fire back into the room was something else entirely.

He tried not to think about what he was doing, who he was targeting, or anything else, only that he could feel that flame begin to flow.

It consumed the room. The heat was enormous.

Cedrick joined him, and Dax frowned for a moment. "Do you think you could add life to the fire?"

"Why?"

"Just a thought I had."

Cedrick frowned, and then held his hands out, and some of the pink began to stream from him. The effect was immediate.

As it mingled with the flames, the fire began to intensify. Shrieks of pain were followed by the sound of stone shattering. Then the shrieks fell silent.

"Did you kill them?" Cedrick asked.

"No. I don't know that I could have. They escaped. At least for now."

Dax began to pull fire out, placing it into the containment rune.

There was still one person here. And he recognized them.

Ames. The old headmaster.

"You have proven quite troublesome," Ames said. "And you've revealed the extent of my infiltration of the Guardians. I'm going to have to deal with you, but perhaps you could be of assistance."

They had come for the essence flare, but why was it so important to them?

"Where is it?"

Dax glowered at him. "Why do you need it? It's just essence. You could've gotten that inside the tower... which means it's more than just essence, isn't it?"

He pointed the blade at Dax. "Much more. And you are too inexperienced to understand. You took away my opportunity with the Great Serpent, but you will not take away my opportunity with her."

Her.

It was the second time that he had heard that.

Her?

The silk shatter.

"Did you really think to take the Queen's essence?" Dax asked.

The look of confusion on the headmaster's face was almost enough to bring a smile to Dax's face. Almost.

"Take it? No. *Trade* it. Once I have *her* essence, then even the Emperor himself will have to parlay with us."

"Why?"

Ames glowered at him again. "I'm done with this. You will return it to me."

"I don't think so," Dax said.

"You don't have Desmond with you now. How do you think you can handle me?"

"We've learned," Dax said.

The headmaster snorted. "You're students. That's all you are."

"But skilled students. And personally gifted by the Great Serpent." He smiled tightly. "Unlike you."

The headmaster glowered at him, and then a beam of power shot from the end of his blade. For the first time in a while, the tingling on the back of Dax's neck seemed to shriek. Dax dropped, but he did more than that. He swept his leg around and pulled his friends down. They went in a heap.

He twisted, rolling, and pointed his own essence blade, drawing upon transference as he did. He summoned each of the essences from around him, and he shot toward the headmaster.

Ames managed to catch all of that on his blade.

He pointed that same blade at Dax.

The essence streaming from the end was considerable. There was a tingling on the back of his neck, a warning from the Great Serpent, and Dax rolled out of the way.

He had to try something different.

The kind of power that Ames wielded was greater than what he had fought before. The others had used runes to augment their essence. He had a feeling that the headmaster did not.

He cocked his head to the side, regarding Dax.

"Had you more time, you might have an opportunity. But you don't understand what you face. You don't understand what we intend. And you cannot stop it."

"I understand that you intend to destroy the Great Serpent. Or you intend to steal power—"

A stirring on his neck caught Dax's attention, and he rolled.

A blast of fire came.

But it wasn't coming *from* Ames. It came *toward* Ames.

Dax popped to his feet, and he saw...

"Mother?"

Ice circled, swirling and joining with the fire, the two building.

"I think it's time that you get out of here, Dax."

"How did you get here?"

"Not now, Son," she said.

He looked over at his friends.

"We can't go without—"

"Go!"

He hurried over to the others.

"What is going on? Who is that?" Cedrick asked.

"That's my mother and... Desmond?"

Desmond strode forward, and he was not alone. There were two others behind him, though Dax didn't know either of them.

He looked around. They didn't have to deal with headmaster.

Others who were more capable of handling him would do that.

"What do we do now?" Rochelle asked. "Do we go?"

"We need to get the crystal to the Queen. That's what this has been about. I just don't fully understand *why*," Dax said.

She locked eyes with him. "You never make it easy, do you, Dax?"

"How is this my fault?"

She laughed, and then they darted toward the hidden wall.

Chapter Fifty-Five

THEY STOOD IN FRONT OF THE WALL AS DAX FOCUSED ON
the essence. He began to draw it off, sensing the fight that
was going on behind him. Casting a glance over his shoulder, he saw his mother and Desmond and the other two
Cult members raging in a battle with Ames. Somehow,
Ames was still holding them back.

What hope would Dax or the others have had in
defeating him?

But he didn't need to worry about that. All he needed to
do was to get the essence flare to the silk shatter. He
squeezed his eyes shut, focusing his essence down tightly. It
was difficult, as he was scared, and he had been trying to
use so much transference, he wasn't even sure what he
might find.

Then he felt it. He jumped and grabbed it.

"What now?" Gia asked. "Do you intend for us to fight
our way out?"

Dax shook his head. "I think that would be a terrible
idea. We need to go up."

"Up isn't out," Cedrick said.

"Nope, not exactly," Dax said.

He found the ladder, and then he climbed, and once outside, he stood for a moment, looking around the university grounds. It was chaos.

Students and professors and creatures all battled.

The steady thumping persisted.

Everything within Dax was on edge.

"Why did they attack now?" Rochelle asked, her voice soft.

"It's all about these creatures. That's all I can tell. Not sure why it is, though."

"How are we going to get down?"

"Gia," Dax said, turning to her.

"What? She's going to catch us?" Cedrick asked.

"No, earth, dummy," she said, turning to the side of the building, where she leaned forward and focused her essence. Gradually, the wall rippled. It wasn't significant, but a very narrow and steep staircase formed along the stone. "I can't hold this very long, so you had better get going."

Cedrick started forward, but Rochelle caught him. "Dax first. He knows these creatures."

Dax held her gaze before scrambling down the face of the building like it was a ladder. About midpoint, it started to tremble, and he hurried to the end, sliding the last few feet before landing with a thud on the ground. He looked up, and Gia was clenching her jaw.

"That's as long as I can hold it. Go deal with this."

He didn't want to leave his friends, but he did need to deal with this.

Dax looked around. The Academy grounds were such chaos that he wasn't even sure where he was supposed to go, only that he had to move. He went racing. He hadn't gone very far when he saw one of the Guardians chasing him from near the university building.

He turned, but there was the strange bearlike creature —or perhaps a different one—racing at him.

He was trapped.

Thump. Thump. Thump.

Thump. Thump.

The steady call.

Thump.

He didn't like the sound of that.

He hesitated a moment.

That last thump had come from someplace close. Someplace *down*.

And it had seemed to reverberate—almost as if toward him.

The library?

He looked around. He could fight his way across the grounds, head toward the transference barn, and hopefully get to the silk shatter, but there was no guarantee that the creature would be able, or willing, to stop all of this.

Was there?

Thump.

That single thump drew him.

Dax headed into the library, racing past the librarians, down to the fifth sublevel and into the hallway once more, where he came to a stop in front of the strange doorway. Once again, he felt the warmth from it. Without hesitating too long, he transferred the power out of it, pulled the door open, and stepped inside.

It was a conduit.

Thump.

The trembling was louder now.

He took a deep breath and stepped forward.

The silver surrounded him.

Thump.

He took another step. With each one, he could feel something shifting, but maybe it was just his imagination. He was terrified.

Thump.

He took another step.

Then there was a door. It was much like the last one, only this one was a deep green color, with what looked like vines, threads that were interlocked on it, forming some pattern that looked almost like a web.

Thump.

It was loud now.

He stepped forward, transferred essence from the door and into himself, and felt something familiar about it. Now he knew that he was heading in the right direction.

He pulled the door open.

The room that greeted him was filled with lush greenery, and an enormous silk shatter occupied the entirety of it. She towered above him, nearly two stories tall, with eight massive crystalline legs. The five eyes that turned toward him seemed to overwhelm him.

Dax could scarcely breathe. He could scarcely move. It felt as if he were in the presence of something as powerful as the Great Serpent.

He reached into his pocket and grabbed the crystal. "I have this."

There was a pause. "Dax Nelson," a voice said, seemingly from all over.

"Please call it off. I wasn't responsible for what happened."

"Your people were to hold it, not use it."

"Not my people," Dax said quickly. He had a feeling that he had to convince this silk shatter that he wasn't responsible, but he wasn't sure how he would be able to do that. "They were a part of something else. The Order that wanted to harm the Empire—and the Great Serpent. We did what we could to stop them."

There was a moment of silence. Dax feared that he wouldn't be freed, but he knew that if he wasn't willing to do what he could here, that he wouldn't be able to stop the attack. The creatures were angry—and for good reason.

All around him, he was aware of other silk shatters. He tried not to look, but even if he didn't, he was attuned to them, feeling them moving with the connection he had to essence. All of them scurried, skittering around, and he found himself trying not to freeze.

He held the crystal up.

"Dax Nelson."

"This wasn't my people, but I will do what is needed."

That was what the Great Serpent wanted of him.

Understanding.

Do what was needed.

And maybe the Great Serpent had known what was going to happen.

"What do you want me to do?" he asked.

Then he felt her presence.

There was no other way to describe it.

He felt as if he were torn into a black and empty void.

And within that void there was movement—a scurrying, a terrifying scratching of legs on stone. Gradually, he became aware of threads of other essence. Earth, then water, then life, then wind. Then he saw the silk shatter. Small, compact, and skittering through some darkness.

He was ripped free again.

The silk shatter was there, larger this time, surrounded by others.

Essence squeezed him, crushing him.

Then he saw another vision. This image was stranger than the last. A light? Brightness. Maybe essence, but it was mixed with other forms of it. And he felt something more.

She wasn't alone. There was another entity.

And it was an entity that Dax had felt before.

The Great Serpent.

"Dax Nelson."

There had been a vision when he had gone after the flare and seen the Great Serpent.

Dax was now holding the crystal.

This was a summons.

Thump.

So he stepped forward.

Dax had no idea what he was supposed to do with the crystal, no idea how he was supposed to use it. He only knew that he could feel that essence, and he could feel that summons. He could feel power from her, from the crystal, and flowing into him.

Thump.

He held it up.

But that wasn't what she wanted. She reared back.

She stood on her hind legs and exposed her belly.

Everything was a crisscrossing of essence, of glowing lines, and it met in the middle of her abdomen.

Thump.

Dax stepped forward, holding the crystal up.

He couldn't move.

Essence seemed to grip him.

No. Not him.

It gripped the crystal.

He released it. Those essence lines began to glow all around him, pulling that crystal away. It was a web. It came from the silk shatter. From all the silk shatters surrounding him. It pulled the crystal, bringing it toward her abdomen. The crystal touched, and there was a flash of light.

Then the silk shatter shrieked.

The sound seemed as if it were going to rip him apart.

He froze.

Then there was a thumping.

Thump. Thump. Thump… Thump.

It came from the silk shatter in front of him, but she wasn't moving. Somehow, Dax was certain, it was still her that did it. Once again it came.

Thump. Thump. Thump… Thump.

Then everything fell still.

"It is done," she said.

Chapter Fifty-Six

HE COULD SCARCELY MOVE.

He looked up at the silk shatter, but she had settled down onto her belly, her legs splayed out on either side of her. She was breathing, and there was a steadiness to her breathing, but it was a strange sort of steadiness.

He wanted to approach, but the other, smaller silk shatters pushed him back, guiding him toward the doorway that he had come through. Once there, he was pushed deeper, the steady scratching sound of their legs on stone forcing him back. Life essence created a web in front of him, and though Dax thought that he might be able to use transference on it, he did not dare. He had no idea what it would do, nor how it might aggravate her, but he was not at all willing to risk it. Instead, he found himself pushed deeper and deeper into the tunnel, until he felt something near him.

He froze.

The silk shatter from the Academy passed him.

"Why?" Dax asked.

"It was a gift to us. A trade," he said. "What you saw

was set into motion long ago. It was a celebration, but your kind interrupted. They thought to disrupt. They thought to steal."

That was what the Order was after. They wanted to claim the flare. They wanted to interrupt the essence parlay, whatever that was. And Desmond must have known.

"The celebration. That's the essence parlay," Dax said, looking back along the hall.

The crystal. The Great Serpent. And the Queen. Or whatever she was.

He had those images. His. Hers. And yet, it seemed as if there had been something more that he was supposed to know.

"What's going to happen?"

"Do not enter the forest."

"What of your kind? The other creatures? Are you still…?" He flicked his gaze up.

The silk shatter regarded him with those strange five eyes. There was a tapping. One. Two. Three. Then four.

The silk shatter settled back to the ground. "It is done. Do not enter the forest."

With that, he spun away and slid down the hall, disappearing with the sound of scraping legs on stone behind the door.

Dax finished making his way through the conduit and stepped back out, closing the door. Realizing that he was still holding onto the transference essence that he had used on the door, he poured it back into it.

It closed, locking once again.

He had no idea who could access it, but he wasn't going to be the reason that somebody broke in and harmed the silk shatter—not given that there was a direct connection to some chamber of hers here. He picked his way through the library, worrying about what he might find once he got out.

But the Academy grounds were quiet. At least, relatively so.

Students and professors mingled on the lawn, but there was no sign of the creatures. He had no idea how they had simply vanished, but it seemed as if that was what had happened here.

Instead of lingering, he made his way toward the administrative building, wanting to get to his friends. He found them leaving the building, shuffling behind Desmond and his mother.

"Dax?" Rochelle asked, racing toward him and meeting his eyes. "What... What happened? Everything just came to a standstill. It was almost as if time stopped."

"What?"

"You weren't here, Mr. Nelson," Desmond said, "so you did not see that some burst of essence erupted and caused everything to freeze. At least, it seemed to do so for us. I suspect that is when the others departed." He shook his head. "And, unfortunately, that is when Ames took the opportunity to escape as well."

"He's still out there?"

"I'm afraid so," he said.

"What happened?" Rochelle asked.

"Well, I can tell you what happened," Desmond said. "A combination of errors. I was given a task by the Great Serpent, and the Order must have realized what happened. They came after the flare. I thought the secondary flare would be enough to distract them, thought that was all that the Great Serpent had wanted." He frowned at Dax. "But perhaps that wasn't what it was about. And perhaps the Great Serpent should have given the task to you rather than to me." He breathed out heavily. "I had not realized that Raisor had learned of the flare. Had I known..." He shook his head. "He's a dangerous one. Nearly as dangerous as Ames. And he understands truths about the world that very few know."

Dax wasn't sure, but he thought that he meant the truths of how the creatures were sentient. At least how some of them were.

"So what now? Why are you back?"

"In the absence of appropriate leadership, it seems as if some of our instructors decided to capture some of the local guests. This caused a bit of a ruckus, and then these guests decided to create some chaos and disruption around the Academy, which drew the attention of the Order." He shrugged. "I believe the issues have been resolved, and I will send word to the Emperor that we can have his delegation move forward."

It was almost overwhelming. "His what?"

His mother looked at him. "That is why I am here, Dax." She turned, facing the forest. "I was sent to serve as a representative of the Empire for the parlay."

"You knew?"

She held his gaze for a moment. "I know many things, Dax. And when it is done, I will speak to you of them. Though your father probably would never admit it, you would have been useful along the border. I think you are much more useful here though." She turned, locking eyes with Desmond. "Thank you for your transport. And your guidance." She flicked her gaze to Dax. "I hope he doesn't cause too much trouble for you in your new role."

"I doubt he will, but he can be a bit rambunctious."

His mother released Desmond's hands, strode over to

Dax, and locked eyes with him before squeezing his hands and pulling him in for a hug.

"Be smart, and keep your eyes open."

With that, she strode away.

"That's it?" Dax said, calling after her.

"I'm afraid that her obligations preclude her from spending the time that I am sure you want her to. I can share as much as I can, so long as my own obligations do not cause too much difficulty. We need to clean up the grounds, get the Academy back in order. I believe you students have a project to complete."

Dax looked at the others. It felt...

He wasn't sure how to describe it, only that it felt almost hollow, empty, as if there were still so many questions that he had unanswered. Increasingly, he wasn't sure whether he would ever learn the truth.

His mother had known about these creatures.

She had been called.

"What about the Order—"

Desmond rounded on him, raising a finger. "We will not speak of it."

"But they were here, Desmond. They knew about—"

Desmond lowered his voice, leaning close to Dax. "As I said, we will not speak of it. Not openly. There is a place, and a time, for such things, Mr. Nelson."

Dax nodded. He wasn't sure what else he could do, what else he could say. It felt strange, though.

"What did she mean about your new responsibility?" Cedrick asked.

Desmond straightened, clasping his hands behind his back, and he looked around at the Academy. "As I said, in the absence of appropriate leadership, we had instructors that were taking liberties that they should not have been. The council has decided that should change."

"Wait," Rochelle said, turning to him. "Does that mean…?"

Desmond grinned at them each in turn. "Yes. I have been named headmaster."

Don't miss the next book in Essence Wielder: The Shattered Construct.

A unique connection to essence is key to protecting the empire.

Dax and his friends have settled into their roles at the Academy. They've stopped another attack, which has gained them notice, but also allows them a measure of freedom in their studies. With Desmond now serving as headmaster, they think everything will be different. Better.

But the flows of essence are changing.

Those who study such things don't know what that means, but all agree it's dangerous.

When asked to travel north during the term break, beyond the unclaimed lands, Dax has little choice but to go. What he finds changes everything he knows about essence —and what it means to wield it.

And it just might be the key to destroying the Order for good.

Series by Dan Michaelson

Cycle of Dragons

The Alchemist

The Tether Bond

Blood of the Ancients

Essence Wielder

Similar Series by D.K. Holmberg

The Dragonwalkers Series

The Dragonwalker

The Dragon Misfits

The Dragon Thief

Cycle of Dragons

Elemental Warrior Series:

Elemental Academy

The Elemental Warrior

The Cloud Warrior Saga

The Endless War

The Dark Ability Series

The Shadow Accords

The Collector Chronicles

The Dark Ability

The Sighted Assassin

The Elder Stones Saga

Made in United States
Troutdale, OR
05/14/2025

31332394R00281